TIME WAS RUNNING OUT . . .

At the scream and thrum of weapons, Megan's head snapped up—just in time to see bright copper hair flash, as Shkai'ra pelted through a clear spot.

"Move!" screamed Megan. "If you freeze, you'll fall."

Other running figures were now visible. One stopped to kneel and take careful aim.

Shkai'ra was halfway between dock and ship when there was a sudden impact below her right shoulder—the blow of a sledge swung overarm. She felt the sharp prickling point of the bolt as it touched her skin, but she leaped and twisted in midair, coming down straddle-stanced along the rope. Her balance was saved, but she stood immobilized for a crucial brace of seconds. She looked back to see the kneeling crossbowman sight; the arrow was loosed, and Shkai'ra watched as her own death approached. . . .

THE SHARPEST EDGE

THE SHARPEST EDGE

S. M. STIRLING and
SHIRLEY MEIER

Ⓢ

A SIGNET BOOK

NEW AMERICAN LIBRARY

PUBLISHED BY
THE NEW AMERICAN LIBRARY
OF CANADA LIMITED

NAL BOOKS ARE AVAILABLE AT QUANTITY DISCOUNTS WHEN
USED TO PROMOTE PRODUCTS OR SERVICES. FOR INFORMATION
PLEASE WRITE TO PREMIUM MARKETING DIVISION, NEW AMERICAN
LIBRARY, 1633 BROADWAY, NEW YORK, NEW YORK 10019.

First Printing, March, 1986

    2   3   4   5   6   7   8   9

 SIGNET TRADEMARK REG U S PAT OFF AND FOREIGN COUNTRIES
REGISTERED TRADEMARK—MARCA REGISTRADA
HECHO EN WINNIPEG, CANADA

SIGNET, SIGNET CLASSIC, MENTOR, PLUME, MERIDIAN
AND NAL BOOKS are published in Canada by The New American
Library of Canada, Limited, 81 Mack Avenue, Scarborough,
Ontario, Canada M1L 1M8
PRINTED IN CANADA
COVER PRINTED IN U.S.A.

DEDICATION

Creativity

> Dance with Siva!
>   In Joy we Dance!
>   We dance destruction
> and creation.
> Fly with Eagles
> Delve in darkness.
>   In joy and sorrow
>   are we free,
> to cleave a Stormcloud
> Ride the Thunder.
>   Laugh!
>
>   For we are Free.

*—to all those whose help
and encouragement made this possible*

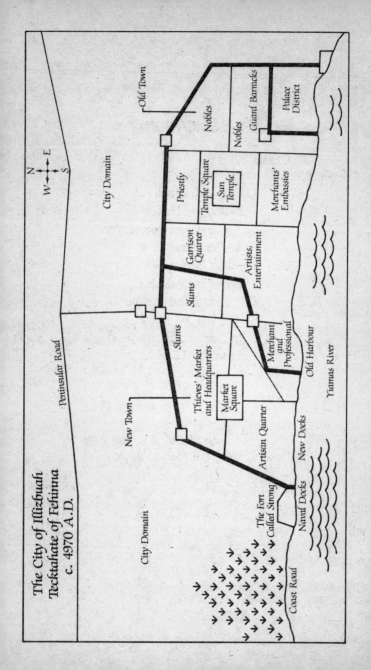

The City of Illizbuah
Tecktahate of Fehima
c. 4970 A.D.

It was interesting how the room looked from this angle. The blond woman slid downward until her head rested on the rim of the sunken tub and studied the view between her toes as they floated and dipped through the light wisps of steam on the surface of the water. Dying evening light slanted down through the skylights, filtering through the hanging plants and striking off the carved screens of black-lacquered sandalwood that divided the bathchambers of the Weary Wayfarer's Hope of Comfort and Delight. Relaxing into the heat, she pondered on reaching for her winecup, then settled for reaching her hand over the smooth marble rim. A furred chin settled onto the fingertips; she rubbed, and was rewarded with a deep rumbling purr from the black tomcat crouching on the tiles beside her.

Ahi-a, she thought. *What to do? Feasting, fornication, and fighting: I'm too poor for much of a feast, too tired to fight. Hmmm, Jaibo's out visiting his kinfast on the farm, Baiwun hammer him, so—*

Feet stepped into her field of vision. Woman's feet, small, well formed but battered and callused. Long legs . . . no, only in proportion; she was small even for lowland Fehinna, no more than four feet. But not a local, despite the long night-black hair; too pale, where the sun had not reached. Good build, muscle clearly defined under the skin, rolling in long smooth curves and flat straps. She noted the way the buttocks curved at the back but flattened even with the thighs at the sides; only hard exercise could produce that. Lightly ridged stomach with an old scar up the center, tight waist, breasts high and rounded,

7

strong neck, shoulders sloping from the deltoids. Scars, mostly on the left hand and arm and thigh; knifefighter's scars, if she favored that hand. And a good one, to have lived a score of years with a disadvantage in reach.

The face was alien here in Fehinna. It would have been more so in the bleak stone Keeps and huddled villages of the watcher's northwestern home. Triangular, pale, the eyes enormous and as black as the hair that torrented past her waist. *Strange*, she thought. And beautiful, and as deadly as a fer-de-lance, coiled in crumbling temple ruins.

She rose, lying with her arms outstretched along the sides of the tub. Water hissed across the blue-glazed tiles of the floor as she reached for her cup; the smell of the wine was pungent, musky, cool against the smells of hot wet stone and perfumed soap.

"Room for two," she said. This was the only tub with less than three, which was no accident; she was known to the Weary Wayfarer's regulars. Still, Illizbuah was a harbor city and strangers were frequent.

"I thank you," the other said, in Fehinnan still more harshly accented. She laid a fingertip to the white strand of hair at her temple and inclined her head slightly. "I hight . . . pardon, am Megan. Called Whitlock."

"Speed to your horse, strength to your lance, a straight shaft to your bow. Shkai'ra Mek-Kermak's-Kin, I am called: late Senior in Stonefort, in the Kommanz of Granfor. On the Sea of Grass, six months' travel north and west." She held up the winecup to be refilled by one of the servants.

Megan examined her speculatively. *Yes*, she thought. *She'll be tall when she stands*. Skin white where the sun had not turned it brown; eyes of a pale smoke-gray, startling against the dark-tanned face. So was her hair, bright copper-blond spilling down over broad shoulders. Thin high-cheeked face . . . a saber cut must have caused that scar; other white marks on right arm and left leg, below where the shield would cover. A cavalry fighter, then. That would accord with the greeting; and a plainsdweller, like those at home.

The appraisal flickered through her mind in the instant it took to slide into the water, submerge, and resurface, slicking hair back from her face. A few suds floated free, from the preliminary cleaning; three weeks in the swamps was more than one rinsing could wash out.

"A titled one. . . . The only rank I can claim is captain of the *Zingas Teik*, the *River Lady*, out of F'talezon in Zakos. Over the Great Sea . . . the Lannic, it is called here. Recently arrived."

"So I thought," Shkai'ra said. Those were fresh manacle marks on the other's wrists. "By your speech. Nice to hear someone who speaks Fehinnan with a worse accent than mine!" She was actually fluent, but the sounds were difficult for her after the staccato gutturals of Kommanzanu.

Resentful at being ignored, the cat put his paws on the westerner's shoulder and kneaded. She smiled, an odd closed curve of the lips, and scratched expertly behind his ears. The yellow eyes closed to slits.

"As for titles, 'penniless exile' would be better, here. Or 'sellsword,' as the Fehinnans say."

"We have that in common, then. . . . Whence comes the little shadowbrother from?" Megan said, regarding the cat. It returned her gaze and yawned, pink and white and cavernous. "In my city, the beggars eat them, the ones they can catch."

"Did any try with Ten-Knife-Foot, I'd bewail them," Shkai'ra said. "I picked him up two seasons ago, on the western border."

The arrows had come out of the scrub oak along the mountain trail at dusk.

"We didn't do too well."

She had shot her quiver empty: the Kommanz wheelbow hit harder than anything east of the Great River, but none of the others were horsearchers. . . .

"I woke up with a broken arm and my horse lying across one leg."

Crusted blood on her eyelids. Yelling laughter from the tribesfolk as they took their pick of heads and melted back into the forest.

"Ten-Knife was sitting on my chest, the next time ı woke up."

The sound the wounded made, when the scavengers found them.

"Wine?" she said, raising her cup and admiring the sheen on the swirling rosewood grain.

Megan reached over to stretch out a hand to the beast, very carefully. He sniffed, twice, then turned and inclined his head, purring as she rubbed the indicated cheek. "Why do I feel as if I had passed some test?" she said lightly, lying back again and letting her hair drift free in the soothing water.

Good to feel clean again, she thought. *Very good.*

That morning the hair had hung in rattails before her eyes, matted with sweat, smoke, grease, and crushed insects. There had been plenty of water in the swamp, and all of it left a greasy feeling on the skin. She remembered killing six mosquitoes with one slap, and feeling a dozen more on her, bloating.

She opened her eyes to the ceiling, glass skylights and mosaics of colored stone showing seaweed and fish, thinking that she never wanted to see gray moss hanging over her again. It went with the smell.

They lounged in silence for minutes, comfortably. "I'm starting to wrinkle," Shkai'ra said. "Odd habits they have here in the southlands, soaking the whole body in warm water. Nice, in limited amounts."

"In so warm a climate, I can ynerstun . . . understand it?" Megan said. "Fehinnans seem offended by smells . . . the wine smells good, but not on an empty stomach."

A too empty stomach, she thought.

The stink of scorching half-rotten meat filled her memory. Again she sat on the swamp hummock, crouched over a smudge fire and roasting the corpse of one of the voracious little toothy lizards that had hounded her through the weeks since her shipwreck. It was easy to catch them; they had the temperament of packfish. Just wade into deeper water and wait for them to attack, being very careful not to go too deep. There were thousands of them.

The memory blew away like smoke from the fire. "I could eat. And then I will drink wine with you, my friend. If I may call you so."

Shkai'ra rose and wrapped herself in the cool fluffy towel held out by an inn servant. "The Weary Wayfarer sets a good table," she said, stretching with unself-conscious pleasure. "Among its other virtues. Neutrality is one—freelances stay here, from the City and the world." She looked down to the smaller woman; standing, the other's head just reached her breastbone. "We are not unfriends. And yes, I think we may become friends." The narrow face lit for a moment in an oddly charming smile. "It would be dangerous for both of us if we were enemies, I think."

Megan looked up and imagined that face over a blade, all angles and planes, with not a soft line in it. And the way she moved . . . "You'd have the weight and reach on me," she said casually as they proceeded through to the changeroom. Attendants handed them long linen robes and cloth sandals. "But I'd be willing to wager on speed, if only for the first pass," she continued, pushing aside a servant and tying the sash herself. The—Kommanza, was it?—would be useful, knowing the city well even if not a native. And she would have to raise passage money, at least.

There was an outdoor dining area, tucked into the angle between two roofs, at second-story level. Seaward, the masts of ships showed forest-thick over the warehouses. Clouds piled above, black and threatening; away to the west, dying sun touched them to fiery scarlet and threw the thousandfold roofs of the city into black silhouette against a horizon gone shadow-blue. Out on the river to their left a wargalley went upstream under bare poles, the grinding of its treadmill-powered propellers snarling over the water. Already a riding light glowed at one masthead, a yellow jewel over the flatness of land and water. Harbor smells were overborne by roasting meat and garlic.

"Ach, that smells good," Megan said. They sank onto cushions heaped around a low table; it bore candles in glass bubbles, salt, spices, a platter of cornbread, a tall beaker, and cups of cool brown stoneware. The breeze blew crisp and strong, damp from the river but cool against skins still heated from the baths. The wind was rising before rain.

"Better than what I've smelled of late," Shkai'ra agreed. "This morning . . ."

The hideship stank. Most did, but the little schooner smelled of more than raw leather. Apathy, ancient grease, sour decay from the timbers; tangled ratlines ran from the rigging, and a thick green skirt of weed followed the hull's labored progress toward the dock.

Shkai'ra leaned back against her seabag and drew a deep breath. "Good to smell Illizbuah again," she said.

The Joisi skipper shrugged and spat over the side. "Ay bean on tis run fi'fif yearz," he said with a nasal north-coast accent. "Caen' smeall antin' but tis pigraper scow."

The rowtug came alongside, warped their cable to a bollard, and set out for the pier. The thick rope came out of the water and stretched taut, crackling as tiny jets of water spurted out of the wet sisal.

"Tiem 't di'bark," the captain said. "Pay passage fee."

Shkai'ra rose and smiled sunnily, hooking her thumbs into the leather belt of her tunic and ignoring the long bone hilt of her saber. Sunlight blinked off the water; her eyes were slitted against it, with the squint lines beside them that sailors have, and steppedwellers. Crewfolk drifted near, in canvas kilts and knitted caps, hefting belaying pins with elaborate casualness.

"You agreed to free passage, for my sword," she said softly.

"Ter waes na ficktin'," he said. "Yaw haef tradewire." Shkai'ra shrugged, sighed, and kicked straight up into his crotch with blurring, unbelievable speed. He gave a single high-pitched shriek and sank to the deck, vomiting greenish bile.

The sailors lunged, then froze as Shkai'ra's hand snapped across her body and near a meter of killing metal appeared; a saber, bright and long, light breaking off the honed edge. The hard cords in her forearm rippled under the brown scar-seamed skin as she twitched the curved sword back and forth through the moist air with a sound like ripping silk. She dropped the point to the fallen man's throat; he froze at the touch of the cool sharp metal, breath wheezing as he fought to control muscles locked in spasm.

The long blade was the aristocrat's weapon; the sailors were afraid, and their pikes and boarding axes were below. Shkai'ra grinned at them as she stooped to throw the seabag over her shoulders.

"Such courage," she laughed, and spat in the captain's face. He barely flinched. "Painful, isn't it?" she said, and added a kick delivered with concentrated viciousness at the base of his spine.

There was a shock and a grinding crunch as the little ship slid into the cooler shadow of the longshore warehouses and thudded into the rope bumpers of the pier. Untended, it rubbed on past and ground into oak timber; the ship lurched, and several of the crew grabbed for ropes. Shkai'ra flexed easily; she had been raised on horseback, and had spent enough time on ships of late to know their ways. She leaped sideways to the railing, then to the wharf, turning and backing on the balls of her feet. One of the sailors flipped her knife up to the throwing grip.

"Wouldn't try it, fishsucker," she called, and ducked around a stack of baled cotton. Leaning back against the rough burlap covering, she considered the sky.

"Ai, ai, so much for winning my fortune in the Middle Sea," she said to herself. "Not even enough to get my second-best set of armor out of hock." She began to giggle, and the sound rose through a chuckle to a full-throated roar.

I could always pawn the fancy shooter, she mused, pulling the shotpistol from her bag and thrusting it through the back of her belt. *Nia, not every day you can find a dead general, unstripped.*

Shkai'ra shook herself and tucked her feet beneath her on the cushions. "Fish stew?" she said to Megan inquiringly.

"It sounds better than what I've been eating lately; crossing the swamps south of the river is no way to eat well, or at all."

She had looked down at the lizard-size alligator as it sputtered, with a grimace of distaste, then reached out and tossed it spinning into the tea-colored waters of the swamp. The surface boiled and seethed, growing pink as the dwarf cayman's relatives devoured it and started in on each other.

Better you poison yourselves with that carrion for breakfast than I, she had thought, and begun wrestling the clumsy dugout toward a channel of open water that wound away sluggishly among reeds and cypress roots. Morning mist lay on it, man-high and white; trees crowded around, cedar and eucalyptus, live oak festooned with gray tatters of hanging moss. They closed overhead, turning the north-bound channel into a tunnel through hot olive-green gloom. Stray beams from the young sun stabbed blinding down to scatter in the fog like white light; sweat lay on her skin in a film of rancid oil. . . .

She shook herself back to the present. "But I have wished for good red meat for many days."

"Truth from the gods, I'd wager, after crossing the Great Dismal Swamp." Shkai'ra shuddered; even the na-tives were wary of it, and the thought of those entangled green marshes made her plainswoman's soul crawl. "Well, then. Hmmm." She signaled the servant over with a jerk of her head.

The red-bean soup with prawns was good, and hot in both meanings of the word. There was a salad of greens to follow; then a roast of pork, honey-glazed and stuffed with truffles and onions; steamed seaweed; baked sweet pota-toes on a bed of scented rice. The wine had a strange musky tang to Megan's palate, but it was pleasing enough for all that.

They both ate with the slow enjoyment of those who have gone hungry often. At last Shkai'ra sighed, mopped up a corner of her plate with a heel of bread, and belched comfortably. Swift, efficient hands removed the soiled dishes and replaced them with platters of cheese and flatbread, more wine, a pot suspended in a porcelain frame over an open flame.

Shkai'ra paused, considered, and poured herself a cup of the tea rather than more wine. "Ahi-a, at home I'd be eating jerked meat in the saddle, while we fought to keep the nomads off the crops. Exile can have its compensa-tions." She smiled, and glanced upward. Now the long twilight of summer was fading, and clouds rolled black along the western horizon.

A woman sat before a silver bowl, in a garden that whispered and rustled as rain pattered down, on vine and leaf and carved stone pergola, somehow avoiding the space where she sat. Long black hair fell in a curtain as she leaned forward over the bowl and passed a hand over the water; eyes that were the color of milk from corner to corner regarded it.

Cold suddenly radiated from it; frost-fog tumbled over the smooth edge and drifted over embossed figures thick with hoar, to puddle and dissipate in the rain outside the circle of protection.

Thunder cracked overhead. The figures rising out of the ice wavered for a moment, then firmed as her concentration took hold. The symbol was the thing; she reached to hold firm the sympathetic linkage between the *here* and the *there*. Ah, General-Commander Smyna. And the High Priest, unmistakable; their voices rang insect-thin from the images of frost. War, then. Her teacher must know of this.

She touched the bowl with a finger, and the metal glowed white for an instant: time present. Then another image arose, unbidden, flickering. She concentrated to firm it, for the unasked Sight was always valuable. A woman—no, two women—sat at a low table, a candle between them. Red hair inclining toward dark, a finger tracing on the table. A gust of . . . not-wind, and the scene vanished. She touched her finger again to the bowl, and this time the glow was red: time past. The blind woman raised her eyes to the garden and thought for long minutes. Two more to play the game.

Faces called up in answer to her question. How were they to deal with Illizbuah? She smiled suddenly and gestured. The cold-formed fog billowed up, obscuring her from sight. Lightning flashed, reflecting a million shining droplets of frozen air as the rain now fell freely everywhere. It puddled in the bowl, mingling with the rapidly melting ice, for there was no one there to hold it back.

"But for all the striving and slaying," Shkai'ra said, an hour later, "I've only what I arrived with, my sword and my wits. *T'Zoweitzhum*, a good brain and the world is a sheep to be fleeced."

Megan leaned back, stretched, braced her arms on the table. Lamplight glittered in her eyes, sheened off hair and the bright inlays of the low table.

"A good thought," she said. Pondering, she tapped one nail against the table with an oddly metallic sound. She decided. "Together, we should be able to shear this flock to the skin. Shall we?"

Shkai'ra smiled, a different expression from the carnivore baring of the teeth she had shown earlier. It was lopsided, raffish, a touch self-mocking, older than the face that bore it; the smile of a survivor without illusions. "Bare is back without comrade to guard it. You have natural talent; I'm a judge of that. And I know local conditions." She hesitated. "And you're pretty, too."

Their fingers touched; Megan opened her mouth to speak. A fat drop of water fell on their hands, and with a rushing blaze of multiforked lightning the storm broke over their heads. They blinked away the dazzle and rushed for shelter, reaching the arcade before the rain became a hissing downpour. The mood was broken; flash followed flash across the sky as the violence on high seized the bowl of heaven.

Megan's expression turned to a peculiar inward bitterness as her face turned upward, bathed pale in the blue flaring light, cast into shadow by the cloud-gloom. Thoughts rose and swam like sharks below the surface of consciousness. "I *hate* storms." she said.

"*Eh'mex mehkagro nai,*" Shkai'ra replied, and shivered slightly. "Baiwun Avenger rides the Plains of Sky tonight." She looked up; the sky was *black*, not the normal dark of a sunless sky; this was the almost palpable darkness of a shuttered room. Light twisted across the velvet backdrop, searing patterns into her eyes. Over kilometers of darkened cityscape the flame of the Sun Temple twisted in the lashing air, three hundred meters above the streets.

She turned to Megan. "We'll meet," she said, and made a curious gesture with her swordhand. "There . . . is a fate in this, I think."

Megan nodded. The weariness of days settled on her shoulders. "Goddess ward your sleep," she said.

It was after midnight, and Baiwun's hammer still rumbled through the night. Shkai'ra sat cross-legged on the great round bed that dominated her room. Hands rested on thighs, and the gray eyes were sightless as her mind turned within. No Kommanza was easy in a thunderstorm; it was the most fearful of natural things to those dwellers on the empty plains. And in thunder the Avenger sought out lawbreakers.

Suddenly a harsh scream broke the silence and the sound of dripping waters. It came from the next room, a long despairing wail of agony and terror.

2

Lightning flickered. The young priest's pupils contracted, throwing the room into shadow as he glanced down from the darkened skylight. Returning vision swept along honey-colored tile to rest on the stocky figure of the High Priest where he sat motionless at the focus of the room.

Cubilano, Reflection of the Everlasting Light, High Priest of the Sun in Illizbuah, Chancellor of Fehinna's God-King, sat in the silence he preferred. *More indiscipline*, he thought, noting the slight movement of the younger priest's eyes. He made an almost imperceptible sign with one finger, and the acolyte moved forward, covered his eyes with his hands, and bowed deeply.

"Young one," Cubilano said quietly, "strength of will can overcome the need to move injudiciously. My child, go from here to the Great Altar; there you may assume the posture of submission, as you now do. And remain there, contemplating what virtue lies in stillness, for as long as it would take the Sun to pass through the width of two hands."

The young priest began to stand. "You are in my presence, and have not been given leave to depart," the hierarch said in mild reproof. "Meditate for a further time on the usages of proper respect. Go."

He watched the boy back out of the room, and slowly his gaze ran past the dozen others arrayed against the

walls. These were the shaven-headed symbols of power,
identical in their robes of orange satin. One did not need
things cluttering one's life in order to show strength.

The furnishings of the room were sparse, as befitted a
man of austerity; a low table, racks for books and scrolls
and the pillows Fehinnans preferred for their cross-legged
sitting posture. Tropical cedar from the islands of the
Middle Sea lay warm against tile, in light that the tinted
skylight washed pale yellow. This chamber was deep in
the temple; mass muted the wild noise of the storm, and
the lamps never flickered on their stands of serpent-carved
oak. The silence had been a physical presence to be felt;
now it deepened to an unbearable motionless tension.

Cubilano might have been a figure carved of gold and
mahogany, here in the centrum of his might. An ordinary
face, at first glance; the wrinkled, dark-brown, thick-boned
countenance of any land-bound peasant lucky enough to
see sixty seasons; but the eyes . . . were not ordinary at
all. Black, emotionless, the gaze that millennia of slaugh-
terhouse history had known, the eyes of incarnate Purpose.

One of the acolytes leaned close and whispered. The
door opened, swinging on ironwood bearings.

That door . . . he thought. How many Sun-turnings had
it been? It had been his second week in the temple, still
speechless with awe; even the little provincial seminary
had been impressive enough, after his kinfast's wattle-and-
daub huts, but Illizbuah . . .

All new acolytes were presented to the Reflection; it
was a tradition, but no great ritual. He had advanced with
eyes firmly fixed on the ground, a stocky boy of ten in a
saffron gown. The hand had fallen on his head; he still
remembered the dry cool feel of the old woman's skin on
his scalp.

"So this is the one who shows such promise," the voice
had said. That had startled him enough to make him
glance up. Their eyes had met, the young boy's and the
old woman's, for a long minute. Her face had looked
incredibly old to him, an aristocrat's face seamed and worn
to a blade of bone and skin, the face of a dying eagle.
Beyond the indignities of hope, prouder than an ocean of
lions.

"Perhaps the reports are correct," she had said at last,

with a dry rasping chuckle. "Who knows? He might sit on this cushion, one day."

As General-Commander Smyna Caaituh's-Kin was ushered in, the room flashed from warm yellow into searing blue-white. Thunder followed, more felt in bone and gut than heard. *A bad storm*, she thought. Hopefully not an omen for what she planned. Then again, when hail fell in high summer, *someone* was struck; it might be her enemies, they were thick enough on the ground. The uncanny figure before her did nothing to ease her discomfort; priests were . . .

She tuned her mind to a meaningless hum of unfocused thought. One never knew how much they could see; the Sun-on-Earth could, that she *did* know, having spent time in the palace. More than one commander of her acquaintance had gone to the flaying tables for disloyal fantasies. She closed her eyes for a moment to allow them to adjust to the dim light and heard Cubilano's voice, dry and whispery.

"General-Commander, enter and be welcome in the House of the Sun." From where he sat, Cubilano could feel the room's effect on the soldier. It was normal enough to the eyes of the uninitiated, but subtle art had gone into the angles, the patterns of roof and floor. They dwarfed any who stood before him, and gave the dais a dominating effect that mere size could not yield. Silently, he commended the spirit of the long-dead Reflection who had built it; had he been alone, he might have smiled. It was the duty of the Servants to increase the power of the Sun-on-Earth, generation after generation—which meant, to diminish such as this.

Smyna waited by the door, feeling sweat trickling down her flanks under the fine green cotton of her uniform tunic. She summoned the arrogance of thirty generations of aristocrats to stride across the floor that reason told her was of no great size. Reason lied, something within her said. It was vast, and she no more than a mote on it. An insect to be crushed beneath a sandal.

High Priest? she thought. A tenant's child, she reminded herself. Scarcely more than a slave, whatever the law might say; bound to the soil, barely fit to serve in her stables, but for the chance attention of some priest in the villages.

"Great Light, I greet you," she said. There was smooth deference in her voice, but her bow was merely that to an equal, and she failed to speak in the subordinate mode. There was a tensing among the acolytes, less a physical movement than a turning of attention. "Fellow Hand of the God Among Us," she added. That put her behavior within the canons, although barely. She had addressed him in private, and in his capacity as Chancellor, which was not a priestly office, in theory. Usually the Reflection held it, but lay men and women had as well, within living memory.

Cubilano watched her as she stood with stiff-spined alertness before him, like a fighting quail ruffling before a rival. *Hard metal*, he thought. But that was needful, for a sharp tool. He gestured to one of the cushions before him and returned the hand to its place in the opposite sleeve.

"Child of the Light, be honored among us"—*for the moment*. He watched unmoving as she lowered herself to the floor. This one, he thought, would bargain toe to toe with the Sun Herself for ambition's sake. Anger threatened to cloud his mind, at the thought of the Servants of the Light seen as a steppingstone to mere power and wealth. For a moment he concentrated on the smells of incense and warm wood and sunflower oil from the lanterns.

"Leave us," he said in his dry, quiet voice; a rustle like that of dead leaves. The acolytes bowed, turned, and glided from the room, the muted rustle of cloth on cloth loud in the silence. The last paused to pull the door shut behind her. Another flicker from the storm outside gilded them both as they gazed at each other. *I have the advantage here*, he thought, looking down at Smyna. *She shows little reaction for one untrained; let us see what bait she takes*.

"You mentioned that you wished to discuss the darkness and heresy that surrounds us?"

Smyna took her courage in her hands: a Fehinnan would have said, caught her soul in her own net.

"Here are the staff studies, Radiance," she said, setting a thick leather folder of papers before him. "Essentially

. . . not to be technical, we can take the Kaailun States to the south in two campaigning seasons. None of them are very large, and Intelligence swears that they'll be slitting each other's throats when our siege trains arrive beneath the walls." A brief smile showed white against the olive skin. "Encouraged by our, ah, subsidies."

She sat, and watched him stare unwinkingly at the folder. Coming here openly had been a statement of intent, and her rivals in the Command would use it. But none of them would seriously suspect that she had given the Chancellor the secret contingency plans; the penalties for divulging them would last three days at least. The factions were delicately balanced in the Iron House; command of the Illizbuah garrison was prestigious, but of less real importance than one of the provincial army corps. But with this, Cubilano could marshal unanswerable arguments with the Sun-on-Earth. Unlimited preferment would come to the commander who had been on the winning side, once the Sun-on-Earth spoke for war.

"The Kaailun are notorious unbelievers, who have rejected our missionaries most obdurately," Cubliano said.

Not altogether surprising, since they preach unlimited submission to the Sun-on-Earth, Smyna thought dryly, then caught herself. That was a dangerous thought, skirting blasphemy, and here . . .

"And the northern powers?" the High Priest continued.

Smyna shrugged. "No great problem, Radiance. We've recovered from the Four Nations War faster than they did." As a girl she had played among the bones and broken catapults in the cleared firezone beneath the walls of her kinfast's stronghold. "The Pensa are too occupied with each other; they've considered it beneath their dignity to fight outsiders since the Maleficent's day." The archpriest made a sign to avert evil at the name. "Maailun and D'waah will fight"—she spread her hands—"but that, however, is what the armed forces of the Tecktahate of Fehinna are for, after all." Smyna used the formal term: Burning Righteous Sword of the Divine Incandescense.

Flattery never hurts, she thought. *Nor unction. Smear it on—"the arse of the mighty tastes of gold."* Fear stabbed at her again; the mind was open to the God of which it was a shadow.

The priest stared over her head, as the lightning cast the room in silver. "All those who do not believe . . . lost, lost in the darkness. The Fire that cleanses must be brought to earth, a healing cautery."

Like the great lens in the temple dome. He could almost see the fierce point of focus trembling in the incense-laden air; almost hear the shocked, disbelieving first scream as another soul was freed to the only God.

Smyna sought to bring the conversation back to practicalities. "Radiance, there are still those who oppose the plan. Many of the landed families are afraid for their estates; loot is desirable, but burned crops and slaughtered workers . . . they remember the last war. And the navy is more interested in the Middle Sea, and the new trade colonies across the Lannic."

Peasant hardheadedness showed on the other's face. For a moment Smyna was reminded of a formidable suspicious old farmwoman at market, shaking her fist over piled yams and raisins and refusing to be taken in by smooth city words.

"Aye," he said. "The shiplords of the city are so inclined; little in landward expansion for them, except higher taxes and smaller markets. For a time, and they seldom look beyond the swell of their fat stomachs. And they stir the shaaids, the city-scum, to complaint over the imposts we must have, to hire troops and import metals." He stared at the soldier. "Only in burning is there holiness. They too will have their moment with the Flame."

Smyna Caaituh's-Kin, who had hunted tigers and humans for sport, inclined her head and fought to hide her shudder. Fanatics disturbed her; they were too unpredictable. And the Chancellor was brilliantly so. To use him was to grasp the knife by the blade . . . but there was little choice. And less glory, and no advancement in peacetime. Few of the officer corps in these days were the heirs to great wealth; the Righteous Sword was a convenient and honorable way of giving them a living without upsetting the delicate matrimonial alliances that were the warp of Fehinnan politics. Plunder would pay embarrassing debts and augment niggardly pay and stipends; casualties and mobilization of cadre units would give the ambitious room to rise in the table of ranks.

Oh, yes, there would be many to follow and support; rotting in the border garrisons, in the endless boredom of drillfields, patrolling the western mountains against starving savages who could hide under an oak leaf and put arrows through a squirrel's eye. . . .

"You are prepared for opposition, then, Radiance?" she asked. She was deeply committed; still, it would be well to be sure that he was not too far gone in mystical ecstasy to attend to the necessities.

He nodded. "They have overreached themselves. Trade is bad enough, with Flaadah and Ky'baa fighting for control of the Straits in the south. Their rabblerousers have provoked the shaaids beyond endurance. There will be troubles; I will use them to swing opinion against them in the Council, and the House of Tecktahs. As you warriors use an opponent's strength against him."

"How does the Sun-on-Earth regard this matter?"

Both Fehinnans drew a circle over their breasts at the mention of the God-King. "The new Avatar of Her has authorized . . ." Cubilano produced a stamped document.

Smyna restrained herself from snatching and read gravely. Cubilano allowed himself an inward smile as trained eyes read the language of the body. "Ah, Radiance, this is everything we asked for!" She looked up, understanding in her eyes. "Ahhh, *that* is why there was an announcement that the proclamation would deal with an increase in taxes!"

Cubilano withdrew a hand from his sleeve and stroked his chin. It was the first gesture Smyna had seen him use; she would have been surprised at the reaction of his acolytes, had they seen.

"The Sun-on-Earth . . ." he paused. How best to explain? "The God is much occupied with other thoughts, of late. This matter is left in my hands. Still, the civil and military hierarchies are separate by wise decree; it would be well to have preparations made concurrently in the Iron House. Both to deal with possible civil unrest, and to use the revenues which will flow automatically, once the new measures are in place. Since you are commander of the Illizbuah garrison, and have access to the necessary communications and staff personnel . . ."

"The shaaids will riot?"

"Of course. My information is definite, and it is in any case necessary." He managed to shrug without movement. "They are not so devout as the peasantry; still, however many you kill, there will be sufficient for the city's needs."

"In other words," Smyna said, greatly daring, "you feel a short, sharp riot will strengthen your hand against the merchants with the Sun-on-Earth. Who will not love those who incite his subjects to revolt. And by association, the navy and peace factions will be covered by the same shroud. But the disturbances must not be allowed to get out of hand; that might convince the Radiant One that there was something to our opponent's predictions of ruin from a militant policy."

Cubilano gave her a smile as cold as duty. "Who are we to question the mind of the God? We serve the Avatar of Her with our human minds and wills." He paused. "Have you made your devotions to the God as the Law commands?" he said sharply.

Caught off balance, she struggled to regain the initiative. "I . . . the Caaituh's-Kin are pious; nobody can dispute that."

"Yet a great kinfast is made up of many souls," Cubilano continued. "Dehanno, your kinelder, heir to the Tecktahship . . . he has been less than friendly to the Servants of the Light. Disputing our ownership of lands." His expression became somber. "Such a one might have to be . . . set aside by the Sun-on-Earth. For a more devout heir."

Smyna bowed her head. Here was the bait, tailored to her alone. Hers if she succeeded; if she failed, there would be disgrace for the one who had callously slaughtered the people of the Divine One, as they rightly protested measures adopted by misguided ministers. The God could do no wrong; Her Servants were another matter entirely. And there was a silken reminder that however high she climbed the temple would have its hand on the ladder. Still . . .

"I will order the regiments into the city," she said. "Obedient to your wishes, Mirror of the Eternal Light."

The priest made a gesture of dismissal. "Further communications had best be by the secure channels we estab-

lished," he said. That was communication itself; she had
known his insistence on a public meeting was a demand
for commitment. She replied with a deep obeisance and
turned to go. At the threshold she hesitated.

"Radiance, I have heard that the Guild of the Wise
favors the merchant guilds, in this matter."

For the first time, Cubilano raised his voice. "The Con-
spiracy of the Foolish!" It cracked out across the chamber. "The Guild of the Damned!" Smyna blinked, dazed
for a moment by the force of will pouring out into the
room. "After the riots, the guilds will have no recourse.
Except the 'wise.' And if they are so foolish . . ." His
hands curled shut. "The Sun has fire to spare."

The High Commander paused as she emerged from the
portico of the temple and glanced upward, slapping her
gloves together. Thunder sounded, and the rain became a
stinging torrent mixed with hail. *Bad for the crops*, her
mind noted automatically. A thin smile crossed her lips;
that was a concern for the head of the kinfast, safe on the
ancestral acres. Not hers. Not yet. The smile grew broader,
and wolfish, until her eyes fell and met those of the
escorting underpriest. He stood, ignoring rain and warriors alike, eyes serene and unblinking. For a moment
they confronted each other, the hound and the serpent,
before she accepted her cloak with a shudder and strode
off in a flurry of underlings.

Priests! she thought.

"Did the meeting go well, High Commander?" The
voice was her chief aide's; fishing for her position, of
course, but still her most trusted one.

"Very well," she said, shark-hunger in her voice "Pre-
pare to activate Plan One."

"War, then!" the other said enthusiastically.

Smyna looked up at the bulk of the temple, shimmering
through the rain, lit by the wavering torch of the hundred-
foot flame and savage flares of lightning across the gilding
of the dome. "Perhaps. If all goes well, if the priests keep
to their part of the bargain, if Old Baldy back in there can
do as he boasts—then we can move the old nearsights in
the Iron House aside."

"Then, for such an enterprise, Fehinna may need a new Supreme Commander of the Righteous Sword."

Promotion for me, promotion for you. And when there's no more rungs on the ladder above me, it will be time to consider the downward kick as you climb behind.

"Yessss . . ." she said thoughtfully. Fire poured across the sky in blue-white sheets; ozone was in the air, and the temple burned hot gold, leaving fading afterimages swimming before her eyes in the wet darkness. "And perhaps a new Reflection?"

There was a snicker of laughter as hands dropped to well-worn hilts.

The door closed softly behind the departing general. From a cunningly concealed alcove an acolyte stepped. She bore the leaf mark of high degree on her forehead, and settled beside the high priest with the ease of long familiarity.

"Analysis," he said.

"Typical of the unLight," she said. "Fear. Also ambition; perhaps already heretical thoughts. Still, a useful tool." She paused. "If this one-in-shadow may ask, is it not dangerous to split the forces of the Iron House?"

Her superior nodded. "Perceptive analysis," he said. Above, the skylight was dark now, lit only by the flashes of the lightning. "As to your presumption in questioning policy," he paused, "that is also acute. Know, any large organization, such as the Righteous Sword, will have conflicts of faction; such will tend to become identified with disputes of policy. Observe, this is regrettably true even of we Servants of the Effulgent Radiance. We do not intend to *split* the Iron House; if division came to actual fighting, there would be disaster. The Sun-on-Earth would intervene, at the least. However, we merely intend to tilt the natural balance of contention; the losers will mostly accept the new leadership, some will be reposted, a few will retire or be courteously requested to open their veins."

"Still, Radiance, this is a two-edged sword; the combina-tion of ability and ambition is dangerous."

"Very true; once used, the tool may be discarded. In any case, when shoveling pigshit one must use a dungfork.

Once the task is completed . . . perhaps a new General-Commander?"

The acolyte nodded and withdrew in silence at his signal. He stared after her meditatively for a moment.

"Very true," he murmured. "Ambition bears watching, in whatever quarter." He withdrew his attention from the matter; there were other concerns for a High Priest, and he was hierophant as well as Chancellor. Ah, yes . . . There was a Ritual of Purification in a tenday; it would be well if the misguided one would confess and recant before then. The Servants assigned in such matters here in the supreme Temple were rigorous and imaginative, but there was no manure like the master's foot. . . . Perhaps a few nights in the cage with the Sniffers?

Yeva sat in the guest room rather than the garden now. Some stern ascetics would scorn to use the Art to keep themselves dry in a rainstorm, or to make ice to render scrying easier. She was not of their number, but there would be no energy to spare for luxuries this time. The glass stood before her, as milk-white as the magician's eyes, held in its frame like a pearl beneath the chin of a dragon.

War had been decided; that was certain. But it was necessary to know more, and alarms had certainly been tripped. She took one deep breath, then another, sank into light trance, and began very delicately to probe.

The circle of priests formed with swift ease once the Watcher had called. Around the walls of a cone-shaped room, eyes focused unblinking on the pinpoint of flame that burned unwavering in the center. And waited, patient as a cancer breeding silently through the nerves.

There! The flame wavered in a certain nonphysical undirection. Hate surged within the circle, building into a swirling vortex, ready to be released when the Damned One of the Guild of Fools showed himself.

Soundless, the Form of the magician drifted over the temple. She scanned the area carefully, averting her consciousness from the shape before her; on this plane one could confront nothing that was not elemental Truth; she had no desire to comprehend what two hundred generations of belief and agony had made of this place. Here as ever, there was no unknowing.

Probing, she met a shell of glass. No, it was alive; pulsing rhythmically, tiny openings gaping for instants. It tasted of sour yellow; she gritted nonexistent teeth and slid along the outer surface, extending a tendril. . . . She stepped sideways, to the plane of Absolute Essence, and considered the Symbol of the Temple. *Ahhhh, perhaps* . . . Walking the time dimension was a physical thing here, studying the manifold branchings of probability. Yes: a high possibility of a gap *here*. Best not consider it too closely, lest the information gained fix the parameters when she returned to the time-in-flow. And it would be of no use to penetrate here, for there was no verbal language among absolute Symbol.

Sideways again, to the original plane. She picked the place/time, pushed, felt a sensation like icy slivers that rasped sadly gray on her skin, and was through. Yeva heard: ". . . not intend to *split* the Iron House; if division came to actual fighting, there would be disas—"

A wave of emotion broke around her, swirling the identity matrix of patterned energies that was she against the inner wall of the temple's protection. Rage, pain, fear, guilt, hate, lust flickered through the pathways of her consciousness, and far away she could sense the response of her immobile body as its glands opened slightly, beneath the iron control her training imposed on the hindbrain. Coppery taste of fear, savage adrenaline exhilaration of anger, gray meaninglessness of depression. With a single convulsive heave she snapped back through the opening of her entry and returned identity to the physical body. That provided a brief channel, a window in time and possibility for the counterstrike. World and otherworld crackled as the bolt struck, and there was an ear-stunning roar of entropic noise as she shouted the words of Containment. Darkness.

And rain. The servants arrived as fear overbalanced fear. They found master's guest sitting unharmed amid the shattered glass and plants of the solarium; droplets misted her hair and seeped into the cushions as she regarded the crushed and smoldering remains of her surroundings. But for fortune and speed, they might have found nothing but charred bone and greasy ash, or a body probability-twisted into something that had no right to exist in time-present-here. As it was . . .

"The lightning rod needs replacing," she said, before signaling her mute bodyservant to carry her from the wreckage.

3

The scream still echoed through the thunder-ridden night as the plainswoman came out of her crouch and flowed smoothly erect. The saber flickered into her hand as she twisted past the bedpost; three long strides brought her to the connecting door. Her dagger thudded into the wood beside the lock, and she threw her weight in leverage against the hilt until the ironwood lock mechanism broke from the softer oak with a rending crunch; it was the sound of tearing cartilage that went with a crushed knee. She kicked flat-footed, then dove forward into the outlander's room, the curved sword moving in a neat precise arc, up into guard position.

Megan had flung herself onto the strange bed, staring at the ceiling. Naked in the damp heat, she lay and listened to the storm, refusing to remember. Denying any thought of . . . no. No! She concentrated on her breath, forcing it to even out into deep slow rhythms; felt the sweat trickling down her flanks, the crisp texture of the close-woven linen beneath her. A pond of still water grew before the eyes of her mind. She slept. And dreamed, remembering.

*   *   *

The rough, prickly fiber of the rope dug painfully into her hands; that was nothing, a welcome distraction from the tearing pain between her legs. She leaned into the coil of rope, grateful for its support as she stared down into the dark track behind the ship, black against the slush-white surface of the freezing river. She was cold; the tears froze on her lashes. Blood trickled warmly down her thighs, cooling and freezing in its turn. Thunder crashed to the north. Muffled now, not close and overwhelming as it had been when it overbore the sounds of her pain. As Sarngeld forced himself into her, heedless of her pain, relishing it.

She looked down at the water with longing as it curled and chuckled to itself under the keel. Peace, and escape, and forgetting.

But if I die, there will be no vengeance, she thought. The tears dried. There was time, and the young healed quickly. Time to learn what she must. *Happy Twelfth Cycle,* she told herself. *May each new year bring such joy.* She shifted her weight, and the blood flowed again.

Shkai'ra scanned the room, instantly aware that there was no third presence. She relaxed as much as was possible for one who had spent her childhood under the Warmasters' instruction and laid the saber on a table before walking to the bed. The outlander—Megan?—ground her teeth and wrestled with the sweat-soaked sheets. Shkai'ra stood, watching, contemplating her own emotions with detached curiosity.

She did not feel pity; her folk lacked even the concept. Concern, perhaps. On the Plains of Night, even the fiercest was driven prey, and she had night terrors enough of her own. What connection? The stranger was interesting, true. And attractive, but no more so than many men and women she met daily.

She sat on the bed and laid a cool strong hand on the other's shoulder. "Wake, Whitlock," she said in a calm conversational tone. "That fight is past."

Under her hand, Megan froze to utter stillness. With a shudder her body relaxed into wakefulness, and her hand went out to trace the smooth line of Shkai'ra's cheek.

"Not him," she murmured, still in the dream's grip. She sat up. Unwelcome sobs forced themselves past clenched

teeth. She had sworn that she would not weep again; shame added to her misery as she turned her face away.

Shkai'ra gathered the other against her shoulder. "Tears are for afterward; they free you," she said. "I've found that, in the outlands."

Megan hesitated for a brief moment, then buried her face in the other's shoulder. The plainswoman felt wiry strength in the desperate grip.

"I . . . I should not." Megan took a deep, shuddering breath and tried to sit up but couldn't make herself let go. The Kommanza was contact that she had not allowed herself for years. "This binds . . ." Her voice also refused to work properly, and it came out so low that she doubted Shkai'ra heard it. Something that she had walled away inside herself long ago finally broke free, and she cried; harsh and tearing, for she fought it still, but the tears still came.

"I felt him die, he who harmed me . . . I felt his life go, leaking out of every wound, but still I must live that time again, when thunder walks. Why?" Then rage welled up in her through grief and she crooked a hand in a slash across the bedding. "*I could kill him again. And still feel pleasure in it.*"

Her tears were gradually slowing and her breathing becoming more regular. "So long. So long ago."

"They never leave us; love or hate, we give them immortality."

Minutes passed. Megan relaxed, becoming aware of her surroundings once more. With a shock, she was aware of the play of muscle and skin held against her. Warm and close and a clean summery smell . . .

Shkai'ra felt the change in Megan's grip. She kissed her, lightly at first, then harder, caressing with the tips of her fingers behind the Zak's ears and then down her spine.

"How strong you are," she murmured. "How beautiful."

Megan laughed deep in her throat, rough with disuse. "Lend me your strength," she said, and returned the kiss. Their lips met, and their tongues. Her hands ran down the lean body with an urgency that surprised her.

"And you are the beautiful . . . so . . . so . . ." She gasped, as long-dormant sensations woke at the feather-light touch of lips on her face and throat and breasts. "Together we defy the storm."

Shkai'ra tasted the tears on Megan's face, buried her hands in the mantle of fine black hair that wound about them as they rolled to the center of the bed, limbs twining, dark hair mingled with copper-bright.

4

Megan woke, to a moment's bewilderment. The knock came again, timid and muffled, from the other woman's room. There was a stirring under the brown linen coverlet and two heads came up on either side of her, one red-blond, the other small and black-furred with slitted yellow eyes.

Shkai'ra yawned, stretched until her joints cracked, and ran hands through tangled, tousled hair.

"Someone knocks, long one," Megan said. "Since it is coming from your room, *you* answer." She disappeared beneath the covers.

The Kommanza rolled out of bed and padded through to the other room. There was a murmur of voices, and she returned, balancing a tray on one hand and frowning over a piece of paper in the other.

"Tea," she said, placing it on the floor beside Megan. Pausing to give the other a companionable kiss, she sat cross-legged and frowned over the Fehinnan cursive with her lips moving slowly.

A snuffle of laughter escaped her, growing to a throaty chuckle as she tossed the paper aside, scooped up her cat, and dumped him in her lap.

"An itemized bill," Shkai'ra said, ruffling the animal's ears. "for Ten-Knife's depredations. A trail of ruin he must have left. Also a trail of black kittens with yellow eyes and terrible tempers." The cat endured her fingers for a moment, then flowed through her arms and stalked away with an air of purpose.

"How much damage can a cat do?" Megan said. "And he must have caught his share of rats."

Shkai'ra picked up the list. "Also a pet dog, a roast of beef, two pieces of imported sharksfin from the table of a shipowner, upsetting a bottle of wine in the process . . . Zaik, how did he do *that*?" She tossed the paper aside and moved to the window, sighing and stretching with contentment. It was early morning, and the rain had washed the air of some of its tidewater sultriness; there was a freshness to the damp, a smell of coffee and food and silt-laden water from the river. She took a deep breath, bent backward until her palms touched the floor behind her heels, did a handstand, and then dropped into a series of exercises, stretching first, then blocks, kicks, and handblows at an imaginary opponent.

Megan watched a moment, then slid out to pour herself a mug of tea. She leaned back against the pillows, heaped high and newly beaten into submission, promptly scalding her mouth.

"Fishguts! I should know better." She put the mug down and watched Shkai'ra for a long moment before gathering her hair to rebraid it. "I knew there was . . . ouch . . . a reason that I seldom unbound this mess. I should hack it all off." She finished winding the braids around her head and fetched her brace of knives as Shkai'ra drew her saber.

"On the lunge, wouldn't it be better to use the other arm as a counterbalance?"

"Not . . . if . . . you're . . . using . . . a shield," she said, between deep even breaths. She shifted her grip to the two-handed foot fighting stance and snapped into the guard-against-spear, then whipped down into the straight cut to the head, the apple-splitter. The moves flowed one into the other, yet each was sharp and definite, ending with a "huff!" of expelled breath at the moment of impact, the long flat muscles standing out under the skin in clean relief as they tensed and relaxed.

"Not that I really know much about those ox-stickers,"

Megan said. She very slowly began a series of fluid moves, one into the other, holding each pose a second or so. So controlled were the motions that it was almost unnoticeable that with each, she increased the speed until she was blurring through a shadow fight that ended with the lunge; throat, heart, groin. She stood up, and nodded at her imaginary opponent, and walked back toward the bed flipping the two knives.

Shkai'ra had finished with a sideways flick of the sword and had stood watching, wiping the steel in her hands carefully. "Ox-sticker it might be, but good for keeping small people with sharp objects in their hands at a safe distance."

Megan had not stopped the spinning knives, but she glanced out of the corner of one eye. "Oh?" Thunk, Thunk, CLANG! "Really." The first two stood quivering in the wall by Shkai'ra's head. The third one, which had glanced off the sword, hung vibrating slightly in the beam above the bed.

"Where you got the last one I can't see. There aren't that many places to hide a knife without clothing on. . . . So now that we've finished impressing the hell out of each other, what do you say to having some breakfast while I try to talk the innkeeper out of making an evening tidbit out of Ten-Knife?"

"I could always eat. Hold still a moment." A step forward, a leap, and she launched herself from Shkai'ra's shoulders, trusting her to hold fast, her weight there only for a second as she reached to snatch the blade out of the wood. Its ridged hilt slapped firmly into her palm, and she curled to land on the bed feet first.

Shkai'ra grabbed her out of the air, sweeping sideways to put arms behind shoulder and knees. She gave a slight *woof!* of surprise at the other woman's solid compact weight.

She kissed her with slow skill. "I'll send for breakfast, and your clothes," she said. "Of course, that leaves us with some time to fill." Shkai'ra licked her delicately behind one ear, then under the chin, and began a series of light kisses interspersed with tongue-flicks down the line of her throat. "Hmmm?"

Megan stiffened, surprised, then turned in the other's

arms, supple as an eel. She began nibbling at the hard smooth curve of her shoulder. "Hmmm!"

The Kommanza stuffed the last bit of bread into her mouth and finished buckling on her saber. The stiletto disappeared up one sleeve, and the dagger rode opposite the sword. Then she produced a stotpistol from under the pillow, a heavy double-barreled weapon with a pistol grip. Breaking it open, she checked the brass cartridges.

Megan disgustedly looked down at the glass she was holding. "Swill!" She threw the contents as far back into her throat as possible, so she wouldn't have to taste it, and shuddered. "Gahh, that's awful." She washed the taste of fish oil from her mouth with a swig of cold tea and sat on the pillow by the desk.

Shkai'ra clicked the firearm closed with a flexing of her wrist and walked over to run a finger around the clay tumbler. She tasted and made a grimace.

"Zoweitz of foulness, what *is* this stuff?" She patted her pouch to make sure the other two rounds were in place; that was the price of a good horse, and the weapon would buy and stock a farm.

Megan held up her hands and looked at the light glancing off the silvery nails. "The wi—one who gave me these warned me that the iron in them comes from me. Fish oil has the most of what is needed, and rather than letting my 'claws' leach me of something I need . . ." She reached out and tapped them on the mug. The sound rang hard. "I've had them only about seven, eight iron-cycles; moon-turnings, you would say."

Shkai'ra looked at her hands, halfway between nervousness and appreciation. That was a good magic, for a warrior; ten knives nobody would suspect and nobody could take away. Even the steel-sheen could have been paint; she had suspected nothing, until she felt them. At that, she rubbed her brown tunic, where it covered five long scratches running from the small of her back to one buttock.

"And *sharp*, too," she said. "You'll have to learn a little control, kh'eeredo."

"Sharp? Oh, I don't have a means of really honing them." She lapsed into silence. The word "kh'eeredo" had a sense of kinship in it, but this one had been a stranger to her just yesterday. *I trust her to a point, but can I?* There was a bond there; something she hadn't allowed herself in years. Bonds could be used against you. They opened you up to feeling and emotion. The old habits died hard; even the donning of clothing had put the other at arm's length. It was safer, but . . . she felt truly well for the first time in years. Perhaps the aloneness wasn't necessary, here.

Her voice was sharp as she turned away, a crease between the eyebrows. "A weapon, I take it?" She nodded at the shotpistol that Shkai'ra still held.

"Ia," Shkai'ra said, tossing it to her. Automatically, the small hand flashed out and caught it by the grip. "You point it, pull the trigger, and it blows holes in things. Magic, I suppose. Expensive, too; a last chance if you're cornered."

She turned and kicked her foot into a sandal, bracing the foot against the bed and winding the soft leather straps around her calf. Boots and trousers still felt more natural, but she looked alien enough as it was, and the Fehinnan clothes *were* more comfortable in this weather. Her back prickled slightly; it was early days, to let the little one behind her with a weapon. Still, she could have opened a vein last night, and Shkai'ra thought herself a judge of people. And it was one unmistakable way to show trust; she could use a partner.

As her other hand came up to support the weight of the thing, Megan looked at the Kommanza's back . . . and felt the fool. The weapon in her hands lay heavy, metal and smooth-worn wood; a means of death. A bond . . . well then, so be it. She would learn what it was like to have a companion.

"I see. I don't think it's magical." She opened her mouth, then stopped. *No, she needn't know everything, yet.* Decision made, she continued, "Would you exchange steel with me?"

Shkai'ra blinked, her people's expression of surprise; that was a ritual they used for deep trust. She drew her scabbarded poniard from her belt and extended it hilt first across her forearm. As she did, she wondered at herself; she was not usually so swift to accept friendship. It came to her that Megan must have been very alone, for a long time, without even the bonds of kin and discipline that gave a Kommanza an iron framework for life. They were both exiles.

Megan handed the westerner one of her belt daggers across her palms and examined the ten-inch knife she had received. The weight of it was less than the emotions it carried. She laughed suddenly, her eyes crinkling at the corners (how much easier that was), at Shkai'ra's expression. "How like our tools we are. That looks like a useless toy, a lady's weapon, but is well balanced and holds an edge well. Cut your shadow on that one, and this . . . simple, direct, elegant in its ruthlessness. *Celik Kizkardaz*, there is Steel between us." There was silence, then she stood suddenly. "So, show me this city that they are so proud of. Walking the streets as a zha-shaaid; what does that mean? Is not the best way to see the sights. I got called that enough to fill me to the back teeth last night."

Last night . . . a roar of crowds. Sibilant words that all made them sound like they were talking with a mouthful of mush. The taste of strawberries and the tiredness. She had seen one of the quieter streets. That had been darker, what with some of the lanterns that stood atop posts of poured stone lying shattered on the street. As the argument between the three at the cross street up ahead grew to a hissing that she could almost understand, she checked the location of her garrote. A flicker of steel, and one of them dropped choking on his own blood. They had glanced at her as she walked by, but her pace hadn't faltered, and they had gone back to their search of the corpse's clothing.

And Delight Street, rather the Street of Dubious Delights Tolerated But Not Approved. Cock fights, the boy who had lured the fat merchant woman in through the pink glass-bead curtain, fruit sellers, toy sellers, the scent of incense on the air. Figures as dirty as she was gathered in sullen groups; the one dragged down from the lamp post, where he sought to harangue the crowd, by the Watch. And the sound of agony as they beat him into a slowly dying example . . . even the well-dressed allowed the Watch room.

Hot oil and boiling onions, meat cooking and bread baking fighting with the odor of the crowd. The splintery-wood texture of the pike of the Weary Wayfarer's door guard barring her way, at eye level. That had disappeared fast enough at the sound of her coin ringing on the cobbles. A strange city.

Shkai'ra turned Megan's giftblade in her hands; it was a pleasure to handle something so well made.

"Shaaid?" she said absently. "Maggot. The poorest, dockworkers, day laborers. Escaped tenants, beggars, children born without kinfast. No money, skill, or lord: a million heads in this brick warren, and two-thirds are shaaid. They die by the thousand down in Low Town; more come in every day, to find the silver bricks of Illizbuah's streets."

"Better to be a—Gaaimun, is that the word?" They laughed and walked out into the brightness of the street, arms resting easily over shoulder and waist.

5

There were crowds along the Laneway of Impeccable Respectability; they turned to throngs as the two women turned onto the eastbound Street of Dubious Delights Tolerated But Not Approved; that was a major artery leading to the Old City. Carts drawn by oxen, mules, horses, dogs, and humans crowded the brick pavement; folk on foot thronged among them—naked porters bent under wicker baskets; robed upperservants; a party of off-duty soldiers in green leather tunics, hands on the hilts of their shortswords; two tall black Haytin from the Middle Sea, feathers nodding from their fantastic sculpted manes of coiled hair. Smells of sweat, dung, hay, smoke, hot brick dust hung around them among creak and clatter and babble, cast back by the three-story brick walls on either side.

Not every building along Delight Street was a joyden,

of course; tiny stores spilled their goods onto the raised side passages, hawkers cried, pedal-driven looms thumped from behind blank walls; a small girl in a loincloth stood and drew rude words on the stucco with a stick of charcoal until a harrassed-looking woman darted out to drag her off by one ear, swatting energetically with her other hand.

Megan dodged around a cart loaded twice head-high with cornstalks, then avoided a priest in a soiled orange robe with stubble on her shaven skull with a whirl that brought her to rest against the counter of a wineshop. Tubs of wine, beer, and fruitjuices were sunken into the counter, which bore stacks of cheap clay mugs, a dipper, and the elbows of a scowling owner.

Crowded, she thought. But the nature of the crowd had changed. People spoke more loudly, and sunlight brightened them; the nightfolk were gone to their pallets. This city at night had a darkness more than material, tasting of smoke and incense and music. A torrent of children passed, shrieking with the excitement of some incomprehensible game.

She reached over to touch Shkai'ra on the elbow. "See, that one there?"

Gawking, a boy of fifteen seasons stood on the corner. Tall for his age, and big in the wrists and ankles; Shkai'ra judged him to be from the Piedmont borderlands, from his long tunic and leggings and the pale freckled skin; perhaps of a yeoman-farmer kinfast.

"An easy mark," Megan said. She slid a tiny iron slug across the counter and took a cup of pomegranate juice, cool and tart on her tongue. Briefly, she wondered at the metal's value. "In F'talezon, the childpacks would leave him stripped and wondering on the Dragonlord's doorstep. Not a healthy place."

"Not greatly different here," Shkai'ra said as they elbowed their way forward again. A woman in a soiled white tunic was talking to the boy. "That's Maihra, of the LowLords. They specialize in kidnapping; that one's kinfast will have to pay well for him."

Megan slipped and struggled back to Shkai'ra's side, playing idly with the strings of her beltpurse. "If they don't notice it's gone," she said with a wink, "I don't have to give it back, do I?" There was a clink, and a coil of tradewire disappeared into the depths of her pouch. "So. What to be doing should we?"

Shkai'ra looked down at her. "You can buy anything in Illizbuah, anything that exists and some things that don't. But I know *just* the place."

The weapons shop was part of the Dark Creatures of the Earth Brought Forth and Transformed by Effulgent Light: one of the metalworkers' bazaars. The whole of it was covered, two stories high on arched glass-fiber-concrete; below were narrow laneways through acres of milling confusion; customers, guards, artisans, fetch-and-carry slaves, apprentices, foodsellers. For all that, it was less crowded than might have been expected; access was limited, and Shkai'ra had had to show her member's sigil in the Guards', Mercenaries', and Caravaneers' Guild to enter.

"*Whulzhaitz,*" she snarled in her own language. "Sheepshit. Sometimes I think it would have been better to settle among unlettered folk. At least if they rob or kill or imprison you, it will be for a better reason than not having your papers in order."

They plunged into the crowd. Shkai'ra's height and sword and alien looks made only a modicum of elbowwork needful; she noted that surprisingly few jostled Megan, and none twice. The air was thick, smoke from the forges despite their fuel of charcoal or city gas; sweat; the vinegary smell of hot metal; the soapy almost-taste of quenching oil. Light was dim through the grimy skylights, and Shkai'ra found her way more by instinct and memory than sight; both played her false more than once, amid booths cobbled of board and canvas.

"Been more than a year; they shift. . . . Ah, here." One alcove opened to a long narrow workshop. It was for display, and a little finishing work; a lathe whirred somewhere in the background, and the teeth-jarring sound of a grindstone came, clear through the endless surf-roar of the crowds echoing from the pillars.

The proprietor looked up from dashing a dipper of water over his head as they turned sideways to enter. The wet glistened on his scalp, bald as an egg, and on skin as black as the soot of his trade and seamed with five decades of forgeheat. He was dressed in a loincloth and leather apron; not a tall man, but muscle bulked huge on ape-thick arms and shoulders.

"Hai, Firehair!" he said, grinning hugely. He had the slightest trace of an accent; native-born, but his mother had wandered in on a ship from the Sea Islands. "No need to ask what you seek."

He waved a hand toward the walls and racks. Weapons, and things that must be weapons from the company they kept. There were swords, short double-edged cut-and-thrust blades; the long single-edged cavalry swords with basket hilts that the east-coast kingdoms favored. Pensa broadswords, as tall as Shkai'ra at the hilt. Curved swords, recurved chopping blades, swords mounted on poles, swords that slid into canes and umbrellas and scribes' bookstands. Knives of every description, from a main-gauche as long as a forearm, meant to do duty as a shield, to a dainty little razor-edge thin and flexible enough to slip inside a belt, with the hilt shaped as a buckle. Spearheads, pikeheads of metal or fiber-bound ceramic or glass. Halberd heads, knife-sharp chainlike fighting irons, throwing stars, blow-pipes that slid in sections like telescopes. Behind lay bits and pieces of armor.

Megan said not one word, but the wall drew her as if the metal were magnetized. *Good work here,* she thought. Layer-forged, from the sheen, with charcoal added. Her eyes were caught by a blade hanging just above her eye level. *Eastern work? Did I not know better I would say that was one of our best. It matches our best; what a market for metal, could I find a way to get it here.* She turned and raised an eyebrow at the smith. "Trade goods from oversea? Worth maybe the iron that makes it."

"Good work," he said. "As good as mine or my kinmates, but different." He lifted it down with huge spatulate fingers that were somehow delicate, and bellowed over his shoulder, "Tea!"

"See," he continued. "Layer work, yes . . . but I think they used iron and steel wire, not twinned barstock. Nice! Firehair's sword is like that, but it comes from the northwest. For this, I could give you, oh, only one-twenty-fifth the weight in gold."

A boy of twelve with something of the man's build came in from the rear with a tray. The tray was grubby leather, but the flask and cups were Naiglun porcelain, delicate and simple and lovely, eggshell-thin. The smith lifted one cup, the scarred and calloused hands closing on it as lightly as on a rose. "The Sun shine on you!" he said. "A pleasure to deal with someone who knows good work."

Megan gently touched the teacup with a forefinger and decided against picking up the scalding-hot utensil. "*Tschchak*. I thank you, but one can see from the color that it is oil- and not blood-quenched, a less, ah, expensive way of cooling. One fiftieth."

"Brightness! The offer is an insult to the weapon. And who needs blood quenching? Superstition! A tub of seawater with leather soaked a week does as well. For that price I could offer this." He reached over and picked out a lesser-quality dagger, still of steel; a rustless one, but laid beside the first the difference was obvious.

She blew gently over the cup she had just lifted and sipped, carefully. This sort of thing she knew. She looked through the steam at the smith, and settled herself for a long session. "Perhaps when we speak of silver rather than gold would I consider this one, or others. The market seems to hold many smithies—perhaps I should look around first." She set the cup down. "I thank you for the tea. It was nicely made."

The smith scowled and signaled his kinchild to replace the cup. A horn cup of fruit juice succeeded it. "Bah. The others would cheat a foreigner on principle. I am a man without prejudice, and nothing is too good for a friend of a friend. Besides, you would care for the steel. For you . . ."

Shkai'ra laughed. "Now you've unsaddled yourself," she said. "Next to working the metal, he loves bargaining." She turned to examine a tray of arrowheads.

It went on for a while, discussing relative worth of workmanship, the smith bewailing the necessity of being generous to a friend's friend, protesting that his kin had to eat. At last, before them lay the eastern knife, three of lesser quality, and a knife harness.

"Ach, we are agreed on one-thirtieth for the one; but for the others . . ." She sighed. "The most I could agree on there would be one-seventh, silver."

"You would have my work for nothing? It pains me. Five."

Megan pondered. "Since you are *Freyat Kizkar*"—Friend-of-kin—"I would be generous. Five and a half if the harness comes too."

He frowned deeply. "You make me cut out my heart on the altar of friendship! May the Sun see my generosity to a stranger! Agreed." And they slapped hands on the bargain.

She turned, buckling on the harness and trying various placements for the blades.

"A heavy investment," Shkai'ra said, replacing a bola with balls of stone set with bronze spikes. She hesitated as another came through the curtain; a blind man, old, with skin like weathered parchment. He wore a patched tunic and carried staff and begging bowl. It was a moment before you realized the eyelids were permanently shut.

"Harriso!" she said.

Megan snicked a blade back into its sheath. "Investment in the tools of the trade," she said. "Another friend?"

The man's face turned toward her, nostrils flaring. Then he smiled, his face a network of wrinkles, the smile of an ancient, wicked, merry child.

"So, you come to the City again, red-hand," he said in a smooth, well-modulated voice. Megan's Fehinnan was just barely good enough to recognize the accent of an aristo-crat, or a scholar. "And another foreigner with you. One who smells of death-to-come, like you."

He turned to the smith. "Kermibo, my friend, today I think we must forsake our discussion of the philosophy of Annitli the Subtle."

The metalworker shrugged. "We're getting in some new barstock, anyway." He smiled sheepishly at Shkai'ra's in-quiring eyebrow. "Well, a person must have something to do in their age. . . . Fare you well." As they pushed aside the curtain, he added: "And bring many more such friends; more business for me than that boy acrobat last year!"

Shkai'ra cleared her throat and turned her head to the beggar. "How goes the city, Harriso?" she asked.

He shrugged, and used his staff to trip a woman who had jostled him into a stack of pots. "In and out, around and about, as ever, red-hand."

"A philosophy?" Megan inquired. "Written, perhaps?"

Both the others regarded her curiously. Harriso opened his mouth to answer, then shifted to a mendicant's whine.

"Alms! Alms and the Light will shine upon you! A copper buys so little, and the Beggar King must have his half of that."

A member of the Watch strolled by, eyes appropriately roving. Shkai'ra broke off a bit from a copper coil and tossed it into his bowl.

"I can smell them," Harriso said. The metal disappeared into his tunic. "You travel in learned company. As to the City—the Sun-on-Earth, in his wisdom, has issued a proclamation doubling the taxes on breadmeal, salt, and fish."

His hand tightened slightly on her elbow, and Shkai'ra choked off her reply.

"So that all may know the wisdom of this, the proclamation is to be read from the steps of the temple. Great is the wisdom of the God Among Us," he added dryly, "but *I* will be content with secondhand knowledge."

The blond woman stopped at a vendor's stall and bought stewed lentils, a round of flat bread, and ground chickpeas fried in oil. Accepting the well-filled bowl, he squatted in a corner and produced a bone implement from his tunic, with a fork at one end and a spoon at the other. Eating with fastidious neatness, he continued, "We will speak later, in privacy, I think." The blind eyes turned to Megan. "May my fingers see your face?" The touch was feather-light. "Ah, younger than the voice. Yes," he added gently. "If you wish to peruse the Path of the Ten True Ways, you may. The printed book does me little good, in these days."

As the old hands gently took in the line of her face, she smiled at his compliment, but she thought of being in dark for the rest of her life and quelled a shudder, feeling sudden anger for the injury done. She could see faint marks around the ruined eyes that spoke of deliberate blinding, yet in him she felt a serenity lacking in most. Wisdom, she thought. Not content but tolerance. She grasped the hand and said, "Old books and scrolls are of interest to me. My name is Megan, Elder." She rose and turned to Shkai'ra. "The temple. The dome? Perhaps we should hear this proclamation. It would, after all, be natural that strangers go to see this place."

6

"What was the old one, before?" Megan said, clinging to the arm of the pedicab. The ride was as smooth as glass-fiber springs and rubber tires could make it, but the four sweating laborers on the pedals were forced to a good many swerves and swift brakings in the congested street. Besides, the machine was new to her.

"A noble, and a priest," Shkai'ra said, reclining at her ease. No Kommanza liked to walk when there was an alternative, and keeping a horse in the City was beyond her means. "He fell from power, but the priests of the Sun are sacred. So they took his eyes, rather than his life. His wits are as sharp as ever, and he hears everything. I saved his life once; not much of a life, he said, but the only one available at the moment."

The machine swerved among horses, carriages, wagons, and swarming pedestrians. Kilometer after kilometer of Illizbuah slid by; tall buildings and low, brick and concrete and some sheathed in stucco or mosaic or stone; streets of weavers, of lensgrinders, potters, leatherworkers, apothecaries; little corner temples; the blank walls that courtyard-centered tenements turned to the streets. The heat grew, and the crowds flowed eastward. Ahead they could see the battlements of the wall that separated the Old City from the New. Helmets and spearpoints flashed from the wall; flamethrowers snouted, and dartcasters. Five centuries ago this had been the city's outer shell, and it served the purposes of its masters to maintain it.

The gates were swung open and the crowd streamed into the darkness of the tunnel, through another set of gates that would close a small courtyard and through the

two dogleg jogs in the road before emerging into the Old
City. Megan took in the arrow slits, shielded slots, noz-
zles, and various other strange openings where the walls
met the ceiling and in the ceiling itself. "A cautious people. Do they have reason to be?" She thought of the
shaaid beaten in the street, raising a shattered no-face to
the crowd, last night. The cleanliness of this city was
strange, but the stink of corruption was just as strong as at
home. The mood of the crowd grated on her, raising
hackles. There was trouble here, for all its fairness.

"Not usually," Shkai'ra said. "I've never seen a city so
strong, and it rules broad lands. Nobody's stormed it since
the Maleficent's time, and that doesn't count; nothing and
nobody resisted *her*." Shkai'ra frowned in the tunnel gloom.

"Odd," she said. "They usually have a guard detail
here, checking papers. And there are more shaaids here
than I'd expect. They have the money to keep slaves for
most rough work in the Old City, rather than hire day
labor."

Past the gate the roads were wider and less crowded; a
relic of previous centuries, when Illizbuah had been a
garrison of administrators and absentee landlords rather
than a center of trade and crafts. High walls covered in
glass mosaic swept by, the tips of trees hinting at gardens
within.

Megan joined Shkai'ra in glancing uneasily at the crowds
around them, sweeping toward the central square. There
was too much purpose here. That faded from her mind as
they swept through the last blocks of offices that surrounded Temple Square. Everything did.

"Elder Brother," she breathed, with almost reverent
awe. There had been glimpses of it, over the intervening
buildings, but . . . not this. The base of the temple was a
block a thousand meters on a side, sheathed in white
marble polished to glass brightness. Above that reared the
gold-sheathed dome, six hundred feet; a hundred feet
more of flame lancing, searing from the apex. The bright
nooning sun blazed off it until it hurt the eye; a huge
blazing pile that left intolerable afterimages scouring across
her eyes and brought involuntary tears of pain. A monolith
that must have taken years to build, and many deaths.

She had awe for the sheer daunting effect that reduced

the people at its foot to less than ants, and the ages of worship, living, dying, and pain that soaked every stone in its construction. But somehow she wished for the feeling of age and agelessness of the Goddess's mountains; as old as the world and scoured by wind and rain, not by priests. In them was no twistedness. And a small voice in the back of her mind snidely asked what all that gilding would bring. Her eyes and all her senses were fixed on the dome, and she paid little attention to the fact that they had alighted. To build such a thing, its roots must reach back into years of belief in their god.

"Gods!"

Shkai'ra nodded. "I didn't speak for half a day, the first time I saw it." She looked around. The crowd was dense, with little swirls of tension erupting around a fight, or a speaker, as the mass swirled to pack itself around the broad steps of the building. "Let's get a good vantage spot."

A pickpurse laid a hand on her pouch. Without turning she grabbed his wrist, locked it, and wrenched the shoulder out of its socket with a twist. Looking up, she saw clouds piled over the city, hot gold towering up into the sky.

"In fact, something tells me that it would be better off this pavement. Let's move, kh'eeredo—I want some height." She slanted off toward a building that formed one corner of the square, making liberal use of her elbows and knees and the hilt of her sheathed saber. Those who turned to take a second look mostly fell silent. Megan moved in her wake, partly in the space she cleared, partly using the vicious minor tricks one of her size had perforce to learn. She looked up at Shkai'ra's back with a mixture of exasperation and amusement. It was like herdbeasts parting for a big cat; not exactly fear, but an instinctive caution.

They turned into a sidestreet, edged toward a wall where it was easier to push against the squareward current, then climbed three flights of stairs past terra-cotta moldings to a wineshop set in the third story of the office building. Megan darted ahead, to be met by a majordomo with arrogantly raised brows.

He looked down on her in every sense of the word, then up to Shkai'ra. She stood with her head slightly to one side, regarding him with detached curiosity. Both women were obvious outlanders, and their tunics no more than modestly rich. There was dust on their feet; he was conscious of the sweat that had plastered the thin linen to the tall one's breasts, and the smell of her, clean but strong, like a horse that had been pulling a cart in the sun.

"This shop is full," he said, in an affected upper-class Fehinnan, using forms new to Megan's recently acquired peasant dialect. "Doubtless there are those who will welcome your custom, down by the docks."

Megan bristled. Shkai'ra smiled. At least, her lips came back from her teeth as she stretched an arm over the other woman and laid a hand on the headservant's shoulder. The long fingers dug in, putting pressure on the nerve bundles; the muscles stood out in her forearm and shoulder and the thick pad around her wrist that told of daily saber drill for most of her twenty-eight years.

"My—arm!" he gasped.

"Not for long," Shkai'ra said cheerfully. With her other hand she dug a piece of silver tradewire out of her pouch. "Now, about the table? The corner one, next the window?"

He felt a coldness in his groin and looked down. The little blackhair was standing closer, and her hand was below the hem of his tunic. It moved, and he felt the blade flat against his inner thigh.

The table was a good one. The mugs of the thick, rather lumpy corn beer of Fehinna arrived, quickly. The crowd among them were mostly robed and shaven-pated; in the white of the lay bureaucracy, or the orange of the temple. Ostentatiously, they ignored the intruders in their midst; they would have been offended to discover that these heeded them not at all.

"Something tells me . . . ah!" Shkai'ra said, shading her eyes against the glare and staring across the vastness of the square to the knot of figures who had appeared on the temple steps. Even at this distance, the burnished steel-plate armor of one was obvious.

"General-Commander Smyna Caaituh's-Kin, wearing the price of a thousand acres on her back. And see the ones in cloth-of-gold? Priests and acolytes, high-ranking ones."

Out in the square the crowd was gathering, clotting into

a brownish-gray mass before the steps and the main entrance. A thin line of guards knelt and faced the crowd, their points a string of order across the front of its chaos, separating them from the building and the lords. The sound of feet and voices was a surfthrob across the stone-paved expanse.

"How many of them are there?" Megan asked.

Shkai'ra thought, and glanced down at her toes in the openwork sandals. "Perhaps . . . five tens of thousands," she said. It was an impressive number; there were not that many adults in the whole Kommanz of Granfor, but even so the crowd did not fill the whole of Temple Square. A broad, vaguely wedge-shaped blot spread out from the main entrance to end crowded against the fringing building at their feet, but to the left and right the mass thinned into individuals.

The glittering figures on the upper tier of steps were addressing the crowd below; a barrel-chested herald with a megaphone relayed the speech to the mob. Who were not taking it well, from the stirring and buzzing that rippled across the sea of heads.

Megan frowned. "Why provoke unrest?" she asked.

Shkai'ra shrugged. "Who knows? Politicians and priests are no less prone to making mistakes than other folk." She finished the mug, wiped her mouth on the back of her hand, and signaled for another; it had been a hot day. "New taxes, that means a new project. War, perhaps. There were rumors of it to the south, as I worked my way up from the Middle Sea. But then, there always are; the neighbor states have been staring at Fehinna like rabbits at a weasel since the Pensa stopped being a power, when the Maleficent died."

She propped her chin on one hand. "Expensive, if they mean it. Of course, the merchant princes would have to pay for most of it, which the landowners wouldn't mind, and they dominate the Righteous Sword. Smyna's poisonous as a whipsnake, but no fool: I found that out when I was an officer in the irregulars. Not like her to let a crowd of city rabble get this big or ugly . . . sssssssa!"

The priests and generals had finished their address. And the crowd made its response, an animal noise that raised the hackles on Shkai'ra's neck with an odd, avatistic thrill-

ing. Starvation itself makes humans passive. They creep
away to die, quite quietly; once the initial hunger is done
there is only an increasing lassitude. But the *fear* of famine, among those who have lived on its edge all their lives,
is another matter. The crowd became a mob, and the
human animal is braver in groups than alone. By themselves they might have cowered. Shkai'ra had seen shaaids
clubbed with hardly an effort to escape. But the mob
poured up the steps, reaching for its tormentors with a
hundred thousand arms.

"Now," Megan said calmly, "there will be a great killing. Of who depends on how clever those priests were."
Her hands tightened on the cup.

Shkai'ra could sense the tension in her, although no sign
showed in stance or movement. This was altogether more
serious than she had awaited. There was no personal danger, but . . .

Around the curve of the temple came a thunder of
drums, and even against the roaring of voices it rolled
irresistibly. The grandees and their guards filed backward
into the temple, and the doors swung shut with soundless
power as counterweights levered. The two women could
see the crowd recoil from the direction of the sound, or
try to. Above their heads appeared a line of bright ob-
longs, sun-flared; pikepoints, a block five hundred pikes
long and six deep, in perfect mathematical alignment.

"This will be a massacre," Megan whispered.

Shkai'ra nodded. "Not much doubt of who, either," she
said. "Watch. About . . . *now.*" Her curiosity was detached;
unlike most Kommanza she cared for those close to her,
but empathy on a larger scale was not a quality one of her
breed could learn.

Across the square came a megaphone-amplified voice.
The phalanx had pivoted on the great building, the outer-
most ranks double-timing. Now it faced the mob like a
solid bar, motionless.

"PIKEPOINTS—DOWN!"

A long smooth ripple, as the first four ranks of eighteen-
foot polearms came down and halted, staggered to present
a row of points. From behind the rigid columns of the
pikes, men and women in light armor ran foreward to kneel
in ranks of their own, under the sharp-honed protection.

The crowd surged forward, back, eddying along the row of foot-long metal points; the four edges of each pile-shaped pikehead blinked, blinding-bright. Suddenly there was a flurry; a ragged figure rushed in to chop at the haft of a pike with an ax.

The next four pikes jabbed forward and back in vicious darts, quick as a trout's snap at a fly, drawing free dark and wet. The impaled body rose, passed backward over the soldiers from row to row on the polearms, limp and dangling twenty feet above the pavement.

"It all depends on how fast the crowd breaks," Megan said. She took a pull at the sweet frothy beer, wondering how such a force might betrained. The troopers were standing motionless under the spatter of blood and fluids from the grisly bundle, and even from here she could sense the unchanging mask of their expressions. She looked down, away from the square.

"Are they fanatics?" she asked.

"Nearly," Shkai'ra replied, sighing into her beer. This was one thing she had never learned to like about Fehinna: her own people brewed theirs from barley, and imported hops. "Those are lifetime regulars. The Bounding Marshcats Advancing Fearless Against the Foe, Protected by the Glorious Light. Or the Bouncing Kitties, as the other regiments call them. When there aren't any of them around to hear."

Megan surprised herself with a chuckle. On its heels came the amplified voice from the square.

"DISPERSE IMMEDIATELY. TO YOUR KENNELS, SHAAIDS!" The tone was bored, the accent a peculiar lisping drawl that the mob recognized. Gaaimun speech, the dialect of the aristocracy.

The crowd snarled, a chilling basso growl. They ran forward, or the rear of the huge mass did, pushing those in front toward the line of steel. For a moment the pikes stabbed, flicking like knitting needles. The crossbows knelt, stock-still.

"AIM!"

The weapons came to shoulders.

"READY!"

A thousandfold click.

"LOOSE!"

Repeating crossbows; they would fire as often as the triggers were pulled, while the six-round magazines held bolts. Those would penetrate two naked bodies before lodging in a third, or even the best armor at close range. Six thousand bolts were fired in thirty seconds, and the endless twanging of the strings was matched by a multifold meaty thumping, like wet hands slapping on fresh liver.

"ADVANCE!"

The drums spoke, the pikes moved forward with a sense of utter inevitability. The killing machine of Fehinna walked, and nothing was left behind it but the dead. Megan's eyes flickered to Shkai'ra. She swallowed and forced herself to lean back, casually.

"How do they deal with the cleanup?" asked the Zak. The missile troops were pausing to crank the springs of their crossbows and collect bolts. "With all those bodies, you'd think there would be a risk of plague."

She turned again to the window. Below, the limestone pavement was awash with red, thick trickles of it running from the long windrow of bodies where the bolts had struck, smaller streams from the thick scattering of shaaids piked as the phalanx advanced across the square. Some of those were still stirring, but not for long. Under the monotonous thutter of the drums the sound of the mob had changed. It was higher-pitched now, more like the monstrous wailing of some giant child.

She had noticed a hush falling on the wineshop; her last remark had fallen like a rock into a pool. Around her the clerks were pasty-faced, their gaze fixed on the horror in the square. This had been unexpected, and few of them were as used to the raw salt latrine-and-blood stink of a battlefield as she or Shkai'ra.

The edges of the crowd below had begun to fray as some raced for the exits to the square. And found them blocked by detachments who knelt with leveled pikes, crossbows ready behind them. There was no escape. Around the temple, another infantry regiment was deploying, herding the remnants of the mob back into the killing ground.

Over the milling slaughteryard below a trumpet spoke, high and sweet. With it came the sound of hooves. Behind the first line of pikes another row of steel points appeared, these still bright, many trailing brightly colored ribbons.

"Wasteful. But then with so many, lives are counted cheaply." For some reason she felt uneasy about the safety of this place. The ranks of the pikes swung open, huge and ponderous and smooth, like some gigantic door moving on greased bearings. The lancer company sat their horses as if carved, until the order rang out.

"READY!"

The lancebutts came out of their buckets; the heads came down as the riders locked them under armpits. The remains of the mob milled and screamed and clawed the smooth walls of the buildings around the square or the locked portals of the temple itself. They spread away from the death facing them to be trapped by walls. In the center of the square a child looked up and ceased pulling at one of the bodies lying like a bundle of rags in the blood.

"CHARGE!"

It began as a clattering. It built to an endless roar of hooves as the sound echoed and reechoed on stone. The dead and wounded were pulped under the stony avalanche, only one or two of the war-trained destriers balking at the uncertain footing. The lancers swept through the bulk of the mob, then the shafts were broken, or left jammed in bone. And the swords came out, bright and long.

"Oh, they grind the bodies up and feed them to the gaspits," Shkai'ra said. "Burn the gas for light, and use the sludge for fertilizer. Smart. Not that I'm surprised the shaaids were ready to riot—death so casually handed down by decree was too much. Stupid of them to riot here, rather than in their own quarter; all it did was attract more attention." She paused, a thought spurred by one of Harriso's comments. "Unless, of course, that was the idea."

From below, over the desperate roar of the crowd, there was a sudden thudding boom.

Shkai'ra started up. "Baiwan Thunderer hammer me flat for a fool, there's a door from here out onto the square!"

"We go up then." Megan glanced out the window. The wall was smooth stucco with no ornamentation. "Where are the stairs?" She slid from the table and headed for the door.

"Out the door, down to the end of the corridor—the stairwell goes right out to the roof." The long curved sword snapped out into her hand. "We can—sheep*shit*!"

From below there was a rending crash as the doors gave

way, and a long baying roar as the mob poured in. The wineshop was three stories up, and there was a broad open stairway from the lobby. *Press of numbers will slow them*, Shkai'ra thought. Even more so, now that they were fleeing in panic rather than attacking. There was a chance, provided they gained the roof quickly; if they stayed here, none.

She tried to force her way forward; boots, elbows, butting head. It was useless, and even the edge of her saber failed. She slashed one man's face, broke another's collarbone with the hilt, and their neighbors hardly noticed. To the respectable of Illizbuah an uprising of the shaaid was an ever-present nightmare from childhood, and even the bright metal before their eyes was less terrible.

7

The doorkeeper was nervous but determined. In Illizbuah, keeper-of-portals was a responsible post, and this was not the first confidential mission she had made. "My master, Milampo Terhan's-Kin the Enterprising, awaits your reply," she said.

The old man bent again over the flowerbank. The yellow of the rhododendrons flared against the creamy white linen of his robe, and a single bee paused to alight on his finger. He brought it close to his eyes and studied the intricate veining of its wings for an instant. "Beautiful," he murmured. He turned to the messenger.

"Even now, people of this city are dying at the hands of the Sun-on-Earth's soldiers, because your master and his kin-in-wealth aroused them to fruitless anger. This would have been a . . . disharmonious deed even if the purpose behind it had succeeded. As it is, the position of your

THE SHARPEST EDGE   55

master's enemies is even more secure. Can unwisdom ever be righteous?"

Around them the courtyard garden spread in sunlit graciousness; not at all what the servant had expected of a notorious sorcerer. Birds fluted in the rich green ivy that covered the brick walls and archways; within, flowerbeds, potted trees, and herbs made coolness and shade in the heat of lowland summer. The mage himself might have been any elderly patrician of scholarly bent.

She straightened her back, courteous and firm. "I am not empowered to negotiate, Honored Wisdom." She hesitated, then dropped the "Effulgent with the Sun's Light"; that might not be tactful, in the house of one the temple declared abomination. "However, my master anticipated your reply. He instructed me to point out that many more lives will be lost if the war which is planned comes to pass; directly, and by the famine and pestilence which follow the armies. Also that the temple will not be satisfied to fleece either the city or the neighbor realms; souls, not gold, are what the Reflection desires."

Her voice dropped a register, unconsciously, as she began to quote: " 'With greed I and my kinmates and colleagues can deal. For fanaticism, we require aid.' "

The magician released the bumblebee, watching its soaring with brown eyes that held a troubling serenity.

"Indeed, we of the Guild of the Wise remember the persecutions. . . . It would not be well should the current Reflection garner too much of the Sun-on-Earth's attention." He paused; it was never easy and seldom advisable to explain the workings of the Art to an outsider. "As to means, perhaps events will take a more . . . fortunate turn."

He produced a leather pouch. "The message, for your master. And for yourself, a gift."

She looked at it dubiously. "Messages can be stolen," she said. The consequences of a message from the guild falling into the hands of the temple, or even the secular authorities, were too obviously horrible to need detailing. "Best written on air. I am my master's trusted servant."

"And messengers may be taken, and forced." Somehow his gesture stilled her protests. "No, I make no reflection on your honor. But none, I think, will read that message until young Yeva lifts the blocking on it; it was for such matters that we consented to her accepting . . . ah . . . hospitality."

Still she looked down at the bag so innocently proffered as if it concealed a poisonous insect; then her hand slowly went out to take it, twitching back as his hand moved. Its weight settled into her sweaty palm, something crinkling under her closed fingers. She tucked it away into her beltpurse, then looked again at the old man. For all the drowsy, sweet-smelling peacefulness of this place, she would be glad to be back in the stink and clamor of the streets. Peace was held here, close and unwelcome to her.

"Honored Wisdom." She bowed and backed up a step or two. "I go." She backed further than was necessary for courtesy and left; fled, one could say, even though she only hurried and never saw the gentle amusement in the old man's eyes.

The street outside was far too quiet for this area and time of day. Normally servants stopped to gossip, dodging riders and carriages as they carried out their errands, as they ostensibly paused to rest their various bundles and parcels. It was still crowded, but only one or two carriages were out, and not a rider in sight. People walked rapidly, with their heads down as if to avoid rain, and tended to keep to the edges of the street, close under the walls and trees. Only occasionally did someone glance up for a second toward the sound coming, distantly, from Temple Square. It was like the sound of one's own blood roaring faintly in the depths of a seashell, with the odd sharper note. The doorkeeper paused just outside the old one's gate, then carefully matched her pace to the flow of what traffic there was. It was not difficult for her to feign the hurried furtive pace of the others. As she vanished down the street, from a rooftop behind her a dark-hooded head rose over one of the ornate parapets and a hand flashed in silent signal to a woman sitting by a shoulder yoke, below. She bent, lifted the yoke with a practiced twist that settled it, and followed in the doorkeeper's wake. Behind them both a shadow flitted across the roof, followed by another.

*   *   *

The room had dissolved into a seething chaos; milling human meat with no direction or purpose save its own survival; no way through. Shkai'ra bounded to a tabletop. "Follow me!" Her voice was pitched to a battlefield shout that rang over the mob noise. She leaped from table to table with a surefooted goatlike agility. Megan jumped in her wake, knife flickering as panic-stricken hands clutched at them.

"I must have brains like sheepshit in shallow water trying to make it to dry land!" Shkai'ra snarled, balancing on the heaving surface of a table and kicking hard into a face. "Megan, if—when we get out of this, you owe me a good kick in the arse."

The Zak leaped clear as the rocking table went over. "A commendable sentiment, but this is not the time to discuss it," she said. A hysterical figure in white clutched at her ankles. Megan slashed, and felt the knife grate on a spine. A clot of bureaucrats by the door were trying to close the frail latticework barrier against the onrush of the shaaids; the basketweave portal would have been hard pressed to stop a single kick. "Fools!"

Pain stabbed through her right leg. "Son of a dog-sucking pig!" she shrilled, and stamped. There was a brittle snapping, more felt than heard.

"I should have thought of it, too," she continued. "Duck!"

They vaulted to the floor from the last table as a chair leg whirred through the air overhead. The folk by the door were too preoccupied to look behind; Shkai'ra slammed two knuckles into the kidney of one, grabbed a shaven head by the ear and rapped it into the brickwork, clubbed a third behind the ear with the pommel of her saber, and then shortened the blade to stab a neat handspan deep beside a spine. Out of the corner of her eye she saw the last figure in front of Megan dropping with a slit hamstring. There was a good deal of noise, which both ignored.

"Right," the Kommanza breathed, wrenching at the locked door before kicking flat-footed beside the mechanism.

The women skidded out into the corridor, just as the first six members of the mob sprinted panting by on their way to the stairs. Below, the surf-roar intensified; this was the first spray cast before a wave that would crush. The last of the ragged figures turned; she bore a wooden club studded with chips of glass, and they could see the lice crawling amid the stubble and mange of her cropped hair.

"Gaaimuns!" she screamed. "Gentlefolk!" It was a curse. Her cry turned the others from escape, and hate conquered fear; they attacked.

Shkai'ra felt suddenly at ease; it would have been better in armor, on horseback, but this was a situation in which she felt completely at home. She flicked the saber forward into the two-handed grip used for work on foot without a shield, filled her lungs, and charged.

"AaaaaaiiiiiEEEEEEEEEEEEEE . . ." Fighting, she shrieked, a wailing falsetto that wavered up into the insane squealing of the blood trill. Her first stroke snapped up from left to right with the immense leverage of both arms spaced on the long hilt; it flickered under the clumsy cudgel and opened the woman's abdominal cavity in a diagonal line. Without pause the sword swept up over her head; her hands shifted, the left to the end of the pommel, right on the back of the blade to give more force. It came down in a streak like a solid arc of silver to carve through the forehead of the second rioter while his obsidian knife was still slipping from its sheath. Shkai'ra's body extended effortlessly in a lunge across the falling form. The point went in under the breastbone of the next shaaid, slicing up through the lungs to lodge for a moment in the shoulderblade.

Megan stepped to one side to allow the first body to fall past her, slipping along the wall. One shaaid, stumbling over the corpse of his fellow, went down, his hands fluttering up to touch the hilt of the knife standing in his throat before he died. As Shkai'ra lunged to skewer her third opponent another grabbed for a blood-slippery weapon, striking from below and to the side. The gift-blade, given just that morning, spun glittering from Megan's hand under Shkai'ra's raised arm to sink itself into his eye. In the roar from behind and below, the sound of his death was lost. She leaped over the slash of the last shaaid, coming down hard on a vulnerable instep. The woman lurched and tried to grasp her broken foot. She arched back in an impossible, spine-cracking bow as the knife slid into her kidneys. As her head came back, Megan reached out, pulled the head down by the hair, and cut her throat, all in one motion. The knives slid out just as easily as they had gone in, and she snatched at the blade standing in the eyesocket of the one corpse. "Move! We'll compare technique later!"

The bodies spilled around them in a tangle of blood and body fluids and liquid feces from slit intestine. Shkai'ra paused for an instant to grab a handful of rag as she stepped over them, wiping the slippery soles of her sandals.

"Let's *go*," she said. The corridor stretched before them, smooth stuccoed brick, to the swinging door at the end. They took it on the run, flinging themselves up the stairs in long strides; Shkai'ra checked herself to let the shorter woman keep pace. Their hands left faint red smears on the scrubbed white pine of the balustrade.

The stairwell exited on the flat central roof of the building. Five stories above the carnage of the square there was only the roar of sound and the clean breeze of the upper air; they stood on a flat courtyard of cracked gray concrete slabs, surrounded on four sides by low-pitched roofs of red tile. At the opposite end of the rectangle was another exit; beside it stood ten soldiers in heavy infantry armor, armed with shortened close-combat spears, huge oblong shields, and double-edged stabbing swords. Bright sun glinted on their harness, yellow trim on the edges of shiny green varnished plates and scutes of leather backed with fiberglass. Their officer wore the same round steel bowl helmet, but his carried a plume.

Shkai'ra traded glances with the commander. "Sheepshit," she said with slow disgust. "Glitch Godlet of Fuckups is with me today."

The Fehinnan officer's dark face was split by a white-toothed smile. "Shkai'ra!" he said. "Such a pity we'll never be able to toss the bones together again. On the other hand, I won't have to pay those thirty silvers the dice lost me, either. . . . Kill them."

The squad trotted forward with bored professional competence, at the regulation pace, with just enough space between them to give support without hindering each other. The shields with the sun-disk blazon covered them from neck to knees; greaves, thighguards, breast-and-backs, gorgets, helmets left not a joint exposed. The broad honed heads of the spears glinted, held ready for the upward gutting stroke that would dart from behind the shields and return like the tongue of a snake. These were not gutter starvelings armed with blades of glass.

Megan wiped the stickiness from her palms onto her tunic, drew a knife, feinted, and threw. Behind the rank of his troopers the officer ducked his head and let the blade ring off his helmet; it was too far for a reasonable throw against an alert opponent.

"Well?" she said to Shkai'ra, as they backed before the line of points. "Any plans?"

Shkai'ra bent to unclip the tags of her sandals, kicked her feet free, and tucked them into her belt.

"We have two choices," she said thoughtfully. "We can fight, or we can run." She paused. "Let's run."

She bounced backward, onto the sloping surface of the tiled roof. Her toes splayed out, gripping at the slick dusty surface as she side-walked back and up, knees bent. Megan joined her; below, the squad turned and paced them. They were on the outer roof, facing the temple; they would have to cross three sides of the building's roof to climb down or gain the next.

The captain opened his mouth, then paused as the stairwell his prey had used echoed to a long howling roar.

"*Aykkuka!*" he snapped. The sergeant backed two careful paces out of the shieldline before turning to face him. "Detachment. Remainder of squad, to the stairs."

The aykkuka looked up. "Shmyuta, Billibo," she said. "Shuck down, take them." Two were all she was prepared to risk, on a task peripheral to the main mission. She hefted her spear overarm and made to throw, forcing the two fugitives to keep to the roofline and circle to reach their objective. The two troopers named hit the quick-release catches on their armor, designed to allow marines to shed their heavy harness quickly on a sinking ship. Naked but for rag loincloths, they leaped agilely to the rooftops, spears in hand.

Megan and Shkai'ra stood to meet them. One was male and the other female, but they were alike in their taut

THE SHARPEST EDGE   61

grins, cropped hair, scarred brown skin rolling over muscle hard as tile.

The short spears they carried were about four feet long, a blade curving outward and broadening toward the front third. Megan could almost see the texture of the rope coiled around the handle. She backed another step, to the ridge of the roof, hearing the sounds of carnage continuing below her heels. A number of possibilities ran through her head and were dismissed. These weren't shaaid to be slaughtered like cattle. She moved forward suddenly to give herself room and saw that the one facing her did not flinch at the sudden motion. Now was a hell of a time to wish that you had trained in another weapon, she told herself. *Several feet of metal between her and me would be nice.* The woman stepped forward, feinting with the weapon slightly. Megan shifted to a low stance that exposed only the narrow outline of her body to the other. She saw the blade begin to move and knew that this wasn't a feint. Time slowed, and she watched the gleaming edge move toward her, then past as she stepped sideways, feeling the rasping shock as she deflected it with one arm. Then she was inside the reach of other, throwing herself forward before she could pull the blade back and cut through her neck from behind. Her momentum slowed as she slammed the knife in just under the ribcage. Slowly, slowly, she saw the other's hand start to move and her mouth drop open, and she was pushing for more speed, knowing that if she had missed she *had* to get past the other or it was all over. The knife twisted in her hand and then she was down on the roof, the peculiar dusty-slick feel of the tiles under her palms as they took her weight and she rolled and slid past, now unable to stop. Her mind was screaming; GET UP, next move, GET UP! And she twisted, driving nails into tile with an ear-punishing shriek. There was no need. The woman was down in a puddle of blood, the body lying at a strange angle, held there by the hilt of the dagger that had cut heart and artery.

Shkai'ra faced her opponent with the weight on the balls of her feet, hilt of her saber at waist height and blade slanting out. The man watched her narrow-eyed; the sword and stance were both unfamiliar, but he knew that in close

combat without protection there was rarely time for a
second passage. You moved, committed, and were either
victorious or dead. He feinted once, lowline, and halted as
the wrists and shoulders flexed into position. For a block,
he assumed—Sun *shun* it, he didn't know the counters for
this one! Once you were in under a straight longsword you
had it, but this thing looked fit to take your hand off
anywhere along the length.

The Kommanza backed her left foot a half-step, breathed
in, and attacked with the overarm cut to the head—the
pear-splitter, the Warmasters in Stonefort had called it.
The short spear spun like a propeller disk in a sweep-
parry, then darted out in a straight-line thrust to the
midriff.

But the first move for the pear-splitter is also that for
the side-downsweep. The long, slightly curved sword halted
and turned ninety degrees from its angle of attack; the
spear met nothing in its parry, and the cutting edge of the
saber ground into the oiled hardwood of the shaft. Even
with the two-handed grip, that was not enough to cut it
through. But the deflection knocked the man offline, with
his weight thrown forward behind his thrust. And Shkai'ra
kicked, the heel of her right foot driving into his kneecap.

The man was brave and stubborn. He ignored the flash
of pain from the dislocated knee, dropping the spear and
trying to grapple and use the greater bulk of his arms and
shoulders. Thus they were chest to chest as Shkai'ra released the saberhilt with her left hand, flip-reversed her
grip with the other, and brought it out to the side, point
in. That settled in just above his hip, and she ran it
through his body from right to left, below the ribs. She
could smell the familiar Fehinnan ranker's odor, sweat and
sunflower oil and leather and metal, the smell of a tool, a
thing, a trade; could watch his eyes as the cold iron slid
through his stomach. For a frozen moment she held him
poised, a soft sound of pleasure escaping her lips, then let
the body drop and withdrew the blade with a twist to
break the suction grip of muscle.

She looked up to see Megan kick over the woman's
corpse to retrieve her knife. Below, the aykkuka snarled,
hefted her spear, then turned and ran to the stairwell,

where the squad were engaged with the uprush of fleeing shaaids.

"Now," she panted, slow and deep. "Down?"

"The streets—" Megan paused to swallow dry phlegm. "The streets will not be too safe." She waved a hand; for the first time Shkai'ra noticed the rips and bloodflecks on their tunics, the brown crusty stains running up her swordhand nearly to the elbow.

"Over, then," she said. "The gaps between back alleys are narrow enough."

The pounding of their feet across the flat roof was drowned by the sounds of screams, shouts, and metal cleaving flesh and bone as they sprang to the roof of the next building, perhaps three meters away, and lower. Megan cursed under her breath as she ran. "Fishgutted, dogsucking, sons of three leperous wh . . . No, this way." She angled to a corner of the building and jumped. It was almost too far, over one of the more major streets, but she grabbed an ornately carved cornice and swung around to land on its other side. There were no carvings save on the corner pieces of this house and handholds were few.

As Shkai'ra leaped she caught a glimpse of someone in the street below staring up at them. Her long legs gave her an advantage and she didn't have to use the ornamentation. The next one was taller, and they climbed two balconies before disappearing over the peak of the roof. Below, the person standing at the corner had seen a flash above and heard the rattle of boots on tile, looking up just in time to see Shkai'ra jump; black and scarlet. He glanced both ways, saw them go over the taller building, looked back over his shoulder toward noise from Temple Square, and put his head down, hurrying on.

"Wasting two of my good steel knives on those pigs," Megan panted. She paused by a chimney and looked down, both sides. "There," she said, pointing to a stone wall below. "Does that give us a way through to a safe street, or are we still in the midst of this rat trap?"

Shkai'ra grinned and sat down to put on her sandals. "Why not?" She went over the edge, hung by her hands, and dropped to the smooth top of the wall. "Strange," she said as Megan joined her. "Usually, if there's something to protect they stud the walls with stone splinters, angled in

and out. No matter." Gripping a drainpipe, she slid downward, landing in a crouch, sword once more ready. Around
her was a formal garden, colored marble flags, fountains
carved in strange shapes, bestial topiaries, potted flowers.
The air heavy with sweet scents, and somewhere incense
burned. This world denied that such things as bloodshed
and massacre existed.

8

The doorkeeper turned from the crowded thoroughfare.
The street that fronted her master's estate held nothing
but the residences of the rich; hence there was little traffic
even in normal times, and none now when turmoil kept
owner and servant in wary guard over their thresholds.
She could feel a prickle of sweat, beyond what the heat of
the day and a hurried pace could account for. When the
market woman with her shoulder yoke of fruit turned into
the street it almost brought a sigh of relief.

Almost, but she remembered that the produce markets
in the Old City were closed this day, and what vendor
would have been given an order for delivery? She crossed
to the other side of the street, one hand to her pouch. The
sound of grit against stone under her sandals sounded loud
in her ears as she hurried past glass inlaid walls.

Only one more turn, she thought. On the grounds of
my master, not even the Adders would dare follow.

As she turned into the laneway the market vendor laid
down her yoke and wiped her face, making a sign with her
fingers. Two dark figures on the roof opposite stood; one
lifted something with a metallic glitter.

Milampo's servant felt only an enormous blow beneath
her shoulderblades. The huge impact threw her forward

onto her face; it was when she tried to rise that the pain began. She moaned, and felt a bubble of wetness break on her lips. It ran down her chin and dropped to the dusty pavement, bright red in the morning sun, one more droplet of blood among so many shed that morning.

It was impossible to breathe. She struggled, forcing her lungs open against the wet, gurgling sounds within, and crawled. One pace, two. Her hand pulled the beltpouch free from its thongs. The toss was weak, and the pouch landed a pace short of the doorkeeper's alcove.

"Hearing . . . and obeying . . . master," she whispered. And there was a long night's falling into emptiness.

Megan hit the ground just behind Shkai'ra, saying, "Wait, now you should see to that hand now that we have a sec," when she felt it. She reached out and caught Shkai'ra's wrist, in a suddenly urgent grip. It was a tickle in the back of her mind. An elusive whiff of power coiled somewhere in this place like the delicate sound of a color or the scent of a song. "There is power here. Tread carefully, my Akribhan, lest we drown in this sweetness." She turned this way and that but could not pinpoint the source of disturbance. "Such power . . ." she whispered.

Shkai'ra bared her teeth and glanced around. The expression was not a smile. "Spook pushers," she said, very softly. "Oh, I don't *like* spook pushers. Never trust a shaman—the truest thing the Ancestors ever said."

They took the path to their left, sweating lightly and breathing deep with the controlled reflex of athletes in hard condition. Shkai'ra sucked at the fleshy side of one hand, below the little finger.

"Should have watched the back shoulders of the spearhead—sheepraping sharp," she muttered.

The paved way turned around a massive bush covered with thousands of tiny blue flowers that moved gently in the warm slow breeze, tapping against the stone of the statue in their midst. Megan looked up at the figure of the leaping dolphin with growing uneasiness; there was a prickling between her shoulderblades, as of approaching . . . peril? Not necessarily, but *something* was about to happen. This feeling was one she had learned to trust.

They padded around the corner and stopped dead. Before them, a woman sat. Long black hair flowed down, over her cream-colored robe, past the cloth-of-gold cushion on which she sat, to coil slightly on the purple and green marble of the dais. A light wooden lattice overgrown with a green vine blossoming scarlet arched over her protectively. From a small brazier on her left incense rose in a blue coil; to her right was a silver bowl on a tripod of bronze. She raised eyes as white as milk to meet them, from the crossed palms in her lap. Without iris or pupil; blind eyes, that saw.

"I greet you, both," she said. The voice was soft, curiously hard to gauge. The face was smooth. Was the voice that of a child, or of middle age?

"I felt you in my darkness. One from afar; another from farther still. I see you in darkness, and darkness follows you; fate, but that I cannot see." Her nose wrinkled. "Blood, the smell of it; now, and in the time to come."

The woman's voice dropped like cool water into the humid stillness of the garden. Shkai'ra backed away, unconsciously, knuckles white on the grip of her saber as the tiny hairs along her spine struggled to rise against the sweat-damp cloth.

"Who . . ." She cleared her throat against the sudden roughness of her voice. "Who are *you?* You're no Sun priest; nor a merchant's clerk."

Megan bowed and made the gesture of respect, a faint clap sounding in the drowsy hum of bees from the lilac. "Lady of Power, you see much. We apologize for disturbing your, ah, meditations." She backed up, pulling at Shkai'ra's arm, searching for a safer distance from this woman. *Shkai'ra,* she thought, *don't offend this one.* She radiated power. Megan felt as though breathless, the sensation of pressure under the lungs almost stifling. Those eyes turned to her, and the woman laughed. "Fear me not, young-kin. I am merely a seeker of wisdom. And a prisoner." The laugh transformed the ageless face into that of a young girl. "Or so my . . . host . . . thinks."

She raised her hands, and a faint nimbus of blue light played around the long, slender fingers.

"This moment was foreseen." Her voice was remote, the laughter faded into a cool monotone that might have come from the idol in a sanctuary carved of glacial ice.

"Now all turns on your actions. Two chance-met wanderers, and on them rests the fate of great lords, wisefolk, merchants, and priests. How, I cannot see; there are too many branches of the Path."

She diminished into humanity. "But it would be best if you left soon." She pointed down the avenue of topiaries behind her, with a sparely elegant gesture. "There lies a gate which will not require you to traverse much of the greathouse; the household is much disturbed."

She turned her head, and at the unspoken summons a man appeared. Middle-aged, he was near seven feet in height and corded almost to squatness with muscle. He picked up the white eyed woman as an adult might a child, and it was only then that they realized her legs hung limp and useless.

"That way, Bors," Yeva said. The milky eyes turned to regard the two. "Go well, I hope," she continued. "Strangely, I can be sure of."

"A most interesting woman," Megan mused, and fell silent.

"Come *on*," Shkai'ra said, waving a hand before her face. Megan started as if coming back from a long distance and followed Shkai'ra down the row of sculpted shrubs to the opposite wall that encircled the garden, and to the heavy door set into it.

Megan paused, felt in her belt, and sighed. "Another cloth gone. You'd better clean that meat cleaver of yours." She looked about, then cleaned her daggers with a corner of her tunic.

Shkai'ra pulled a silk rag from her belt and wiped the long patterned blade lovingly. The dappled patterns in the steel shone as the red-brown scum came away.

"Ahi-a, I never leave blood on Swift-Kiss here longer than I must," she said, buffing the metal again and sliding it back into the sheath, a practiced motion that didn't need the guidance of eyes. "Getting good Minztan steel this far east is near impossible. Besides, even in Illizbuah walking the streets with a bloody sword is a trifle conspicuous."

"What, it isn't the universal practice? I'd have thought—" She broke off, intent. Beyond the door: a muffled sound, perhaps a whisper . . . and from the other side.

She looked at Shkai'ra; the Kommanza shrugged, drew,

the point of her saber making small neat circles in the air.
"The doorkeeper, maybe. Go on."

They opened the dark mahogany panel, and met silence. Projecting walls made a U-shaped nook for the
guardian, but it was empty. The liveried figure of the
servant lay beyond in the street, one outstretched hand
touching the threshold; a crossbow bolt behind one shoulder showed the reason. She was very recently dead, still
bleeding in a slowing trickle, and at their feet lay a
beltpouch. They both moved toward it by reflex; Megan's
small deft hand arrived first, tucking the leather bag under
the hem of her tunic.

"Time to count it later," she said. "No sense waiting for
whoever shot her."

Shkai'ra bent over the corpse for an instant as they
passed. "Ahi-a—House of Milampo Terhan's-Kin. The fat-
test pig among the merchant swine-princes."

A dark figure clung to the roof above them, straining
after their departing voices. Two more joined him, and
they dropped softly into the street beside the body of their
victim.

One knelt to run quick expert fingers over the still form.
"Shadowed One, it is not here."

The leader cursed softly and flipped the body over with
her toe. "Search about," she said to the others. "Our
informant said this one would have it." Her head swiveled
to where the two outlanders had passed. Or could they
have taken it? A fine sweat broke out on her forehead. She
would not envy the subordinate assigned to take *that* news
to the Adderchief. "Perhaps those two should be ques-
tioned," she mused.

9

Megan and Shkai'ra strolled along the brick sidewalk, a luxury of these affluent quarters of the Old City. Folk were about their business, seeming to ignore what was happening only a half-kilaahm away. Or perhaps not seeming, Shkai'ra thought. Old City dwellers were not all rich, but the poor here were mostly the servants of the wealthy; the unfree mostly not even Fehinnans. A quiet existence, ordered, secure; it might have been a different continent, a world invisible from the desperate daily scramble of the lowtown slums, their sweated trades and the vicious predators that lived off them. Massacre did not really touch their lives; unless they were physically involved, it was not real to them.

The traffic of the street parted for a laaitun of cavalry, bright gold-lacquered armor and ribbons wound in the horses' manes. Shkai'ra put an arm around Megan's shoulders and nodded to a laughing group about the entrance-way of a shop.

"Nothing stops Fehinnans when Festival is coming," she said. Gaily painted masks were being passed from hand to hand: faces of saahvyts and paancahs and waybaycs, the devils and pranksters and house goblins that lingered still beneath the austere monotheism of the Sun. There were other goods for sale: leather wine flasks for squirting into the mouths of passersby; handpumps for showering colored dust and strange powders; bladders well blown for banging on heads; and feathered cloaks worked with the grapes and ears of corn that symbolized the season of growth. Even in Illizbuah the City Solstice, High Sun, was still largely a fertility rite.

"Much like Jyahrant or Dahgde Vroi at home," Megan said. "Year's Ending and Days of Fools." Her eyes narrowed speculatively at some of the powders displayed. "One of my kin," she spat. "Makes things like these, but for more serious purposes and higher prices. If I'm lucky she'll have died before I get back." Suddenly she laughed. "*She* would be lucky if she did!"

Shkai'ra's smile died as she looked down at her companion. "Hoi, you're limping? Did you take a wound?"

Megan twisted her leg to one side and looked at it with annoyed impatience. "Nothing serious, I didn't notice it at the time." Her unaccustomed chuckle lapsed into an almost hysterical giggle. "It must have been in the eating shop. To go through all of this and be stabbed in the leg with a table tool, with a fork! The burghers of this city are more dangerous than the soldiery. Don't worry, it's hardly visible."

Shkai'ra grunted skeptically. Megan must have good natural resistance to infection, to have lived this long; still, even a small wound could bring the green rot, or poison the blood. "Best we see to it, though," she said. They were in a district of shops, expensive goods for the Old City trade. Among them stood a small park, tessellated brick pavement with dwarf flowering shrubs in carved stone pots.

"I'll take a look," the blond woman said. Megan leaned against one of the man-high flowerpots and extended the leg behind her; the wound was in the calf just above her right boot, difficult to reach.

"Remember, that fork was in a priest-bureaucrat's mouth—no telling what was on it," Shkai'ra said as she knelt to examine the puncture. Two small red dots, side by side; she ran her fingers around the affected area before applying her mouth. "Hmmm, there was something in there," she said, spitting. "Tines probably broke off."

Shkai'ra worked the wound with her fingers until the blood flowed clean, then produced a tiny bottle from a beltpouch and poured green liquid into the holes, ignoring Megan's startled twitch.

"Fishguts! What are you doing, woman, whittling it deeper with a hot needle?"

"Stings, doesn't it?" she replied, grinning up at the Zak, teeth white in her tanned face. "The Fehinnans make it from seaweed. Good for cuts. Now, food."

A copper bit stirred the vendor of a nearby pushcart. A big ceramic vat bubbled in its center, sending a scent of hot peanut oil into the warm still city air. Into it the streetseller flipped a double handful of meat chunks, onions, peppers, and pieces of yam. A few minutes later he scooped them out with a slotted wooden ladle, rolled them in flatbread, and doused them with a hot brown sauce. Cornhusks served as platters; an extra bit brought two wooden cups of peach juice from a sweating clay jug, cool and tart.

The two women lounged back into the shade of plants and buildings, sitting at their ease on a patch of coarse grass. On the street outside a group of retainers trotted by, in the livery of the Terhan's-Kin. Swords were forbidden to such as they, but there were ceramic-headed spears in their hands, knives at belts, worried determination on their faces. Shkai'ra juggled the hot food in her hands, watching with interest from between the leaves of a potted eucalyptus tree. Happily she inhaled the smells of warm stone, garlic, hot oil, and flowers. Patterns of sunlight shifted across her face, dappling as wind shifted branches.

"Here," she said, handing Megan the second roll. "If that pouch was missed so soon, it had something in it besides the doorward's wages, or I'm a kinless sheeppraping nomad." Her eyes narrowed in amusement; a Fehinnan friend had told her once that she loved strong happenings more than wine, and there were times when she saw some truth in that. And an exile with nothing to lose but her life could play such games with no regrets.

"*Rauquai!*" Megan exclaimed, blowing gingerly on her portion. "And I thought to *rest* in this city! You realize, Shkai'ra-my-friend, that since I arrived I've scarcely stopped running? Well, nothing more is likely to happen; soon I'll be able to raise passage money and sit on my butt, the fine lady passenger."

Megan finished the fruit juice and peered over the rim of her cup at the Kommanza, eyes snapping. "Since you are my Akribhan, perhaps there is something you should see."

Shkai'ra set her own cup down on the yellow brick, circling her arms about her knees. "See?"

The Zak nodded at a man dozing in the heat. He lay on his cloak, a broad-brimmed traveler's hat over his face; beside him at waist height was a winecup, securely planted on the rim of a treepot. She dipped a finger into the dregs of Shkai'ra's cup and drew two lines, one around the base and another on the rim. Words dropped from her lips, half-chanted. "Watch," she said.

Very gently, she put a finger to the edge of Shkai'ra's goblet and pushed. The cup five meters away leaped in a parody of the tiny motion, and the cool liquid poured unerringly into the man's lap. He leaped to his feet with a wild, strangled yell, fist upraised. Awareness blinked back into his eyes, and the realization that there was nobody within five meters of him. His mouth worked silently; the fist fell, and his eyes with it to the purple stain on the brown cotton of his tunic. He wrapped his cloak about his middle and stole away hurriedly.

The Zak picked up the cup and emptied it with a sly almost-smile. "Not everybody who can do a little magic sits under bushes and makes prophecies," she said impishly. "Better to have a little fun now and then."

In a chamber overlooking gardens, beneath a dome of crystal, a robed figure sat motionless above a brazen bowl of water. Others had watched here before him; there would be a relief when he tired, and that would not be soon. Sensation/experience/perception drifted through the still pool of his mind, without rippling its perfect receptivity. Leaves brushed against the brickwork of the tower; a breeze soughed through the latticework supports of the dome, laden with the scent of flowers and baking bread.

Suddenly, a spot of light appeared in the clear water. He rose smoothly from the cross-legged position he had kept for a hand of hours. Another figure appeared on the spiral stair below.

"It has begun," he said to the one who came. "Summon the adepts."

His gaze returned to the water. The workings of the Patterns were a never-failing source of wonder. This was the nexus of probability they had sensed; he closed his eyes and ran fingers of thought over the skein of branching alternates that ran forward from the fixed point of *now* he occupied. There was every delicate work ahead, a nudging at the workings of fate and chance to ensure that events fell as they willed.

Shkai'ra blinked, narrow gray eyes slitting as she turned to glance down at Megan. One eyebrow lifted.

"You didn't tell me you were a witch," she said.

"Witch? Scarcely. I know a few tricks. But our people don't like to show them outside the walls of the city; it tends to get them burned."

"Hmmmm? In the Zekz Kommanz the dhaik'tz, the shamans, sniff out any witchcraft but their own; then eat the witches' hearts, mostly." She paused. "Silly custom." Long fingers rested on the Zak's brow for a moment. "I trust you," she added soberly.

The adepts filed into the chamber and stood circled around the bowl. One touched the bowl; it rippled, cleared, and revealed the two women in the park.

The magicians waited in silence, their minds studying the scene and its implications on the ramifying planes.

"So," one said at last in a manner not available to ordinary folk. "It seems that our message to the money-hunters is a communication of more significance than we assumed, perhaps. But if we have found them, can the priests"—they all made a gesture of execration—"be far behind?"

"What matter?" another asked. "I still contend that we waste our strength here. These are all ephemera; what are their wars and quarrelings to the wise?"

"The self-christened Wise," another mind added dryly. "Still, this matter has been decided. If you wish another Council . . ."

Negation.

"Young Yeva would be the one to deal with this matter," a woman whose appearance was that of sixty years said. "Their worldlines have already touched hers, and she does excellent work, for a journeyman. At present, we can only see that these will somehow give an opportunity to accomplish our purpose without attracting the attention of the Undying One. With his Servants we can deal; with him . . ." A collective shudder passed through the group.

"And let her not interfere more than the minimum," the first agreed. "Too much, and we may abort the seed of chance that we seek to nurture."

agreement/hope/action

10

The solarium had been repaired, quickly. There were new plants, and the shattered glass had been replaced; all that remained was the zigzag scorchmark, snaking its way across the paneling of the wall.

Beginners, she thought. Lightning was such a showy working, and so easy when the potential-paths through the air were ready, in a storm. All you had to do was . . . connect. Still, a priest would approve of retribution from the sky.

"Here, Bors," Yeva said. With infinite gentleness the huge man set her down on the cushions and helped to arrange the unresponding legs. She looked up at the scarlet blossoms of the trumpet flowers and let them brush against her cheeks, feeling the structure of the plant, its enjoyment of sun and water, the thoughts of the gardeners as they planted and tended it. Yeva inhaled the smells of flowers and burned cedarwood, a melancholy pleasure.

Milampo, she thought with a sigh. Not all visitors were as pleasant as the two women. There had been something strange. . . .

The merchant bustled in, with the inevitable swarm of attendants. Several were members of his kinfast, along with clerks, bodyservants with pitchers of wine and juice, and four mercenary guards. Those were fitted with standard leather armor, but trimmed with bullion tassels along the fringes of the glossy varnished plates. And their spearheads were cheap mass-produced ceramic bound with implanted fiber; she thought with mild amusement how like the man it was to spend on show and neglect utility. But they all had steel swords, which meant a certain degree of competence, those being personal property.

"Honored guest," the merchant began. He was a short man, and the afternoon sun glistened on the sweat film that covered his skin. Rolls of fat overlapped the stiffly embroidered collar of his maroon velvet tunic, and the thin vein-embossed legs beneath were trembling visibly.

"Milampo, my host," she said in a voice pitched to carry soothing tones below the conscious level. "A man of your years, unused to exercise, should not run up stairs so quickly. See, the veins in your temples are throbbing visibly; this is not good."

The merchant swelled. She was surprised that he had the courage to confront her thus, although from the smell his nerve had been heavily reinforced with firewine.

"Slaughter!" he blurted. "Temple Square—blood—"

She raised a hand. "Need we discuss these matters with so much company?" she asked mildly.

He paled slightly and turned, with inarticulate shooing motions. The hangers-on departed, except for the guards, who stood and leaned on their spears. Members of their guild were oath-bound to their employers and could not be summoned against them even in a temple court.

Milampo breathed deeply, and when he spoke again his voice was steady. "There has been a massacre," he said.

"Which we predicted!" Yeva replied, and her tone sharpened. "Milampo Terhan's-Kin, did it not occur to you that your intrigues with gold and favor could lead to *real* blood being shed? Or did you see it as more columns of numbers in your ledgers?"

"Enough of that," he said, waving a hand. Amethysts glowed on his fingers. "They are only shaaid; no shortage. But if the Sun-on-Earth"—his voice dropped unconsciously—"should investigate, the others will blame *me*."

"As the leader in this policy," she said. "Also as the one who proposed calling on the Wise. In which you were

yourself wiser than your wont." *With suitable encouragement,* she added to herself.

"And you and your kin will go to the tables, and your
wealth will be forfeit to the state," she added equably.

He wilted, then darted a glance of suspicion at her.
"Never forget, if I am betrayed, none of my wealth will be
yours," he said. "And . . . I have you, as guarantee of
good faith. I could order you speared this instant."

Yeva caught the glance the guards exchanged behind
their master's back. One tapped a finger to her brow.
These were not temple guards, or even regulars.

"Come, come, have we not agreed to aid you?" she
soothed. "No need to talk of disharmonious violence."

"Agreement? Where is my message? Just now I found
my faithful servant dead beside the west gate, and no such
message upon her."

Yeva started, with a look of dawning interest in her
eyes. Then her gaze filmed over, and Milampo shrank
back with his next sentence unuttered, making the Sun
sign on his breast.

information/essence/confirmation flowed through her
mind. This was not speech; it was what speech imperfectly
counterfeited. Ah, then her suspicions about the two were
correct. The message stumbled slightly.

apologies, eldersib.

*calm yourself. all who are masters were apprentice
once. inform the council i have their message.*

gratitude/appreciation/obedience.

She returned to the world of phenomenon that most
thought of as real. "Be at peace, my host," she said tran-
quilly. It was difficult, this stumbling with words. "The
message which links you to us has fallen into the proper
hands."

"Whose?" he asked, paling. That message, and the cir-
cumstances of it, were enough to earn him three days of
dying.

Yeva considered, and decided that it would be cruelty
to inform him that the proper hands were those of two
wanderers who would doubtless attempt to sell it to the
highest bidder. How could she explain? Even to those
with the inborn talent and long years of painful mastery, it
was no more than trained intuition that those two would

use their burden to bring a favorable resolution. And that was merely likelihood, not certainty. It was her duty to turn the probability into fact under the bright focus of the *now*.

"That will be revealed at the appropriate conjunction of the planes," she said. A yellow bird fluttered in, to land on her outstretched finger. She slipped a feather from the sleeve of her robe and stroked the tiny creature beneath the throat, enjoying the total submergence in sensation that the bird was feeling, possible only in a creature beneath or beyond self-consciousness.

"Observe, my host; never stroke a bird with your finger, for fear of disarranging its plumage or the subtle oils thereon. Instead, use a feather in the hand."

Milampo made a choking sound and wheeled from the room, followed by his guards and a lingering smell of oily, overheated flesh, rose-scented soap, and expensive musk. She smiled at the memory of his appearance, bouncing like a paper balloon filled with hot air at a child's festival. At least he had taken his noisy mind and body away. . . . She chided herself at the thought. Every human soul had its purpose, and it was no more just to despise a merchant for being a merchant than a dog for being a dog.

Still, she was heartily sick of being the trader's "guest." The only interesting conversation he had was on matters of trade, and with the laborious gentility of the second generation he avoided that as ill-bred. She glanced at the forked scorchmark the bolt from the storm had left. The stroke had been clumsy, but what did Milampo think to threaten her with, if she could block *that*? Would he have the gardeners beat her to death with hoes? The mercenaries would be as likely to spear *him*; he was not the sort of employer who would inspire devotion beyond death, not in strangers.

Calming, she settled into a light trance. The minds of the guild washed around her, and she traced the lines of force out over the city. The palace was like a beacon to her sight on this level, one she carefully avoided: minor tricks of seeing and lifting were beneath His notice, but any major alteration of the webs of probability would draw attention like a wasp to sugar. For the sake of balance she could endure the contact of those on the Left Hand of the

Council; the guild existed for their common interests, after all. But the God was truly mad and very dangerous; as well provoke a bull elephant in rut. Yet . . . at the far edge of perception, where entropy faded the lines of *might-be* into a chaotic fog, there was the unmistakable presence of the Sun-on-Earth. He would have a hand in this, at the last.

She sat, tracing the possible consequences of one course of action after another. Some she might have anticipated; others were bizarre. *Yellow-skinned foreigners disembarking from ships drawn by whales?* No, that was vanishingly unlikely. Still, it had its origins. Yes, try eliminating the stranger women—*light brighter than noon, then black ruins under black sky, birds falling to lie unrotting where even death was dead. . . .* Shuddering, she pulled her consciousness back and scanned the time dimension. The future, more than a double hand of years, impossible to tell how much further. Now, nobody had ever seen *that* before; no force on earth could produce such effects. How could the elimination of two outland mercenaries make such a difference?

The bondservant's mind interrupted her with a blast of unconscious fear. She set about trimming one of the newly placed shrubs, that clearly needed no such attention. *Will he never learn?* the sorceress thought. A direct lesson was necessary; next time something more important than mere free-association scrying might be lost by jostling her concentration. Sensitivity had its price; she found screening more difficult than most.

Motionless, she made a complex and completely non-physical shifting. In a room several minutes' walk away, Milampo Terhan's-Kin started violently as a voice spoke behind his ear. A young voice, breathless and sweet.

"Silly. Why bother, when that-self Yeva cannot walk." A silver bowl sat on a window ledge; it was a simple curve of metal, and a part-perception of the sorceress's mind admired its restraint. Gracefully, it moved away across the room and down the hall toward the solarium garden, leaving the merchant crouched on his cushions, the knuckles of one hand pressed to his lips.

The gardener dropped her shears with a clatter as the bowl carried itself into the still-scented warmth of the roof-level chamber. One blade shattered on the marble tiles, the edges of the vitrified clay glinting with silica in the sunlight. Yeva took the bowl in her hand and extended it.

"I wish this filled with water, from the spring against the south wall, the one that cannot be seen from here. Do not let the water or the bowl touch the ground. When you return, place it here and then go to your master. Tell him—again—that I do not wish to be disturbed at my work. And, that he has merely annoyed me. Have him contemplate the consequences if I become *angered*."

She retreated into herself, monitoring breath and heartbeat, feeling the thrill of fatigue along her nerves. Even to move a metal bowl in the physical universe was savagely tiring; magic was rarely useful for such gross manipulation, particularly without preparation or patterning.

Afraid, she thought. All of them, and of what? One without the use of her eyes or legs. But that was part of the fear; that one such as she could be a figure of power, rather than another beggar on the temple steps. She sighed. In the guild, there were few enough who could look past the surface of things; outside, almost none.

The bowl was extended toward her on trembling palms. "Young one, I thank you for this service," she murmured, taking it. There was a rapid patter of departing feet.

She placed the curve of silver in the tripod before her and waited for it to be still. She was weary, but it would be as well to be informed. The red one first . . . a pattern of thought wrapped in black, tempered. A name rose into her mind: Shkai'ra Mek-Kermak's-Kin. The dark. Force constrained, and a place of age. Ice and iron, the sound of a waterfall, sunlight on water. Creak of rigging. Megan Whitlock.

Holding the images in her mind, she gestured at the water and spoke certain words. It rippled and smoothed, to show . . . nothing. A wry grimace crossed her mouth; she had never been very skilled at scrying in water. There was a sudden flare from the brazier at her side as she drew heat from the water and cast it into the charcoal. The silver clinged and sang as the water within it shifted from liquid to crystalline ice in much less than a heartbeat. The beads of moisture on its outer surface flashed into crystal, and the wrought metal rang in protest at the swift change in temperature.

Yeva smiled, remembering the pride she had felt at first mastering the little trick. Then she spoke again, weaving the names of the two she sought into the chant. Names were a thing of power; the symbol *was* the thing it represented, that was the core of magic. Lesser to greater, and distance could not sunder the bonds between objects linked by similarity. . . . A complex form grew in her mind, as structured as a snowflake with interlattices of meaning, glowing with the color of hot steel as she pushed energy through it. To the Sight, images formed.

Ice is much better, she thought.

11

"*You* trust *me*?" Megan said incredulously. "Who do you think *I* trust in showing this? And is there need of talk of trust between us?"

Shkai'ra inclined her head, accepting the implied rebuke. "True. But my people . . . fear magic, wherever from."

She laughed suddenly. "And they cast me out, so sheepdung on their customs. Why don't we go back, count our loot, and feed my cat?"

A sound echoed down the street to their left, from the direction of Temple Square. A rhythmic stamping, thousandfold, the sound of three thousand sets of ceramic hobnails striking the ground in unison. It was more a blow through the air than a sound, thudding against chest and gut. It overrode the crowd-murmur, flattened clatter of hooves, creak of wood, even the slow pounding of the pace drums.

And a chanting accompanied it.

"Earth, sky, fire, stone,
Steel cuts to bone.
Earth, sky, fire, stone—"

Endless, the droning marchsong echoed back from the fronts of the buildings. The first regiment swung down the avenue, six ranks broad, pikes a perfect vertical forest of poles with the butts resting in slings braced around the neck. Behind the soldiers came a line of carts, six-wheeled and massive, grain-movers in time of peace. Now they bore another burden, one that drained in threads of red onto the paving stones, like the pressings of grapes piled high in the harvesters' baskets. Death's vintners escorted their fruits. The heavy butcher-shop smell of fresh meat hung on the air.

"I agree." Megan said. "As soon as the road is free. The cat will probably not forgive you for, oh, a day or two if you neglect him so shamefully, and somehow this place seems improper for the counting of monies." She pulled two of her knives free and laid them on the bench, searching for a polishing cloth in her pouch. "These new toys don't need to be tested now." She scrubbed at a drying bloodstain around the hilt of one. "I'd say they've been well tested already."

"Hmmmm, don't forget some might have gotten in along the tang. Had a blade rust out and snap at the hilt once, that way." She looked down critically at the knives. "Good weapons, but haven't you ever wanted to put a little more steel between you and the nasty people?"

Megan nodded at Shkai'ra's long saber. "Not the weapon for someone of my height," she said.

"Ia. Nor the Fehinnan tools, either. But over the mountains, in the cities along the Ah'yia River, they use"—her hands shaped the air—"a long slim blade, with a bell guard. For the lunging thrust, and just stiff enough to slide-parry a cut—nearly got one through my lungs, once. That might be useful for you."

"I suppose it might be useful. To learn a new weapon, though . . . show me one in the market and we'll see." She cleaned the other knife slowly, considering. "I wonder what was so important to the merchant that his servant strove to deliver it, dying." She looked up into the Kommanza's impassive face. "An interesting morning, say you not?"

"And we are doomed to live in interesting times," she said, sliding a hand under the other's hair, rubbing companionably. "A small sword; perhaps Kermibo would know. . . ."

Shkai'ra kicked the door of their rooms at the inn closed and dropped the bar home. With a sigh of contentment she racked her saber and shotpistol, peeled off her sandals, and kicked her tunic into a corner.

"Summertime in Fehinna, I always feel about to sprout mushrooms from my skin," she said, stretching and yawning. Tapping a cup from the clay jug of fruit juice in a corner, she stretched out on the bed and fortified it with a small dollop of cane spirit from a bottle of twisted black glass. "Want some?"

"Yes, assuredly," Megan said, following her example and setting the cup down on the floor while she pulled off her short boots. "You take a look at the pouch. How much for passage from here to the Middle Islands?"

"That would depend," Shkai'ra said, teasing at the tight-wound, intricate knots that Fehinnans used to foil pickpockets. "I know some captains who'd sell you passage cheap. Then sell *you* at their next port of call; who cares if a wanderer without kin or lord disappears? The ones you can trust don't come cheap. Why hurry?"

She rolled over onto her stomach and frowned with concentration; one foot reached out absently to stroke lightly down the back of Megan's leg. "Faster just to cut *tuk t'hait whulzhaits zteafakaz* . . . Hau!"

Megan looked up at the exclamation of delight. Two whole coils of stamped silver tradewire had rolled out onto the coverlet. Two hundred silvers, the yearly wage of a six-master's captain or the price of six fine horses. And there was ten gold in loose bits underneath, half as much again.

The tall woman swung her head back and wolf-howled at the ceiling, softly. "Megan, comrade's delight, take a look at *this*."

The Zak narrowed her eyes and scraped the money

together. "Ahh, precious metals buy more there. Quite a haul for a servant; I was beginning to think I'd have to sell my luckbit to get home." She touched a piece of silvery metal that hung around her neck. "One place I've been, the natives throw it into the river and hope it will ripen into gold. They call it palidum. This I'll spend. And the next captain who tries to sell *me* off is going to dine on his own tripes."

Shkai'ra grunted and fished in the bottom of the pouch with her fingernails. "Something in here." She pulled out a folded sheet of heavy paper and spread it on the yellow fabric of the sheet.

"Sheep*shit*!" she yelled, flinging it away and bolting upright. The caressing toes bit suddenly into the inner surface of Megan's thigh in savage reflex.

Shkai'ra could read Fehinnan, a little, but it was not the content of the message that made her recoil, feeling cold sweat rank on forehead and armpits. The letters . . . could not be read. Not that they were in foreign script, but they *moved*. At the edge of vision they seemed clear, but wherever the eyes tried to rest, outlines shifted into images not-quite-seen. For a moment she thought they formed a face that looked at her—and winked.

"What the Rokatz is wrong with you?" Megan snapped, rubbing at the red mark on her leg and glaring. Then her eyes fell on the paper. The seal on the pouch had been sufficient symbol to shield it, but now the smell of power drifted like unseen smoke on the still air.

"Fishgutted fool that you are, Megan," she muttered to herself as she reached cautiously for it. "I should have warded the room, even if it disturbed her. Probably too late, but—" She picked up the paper between finger and thumb, sliding it neatly back into the pouch.

Then she walked to each of the doors and windows in turn, setting a hand to each and concentrating for a moment. She moved to the center of the room, as nearly as possible with the bed in the way, and spoke a single word that rebounded against the walls, showering the air with silver that shrank to a red line around the openings and then faded altogether. Somewhere there was a shifting, as if the foundations of the room had twisted marginally out of alignment with the world.

"There, the Zak said with satisfaction. "Now *most* people won't be able to think about this room, much less disturb us here. Of course, those with the power will see the 'hole,' and know."

Shkai'ra stared, shivered, then shook herself like a hound climbing out of cold water. The gooseflesh that had mottled the pale flesh of her body faded, and she unclenched fingers knotted about the hilt of a nonexistent sword. The swordhand made a curious, complex gesture.

"*ahKomman mitch'mi,*" she muttered. Then: "Well enough. If we're to have spookers after us, better that we know somewhat of their tricks." She considered for a moment.

"That message," she said. "That message will be wanted, and badly. Protection like that doesn't come cheap." She pulled at her lip. "We might just throw it in the jakes and make a run for it. . . . No, the gates and docks will be watched, and if we were caught nobody would believe we'd thrown it away."

She looked up at Megan. "No one will notice this room? As if it had never been?"

The small woman nodded, and Shkai'ra grinned. "Then they're going to have a problem down in the kitchens. Best we move back into my room, and use this as a refuge."

Their gear was light and easily moved. Shkai'ra laid herself out on the cool sheets and watched the slit where furnace-hot sunlight poured through the rattan blinds.

"Glitch godlet of fuckups was with me this day—not thirty hours back in the city; three fights, a pitched battle, a spook pusher and a cursed letter. And I was expecting to *rest.*"

As she dropped to the round divan, Megan made a strangled sound as if a long-disused chuckle were forcing itself through time-seized machinery. Shkai'ra reached out and touched the red mark on her thigh.

"Sorry about that," she said. "I was startled." She leaned forward and kissed the spot where the flush was fading into the beginnings of a bruise, pushing back the hem of Megan's tunic. Then she paused, a small smile bending her lips. "Does it strike you," she said with the air of one considering a sudden inspiration, "that your legs would fit nicely over my shoulders from there?"

Megan considered a moment as if it were a major decision. "Yes, I suppose they would. . . ." She tweaked one of Shkai'ra's ears and caught her breath suddenly. "You seem to have one thing of importance on your mind all the time. Goddess! I can't stand it!" She pulled away. "Here, try this."

She slid down into Shkai'ra's arms and held her. "I'm not used to such intensity." She drew her hand down the face and neck of the Kommanza. "Just closeness is good too." She hugged her fiercely.

Shkai'ra returned the embrace, nuzzling into the dark cloud of Megan's hair with a warm murmur. "Odd, how holding close gives comfort-warmth even in this heat."

They lay together for a quarter hour quietly. After a while Shkai'ra began tracing along the muscles of the Zak's neck and back, massaging gently at the edges of the long sheaths and straps of well-defined sinew with her fingertips.

"Beautifully developed," she said softly, with her mouth next to Megan's ear. "Like metal under velvet. It's like holding a woods-lynx in my arms." She chuckled. "Complete with claws!" She continued the slow, expert caressing with infinite patience and unfeigned quiet delight.

A black shape leaped onto the bed and swatted at Shkai'ra's bare foot with a peremptory paw. She laughed gently and pushed him away, whereat he settled in a far corner of the circular mattress and folded his paws under himself with an air of offended dignity.

She rolled to one side to let cooler air flow between their bodies, and transferred her fingers to the area under her companion's ribs. Continuing, she looked down into Megan's half-shut eyes.

"You haven't done this very often, have you?" she said. Her hair had come unbraided and hung springy and rippling, silk-fine. She let the ends touch across the Zak's face and throat and breasts, as lightly as the brush of hummingbird feathers. "Not for pleasure, I mean."

Megan sighed, and her eyes crinkled first in a somber mien that lightened rapidly. "No, and having been forced is not a way to cultivate a taste for sex." One corner of her mouth quirked into a half-grin. "Though if you keep doing that I might get to like it." She stretched her length against Shkai'ra and relaxed, leaning on one arm. "Muscle degenerated to fat is disgusting. I'm glad that you are in no way soft." She paused a minute, "That word wasn't quite right . . . it implies no sensitivity as well." There was the droning buzz of a summer beetle on the damp air, and haze was thickening outside. Megan sat up and moved Ten-Knife, who had crept up to plaster himself against them, she and the cat now almost encircled by Shkai'ra's form. She looked down at the tall one's sleepy smile and said, "You're as lazy as a steppe-tiger and twice as nasty . . . I think that's what I like best about you."

Puzzled, the servant looked down at the afternoon tray. "Why am I carrying this tray?" he asked of no one in particular. "Only four rooms on this floor."

Shrugging, he turned and trotted back to the stairwell, through the guest levels of the inn to the subterranean kitchens.

"Extra tray!" he called cheerfully across the smoky chaos of the great brick-lined chamber.

The chief cook was working over one of the ceramic stoves that lined one massive wall. She was huge, inches taller than most Fehinnans and almost square, with muscle under enormous pads of fat. Dressed only in loincloth and leather apron, she was a formidable figure as she turned in wrath from the vat of smoking peanut oil in front of her.

One hamlike fist rose to point at the chalkboard, and a bellow roared out. "ROOMFIVESECONDFLOORWEST NOW!"

The servant would have turned pale if his natural complexion had allowed; as it was, he had to settle on gray. Backing out, he fled up the stairs to the second level. Of course, there were five rooms on all the levels in the west wing!

He stood at the door of room four, second level. "Why am I carrying this tray?" he murmured. "Better get back to the kitchens; the Sea-Cow is likely to drop me into an oil vat if I'm late about my rounds." Cheerfully, he trotted back to the stairwell.

As he pushed through the swinging doors of the kitchen,

a curious expression crossed his face, very like that of a man who, when deep in thought, realizes that a hyena is licking one of his feet and sighing.

"*Why are you carrying that tray?*" the cook yelled. Then, smiling gently, she crossed the room, weaving between porters carrying whole pig carcasses and sides of beef. Quietly she laid one hand on the bondservant's shoulder.

"Himo," she said in a sweet tone. With an effort he controlled his bladder. "You like to run; I should have remembered. We need"—she picked him up by the front of his tunic—"another two hundredweight of cornmeal ground, and the treadmill waits!"

In an aside, she called to another of the kitchen slaves as she carried the blubbering man toward the grainstore. "You, girl! Get a fresh tray, and take it to second-five-west, smartly now!"

As Megan and Shkai'ra sauntered down to the exercise ground, Megan saying, ". . . you only use four knives, but . . ." they passed one of the ubiquitous inn servants as she scurried in the opposite direction. They did not see her halt by the fourth door in the corridor.

Puzzled, she looked down at the tray in her hands. "Why am I carrying this tray?" she murmured. Well, it could not be of any great importance. Best to get back to the kitchens; it wouldn't do to be caught idling.

12

Megan woke in the dead time of early morning, the time when old men die. It was quiet, quiet enough to hear the sounds that daytide drowned; a single set of hooves falling hollow in the distance, clap-*clack* against pavement;

the sough of a slow-heavy sea wind over the fluted tile
roofs. Even the insistent chorus practicing their High
Festival songs had stopped, perhaps because they were
too drunk to remember the words. The air in the room
was thick, pressing on her like hot wet towels; it smelled
of sweat, wine, fruit rinds, and sex. Her bladder was full
to bursting, and the heat suddenly made her skin itch. For
a moment she lay still, listening to Shkai'ra's slow even
breathing, then slid carefully out from under the arm that
lay across her stomach.

She relieved herself and pushed the chamberpot back
under the bed, pacing restlessly. Goddess, she thought,
even the floor isn't any cooler on the feet under all these
rugs. She padded to the window; behind her Shkai'ra
muttered for a moment and rolled over.

The window opened noiselessly, but the air outside
held no hint of the breeze she sought. There was little
light, and the stars were huge and bright in the cloudless
sky. She sat on the deep ledge and looked out over the
city, brushing back sweaty strands of hair clinging to her
forehead. *The silence*, she thought, *It feels as if I were the
only thing in the world still living*.

Across the way she noticed that someone else was lying
sleepless, and a curtain twitched in its windowframe. Ten-
Knife landed beside her on the sill, and she petted him
absently.

"You know, beast," she whispered in one ear that jerked
as her lips tickled the long hairs, "I really don't need you
here shedding heat on me."

The cat purred loudly, then moved its head up with a
quick inquiring movement, both ears pointed forward.

It was odd, Megan thought: he seemed to be staring *up*
the wall. Could he be hearing something from the floor
above? And there *was* a sound from above, the sound of
leather-wrapped metal on brick. . . .

She pitched the cat into the darkness behind her and
flicked up to crouch on the sill; the movement was not
even conscious, a response her life had coded into the
neural channels of her hindbrain. Even so, she was barely
ready when the dark figure dropped from above.

It was dressed from crown to cork-soled sandal in form-
fitting black, eyes a slit-hole in the tight hood. One hand

still held the clench-claw that had held him on the brick wall; the other clutched a glass vial that glowed dully, rotting-green. The stranger's motions were swift and very quiet, a barely audible scraping on the oak of the window-sill as he crouched for balance. But he had been expecting to be alone on it, with only the shutter between him and his sleeping prey.

Megan stayed in her crouch, pivoting on the ball of one foot. The other lashed out, the heel catching him on the side of the knee. There was a muffled sound as the carti-lage gave way, and the man toppled off the windowsill to fall two stories to the concrete pavement below.

She had been reacting on reflex, her mind oddly distant from the brief explosion of violence, hearing with one corner of her mind the cat's yowled complaint at her treatment of him and the sound of the breaking joint. There had been no other noise; even then, it struck her that the man should scream. And he did, just before he hit the ground. But it seemed to Megan that it was not the ground he was staring at, but the vial in his hand. That broke, with a pop lost under the melon-on-stone impact of a human body falling thirty feet. Green vapor burst from the shattered glass, then slowed, seeming to sink into the broken form.

The corpse writhed with life, twitching and shuddering in ways that Megan knew were impossible. Suddenly thread-like tendrils of white errupted from wounds, nose, mouth, ears, and eyes, wriggling out and puffing into dead-white pseudopods even as she watched. The black-clad body began to sag and shrink as the fungus spread.

Swallowing bile, Megan retreated from the sight of the obscene puffball mass that lay on the roadway, already no longer even vaguely human in shape.

The curtain across the way twitched again, and a small dart slammed into the wood just above her hand; the darkness and flickering lanternlight having thrown the aim off. She tumbled off the ledge, and felt the shutter jerk with another blowgun missile as she wrenched it home.

Shkai'ra had rolled up on her knees at the sound of Ten-Knife-Foot's yowl, the saber flowing into her hand at the sound of the assassin's breaking knee; by the time his brief scream ended on the road below she was beginning to wake.

The corridor door burst open, the bar almost shooting back. Two figures in black came through at a run and slammed it behind them.

"Nevo!" one barked. "Did—"

They had one glimpse of the two women, alive and hale, before Megan plunged the room into darkness. It was an absolute blackness, the color behind closed eyes under forest on a moonless night. Patterns of false light drifted before retinas deprived of all stimulation.

The assassins were well trained. To make noise would be instant death; so would staying in the same spot they had been seen in. Quiet as malice, they separated and began drifting along the walls on either side.

Megan froze as she landed and tried to control her panting. *This is what I get for relaxing my guard,* she thought. *Not a weapon in my hands and someone trying to kill us in the dark.* She rose silently and moved toward where the low table stood by the wall. Her knives were there. She heard the rope springs creak on the bed and thought, *Good, Shkai'ra's moved.* And then: *Fishguts— now that she's moved I won't be able to find her.* She seized her daggers and froze again, every nerve straining to hear where their enemies were. All she could hear was the thunder of her pulse in her ears.

Shkai'ra froze as her feet touched the floorboards, toes splaying out like fingers to grip. Tiny puffs of air slid over her bare sweat-slick skin, illusions of coolness in the still, hot blackness of the room. Her mind coolly calculated chances; she was taller and heavier than most Fehinnans, and so more likely to squeeze a betraying groan out of the floorboards, no matter how carefully she moved. And while she was confident that no Illizbuah blackcoat was faster, reflex had sent her hand to her saber, rather than the knife that was better for this work.

Now, where had Megan been? Hmmm, best to move before she came out into the room and gave Shkai'ra *that* to worry about as well. . . .

With an earsplitting screech she jumped straight up, bounced flatfooted on the floor, and then cartwheeled silently to the left, toward the entrance. The Adderfangs would have cleared the door area: it was the last place they had been visible.

Shkai'ra came smoothly to her feet, whirled, and lunged *through* the spot where she had just stood, right foot and hand forward, left leg reclined in a tremendous line that took full advantage of her greater length of limb. And her point touched cloth, just as it reached full extension. An expert could calculate her position from that. She pivoted on the ball of her right foot, left shin sweeping around at knee height in the second half of a pirouette that would take her halfway back to the bed.

The edge of a knife touched lightly over the wood-hard muscle of her outer thigh as it pushed her across the space, just parting the skin; for a moment she *knew* where the Adder must be, but the balance factors made a stroke impossible.

Sheepraping dung of a noseless nomad pi-dog, she thought in disgust as she landed. The bed *should* be just about two arm lengths behind her, and the knifeman just beyond sword's reach back toward the door; they had traded positions twice in the last six seconds. Sweat fell into her eyes, stinging; one or two passages of real combat wrung you out worse than half an hour of practice. She gaped her mouth wide, concentrating on keeping her breath soundless. There would be no second chances here, and it could not last much longer. Not in a space this confined.

Megan considered for a long second, then thought: *If I were they I'd concentrate one on one. If I'm right then she (he?) should be coming up the long wall.* The shriek from the middle of the room punched through her ears, and she used the unexpected sound to cover her motion around the corner and past the desk, thinking irritatedly that Shkai'ra *would* be the only one making one hell of a noise. *Now*, she thought, carefully extending the knife before her and moving forward slowly, straining for a noise of some sort, *let us see if we can persuade this one to spit himself*. She heard a faint sound before her and dropped lower into her crouch, pulling the knife slightly closer to give her more play on the extension of the blade.

There—a whisper of something swinging over her head, seeking, and she felt him almost walk into the knife. The down-swinging hand couldn't stop the blade but wrenched

it to one side, tearing. As the hammerblow of his arm sent
her lurching off balance, she rolled forward, feeling bone
smack sharply on her back muscles as he went over. She
reached blindly with her other hand and slashed as he
rolled to break his fall. Her claws caught and shredded
something as she followed the motion that sent her skidding out into the room. She stopped on her stomach and
inched to one side, the assassin choking back a cry as
much of surprise as pain.

Ah, Megan thought. *She. We'll see if the attack from
below works again; I don't think I hamstrung her*. She
crawled back and toward the desk half a meter, spreading
her weight so that no boards would creak under even her
slight weight.

An easy job, they said, the assassin thought bitterly.
Just back up Nevo, they said. She held her abdomen with
one hand. *Nothing strenuous now, or the cut muscle might
split and I'll spill my guts. If the dagger knicked a bowel,
I'm dead meat. What did she have on her fingers? Whatever it was, it was sharp*. But the job still had to be done,
and blades waited out there in the darkness.

The Adderfang backed toward the door, sliding each foot
a careful millimeter above the boards, then bearing down
with infinite patience. The big barbarian would not expect
him to continue back in a straight line; his stomach muscles contracted reflexively at the memory of cold knife-
sharp swordmetal touching him on the ribs as she lunged.
But if he backed, he could circle along the wall. . . .

A sharp sound came from his right, toward the far wall
and across the bed. Tahlni had made contact! He shifted
his weight more rapidly, covered by the hard smacking
sound of a sweep-parry hitting a forearm and—there was
something soft under his foot, but he was committed now,
balance shifted back. Something round and soft, with a
firmer core.

ERRRRROWERREEEE!

The Adder had a moment to stand frozen by the scream
of feline outrage before ten claws and a mouth fastened
themselves in his calf. A cat can turn at a very acute angle
and attack, even with its tail pinned to the floor; and in
any case, the confining weight shifted quite rapidly. If
there had been light, the others would have seen a man in

black dancing in place on the ball of one foot, with a leg flailing madly in the air. And Ten-Knife-Foot managed to produce an astonishing volume of sound, between mouthfuls.

A random twist saved the Adder as a curved Kommanz sword split the place his abdomen had been a moment earlier. The same movement spun him to face the door.

The oak door slammed open. A lean blond figure in a loincloth stood there, with a long slashing-sword in one hand, peering blearily from between sandy eyelids.

"WILLYOUPEOPLESHUTTHEFUCKUPI'MTRYINGTO-SLEEP!" he screamed, and slammed the door shut once more with a bang.

None of the combatants moved, as the sudden blaze of light speared into dilated pupils. The Adder recovered just enough to see Ten-Knife-Foot streak through the closing slit of the door as he turned, did a vault-handspring over the bed, and rolled forward in the renewed darkness to come to his feet by the outer window. He explored the wound with the fingers of his left hand, not wanting to risk wetting his knifegrip. The flesh was ragged and oozing, but not enough to weaken him with blood loss in the next few minutes; he could force the ravaged muscle to operate. And afterward, he would try the taste of cat.

Megan threw herself back into a crouch as the room was again plunged into darkness, wiping streaming eyes. The sight of the room a second ago was burned into her mind, and she knew that the desk and the folding screen lay close by. The Adder had seen her on the floor, so the place to be was high. She leaped to the surface of the desk, a board cracking under her as the weight shifted. The Adder would be coming from that way if she came. *Again*, she thought. *Let her come to me.* She toed a weight off the desk to keep the other coming and felt the change in air pressure as someone lunged past her at the noise. With a wrench she pulled the light wickerwork-and-paper screen down on her and followed up with the dagger. She felt the blade catch on a rib, and the knifehand, driven deep, touched cloth. Blood splashed hotly on her skin, and she sprang to the floor by the wall. *Lousy merchant*, she thought. *He swore left and right that the poison he sold me for my claws was quick-acting. That one's still thrashing around.* Her fingers took stock of the knives left in the harness: three. *If Shkai'ra finishes the other one this one will likely be alive to give us some answers . . . but how can I help her other than simply by staying out of her fight? I'd get us both killed.* She stood in the dark, feeling powerless.

Shkai'ra tried to follow the Adder's probable path, running lightly in the dark and blinking her eyes against the smarting and watering. But the confusion had thrown off her sense of distance; the hardwood rim of the round bed barked her painfully on the shins. It was a solid, substantial sound, heavy wood fiber pounding into the bone and hard rubbery muscle of her leg between knee and ankle.

That would bring the shivman. She fell to the ground and rolled under the bed, easing herself backward until only the spread fingers of her left hand edged out from underneath, and the poised tip of her saber, slanting up.

I should have realized this earlier, she thought happily. *And no mistaking who I touch: we're both still naked.*

Here close to the floor she discovered that she could just make out the creaking of cork-soled sandals as the Adder approached. There was a sudden crash from the corner, and an involuntary grunt of pain. The stealthy footsteps approaching the bed halted. And her hand shot out, to close around a tattered trouser leg, wet with blood. Her blade flashed upward, under a knifestroke that just split the skin along her collarbone, to go in just over the pelvic arch.

Close, she thought as she felt the soft yielding resistance against her sword. If that knife had been a tenth of a handspan higher, it would have opened the vein in her throat even as she killed him. She held the thrust, up into the ribcage from below, until the point sank into a shoulderblade at a glancing angle. Then she used the leverage of his ankle to whip the blade back and forth in the massive wound; it was rare for a single swordstroke to kill immediately, but then this was an unusual angle.

Blood and fluids poured down and spattered face and shoulders and breasts; she could taste the coppery salt as she panted in the dark. The sword slid free with a wet sound, and the outhouse stink of cut bowel flooded out into the humid warmth of the room. The Adder's body slid limply to the ground.

Against the wall, Megan heard the body fall and hoped that it was not Shkai'ra's. *Powerless*, she thought; then, *Power? Of course. Light we need and light we shall have*. She set her back against the wall, pulled out the last three daggers, and concentrated. At equal distances around the room a solid *chuck* sounded as a dagger vibrated in the walls. Each glowed a low, eerie red. A risk she took, but one that was needful.

Shkai'ra looked up, blinked. The Adder lay before her, very thoroughly dead. The odd position had meant that she could wrench the outer cutting edge of the blade up through his ribs, acting like a giant scissor blade. It was Minztan steel from the far northwest, the curved cutting surface forge-hardened and mirror-polished on a softer core; there was no metal that would take a better edge. This had sheared through bone, from the floating rib to the throat; he lay staring on one side, and the whole contents of his body cavity had slumped out onto the floor, a stew of organs in a bath of blood, more blood than Shkai'ra had seen from one corpse before. The body had bled out like a deer strung up to a rack. She picked herself up, her body glistening darkly from chin to hips.

"Don't worry, not much of it mine," she said at Megan's quick glance. She raised an eyebrow at the cold flickering glow from the knives. "Interesting, but why did it take you so long?"

The fallen screen rustled as the wounded assassin stirred and groaned. A quick stride took Shkai'ra to the spot. She gripped the fallen woman by the back of the neck, searched her with swift efficiency, and dumped half a dozen assorted weapons onto the floor. Then she seized one arm and broke it over her knee.

"I don't *like* people who try to sneak in and kill me in my sleep," she said. Her bladed palm slammed down twice, breaking the collarbones; then she pinned the other's jaws in one hand, propped them open with her sword hilt, and probed. "Ah, poison tooth—but we want you to *talk* to us first. Why should we let you die before you earn your favors?"

Megan came up behind and said mildly, "Treat her *too*

roughly and we won't have her company for long anyway. Perhaps if we pulled her soul out and asked questions of it?" She had a distracted look on her face as she held the light level high enough to see by, and the woman would never know that she was bluffing. Anything not able to reflect the red light must needs be black, scarlet and darkness. She put a hand on Shkai'ra's shoulder and leaned over to look more closely at the writhing assassin, the scarlet light dancing in her eyes. "Well?"

Shkai'ra stiffened slightly, then forced relaxation. The assassin's eyes flickered wildly; her captor brought her face up to eye level, thumbs driving into the shattered collarbones. There was an unpleasant grating, grinding sound, much like that of two roughly shattered pieces of wood being forced together. Blood and matter dripped off her onto the captive.

"I think you'd better tell us who put the engagement out on us," she hissed. "Or I'll let my friend do some interesting things to you . . . and *she* doesn't have to stop when you die." Unconsciously, Shkai'ra's hand made the warding sign against magic and ill luck, but she had never been the sort to reject anything useful. As the Warmasters said, the true warrior could make grass and sand serve as weapons.

A glow matching the color of the knives appeared, puddled in Megan's hands. She pulled her hands apart, drawing it into a ropelike strand that looped and coiled in the air before the assasin's face. A humming came from it, a low deep note, eager as the light-snake strained toward skin drawn tight with pain and slick with blood and mucus. The Zak's voice was cool and reasonable, dropping like the water that wears granite.

"Priest's . . . gold," the Adderfang said at last, in a husky whisper. She swallowed, choked, fought for air. "Guildmasters . . . Adderfang brothers . . . merchant's letter. Wi . . . wizard's letter! You took . . . told to recover. Kill you." She rallied suddenly. "*Kill you!*" she snarled, and spat pink foam at Megan. The wracked body went boneless, and the black eyes glazed. Her final words were almost too faint to hear.

"I curse you . . . witch."

"Ah," Megan said. "The poison was fast-acting after all."

The taut look of power faded from her face as she walked over to the bed and slumped down with a creak. The red light faded to ember glow.

"Tired," she said. Pain shot through her head, spearing from behind her eyes to explode off the back of her skull. *Small use in sorcery if it makes you feel like this*, she thought wearily.

"Shkai'ra, could you get a conventional light going? This tires me, and I'd rather explain to the innkeeper about bodies than magic." She stared down into the flickers of red that danced around her fingers. When she spoke again it was softly, in a musing tone: "I wish I could call up a gentler color than this. Green perhaps, or blue. If I had the power."

Shkai'ra looked at her for a moment, then sighed and laid the limp body on the floor, wiping her hands on the black cloth.

"It's a swamp in here," she said, pushing a lock of hair back from her forehead with a hand that left a smear of blood. Opening the shutter, she flooded the room with moonlight. The vague shouts of the watch slaves over the body of the first assassin below on the street came through it; the Kommanza whipped her head back as a tiny feathered dart flashed past.

"Zaik Godlord!" she said. "Blowgun, poisoned dart—that message must be *important*, for them to want us dead so badly. The brotherhoods don't hire cheap. And they sent four, for the two of us; they boast two of theirs are enough for four strangers."

She moved, winced, and looked down at the cut along her collarbone. It was shallow; the edge of the blade had just touched the skin, cutting only because it was honed to a thread. Still, it could infect if not cared for soon. There were streaks and patches of sticky thickening blood over her breasts and stomach; she could feel it clotting in the ends of her long mane and the pubic triangle. She grimaced. "It will be good to be clean again." More slowly, "And if it's worth this much to guard the secret, how many must be willing to pay for it?"

She picked up a lighter from the table and chuckled. "And how highly they must think of us!" The round ceramic ball that held alcohol, with the cotton wick and thumb-struck flint, sparked, and she set the flame to the fishtail methane lamp fixed to the wall by the door.

Blood pooled on the floor, bright liquid red already turning to scum at the edges, soaking darkly into the rugs. The room smelled of blood, excrement, and musky fear-sweat, close within the enclosed space. Shkai'ra wrinkled her nose slightly, but hers were not a fastidious people.

"Best we get someone in to clear up the mess," she said. Megan looked up, rubbing her temples, leaving a blood smear on one cheek.

"No need—hear the uproar down the hall? I think that someone finally noticed that something wasn't quite right." She got up and started pulling her daggers free of the wood paneling. The door opened a crack; light spilled through as the house slaves relit the lanterns. A watch-slave's eye peered in, then gave place to a member of the kinfast that owned the Weary Wayfarer. A black shadow padded through and sniffed disdainfully before settling at the edge of a red-brown pool of coagulating blood and lapping.

"Oh, gods!" the innkeeper groaned, clapping her hands to the sides of her face and staring at the carnage. "Sweet Sun, Beneficent Light, *look at my floors!* The rugs are *ruined!*"

She shook a fist at the ceiling, as servants crowded around the doorway, peering in awe. "Protection money! Protection money!" she raved. "Ten percent before taxes we pay—to every daggerguild in the city and the Watch as well we give our hard-earned trademetal, and look what happens! You can't even get them to protect you against *themselves.*"

She opened her mouth to continue the tirade, then hesitated and trailed off as she caught Shkai'ra's eye. Shkai'ra nodded, finished cleaning the blade, and nudged her cat aside from the blood.

"Stop that—it's probably diseased," she said, picking up the animal and draping him around her neck. "Now, if we could finish our night's *rest* . . ." she said to the inn-keeper, who bowed nervously. The servants dragged the bodies out, after an expert search revealed a round dozen weapons, sealed vials, and instruments neither of the women could identify.

"Sleep would be easier if this mess were cleared up," she concluded.

The innkeeper considered them, and then the Adderfangs and their reputation. "Of course," she said, rubbing her hands on her tunic. "And of course, consider the . . ." She winced. "Consider the week's rent abated, for the sake of the disturbance." A pause. "I will have bowls and towels sent, as well."

Later, she stood in the corridor, shaking her head and sighing. Perhaps the kinfast should go into something more peaceful; secret fencing of pirates' loot, for example, or counterfeiting.

Across the corridor a fair-haired man closed the door of his room with a silent whistle. *And I nearly blundered into that,* he thought, stroking a small mustache with paint-stained fingers. Well, he had been lucky. That sparked a thought; he shrugged back into his tunic and began searching for his dicebox. Luck didn't come your way that often, and the game might still be on. . . .

As the door closed, Megan turned on her heel and walked into the other room, kindling a light there. Shkai'ra followed curiously and found her rooting to unearth the pouch from its hiding place. She crossed to the smaller woman and took the sack, tossing it in her hands. "I think that someone wants this rather badly." Megan snagged it out of the air as it was tossed again.

"It nearly got us killed in our sleep. I'm going to try to find out what is of such importance. If someone wants to send me to hell, I want to know why so I can put up an argument." The headache had subsided to a dull pounding that she savagely suppressed. The anger helped. It also called to mind an earlier comment by the Kommanza. She turned on the larger woman and said, "Look, my *friend*, you can say what you like about my use of power once you know the Manrauq yourself. . . ." Her voice faded in the face of Shkai'ra's wry grin as she realized that the comment had not been meant to prick. She sighed and turned away, unknotting the pouch. "You don't have to stay and watch. Not that there will be much to see either way."

"I'll stay." Shkai'ra hung Swift-Kiss on the bedstead.

"We have to start somewhere, and all we have now is the Glitch-taken Adder's word. Not that I mind a fight, but even I'm not lucky enough to kill every hired sword in the city." Now she watched Megan with more curiosity than alarm.

The Zak took the paper from the pouch, and concentration settled like a wall between them. Nothing seemed to happen for a long moment, then Megan's hands began to tremble, slowly at first, then with increasing violence. She was struggling to contain the power that hid the message and bend it to her will. And was not succeeding. There was an almost audible snap as she sagged, the tension in the room gone as if swept away by a brisk wind, defeat on her face. "Whoever did this was a master. I cannot break it."

Shkai'ra leaned back against the pillow a moment, then reached over to tap Megan's hand just above the parchment, still careful not to come in contact with it. "No matter, for now. I have a thought of what we could do with that." Megan was still staring absently at the wavering, creeping letters, her brow furrowed. "Kh'eeredo, cease. I doubt that we would be attacked twice in one night, so we have at least a day in which to think on it. Tonight we deal with the message, not now." She chuckled. "And you look as if you could sleep again. This magic seems to be more tiring than swordplay."

Megan thought for a moment. "I haven't much to boast of with my magic tonight," she admitted ruefully. "However good my knifework was." She looked down at the leather pouch, her face hardening. "I *will* break this. I don't care how long it takes; I *will* do it." She hurled the pouch across the room; it made an unsatisfying small *put* against the brick and fell to the floor.

Shkai'ra yawned. An overwhelming weariness was on her, and a feeling of cold. She controlled the shuddering. Violent death was no stranger to her, but this was getting to be nearly as bad as a campaign. As bad as the trail barricades in the Forest War, and that was one of her less pleasant memories. Sighing, she forced the taut nerves to relax and allow fatigue through.

"Dark One, take it," Megan said softly as she collapsed to the bed, head in her hands.

"Perhaps he, she, or it will," Shkai'ra muttered.

"He," Megan clarified absently, then shook her head. "Ach, you're right. Last one up has to scrub the other's back, agreed? Shkai'ra?"

The tall woman turned over, murmuring, at her touch and curled into an unconscious ball. "We'll settle that in the morning."

Night was soft and deep.

13

Megan had had to spend considerable time getting the brown crust out from under her fingernails; going back to sleep after a fight that messy was, she told herself sternly, nothing less than slovenly. After so long in the steamy heat of the baths, the tepid water of the plunge-pool was shockingly cold, then comforting. She plunged through the thin scattering of morning bathers with a doggedly competent breaststroke and hauled herself out on the central fountain, lying back on the smooth marble and enjoying the sensation of water drying on her skin as she wrung out her long hair.

One of the few ways not to sweat in this swamp of a city, she thought luxuriously.

A figure waved at her from the edge of the pool. She ignored his waving, slid into the water with a sigh at a strangled, embarrassed shout. For a moment she clung to the stone at his feet and watched his lips move silently before the water released its tension grip on her ears and ran down her neck in warm trickles.

". . . rry to disturb your cleansing, Brightness," he said nervously. "But one of the Shining Servants of the Glorious Light wishes to speak with you." He paused. "A *prominent* Servant." Devoutly, he circled his chest; perhaps the stupid outlander would take the hint. In any case, it would be *his* back that would feel the cane if the Weary Wayfarer attracted another temple fine.

Megan watched with cool detachment as the nervousness increased. Jumpy people said things that otherwise would stay behind their lips; it was a great advantage to be one of those undisturbed by silence.

This one is almost as afraid of offending me as he is of angering the priest, she thought. Last night's affray had improved their reputations considerably. She began drying herself, and took pity on the youth as he shifted from foot to foot and made unconscious patting motions to hurry her. It was unlikely that clerical doings were included on the inn servants' grapevine, after all.

"This priest," she said. "A high one? Rank?"

The servant searched for words. A priest was, after all, a *priest*. It was warm in here to be fully clothed, and he felt sweat trickling down his flanks. *O Sun,* he prayed. *Get me out of this, Divine Effulgence, and I'll never complain about swab-out detail or guests with strange pillowhabits again.* Just for safety's sake, he added an invocation to Ribbidib, gull-headed godlet of Illizbuah, the City and to Haaichedew, the Provider of Maailun.

Megan frowned and considered her words. Her Fehinnan had improved rapidly, but somehow she doubted her mastery of the social inflections was equal to dealing with the shavepate.

"I will not see him alone," she said. "Tell him to wait until Shkai'ra—my friend with the blond hair—gets back." The servant turned gray under the natural olive brown of his skin. "My apologies, of course. Just tell him that the stupid foreigner doesn't understand a civilized language and would be a waste of his time. Use the high forms, tell him what you like," she ended with a small mocking grin, imagining the scene. "Just see that he waits until we're ready for him."

She wrung the last drops of water out of her hair and thought over the book she had found that afternoon. There were fascinating similarities to some very old inscriptions she had seen across the Lannic; even to her native Zakos. It would bear more careful examination, and her hair *did* need a trim at the ends. . . . She turned to go, followed by a small, hollow moan.

Shkai'ra opened the door of their room and paused for a moment. Megan lay on the bed, her chin propped on her hands, staring at the crumbling remains of a book lying open beneath her on the floor. Her hair was unbound, still slightly damp; the ends pooled beside the yellowed pages and fanned out across the linen of the coverlet, neatly trimmed. Lumpy bundles were scattered about, sagging open to show the marks of various guilds; the clothiers', the leatherworkers'. Two boxes showed the ridged ends of bound volumes through coarse brown wrapping paper. A rapier leaned against the bed, needle-pointed and double-edged, with a scrolled cup guard and long quillions. Beside it lay a severely plain leather sheath and tooled baldric.

Ten-Knife-Foot pulled an inquiring nose from a bundle and sprawled across the fragile book, twisting to present an imperious chest for scratching. The warm afternoon light slanted in through shafts of dust-flecked brightness, bringing out the deep highlights of his pelt, matched with the shining black of Megan's hair. Shkai'ra closed her eyes and sighed slightly, content.

The Zak looked up and ceased tapping her teeth with the writing quill in her hand. She smiled: it was visibly the result of conscious choice, but the expression was growing more natural.

"Did your knowledge-hunt find quarry?" she said.

"Nia—no none dares even whisper the hint of a trace of a rumor. Not a word on what the sheepraping message might be, except that it's valuable." She shoved mounds of parcels aside to clear a spot on the bed, sat down, and began unlacing her sandals, until she could work hot and dusty feet into the pile of the carpet with a slight groan of pleasure. "Almost better in boots; the sweat keeps your toenails from splitting. . . . And I see you spent every tenthbit of our loot on the merchanters' rows."

Megan plucked at the hem of her tunic. "The tailor says that I'll have breeches again tomorrow; I shocked him with the outlandish design I wanted."

Shkai'ra slapped dust out of her own trousers, light Fehinnan cotton done to a pattern made in wool and horsehide three thousand kilometers north and west. "Clink the metal, and even an outlander's whims are law. What's that moldy thing?"

"A *book*, ignorant one," Megan said dryly. "It seems to be an old tale, of a hero named Nixo; one who rose to high estate, then was cast down, but rose again to be a demigod of wisdom in the afterlife of Sainclem, in the Uttermost West. I'm not familiar enough with the language to be really sure; and it's been transcribed so often. The words . . . some of them sound familiar, which is strange; languages usually don't spread that far."

Shkai'ra shook her head. "I can read enough for a trade-tally," she said. "Four hundred bales of wool and thirty sacks of grain. Or 'The village of Zh'airzfurd owes service of thirty lances twice each season.' But the gods never intended me for a shaman."

Megan closed the book. "I believe someone who knows the answers to our little problem waits. Someone with a shaved head. I don't know Fehinnan well enough to talk to him—at least that's what I had the bondboy say—so the priestling is cooling his heels somewhere in the inn, if he hasn't stalked off in a huff. I told them to bring him when you arrived."

Shkai'ra stared at her for a moment, then fell back on the bed with a shout of laughter. "*You* told a *priest* to await *my* arrival? Glitch, I wish I could have seen his face when they brought that news; almost enough to be worth going under the Lens for."

Megan curled to her feet and rummaged through one of the bags. A pair of soft boots appeared. "These I found also," she said. "A good grip on the soles, perfect for my line of work. When I don't have a ship. And this." She produced a small flask, a tiny brush, and began very carefully to paint over the hard, metallic, knife-sharp edges of her nails.

A timid knock sounded at the door. "You deal with him," she said, waving with the brush. "I won't say a thing, unless to help you keep your teeth from your knee-caps. Or unless you want him killed."

She repaired to the windowledge to complete the brush-work, taking exquisite care to avoid touching the clear liquid to her skin.

Shkai'ra shrugged and lay back on one elbow, facing the door. It opened to reveal the pained gaze of an inn servant and the imperturbable face of a temple priest. A third-degree Spark, Shkai'ra thought, from the sign above his brow. His face was completely expressionless, but somehow conveyed an impression of bad drains and sacrificial devotion to duty.

The Kommanza scratched under her short ribs. "Will the Spark of the Shining Light, Effulgent with Truth and Justice, deign to enter?" she said. That was precisely what the codes demanded; of course, she should have delivered it on one knee, not nearly prone and tickling a cat beneath the jaw with the toes of one foot.

The priest stepped in, smiling gently. "Of course, One Lost in Darkness," he said. "A Servant need fear no pollution." He sank slowly on the cushions near the desk, his eyes scanning automatically across the room. Not that he expected to see it in plain view, but the urgency . . .

He matched discourtesy with insult and came directly to his business. "Yet the Reflection of the Divine Light is merciful with his priests, and exposes them to heresy as little as he may." Ignoring the snigger from the window-ledge, he continued, "You have what is ours. We want it."

Shkai'ra began picking her teeth with a thumbnail, regarding him sidelong. "Ours, yours, someone else's . . . these are merely words. Even if we should have this item, would I say so? Indeed, I know of nothing in our possession that could interest you or your master." She paused, looking at the matter under her nails, starting to clean under the one index finger. "We are only poor mercenaries in the Sun-on-Earth's, ah, occasional service. I hear, Shining Splinter of the Divine Light, that what the temple has is its forever, while what is ours is negotiable." She grinned at the disapproving priest, who looked as thrilled as a guest discovering ratbones in her soup. "The God's call on our services has been slim of late." And there she left it.

There was silence for a moment; the cry of a street vendor floated through the window as the Servant of the Effulgent Light forced an expression of indifference as carefully crafted as a temple mosaic, and as false.

"I," he said, and coughed before forcing himself to

complete the sentence, "am directed to offer a certain sum for our *item's* return."

Shkai'ra looked at him coolly, curled one leg over the other knee, and began to strop a knife on the hard leathery callus on the sole of her foot. "I like hearing about money," she said genially. "But take pity on an ignorant barbarian, O Lightener of Shadows: be more concrete."

The priest smiled. "Ah, admission of ignorance is the first step to wisdom. One thousand."

Shkai'ra's knife continued its smooth, even movement. A great deal of money had flowed through her hands these last ten years of exile; very little of it had stuck. But this! For a thousand, you could buy a good farm, fully stocked and with half a dozen slaves to work it. Or a horse stud; or fit out three cavalry fighters; or buy a half-share in a middling merchant vessel. Greed warred with wariness; her own people did not use coined money, and her caste had little to do with trade, but she had learned never to accept the first offer.

"Not enough," she said and smiled broadly. The priest, who had not flinched at the knife, swallowed and forced his spine to stiffen.

"It is wealth beyond your dreams," he said.

"Priest, little priest," she said, rising to her feet. The man in the orange robe was of average height for a Fehinnan; Shkai'ra's five foot eleven topped him by four inches. "I dream more grandly than you imagine. And I am not a coastlands peasant, or a merchant, to pleasure myself with haggling. Tell me what you will give, or go."

The priest flushed. *Peace through contemplation of the Light*, he chanted silently. *Peace through contemplation of the Light. Peace* . . . Presently, he won back enough self-control to speak.

"I am a Servant of the Effulgent light," he hissed.

"And I am Mek-Kermak, godkin, descended from the Ztrateke ahKomman," she said. *"How much, priest?"*

"Two thousand. And passage money to anywhere, so it be four hundred kaahlicks from Fehinna's boundaries. Death if you return."

"Nice place," Megan said. "They pay you to leave. Shows their bad taste in people."

"Disobedience to the Sun's will can lead to—"

"Sunburn?" Megan said.

Astonishingly, the priest smiled. "Oh, yes," he said. "A very severe case. Think on it."

He swept from the room; Ten-Knife followed, sniffed suspiciously after him, then turned and made a burying motion with his forepaws.

"He looked as if he was sitting on a caltrop," Megan said. "When he didn't look as if he was imagining us less our skins. But was it necessary to offend him? A certain barbarian of my acquaintance said that was dangerous."

Shkai'ra looked past the closed door, teeth showing between slightly parted lips. "You'd already offended him, Kh'eeredo," she said. "I wanted him so angry he couldn't think straight. As the Warmasters said, the only time it's safe to lose your temper with an enemy is when they're tied and under your knife. But I think in the end our existence angered that one; the priests of the Sun don't like outlanders."

"Two thousand," she said. "They must want it *very* badly. With that much, I could . . . But that offer of passage money! I'd risk Baiwun's hammer if that doesn't mean a rope around the ankles, and a rock tied to it over the side."

She sighed happily. "What would you wager that isn't the last offer? Troubles follow each other like packhorses today."

The sun moved its slitted bars across the floor, through the blinds. Megan returned to the crumbling pages, puzzling slowly over the ancient words. Shkai'ra lay, her hands laced behind her head, happily running over uses for that much silver, and ways of staying alive with it. Less than a tenth-day passed before the next knock.

The tall woman turned to her companion. "Do you want to insult this one while *I* watch?"

"No, no," Megan said graciously. "Merely offending through ignorance cannot hope to equal the effects of deliberate provocation."

The door opened. This man came unescorted, a tall, lean figure in a green undress tunic that had as much embroidery at neck and hem as the regulations allowed, or rather more; he wore a fox-faced festival mask that left only his mouth visible, curled in a smile that matched that of the animal above it.

Bowing slightly, he swept off the mask and tucked it under one arm. His dark-brown hair was foppishly curled and waved, with a slightly tousled air that owed nothing to chance; jewels glinted on fingers and the hilt of his shortsword, and in one ear; some of them were genuine. He smiled engagingly out of a face paler than most lowland Fehinnans', and in a pleasant way remarkably ugly.

"Shkai'ra!" he said, rolling the glottal stop off his tongue with an ease few of his countrymen could have matched. "Won't you invite an old friend in? Surely you're not still sulking because of the dice god's partiality to me?"

Shkai'ra glanced at him sidelong. "Odd, how Ribbidib always smiled on you when you used your own dice." She grinned, and the man relaxed fractionally. "Come in, Sammibo, and consider it payment for that little . . . accident, when I taught you to play bannock."

Curled on the bed, the Zak saw him flush; his swordhand twitched, and she noticed that the little finger was missing a joint.

"I'm sure it must have been a very *little* accident," she said, slyly thickening her accent and dropping into the superior-to-inferior inflection as if by accident.

He turned to her with an eyebrow lifted in aristocratic disdain, which turned to a stare of frank interest; he suppressed the jest about cradle-robbing that sprang to mind. Shkai'ra would take it in good part, but the little one . . . Snakes didn't have to be big.

"Sammibo Haadfayul's-Kin," he said curtly. For a moment he struggled to keep the pose, then sank down laughing on the bed between the two women, dumping the cat onto his lap. After a moment, they joined him.

"Ahi-a, the gods make jesters of us all," Shkai'ra gasped at last. "Still running errands for that tightarse Smyna, or are you full-time Intelligence Staff now, Sammibo?" She lifted a hand as he began to speak. "Bid high, you're not the first, and I—"she glanced at Megan—"*we* intend to squeeze this melon dry."

He looked down, ruffling Ten-Knife-Foot's ears. The animal bore this with a pretense of aloof dignity, sniffed at his hands to prompt memory, then began to rumble.

"Shkai'ra," he began, and looked across at Megan. She touched a finger to her hair.

"Megan, called Whitlock," she said.

"—and Gaaimun Whitelock's-Kin," he continued. "Seriously, you've wandered into deep waters this time. This goes all the way up to the Iron House, on the military side, and you've seen the flameflingers are in it up to their shining pates. I'm authorized to offer seven thousand silvers, an estate near Shaarlosvayl, and reserve commissions in the irregulars—"

"Sheepshit, Sammibo," Shkai'ra said easily. "I know the border country; the 'estate' has probably been bare since the tribes broke over the border in the Three Nations War, about the time I was born. Seven thousand would put it back in operation—and we could then spend the rest of our days fighting hillfolk raiding parties, saving the regulars the expense.

"You'd not be this stupid. Iron House? Anus of a diseased packmule, you say: this has Smyna's grubby pawprints on it. I don't mind that she's greedy as a fish, or treacherous as a crocodile, but she's *cheap* to boot; she's trying to get the High Command with the methods of a New City joyhouse grifter. Now, tell me something *serious*."

"Something *portable*," Megan said. She spread the fingers of one hand before her. For a moment, out of the corner of his eyes, Sammibo thought he saw a reddish glow outlining them; when startled eyes swiveled around, it was gone. "*I* prefer travel, and clean fingernails; growing cabbages was never my ambition. And to be sure, we are not ignorant of the *complexities* of this situation, good Zav'mibo . . . Sammibo? Talk to us as among the . . . wise." She laid a slight, significant emphasis on the last word.

Sammibo ran his hands through his hair, a spontaneous gesture that left the fashionable coiffure disarranged not one whit. "You'll regret this," he sighed. "Always did think you could raise to a three-quarter-five hand, Shkai'ra."

She nodded. "And you always thought you could bluff your way out of a wolftrap, Sammibo," she replied affably. "Go back and use the golden tongue on Smyna—get authorization to raise the offer." She smiled lazily, leaning back with fingers laced about a knee. "Use it to *talk*. Some things I wouldn't wish on my worst enemies."

He looked from one woman to the other. Shkai'ra relaxed, friendly, and lynx-ruthless; she would probably wade into a tavern fight to save him for acquaintance's sake, and just as easily leave him holding a double handful of intestine if it suited her. And make some heathen offering for his ghost; he had never pretended to understand her. The other—he struggled to pronounce the foreign name in his mind—*Megan*. She was sitting cross-legged, black hair fountaining to the sheets, one strand startling foam-white against its darkness. Her nails tapped on an expensive metal beltbuckle. He frowned inwardly: *Why are her fingernails making that clinking sound?*

The Fehinnan officer rose to his feet, shaking his head. "Well, if you think better of it, you know where to reach me," he said. "If not . . ." He shrugged. "I'll pour a bottle of brandy at the cremation."

His bow was elegant, a slight incline of the back that managed to take in both of them. At the door he paused for a parting shot: "Wizards and priests—Smyna backstabs for advantage, but *they* do it for the treachery's own sake."

The door shut behind him with a sough of air. Megan turned to her companion; her lips had opened when they heard the laugh behind them. Reflex brought them to their feet, the Zak blinking incredulously as she realized it was coming from the second room, the one protected by her wards.

Standing just past the locked door between the rooms was a girl-child, no more than seven years from her height and face. She gathered long silver-white hair in her hands and danced a few steps, holding the silky curtain about her like a veil. She laughed again.

"He was pretty, wasn't he?" she said in a singsong voice, skipping past Shkai'ra. "You don't care right now, but *you*"—she flitted past Megan, touching one finger to the tip of her nose—"you noticed how pretty he was."

The cat had ignored her. With a light, butterfly motion of one hand she stroked across his ears; there was a momentary expression of startlement, a hiss, and Ten-Knife-Foot was gone beneath the bed. The child began to hum as she moved, her audience locked in staring silence as she darted about the room.

"The other man I didn't like at all. No, he looked *nasty*. Don't give it to him; they'll just kill you anyway. Oh, before I forget, you *will* sell it, but still give it back to us, too. I know, Yeva knows, I know."

Megan shook off some part of the feeling of strangeness and leaned forward with her questions. Some part of her noticed a coolness, and the scent of jasmine.

"Little one . . . child . . ." she began.

"Child? *Not* child, I think. *Look*. This is the 'not-me' that goes out. You have seeing enough to know that." For a moment she ceased the darting grace of her movements, standing before Megan. "*Look* and see who I am."

Her eyes were dark, as black as her hair was impossibly white; they seemed to drink light as the mane threw it back in blinding fragments. Yet there was a familiarity.

She began to whirl around them, faster and faster, her silver hair swirling out in lines of brightness. "Learn from the mistakes you will make," she said. And pirouetted, spun between them, laughter fading into distance. Silence.

Shkai'ra scanned the room with slow care, as if to make sure that the child was truly gone, licked fear-sweat off her lips, spat.

"I. Don't. *Like*. Spook pushers," she said. And jumped at the hand on her arm, half-drawing her saber before she realized it was Megan. The Zak looked up at her levelly.

"I did know her. That was Yeva." Her voice was utterly without levity. She turned and looked around the room as if seeing a strange place. "The astounding amount of power that woman has." Her eyes followed something unseen about the room a moment as the cat cautiously emerged from under the bed. His eyes also followed the movement of nothing to the corner of the wall; then he fell to washing himself.

Shkai'ra snorted. "Nomad shit. Yeva's adult, black-haired, white-eyed, blind, and can't walk." She paused. "Oh, 'the not-me that goes out.'" She shivered. "Oh, I don't *like* spook pushers."

She propped her head on the heels of her hands and cocked an eye at the window, where the light of the westering sun was reddening. She tossed the pouch in her hand.

"Whoever we decide to sell this to," she said, "we ought to get it out of our hands. I can live without more visitors of the sort we had last night; in fact, we'd be much more likely to . . . Best we drop it off, then let it be known that it's not here."

Megan looked dubiously at the leather sack with its cryptic contents. "Yessss . . . but somehow I can't imagine asking the innkeepers to put it in their fastbox for us."

"Harriso," the Kommanza replied.

"Harriso?" Megan echoed in suprise. "But . . . anyone can kill a blind beggar."

"Yes, but no one has, and Harriso's been working the alleys for many a year. Most beggars don't live long; but somehow when it comes Harriso's time, he doesn't go. Anyway, who would suspect a blind beggar of having the treasure that's set all Illizbuah on its ear? If you want to hide something, put it where folk *won't* look. Best we go after dark, to keep it discreet."

Megan shrugged. "Well, you know this city better than I. But it's still two hours to sunset, and we've slept, bathed, and eaten. What shall we do until it's time to leave?"

Skai'ra gave her a slow smile and reclined back on the round bed, running a finger down from chin to hip.

"Hmmm?" she said.

14

The Alley of the Long-Dead Dog glistened slimily in the dim light of the fading sun. It was never bright here, where the decaying buildings slumped toward each other above the uneven pavement of broken brick. One end of the alley was blocked by the blackened hulk of a burned-out tenement, and in the exposed, rubble-choked pit a hut had been built of timber scraps, old paving, and shattered marble facing. The little structure leaned tiredly into the rubble, always seeming on the point of losing its frail identity in the entropic chaos of decay around it.

Megan and Shkai'ra slid down one wall of the alley, cautiously. Not that the sort of blade who could find no better territory than this was anything to fear, but predators who do not learn wariness seldom live to any great age.

The Zak looked down at the hovel with distaste; it was the perfect setting for the King of the Rats to hold court in filth and squalor; she could feel the soles of her soft boots slipping greasily in the moisture beneath.

Shkai'ra looked sidelong, reading the other's face and keeping her own carefully masklike.

"Odd," she said, tapping the roof below them. "He should be in; in this part of Illizabuah a beggar walks soft at night. The meat on their bones is valuable, if nothing else." She leaped softly down to the overlapping stone shards of the roof, crouching. Her face turned up, dark in the shadow save for eyes and firecoal-bright hair. "Come down, see if you can get this door open."

"Hmmm? Ah, I see." Megan landed, ran fingers feather-light over the surface, and began to probe delicately with a small tool that had been part of her belt buckle a second before. "But this is beautiful work; why does he . . . there!" There was a click, and a meter-square section of the roof lifted fractionally.

She turned to look at Shkai'ra, one hand still on the door. "Now why does he have a lock that would do justice to a Gaaimun's home? And on the roof?"

The Kommanza lifted the square. "You should see his *alternate* door," she said, dropping through the opening like a long-limbed shadow. Megan followed; head and shoulders first, then a backflip that landed her on her feet. A knife disappeared back into its sheath.

The interior of the hut had a spare, scrubbed cleanliness that made bare stone and wood elegant. A hearth was built into one wall; beside it in a niche was a vase that held a branch and two half-open buds. Three closed cupboards were built into the walls; a woven mat of creamy wool served as hearthrug and sleeping pallet, with a small carved chest for storage and pillow.

"How does he do this?" Megan asked, settling herself where she could see the Tatabana and admiring the clean curve of the branch. "And why . . ."

". . . does he trouble himself with the creation of beauty that he cannot see?" The dry voice came from the street door. Harriso strode in with a confident step, leaned his staff against the doorframe, and slid a bar across the plank barrier. The ruined eyesockets turned to Megan.

"Observe, young one," he said. "Observe, and all the worlds and Otherworlds are open, even if your eyes are blind. A blind beggar is what the world sees; this does not mean that I must live or think to match my role. Surface appearance is seen; the assumptions follow. Blindness increases one's perceptions in other regards, not least by revealing how much of what the sighted think they see is the reflection of their expectations."

Harriso stirred the fire, and used a splint to light a lamp of courtesy; the tea service moved through his hands with the familiarity of many years.

"As for this place, there are those who would hear the teachings of the elder days; better students than I had in the temple, many of them. If they have little trademetal, there is the skill of their hands. . . ."

Shkai'ra motioned with her eyes, drawing Megan's attention to the location of the staff, within easy reach of the blind man. "I *thought* I would have heard your stick on the street," she said admiringly. "I still can't see where your bolthole is, in here."

Harriso's brows rose. "One is supposed to stay within, if hooves thunder on the roof above? In the Alley of the Long-Dead Dog?" He reached over, and the dark wood of his staff prodded one wall. "Also, notice that if the roof moves, the walls do also." The staff went back into its corner, and he turned back to the fire, lowering himself carefully onto the other end of the mat. "Hai, old bones are brittle."

Megan, noting the ease with which he still moved, snorted slightly. "Elder, at the smith's you mentioned a book, words of someone called The Subtle? If you would indulge my interest, I'm sure that we can be persuaded to fetch your shawl and a nice warm brick for your old feet."

"Child, I began my study of the Precepts of Annitli when . . . I had considerably fewer Sun-turnings than you do now. By all means, every journey begins with the first step, but . . ." The unexpected smile flashed again, and there was a glimpse of the boy who had sat big-eyed beneath the weight of his scroll. "At that, you would be a better student than Shhhcaair' here, who remains convinced that the best way to study eggs is to open them with a saber."

"Ah, one must make allowances for the savage, Harriso, if I can be so free with your name; but I *am* trying to train her to speak, and wear somewhat besides goatskins." She winked at Shkai'ra's mimed outrage.

He served the tea and sank back to the rug. "It does this ancient one good to sense the children at play; but what is it that you want of me?"

"Ahi-a, the pleasure of your company and the sweetness of your smile, Har'hzo," Shkai'ra said.

"True, just as all priests are naturally bald," he said, throwing back his crisp gray mane. "For the pleasure of company you are well provided, since you returned to us, red-hand. Strong happenings, of late: you escape the great killing in the square, strange events at the Weary Wayfarer, of which I have heard surpassing little . . ."

"We thought you might hold something for us, Elder," Megan said quietly.

There was silence for a moment, save for the soft crackling of the fire. The little room smelled of lamp oil and incense and tea; the blind man's nostrils expanded as if to catch a scent beyond.

"I am not a banker," he said at last. "Besides, the pawnbroker tells me that you have not quite enough to redeem your second-best suit of armor." He held up a hand to forestall Shkai'ra's response. "I know."

"It's just that I never have money for *long*", she finished. It was an old ritual between them. "Besides, I hate to waste good money on paying bills; when I need it badly, I'll steal it back." Her manner became serious. "There is some risk involved. The Adderfangs tried to take it from us; on temple commission, we think. Or military."

An old anger tightened the wrinkled face. For a moment they could see what he had been like in the day of
his power, a cold pale anger as dangerous as ice.

"The Reflection should be as a shepherd to his flock;
instead he is a ravening wolf." The remains of eyes swung
to Shkai'ra. "You are not of this land; you have no obliga-
tions here, and your nature is as it is. But *his* . . ."
Control clamped down. "Why the God Among Us permits
this . . .

"Yes, I will hide your . . . treasure. Nor seek to know
what it is."

Megan laid the pouch before his knees where he sat
easily on callused heels. His fingers touched it lightly, and
drew back for the merest instant. "Yes, I will hide this for
you. But more is involved here than swords, or than the
Right Hand of the God Incarnate dreams, I think." He
noticed the boiling water.

"For now we will speak of other things. Maaigan, Annitli
said: 'Consider the serenity that may be found in the most
commonplace of actions. For example, the brewing of tea,
and its pouring. . . .'"

15

"Your sword, O soldier," the Adderfang said with patient
courtesy. Jaahdnni Layee's-Kin, Squadron Commander in
the Triumphant Steeds Silhouetted Against the Morning
Sun, detached from her cavalry regiment for intelligence
duties, glanced around the antechamber. Her escort stood
stolidly, six troopers from the special-forces section of the
city garrison. There were only two blackcoat Adders present, that she could see, but . . .

"By all means," she said from between tight-clenched

teeth. *Control*, she thought. *Let the city rabble see how a Layee's-Kin behaves under stress*. The assassin took the long basket-hilted blade with a bow; was there a smirk behind his facemask? The door of the sanctum swung inward.

The interior was a surprise. This was the fifth headquarters the Adderfangs had established, a mere seven hundred years old. Once it had been a suburban retreat, a place of privacy and relaxation for a kinfast of wealthy wine merchants. The city had grown around it; the level of the land rose; when the time came to pave the streets of the New City the new avenue ran past the first-story windows of the older structure. The maps that moldered in the archives of the muncipium showed only fill and sewage pipes; considerable gold and a sharp curved knife had ensured that. More gold had emptied the extensive cellars and raised supports for the tenement above; the sewer pipes had proved useful for carrying away the dirt, and later the bodies.

Jaahdnni had expected new-rich showiness. Instead there was dark paneling, flamewood shining with oil and polish. Scrollracks and modern bookcases covered two walls; a terrestrial globe stood in one corner, an ancient thing; she could see the differences, how ice had waxed and seas waned since it was made. A low desk piled with neat stacks of correspondence occupied one end of the rectangular room. Behind it . . .

She swallowed nausea at the obscenity. Shamelessly portrayed in mosaic of crystal and onyx, *a solar eclipse!*

The soldier forced her eyes down to the desk's occupant. And that one was so ordinary, reclining easily on her cushions in a neat dark civilian tunic. The marks of childhood malnutrition still showed, around her eyes, along the darkened fingers; perhaps also the memory of hunger prompted the open box of sweetmeats and the pug-jowls of the Adderlord's face. She smiled, showing bad teeth.

"Jahlini, of no kin." she said. A hand twitched, and servants appeared. Twins, a boy and girl of perhaps fourteen. Jaahdnni was impressed; matched blonds of that comeliness were not easy to find. They bore trays of tea and small seedcakes, setting them before the two women with fluid grace and retiring silently.

The soldier introduced herself, consciously avoiding the superior-to-the inferior inflection, then drew papers from her waist sash.

"General-Commander Smyna is most displeased," she continued. Carefully polite, she sipped the tea. And after all, it was better to be within the sacred bonds of hospitality that protected a guest. Especially if you were dealing with city scum . . . lowlife city scum at that. She leafed through the papers by one corner. Only under orders would she lose face like this, to actually speak to one of *these*. "I have been told that your latest commission is quite late. We *had* hoped that your organization would have been more. . . . adept, shall we say, in carrying out so small a project as a retrieval." She looked up, her face blank, asking innocently, "After all, your artists are said to be much better than any outlander. Was I mistaken?"

Jahlini sighed mournfully. "Alas, recovering the message from the two barbarians proved to be somewhat more difficult than at first imagined." She ran a casual finger down into the interior of her cup before pouring; good, smooth. The kitchen staff were loyal, but one never knew. "Perhaps we have become somewhat oversubtle in the pursuit of our art; after all, for the most part we deal with persons of refinement, residents of Illizbuah, the City, who appreciate subtlety. Not barbarians or country bumpkins. . . . Ah, you shame me as your host; do drink." She poured herself a cup from the common pot between them and drank; the soldier followed suit.

Jaahdnni held the cup just below her chin and regarded the Adderchief through the gentle steam. Suddenly she realized one thing that had bothered her: the wet smell of stone and concrete that lay under the scents of wood and linseed oil. The scent of the herbal tea was pleasing, and she sipped again; perhaps dealing with this one, city though she was, wouldn't be that difficult. *I am so far removed from her that there's really no point in taking her tone as an insult*. And demanding her sword! That was for nobles.

"A lovely blend." She inclined her head to the other. "You do your guest honor." She sighed. "I fear, however, that I must return to necessity. If the little item is not returned to us, then I fear we will have to ask for the return of the fee—oh, very politely, of course. My commander is most concerned that this trifle not fall into the, ah, wrong hands, shall we say." *Namely yours*, she thought, and pasted a smile on her face. Strange, the room that had been so cool was becoming stuffy.

"Yes, indeed. I have prepared a letter of apology which will be delivered to the General-Commander. Now, what—ah, complexity. I fear we *are* too given to it. Take the use of dhilmaan, for example. Honey?" she added, holding a spoon above the pot. The soldier hesitated, noted that the Adder was taking none, and shook her head.

"No, thank you. Dhilmaan?" The word was curious; in city dialect, it meant "loving twin."

"A poison. Two-stage; one part is administered as a solid, the other as a liquid—or in crystalline form. One is insoluble in stomach juices; the other dissolves and activates it. Any systemic poison will do."

Jaahdnni looked down at her cup. "But . . . you drank from the same pot," she said weakly. Her breath caught; that might be fear. Pain shot down her left arm, then lanced into her chest as she toppled and arched, straining for breath. Air rasped into her throat, past muscles locking and contracting on the yelding cartilage of the windpipe.

"Oh, the activator was deposited in a thin film on your cup," she said, nibbling delicately at a seedcake and picking up a sheaf of papers. "Hmmm, fortunate that the temple won't allow really potent aphrodisiacs sold for festival use—that would cut into our profit margins severely. . . . Where was—ah, yes, the poison in the tea. From beyond the Middle Sea; HammerHeart, they call it. The doctors say it brings the most intense pain that a human being can feel; no doubt an experience rich in fascinating sensations." She glanced over her file of documents.

"You seem to be short of breath. Perhaps if you lay down for moment, my good Gaaimun? Yes, like that." The soldier was lying on her back, only the crown of her head and her heels touching the floor. The lean body arched like a bow, thrumming with muscle spasm; veins swelled in her throat as she strove to scream, a pressure so intense that a fine red mist burst from the capillaries beside one eye. "Now, as I said, General-Commander Smyna will be receiving the letter of apologies tomorrow. Also a regretful

notification that we cannot allow outsiders to dictate the
time or manner by which we execute a commission. . . .

"But enough of these social pleasantries," she concluded,
when the twisting figure in army green was still.

From the antechamber came scraping noises; the door
was too thick to let through the hiss of blowguns, but an
armored corpse made a good deal of noise. At the last,
Jahlini clapped her hands.

"Niccibo," she said. Her secretary picked his way into
the room, stepping over the emissary's body with an incu-
rious glance.

"That letter of apology," she continued. The thick folded
paper slid across the desk. "See that it arrives tomorrow,
at her bedchamber's threshold. With the heads, of course.
To remind her not to instruct us in our business." She
finished the tea. "And send me the *new* Overseer of
Terminations; perhaps he will prove more competent than
his predecessor." She looked down at the body. Dhilmaan
was such a *tidy* method; it prevented the sphincters from
giving way on death.

16

Megan touched the crown of her head and winced; the
thick coil of braids was almost too hot to touch, and thick
trickles of sweat ran down the flushed skin of her face and
neck. It was hard not to give an audible sigh of relief as
they passed into the shadow of the colonnade that fronted
this side of the temple's bulk. Peering around one of the
thick stone drums, she studied the work gang toiling with
outsized mops to remove the last bloodstains from the pale
limestone flags of the square. The aqueducts had been
opened to flush most of the residue away; looking out over

the bright scene, it was difficult to remember the sights and sounds of so many dying, only days ago. But flies still buzzed in moving carpets around the thick brown crusts on the storm drains, and faint under water and carbolic came the sweetish smell of rotting blood.

She shifted uneasily, very conscious of the looming bulk of the temple. It seemed to crouch, despite the height; crouch above the city like a beast on the body of its prey. Firmly, she took control of her imagination. When she spoke, it was without glancing back at Shkai'ra.

"It is past the time agreed," she said, scanning constantly. "And if all these so-high wish what we have, why haven't they arrested us?" There were uniformed figures aplenty on the great expanse of the square, but they were patrol or functionary, going about their business. And there were many priests, of every degree. For the rest, traffic was sparse and furtive; it would be some time before the center of Illizbuah's life bustled once more. Megan felt curiously naked; she was unused to having ten acres of open space about her in the center of a city.

"And still no sign of them. I still don't like the idea of selling it to the General-Commander. You said she had reason to dislike you."

"And I, her," Shkai'ra said with a shrug. "But *I'm* willing to deal. And the Reflection probably likes me even less, on principle. Our best chance; nobody would believe we haven't sold it *somewhere*." Her lips pursed. "From the way things have befallen, I'd say it's some interesting piece of dirt. Factions want it, to discredit others, but quietly, no open seizure. I wonder if any of these so-friendly parties know the details of the others' offers."

Megan snorted. "Wouldn't it put a weasel in the henhouse if they didn't, and we told them?" She stepped back another pace, unconsciously shunning the bright expanse of openness before them. "Although my life would not be worth the satisfaction; besides, I am not in the habit of *giving* information to anyone."

She leaned against the cool stone of a pillar and looked over at Shkai'ra, concealed by the bulk of the next. "And if you were they, would *you* pick this spot to trade it in? Coming here was like bending over and inviting the world in general to kick you in the arse."

Listen to yourself, she thought, forcing stillness. *Blathering. Voice and body; it seems one or the other must be moving.* The feeling of wrongness grew, and she had not survived to adulthood by ignoring such warnings.

Shkai'ra spread a hand; Megan could see the fingertips protrude from behind the column. "So long as they pay, why not? Even now, there's a good deal of coming and going here; two more are unlikely to be noticed. And who would expect them to make deals on their rival's doorstep? It makes sense."

"Ha."

Two figures in dull-green uniform tunics with shortswords at their belts separated themselves from the guards around a work detail and sauntered casually in their direction. The two women straightened to meet them, maintaining their careful positioning on opposite sides of adjacent pillars.

One of the army officers smiled, yellow teeth against the sallow olive of his face; the skin sheened with sweat, but that was natural enough in this weather. He loosed a pouch from his belt and hefted it encouragingly. Megan stepped forward, and felt a crinkling sensation on the back of her neck.

"This smells like the Dragonlord's compassion," Megan muttered. The feeling of tension grew; she half turned.

Shkai'ra stiffened as she walked, keeping a smiling face. Behind them there was the faintest clink of metal on stone; from behind and to their right, down the arcade. The sort of sound an overeager archer might make, the crossbow sounding as she twitched at a target's motion toward escape.

"Shields," Shkai'ra said, in any easy, conversational tone.

"What?" the Fehinnan soldier on the left replied, the smile slipping away from his face.

"You," she continued. And launched herself forward from a standing start, body horizontal to the ground and one hand outstretched before her, stiffened into a blade. The spearpoint of her fingers slammed into the vulnerable soft spot just below the breastbone, and the man halted as if flung at speed into a stone wall, his face purpling as shocked heart and lungs struggled to function. The Kommanza landed cat-stanced, feet braced wide; her crossed hands gripped the man by the belt and swung his passive body around the pivot of her heels, to stand between her and the side of the temple. The pulse thuttered in her ears, and the sudden coppery taste of combat excitement was on her tongue.

This is what I was born to do, she thought briefly before conscious thought surrendered to reflex. Eyes, hearing, other senses scanned; the data flowed in to be interpreted, collated by the organic servomechanism the Kommanz Warmasters called mind-no-mind. Time slowed.

Megan only had a flash of what Shkai'ra did as she ran. The man was too big for her to hold. He went for his sword, his weight going forward. One step, two, and her body left the ground in a kick. He never had time to drag the sword free, because his elbow broke under the impact. His body caved in toward the agony flaming through his arm, and Megan landed, taking the single step that put him between her and the others, one hand grabbing for the broken limb. As her hands closed on a forearm, solid and almost too big to get a good grip on, she was reminded of the sensation of deboning chicken, the grinding felt through rubbery flesh. She twisted a little to hold the man's attention and shifted her hold to the wrist. She wasn't sure, but the slamming of the arm against the swordhilt might have broken some of the small bones in it. The soldier was rigid and sweating with pain, a muffled whine trailing from his throat as he fought to keep from crying out. She dug the claws of her other hand into the opposite side of his tunic, feeling cotton give under her tense hands and smelling the rank sweat that had broken out on him. She looked over his back toward the temple, very conscious of the immense open space behind her.

"What now, O master tactician?" Megan snarled.

Before the other woman could reply, a voice called out from the arcade. "Shoot!"

There was the barest second before the crossbows spoke. Megan felt the tense body between her hands quiver and jerk as three solid blows hammered it back against her grip. A four-bladed quarrel punched through breastbone and spine to spatter blood and chips stinging into her eyes; she tasted the hot salt of it through opened lips.

Shkai'ra drove backward the six paces to the pillars, holding her once-living shield between her and the squad of crossbows that fanned out from the row of columns. It would not be long before a lucky shot whipped through soft tissue and struck her with killing force; even armor of proof would not stop a bolt at less than a hundred paces. From the corner of her eye she saw Megan shed her protection and dive scrambling for the same cover; the dead man had twice her bulk or more.

No words were necessary as they dashed down the line of pillars, ducking and weaving with rabbitlike randomness, spending the minimum amount of time on the vulnerable outside arcs of their flight. Less than two minutes had passed, but they were panting with the total exertion that only a death-fight can provoke. Bolts snapped and skittered around them, knocking chips from the stone sheathing of the concrete pillars. Dazed with the chase, the soldiers did not take the time to fan out into the square and gain a better vantage for their fire. And the six rounds in their magazines were quickly exhausted.

Megan clutched at a line of red on a thigh as they rounded the corner. "Nothing, scratch," she gasped at Shkai'ra's unspoken question. They looked out across the open expanse of the square, with its scattered parties of guards. Their eyes met.

The blond woman jerked her thumb down to their left, along the front face of the temple itself, to where the great double doors stood open. "Only place they won't expect. No time—now!"

They pounded down the frontage, past startled groups of worshipers, and up the broad shallow steps. There was no guard on the door; they plunged into shadow night-dark after the blazing sun of noon. A corridor lay before them, twice forty feet high, near as broad, the main avenue to the interior of the dome. There was no succor there. Shkai'ra turned toward a secondary door on their left, with a quick fistblow to the throat of the robed guard and a swinging kick to the latch that held it. The rending tear of ironwood was loud in the scented gloom. Choking, the underpriest barely noticed the smaller figure's trampling feet.

The soldiers poured through the door. An upperpriest glanced at them, then returned his attention to the prostrate doorguard. His hands moved with swift skill, examining the injury; the larynx had folded back on itself, rather than simply crushing. Now, if he was skilled and she was still lucky . . .

He placed his thumbs on either side of the prostrate figure's throat and pushed. There was a subdued *pop* and the cyanic blue of the underpriest's face began to fade. Her superior rose and folded his hands in the sleeves of his robe.

"What is this?" he said evenly. "Weapons and violence in the house of Her?"

"ShiningRadianceoftheDivineLight," the captain gabbled. He jittered from foot to foot, and even in the temple the troopers behind strained forward like hounds on the leash. "We pursue two, ah, heretics. Unbelievers! Yes, profaning the temple, offering violence to a Holy Servant. Please, let us pass."

The upperpriest became utterly still. A slight sign sent one of his attendants noiselessly down the corridor; the rest ranked themselves behind their master, faces as blank as their shaven skulls.

"And what manner of persons were these, Child of Light?" he asked.

The officer strained in an agony of frustration. Failure was not going to enhance his record; besides, one of the dead outside was a friend. "Ah, females, two, one tall and fair, one short and dark, ah . . ."

He stopped, appalled. The priest nodded, once. "So, you too know of this," he said somberly. "Even among the Righteous Sword, true God-respecting obedience is seldom to be found." He sighed. "Return to your lord, and assure her that these miscreants will be found, and their secrets plumbed." He paused. "All their secrets."

17

The corridor was long and narrow, lantern lit, tunneling deeper into the massive outer wall of the temple, lined with gray stone. Panting slightly, Megan and Shkai'ra paused at a junction.

Shkai'ra rose lightly on her toes, peering about, the tip of her saber making small precise arcs through the incense-laden air. It was close and still and absolutely quiet, even more silent than the steppe or deep forest, for there was no movement of air.

"Well?" Megan demanded.

"Well what?" Shkai'ra asked.

"Where are we?"

Shkai'ra shrugged eloquently.

The Zak snorted. "Up or down?"

"Up, I think. We may see the dungeons soon enough."

Ghost-silent, they slid along the upward-tending corridor to their right. Deep-recessed niches held doors every ten paces or so; for minutes they passed locked doors, skyshafts, silence and bittersweet sandalwood smell and unpeopled immensity.

"Where are the priests?" the Zak asked.

Shkai'ra snarled wordlessly. This was worse than being shrunk to hand height and lost in a prairie-dog warren; she was a creature of the open plains, cities were bad enough, but this . . .

"Zailo Unseen knows," she said. "This stone dungheap has as many rooms as half the city; the priests swarm in it like maggots in a greenrot wound, but they can't fill it. Most must be at the noon service, anyway; still, only a matter of time until we run into one."

A murmur began. Directionless, it seemed to hum through the thick poured stone around them. Faint at first, it worked its way into bone and thought; not until the sounds were almost separate words did they consciously notice it.

"Perhaps we should find the source of the chant," Megan said.

Shkai'ra paused with one hand on the slick stone lining of the hallway. "I wish . . . demonshit, I don't even know which compass point we're facing, or how high we've come! All right, then. But quietly."

Megan lifted a silent eyebrow and moved forward, hugging the inner, right-hand wall. There was little sound, save for the soft scuffle of her moccasinlike boots and the harder click of the rigid leather on Shkai'ra's feet. The upward tilt of the corridor grew stronger, then ended in a staircase.

The Kommanza took the treads two at a time, her feet touching lightly to push her upward; once the polished wooden tip of her saber scabbard went *clack* against the wall, and she swallowed a curse past barred teeth. The smell of incense grew stronger. At the top was a landing; another flight of stairs above, another corridor on either side of them. And directly before, a portal of thick green glass with the light of an open space glowing through. Shkai'ra dropped forward at the last step and crawled forward at floor level to peer through the pebbly glass. Megan was beside her almost before she noticed. Before them was the open vastness of the temple interior; a few steps below was a broad balustraded terrace that ran a hundred meters above the floor-level altar, just where the dome rested on the square bulk of its support. Shafts of light stabbed down from the lenses in the dome ceiling, five hundred meters above, diffusing softly over the vacant altar block. Ordered ranks of priests stood about, their endless chant rumbling through echoing space, relays of replacements slipping in as others left for food or rest.

The two women slithered backward, their eyes fixed on the door. Shkai'ra put her lips next to her companion's ear. "We've come around to the north side," she breathed. "If we can get straight down, there should be an exit, and an unsecured passageway for worshipers."

They rose, turned, and froze. A priest stood below them on the steps. Shkai'ra's mind struggled briefly to reject the evidence of her eyes; it meant an untrained citydweller had walked to within a body's length of her without enough sound to alert her.

"I fear you will have to postpone your departure," the priest said, her face and voice calm. "My mentor would speak with you."

She stepped forward, beginning a gesture that commenced with the raising of a hand. There was an utter confidence in it; the priests of the Sun were inviolate, and she had other reasons for unconcern. The two outlanders felt a tightening of their skins.

But Shkai'ra's reaction had begun even as her mind blurred in bewilderment, guided by reflexes encoded at a level that knew neither doubt nor hesitation, only stimulus-response programming. The rough dimpled bone of her swordhilt rutched against her calluses as the left hand flicked along it, looped thumb and forefinger under the pommel. The blade came free from its sheath of leather-bound wood with a hiss of metal on oak greased with neat's-foot oil. Her right palm slapped home on the long grip just below the circular guard, and her foot stamped forward as she lunged with a guttural grunt of effort.

There was a moment's coldness, and a smell of wet salt. The Kommanza found herself kneeling, shaking her head to clear it of a lingering musical tone. Megan gripped her by the back of her tunic and hauled.

"The image is gone. I don't know how or where, but I *do* know we'd better go as well."

The copper-haired woman looked down dumbly at the sword. The curve of the cutting edge glittered cold and clean in the lamplight; she thought dazedly of how it had been hardened while the rest of the blade was packed in insulating clay and then polished to a mirror finish. A swelling clamor broke out below as she sheathed it and jerked her head toward the upward stair.

The tumult behind them rose to a dull, muffled throbbing, like the sound of the sea through thick forest, then faded as they trotted down the corridors. They took the left-hand turnings, trying to work their way back toward the outer shell of the temple, but found themselves forced to climb, ramps and staircases turning up and inward. The concrete of the building's substance was sheathed everywhere with stone, polished granite and marble kept immaculately clean but faintly greasy to the touch in the manner of rock in a humid climate. The air was as cool as a cellar; the Sun Temple was large enough that most of its bulk kept to the ambient temperature of the foundations, and the air smelled of incense and damp and the faint indefinable odor of age.

The corridors began to narrow and curve more sharply. "We must be inside the dome itself now," Megan said, between long deep breaths. She was making two steps to her long-limbed comrade's one, only the trickling sweat marking exertion as they wolf-paced up the steepening slopes, trotting a hundred paces, then walking the same.

"Ia," Shkai'ra said. "Best . . . we . . . stop . . . and rest, soon. We may need our wind."

They reached the end of the ascending passage, passing through a holelike exit in the floor of a horizontal corridor that stretched off to either side, curving gently inward to right and left. Shkai'ra stood blinking for a moment; the lanterns were more closely placed here. She paused to examine one.

"Getting on for empty," she said. "They can't keep all this up without much coming and going. We've been too lucky for it to last." She made the averting sign with her swordhand.

Megan tried a door to their right. It swung open easily; she ghosted it wide with a finger and stood back, alert, before venturing within. A four-meter alcove stood revealed; a knee-high jade balustrade was all that separated it from the huge lambent yellow cavern of the inner dome. They edged through and swung the door home behind them; from this vantage three-quarters of the way to the top they could see that the alcove was one of a ring that circled the dome, disguised in the ornate inner carvings. From below there would be only a pattern of light and shadow.

A strange tubelike machine was bolted to the balustrade, pointed at the floor three hundred meters below. Megan touched it gingerly and bent a look at Shkai'ra.

"A toy for keeping watch on the faithful," she said. "A

farlooker." The Kommanza put an eye to the upper end and adjusted the focusing screw. "Hmmmm, and a strong one: you could almost read the lips." She paused. "Why, the sheepraping croweaters," she said with reluctant admiration. "So *that's* why they tell folk to make their confessions with their faces to the Sun!"

Megan stepped casually onto the balustrade and looked down past her boottips to the tiny figures below. The hunt seemed scattered, disorganized, groups of yellowrobes blundering into knots of bewildered worshipers on the acre-broad pavement. She leaned over to the telescope and appropriated the eyepiece. "But this is blurred," she said. "Is there a magic to it?"

The Kommanza grinned. "No, try turning that, there."

"So." She fiddled a moment with the knob and scanned the mob below. A second later she stiffened and started cursing in a number of languages. "Lady of Winter! I've never seen that before, but I don't want a closer aquaintance. Look and tell me. I want to know what I'm fighting."

Shkai'ra squinted downward. "Oh, Glitch of the Inspired Perverse! They've brought out a Mind-Sniffer. It can follow us anywhere—and turn our brains into worked-over oxturds inside our skulls if it gets close enough." She spat on the marble floor. "I think it's time we left; they don't take those out of the temple, not in daylight, and there aren't many, or so I've heard. Thank Zailo Protector."

Megan had backed up from the edge and was running her fingers over her knives. *Fishguts!* She thought. *Magic is what I need . . . and don't have. Nothing I know would fight something like that.* She opened her mouth to call Shkai'ra on. No sense in waiting for it to find them.

"What are you doing here? I have done nothing wrong to be replaced. This is my post." She swung around. Did they all creep around silently? The old man's eyes were unblurred but vague. "You are . . . not of the Sun. I really should do something. Yes, maybe I should call someone. Yes, yes." He mumbled on and turned as if to do just that. Megan hated to kill the old fool, but he was going to call out and bring the others down on them.

She lunged, caught a wrist, and pulled sharply, twisting as she did so. He staggered off balance, his free arm flailing as his knees struck the balustrade. She doubted he was conscious when he hit; he had only screamed once on the way down. The floor below was suddenly bright red. "I didn't mean to do that. Now I've really announced our presence." She looked over her shoulder and thought of the warren behind the door. She stepped up and stood on the railing the priest had just fallen over. "We can't risk getting caught in that maze again. This railing is unbroken by the walls."

Shkai'ra looked down at the confusion so far below. "And you were a thief," she muttered. "Who did you steal from, the blind?"

Megan snorted and tapped a foot against the slick oily smoothness of the balustrade as her companion struggled with tight riding boots. Grumbling, the Kommanza slung her footgear around her neck and stepped up, her toes curling to grip. She looked to her right.

"A long way down," she said quietly. "All the gods curse these people; mountains are bad enough, but they have to *build* them. Earth should be flat."

Megan shrugged. "It wouldn't kill you any deader than falling thirty feet."

"But you'd have longer to think about it. . . . Lead on."

Swiftly, almost running, they trotted around the inner surface of the dome, passing chamber after chamber opening into the dark corridors. The top of the balustrade was less than half a meter thick; thinner, where it passed the partition walls between chambers.

"Hai, about here," Shkai'ra called when they had reached a point across from their starting place. "The main downshaft should be around here."

They skipped down to the floor, Megan waiting for Shkai'ra to replace her footgear. A risk, but being lamed was a worse one; and they might have to move without care for their feet.

"I thought these 'glove shoes' would be useful!"

Shkai'ra unclenched her teeth and looked resentfully over her shoulder; it was unfair, that cities should be where the best loot was. Especially when you couldn't just burn and sack the accursed places: too bad Eh'mex the hammer of Baiwun hadn't come down on this rat's nest long ago.

They moved out into the corridor; this was broader, and

it ran directly away from the inner chamber of the dome.
Shkai'ra put out her hand. "Wait," she said thoughtfully.

Megan raised a brow. "Priestkillers should wait to be
discovered?"

"No . . . I've heard of this. This corridor must lead
directly to the main buttress, then down to the underlevels."

"Good!" Megan answered. It would take a while for
search parties to climb up to them, but much less time to
block off the possible escape routes.

Shkai'ra looked at her. "This is the fast way down."

They ran forward, swift and silent and cautious, like all
predators that live to any age. The dim sounds of chanting
followed them, and the dusty smell of incense; the sound
of their breath and footfalls gradually became the loudest
thing in a world of stone-rimmed narrowness.

At last they came to an alcove more brightly lit than
most of the warren. Stacked along one wall were wood and
wicker containers, much like openwork coffins, with a
greased oak runner down each long edge, and on the
other wall a dark, narrow square hole left the corridor;
they could see that it ran just under the surface of the
dome, in a huge curve to their left around the surface and
down.

"Don't tell me *this* is your way down! No. Don't even
not tell me!"

Shkai'ra laughed silently. "I've only heard of this; it's
not well known." She examined one of the coffin-sleds.
"Yes, it slides down. . . . Ah, this must be the brake; see
how you can press it with your foot." She paused. "There
may be someone waiting at the other end, or death along
the way." She lifted one of the vehicles to the flat stone
launching stage and climbed in; Megan waited behind
her. "It's been . . . a good time, knowing you."

She winked, latched the cover of the sled, and jerked
her body forward. The sled moved, slowly, then beginning to gather speed even as it carried her into the blackness of the hole, feet first.

Megan stood stunned for a moment, shocked by the
strength of her own emotion. There had been so many
years of solitude. So many years since her parents died,
and everything she cared for had died; the risk, the
risk . . .

Abruptly, she unfroze, cursing herself. Mechanically, she followed. The hinged wicker framework of the capsule swung shut over her face; it was more solid than she had imagined, a hot musty smell of reeds catching at nose and throat. She felt the runners catch, then begin to slide as the wicker bullet moved forward under the impetus of her weight. The first sensation was speed, pushing head and shoulders back against the padded rest. Then she was floating, hair bristling over her back at the strange weightless sensation.

Suddenly she had a wild urge to shriek in exultation; suppressing it in the shuddering, bucking darkness, she grinned at the black pressing down on her eyes. There was a wild lurch as the sled turned a corner, frame groaning under the strain, runners screaming protest at occasional greaseless spots. Acceleration threw her against the side of the sled, back again, and around until up and down were lost in plunging chaos.

Suddenly a scene that could not be *was*. . . .

Something turned from the straight trail and lunged at the wall, straining against its leash and drooling a curious hunger. Hot claws lifted the top of Megan's head and scraped behind her eyes.

She threw the image of a wall at it; a fastness, keeping her mind safe while it mewed outside the gate. It became an oozing thing that worked in, and around, and under, and through her defenses, smelling of battlefields and rivers thick with decaying fish and flies. Desperately she thought of clean water, sea and ocean, as her muscles locked into an unconscious spasm, rigid and clawing into the wickerwork. It plucked at nerve centers, scrambling for access. *Pain*. Her hands began to move without her volition; her defenses beginning to crumble, as it began to force her mind to its mold. Then she was again aware of the sled, wickerwork splintered under her hands, and her blood pounding in her ears.

Shkai'ra plunged through darkness, the speed picking up until the sled bucked and vibrated with the slight irregularities of the stone. The smells of hot oil and scorching wood flew up at her; she touched her foot to the brake on the curves, just enough to keep control. And still the speed increased.

Faster than a good horse, she thought. *Faster than the Great River in spate.* Then with a sudden realization: *This is wonderful!* She threw back her head and screamed, the high, exultant, falsetto screech of the Kommanz warcry.

And then the rattling banks turned into a prolonged hissing as the curve flattened out and the sled barreled into a long flat stretch an inch deep in water. The sled braked to a stop, and an attendant scurried forward to guide it to the landing and throw open the cover.

He paused for a moment, paralyzed, at the exceedingly unpriestly occupant. Still laughing with the thrill of the ride, she shot up one hand to grip him by the throat. The other, fisted, flashed up to land under his nose. She tossed the corpse to one side and rose in a crouch, eyes darting around the cavernous underground chamber.

An instant later the second sled rocketed around the corner and slowed to a stop. As the rush of the disturbed water died there was no motion for a long moment. Finally the cover swung open slowly and Megan stepped out, pale as snow and tension showing around her eyes. She just stood and looked at the scene before her.

Shkai'ra caught her by the shoulders, lifted her to face level, kissed her soundly, and deposited her on the dry surface of the landing stage.

"That was *fun,*" she said. "Kh'eeredo. Let's get out of here before they bring on their tame spook." She jerked a thumb at the exit, a barred wooden door set in plain oozing concrete; they were far below the level of marble sheathing. "There'll be an exit to the sewers—risky, but better than breaking for the surface." She sobered, the exhilaration of the ride fading. "It's that damned monster of theirs that bothers me."

Megan's answer was harsh laughter. "It bothers *you!*" They hurried down a corridor chosen at random. Megan felt along under her jawbone to the spot behind the ear where the carotid pulsed and wondered if she would be quick enough once the Sniffer got close again. *I will not become a beast of theirs,* she thought, and concentrated on running.

*   *   *

Shkai'ra pressed her shoulders back against the weeping concrete, feeling the slow drops soaking through the linen of her tunic and mingling with the clammy sweat on her flanks. Pulse hammered in her ears, and her training fought to slow the quick harsh sob of breath. The priests were close now, no more than two corridors away . . . it was so difficult to estimate distance in this stone warren! She bared her teeth. There must be weirdwork on the tracking; hounds would have given themselves away with their noise by now.

"Where are we?" Megan whispered.

"Lost. Back to the turn and right this time."

They padded back and took the other turning, straining to sense the downward slope they sought. The lanterns were few and far between here, hurtful to eyes night-adapted by hours beneath the earth. The sad smell of wet stone had been with them so long they scarcely noticed it; despite the underground chill the air was close and sticky with moisture. They came to a crossway in the low tunnels, and Shkai'ra eyed the arch above her head with hatred. She could stand erect only in the center, which put her feet in the drainway, a wet cold chaffing inside her boots. This level was all beneath the water table, kept open by drainage to the sewer tunnels and the pumping system.

Behind them the noise of the temple search party grew. And then it was answered from the right, downslope. Megan turned toward the rising left fork of the T-shaped junction.

"No!" Shkai'ra said. "Death that way; too many of them on the middle level above, the tunnels are too wide. Better we chance a fight, try to break."

Just then the sound began behind them. It was a whining, saw-edged shrilling along the nerves. And there was something else behind it, something that drove needles into her ears and blurred the darkened scene before her eyes.

Baiwun be with me now, she thought desperately. She invoked the mental disciplines of the Warrior's Way, then slapped herself savagely across the face. Weakness swam in her, leaving her barely conscious of falling to her knees. A metallic sound came to her from a vast distance; she knew it was her saber clattering on the floor, but somehow it was too distant to matter.

The sound leaped into her mind, forcing its way in through channels burned, with pain, from the last time. Megan stumbled and almost cried out. Acid seared its way into her, and the vague sound of metal on metal did nothing to shatter the hold the Sniffer had on her. She brought up her hands, crooked into talons with the effort, as she felt her mind start to crumble. Her teeth were being driven through rusty metal, she was smothering in broken glass, it hurt to breathe, it hurt to think, it hurt . . . *No. I am. I think. Megan is my name.* She was down on her hands and knees, striving to rise. *I decide. I. I.*" It became an anchor. A fragile thread that grew thinner moment by moment. *I.*

The pressure eased. Awareness returned. Shkai'ra shook her head and groped for the familiar bone grip of her sword, staggering back to her feet. The taste of blood was in her mouth, and she felt the pain of the wound her teeth had made. Vision cleared—

She started backward a step. She and Megan stood in the rising arm of the T; the two parties of priests had met before them. She could have reached out her blade and touched the foremost of them, or the . . . creature it held on a straining leash. And none so much as glanced at her.

"They must be here: they were seen! And the beast *says* they're near, very near, near enough for us to see with the eyes that see light." The priest gave a savage jerk at the leash.

"Someone must be feeding it shit, then, because that's all it's got left for brains. About time to make a new Sniffer; you must have let them slip by you, somehow. His Radiance is not going to like this. Or us."

There was stone under her hands. The Zak raised her head and opened her eyes, blood trickling out of one corner of her mouth. The first thing she saw was the Sniffer's stare. The bulging eyes had once been human; now they were distorted, oozing and bloodshot. It was hairless, limbs stretched to gauntness, pallid white. Skin hung in loose folds under its chin, and it crouched, beastlike, staring at her and drooling greenish spittle on itself, mouth working loosely as it chewed the air. For a second she thought that the priests had them. Then her ears started working again. She moved to brace herself as the priests argued, unseeing. The motion sent the monster—she could not call it anything else—into a frenzy, twisting and backing to be free of the chain. The one priest cuffed it and it snapped at him, then cringed.

"Stop it!" the priest said sharply. "No headaches unless needed. They are *not here*."

"Bring your pet worm," said another, who seemed to be in authority, running a hand over her shaven scalp. "They can't have gotten past us downslope; you must have lost them back in the crosspassages. Quickly!"

They trotted off down the two women's backtrail, leaving the downward slope free. Shkai'ra looked after them, suppressing a hysterical giggle.

I saw that, she thought. *I won't think about it. Not now.*

Megan pulled herself to her knees. "We . . . ha . . . have to get out now." She braced herself against the wall. *We can't expect her help again*, she thought. Yeva's power had, in that instant, joined her own frail defense, a blue-violet surge of power that shielded them.

They took the downslope, slowly recovering from the battering their minds had taken, picking up speed. Then, like a nagging tooth, Megan was aware of the Sniffer, at first fading, then growing stronger, trying to settle a hook into her brain. "They'll find us if they follow the Sniffer. It just tore the chain from its keeper's hand and hunts us alone. *Na Korucai, Rozhum.*"

18

The mildewed lattice, swollen and heavy with dampness, took the two of them to wrench loose. As it swung back with a crash and the raw, sharp smell of urine and rotting garbage welled up, Megan looked at Shkai'ra.

"So these are the sewers. Why aren't I glad that we've reached them?"

Megan eased the grating down and followed Shkai'ra into the rough brick shaft. The stream of water from the drainage channel fanned out in the cracks in the wall, running cold over one hand and trailing down her forearm. The way was closed behind them, if the priests delayed in following their monster.

Shkai'ra was moving down the wooden handholds as quickly as caution allowed. "Hurry. They group around the waste chutes."

"They?"

"Come *on!*"

A rung gave way under her foot, loosened by the heavier woman's weight; Shkai'ra had just set her feet on solid stone when Megan's cry of "Look out!" came down the shaft.

Megan followed, coiling out of a ball to land on her feet. Springlike, her legs absorbed the impact of her weight, but the force of her landing was still enough to drive a small sound from her lungs.

As she rose from her crouch, Shkai'ra's eyes and teeth gleamed in the darkness. "Who do you steal from—the deaf?" she whispered. Her voice scurried around the tunnel, sibilant and cut by the drip of water and a rustling noise in the distance.

"We have time for jokes, *heavy one?*"

"No—follow me."

They edged along the narrow path barely wide enough to stand on; the sluggish flow of water only inches from where they stood. The darkness was not quite black; enough reflected light filtered through to suggest an oily sheen on the rippling surface but not enough to guide the feet.

"Do we have to swim through this?" Megan choked. The stench was heavy, palpable, not raw as it had been in the shaft, but oily and rancid, clinging to the inside of nose and throat like the scent of overripe bananas. She twitched as something multilegged and slimy dropped from the ceiling and tried to crawl into her mouth.

"Nai," Shkai'ra said, dropping back into her native language. The slow drip and splash of the water had changed slightly, sounding against something other than stone or water, a hollower sound. "Canoes," she continued, guiding Megan's hand to the side of a small dugout. "Quick— we're not safe yet."

"This is so difficult to see that you have to tell me?" They pushed off into the current. Shkai'ra set a relentless pace, pushing the paddle deep into the thick fluid. "Paddle hard," she gasped. "But don't let your hands touch the water."

Megan labored to match the taller woman's stroke. "Stop making . . . dark . . . hints . . . and tell . . ." she breathed, matching word to effort.

At that moment a heavy crunching twitch struck at her paddle; the sensation reminded her of a fish striking at a hook. She raised the suddenly heavy paddle, that twitched and jerked in her hands. Straining through the dimness she could make out a small wiggling shape. An alligator only twice a handwidth long, the twin of the voracious little pests that had hounded her through the swamps. Perhaps a trifle smaller. Behind them the rustling was growing louder and the water began to seethe.

"Why have you . . . oh, kill it. Quick, the pack will be here soon."

Megan had shaken the paddle as Shkai'ra spoke, then, realizing that it, in mindless ferocity, would never let go, she crushed it against the body of the canoe. She felt the bone splinter as it came away in shreds. The others were close enough now to snatch at the remains as she used the paddle again. Faintly, in the fetid darkness, she could see that there were only teeth left still clamped deep into the wood of the blade.

They had slowed, and the rest of the pack had converged on them.

"Korucai, Guardian of Lives, give us strength! Shkai'ra, paddle faster!" She tasted the cold salt of sweat on her upper lip. "I've no will to be eaten alive—" She paused an instant to beat off two of the beasts clinging to the side of the canoe. Behind, a sliding, scraping noise was building. "And in such small bites!"

"Can't go faster," was the panted reply. The boiling sound of foul water whipped into froth was close now; the outriders of the horde jerked upward along the gunwales, and the Kommanza smashed the handle of her paddle across their bodies as she switched the blade from one side to the other. "There is one difference between these and the swamp breed."

"What?"

"These . . . their bite is septic."

"Wonderful! *Move*, woman—we're clear of most of them."

I could scream, Shkai'ra thought. *Or vomit*. Her eyes were probing the darkness overhead. "There should be an access here . . . ah!" A movement in the air and a hollowness in the darkness marked the way out.

A thrust with the paddle against brickwork stopped the canoe. "Hold. There must be a service ladder here in the shaft. . . . Sheepshit!" The relief in her voice shifted to disgust colored with urgency. "It's broken off." Her fingers traced old brick, crumbling in the wet; a trickle of oily liquid fell on her upturned face.

Megan rammed down a surge of panic. "If we can't get out here, can we reach the next one?"

The canoe thudded against the wall and rebounded. Shkai'ra had not answered; there was a dim flash of metal as she jammed her dagger into the ancient mortar of the access shaft and hammered it home with the butt of her paddle.

"Climb over me, quick," she husked.

Megan reached up to the Kommanza's shoulders, her fingers sinking into the hard rubbery deltoids. Careful not to shoot the uncertain footing of the boat out from beneath the other woman's feet, she jumped to precarious balance on Shkai'ra's hips, then climbed lightly to place her feet on the shoulders. Reaching up, she wove her hands through the lowest secure rung and braced a foot on the dagger hilt. Arching her back in anticipation of the strain, she looked down into a deeper blackness.

"Climb," she said.

There was an instant of joint-cracking tension as the Zak felt her companion's full weight; she bore the brunt of it on her arms, not daring to throw strain on the sodden mortar and eroded brick imprisoning the Kommanza's blade. Hands clamped her ankles; an arm reached up to circle her thighs, tightened to bear weight, and the other hand reached for her belt. The long body slid over hers, and she gave a grunt of relief as Shkai'ra's hands reached the rung above hers. Her feet gripped the hilt of the dagger, worked it free, and brought it up for gripping as she hung one-handed. Below, she could hear the canoe capsize under the scrambling impact; the slow current bore it away.

Megan tossed the knife upward. "Here," she said. "The walls curve inward to the ceiling; can they reach the access hole?"

Shkai'ra caught the hilt, more sensed than felt, and paused to hawk gummy phlegm into her mouth and spit into the water below. "Yes," she said. "There's growth on the brick lining, and the surface is rough. Take a little time, but they won't stop on a hot trail. At least there's no blood, to drive them into frenzy. Couldn't you do that glowing-knife trick? We could use some light."

"True, but do you suggest that we wait for *them* while I concentrate?" Megan replied. Below, the thick viscous liquid at the sides of the tunnel was being whipped into froth as the caymans scrabbled at the slick growth that covered the bricks. Soon it would be stripped away, and the claws would grip.

Unseen in the darkness, Shkai'ra spat in the direction of the noise. "No," she snarled. "Only one way to go."

"Let me go first."

"Why?"

"If those shoulders of yours get stuck, I don't want to be

behind you, like beer behind the bung. And if *I* get stuck
. . . well, you will just have to use those stilt legs and
push." She paused a moment. "Hard" she added.

Shkai'ra stared up into the darkness, and knew that it
would need all a warrior's sense of shame to make her
follow into the narrow lightless filthy smallness of it. She
bared her teeth and began to haul; just then a small shape
thudded into one leg. White-hot needles punched into a
calf just above her boot.

"Sheepshit!" she yelled. "Glitch take all vermin."

Twisting into a U, she hung by one hand and reached
down with the other as the four-inch alligator thrashed
wildly, trying to tear a mouthful of her flesh free and drop
clear. She snapped its neck, then levered at the angle of
the jaw to force the cartilage-locked teeth out of her flesh.
Grimly, she scrambled to follow Megan. The shaft still
loomed like a mouth waiting to swallow; but there were
too many real mouths below. *At least this one is toothless,*
she thought with a wild inward laughter.

"All praise to the Mighty Ones," she muttered, in her
people's standard response to bad luck. " Now they've got
a blood trail to follow." The noise below rose to a frenzy as
the warm red drops spattered their maddening scent into
the water. A few lucky ones took bites from their dead
cousin; the others drove forward in a slithering hill against
the walls of the tunnel, their combined thrashings raising
the mound of living flesh out of the water.

"Faster—they're climbing the walls after us." An endless scuttling of claw on brick underlay her words.

The shaft climbed vertically, then angled over toward
the level. The darkness was absolute now, pressing wetly
on the eyes. The only sound was their own hoarse breathing, falling muffled and dead into the still, confined air of
the drainage shaft.

Shkai'ra could feel the weight of city-sour earth above
her; it pressed on her chest, made each breath a labored
effort. Instinct fought reason, told her to draw knife, and
smash, tear her way clear to air and light before the walls
shifted and crushed her into darkness forever. Not even a
soul could escape from here; it would be trapped with the
rotting body, eternally unfreed by cleansing fire, never to
be reborn.

The training of the Warmasters saved her. *The true killer should hate all that lives, and that hate will make you strong.*

"I hate," she whispered, harsh and hoarse in the meter-high roundness of the shaft. "I hate you all. I hate . . ."

Megan heard the grating whisper begin behind her in a language that she did not understand; hate and fear and lostness beating through the alien tongue, powerful enough to carry meaning. She could almost see the red flare of rage around her, and every sense cringed from the terror within the sound.

". . . the miserable spook pushers and their ratshit message, and I hate the bungling incompetence that got us into this, and . . ."

It was the last, desperate grasp of someone falling into hell. This is hell, Megan thought. Darkness and that sound will be with me forever and this tunnel will not end.

". . . and I hate the priests and everybody breathing free above. And I hate," Shkai'ra hissed, her voice shrinking into a singsong chant. Memories opened and bled; it was the voice of a child alone in the dark with pain and fear.

No way out. Megan thought. *No opening.* In a cold sweat she imagined her groping hand suddenly finding a wall in the dark. In the blackness. To be eaten alive.

". . . but *I* live, *you* die. *You* go, not me. I'm strong now, not weak . . ."

The hair rose on Megan's back, and she fought down the trembling fits that threatened to lock her here unable to move, either forward, or back.

". . . no one will hurt me again; *I'll* live and kill, until the gods come to eat the world. *And I'll dance in the flames* . . ." The Komanza's face worked into a rictus of pure murderousness, but her body moved forward without pause, its movements guided with a preternatural calmness even as threads of spittle drooled down from her lips. And in her mind, the ancient Litany of Hate continued.

The force of Shkai'ra's fear clawed at Megan's mind, but she could not draw strength from it or anyone else to "touch" her and perhaps ease the fear. It was like reaching for a wall glowing with the force of hate. Megan opened her mouth dazedly and shook her head. Sweat ran down her temples and under her hair as she fought off Shkai'ra's emotions. She gasped again, aware that the air no longer moved at all. From somewhere inside herself she pulled a defense against the other. *Fishguts,* she thought. *That might be helping her but it's not helping me at all.* She pretended that it was a challenge, issued in the childpack; one to perform or loose face and position. She crawled on.

In the blackness before her, suddenly there was no floor. She stopped and felt around the edges, fingers sliding in slimy softness. Her breathing was reflected back to her with an odd metallic ring, cold, and shifting slightly. So *that's* why the air is dead. She clamped her teeth on her lip a second. Blocked.

Shkai'ra ran into her feet. The sudden interruption of the steady mechanical crawling shocked her consciousness back into control.

"Move!" she rasped, then realized that the command had been given in Kommanzanu. "Get *going,*" she repeated in Fehinnan, uncertain this time whether it was a command or a plea.

"Shkai'ra, we, ah, have a bit of a problem." The Zak's voice was oddly muffled, carefully calm.

"*Now* this is revealed unto you?" Shkai'ra said, the rhythms of her cradle-speech rubbing through the tongue she had learned. The effort of talking helped to bring her back to herself, a little.

"The passage ahead of us—it goes almost straight down. And there's water at the bottom."

Shkai'ra choked off a sound that might have been a whimper. Turning her head, she sank teeth into one arm hard enough to draw blood, then clenched a fist and slammed it across the three inches of space available into the side of the tunnel.

The pain overrode fear; to a Kommanza, pain was deeply linked to discipline and mastery. "The . . ." She hawked and spat. "The kinless cowget turd-eating Fehinnans build these tunnels shaped like a *shuh* rune. Down and then up again, farther up on the other side and out to the cellar levels."

The Zak felt sudden shock as if solidly stopping a blow and began to realize how close the tie between them was. I. Am. Not. Afraid. Of. Small. Spaces. She put her head down a moment, her forehead on the weeping concrete, and began to separate herself from her friend. Sympathy so close would not aid them. Water. "An S-curve?" Already she imagined the icy feel of scummy water forcing its way into her lungs. "We don't know how deep either, after that fishgutted storm." She drew a deep breath. "We'll have to turn on our backs and go down head first, to bend around the curve." She froze a second, then with a hurried scramble she edged around and started down the shaft, frantically forcing her body to do what was necessary. *If I stop I'll never make myself do this*, she thought as the water oozed through her hair and touched the top of her scalp, rising only as fast as she could get purchase in the slime.

The sick, tight feeling in her chest got worse as she forced her way under and something squirmed away from under one hand. It was as cold as the Dark One's breath. She thought of breathing. Hold your breath. The blood rushed to her head and pounded in her temples, the darkness behind her eyes pulsed red. There was no air. She scrambled and shoved through sludge. Her nails caught at projections and gave her purchase as she realized that the curve was scraping past her knees. Fighting painful constriction, she lunged upward, striving for air, and life.

Shkai'ra waited long moments before turning. And even so, it was not until the scuttering from behind grew close that she drew a quick dozen deep breaths and pushed herself forward and down.

If I'm going to be eaten alive, I want to drown first, she thought as the oily water closed over her face.

She jackknifed her body to bend around the downcurve, braced her feet against the ceiling, and pushed with all the strength of her long thigh muscles. The impetus carried her to the bottom of the straight section, to where the shaft curved level once more at the bottom of the U. And there she stopped; the tunnel was partly blocked by sediment, and the buoyancy of the air in her lungs kept trying to drag her up and back. Her face scraped against the concrete of the tunnel's roof; her shoulders jammed and sank into the slippery softness of the bottom. Outstretched before her, there was no room for her arms to gain leverage; only the strength in her fingers and wrists was in play against the slick-slimy surface. Her boot toes scrabbled, but her shins were still braced against the curve of the shaft, and it held her feet flailing almost uselessly in the water.

She ignored the overwhelming urge to exhale, knowing that the burning in her lungs would be tenfold worse if she gave in. Years of labor and training had given her lungs that would scavenge the last scrap of life from the air in them, and she held them to their task as her efforts drew down the reserve.

In the end it was the mush resilience of the fermenting waste along the floor that saved her; bone could not give way, nor concrete, but the thick organic mud flowed away from beneath her straining shoulders.

Zaik Godlord, bad enough to drown, but to drown in shit . . . An insane giggle at the thought almost killed her, filling her mouth with cold rancid water as she pulled herself along the bottom stretch. Little strength was left as she broke free and floated up the vertical rise; she might have drowned on the surface itself if fingers had not wound in her hair and held her mouth above water as she retched and coughed.

Megan's voice came from above her head, harsh and strained but with a note of relief. "Just think. If I hadn't had you as a guide I would have missed these glorious sights of this wonderful city. Do you take all newcomers through the best parts?"

She was braced in the vertical upshaft, knees and back preventing her slide back down into Shkai'ra. She looked up as the Kommanza braced herself. Faintly above, she could see a dim light that seemed brighter than the glowing slime that rubbed off the walls. The comment drew nothing from Shkai'ra save a strangled "OUT. Get *out* of here."

They resumed the climb, the phosphorescence fading as they climbed higher. They had reached bare concrete when the shaft grew slightly wider. After the first few feet Megan felt one hand slide again and knew that the dull ache spreading through hands and knees was more than just the pressure of climbing straight up. A slight projection in the wall gouged into one kneecap, and she wished that she had her own leather breeches rather than this useless shift. The Zak levered herself up another foot on flayed knees and realized that she could see the wall in front of her.

Another foot, and another. The light was strong enough for her to see the damp patches where her hands had touched the roughness of the concrete; a little brighter, and she would be able to make out the redness. She was cold, and sweating with effort. Her hand hit the wooden grille covering a side passage and clung to the hard smooth bars as to the promise of salvation.

"Zailo Unseen, don't *stop*," Shkai'ra panted behind her. Leather saddle-trousers had left her knees at least in better condition than her comrade's, but the need for escape was a physical hunger now. And below she could hear a plopping and splashing as the first tiny fanged heads broke the surface of the water; soon claws would scrabble at the walls.

"There's a grating," Megan explained as her fingers ran over it. Woven tightly, it would pass water and air but nothing living larger than a flea. The surface of the wood was oddly slick under her hands, treated somehow to shed the damp and resist rot.

"Of course there's a grating—d'you think folk want to wake up with the little crawlers sharing their straw? Open it!"

Megan braced herself and strained; her face was pressed to the unyielding surface, and she could see dimly up a sloping square tunnel. "I . . . can't . . . budge it," she gasped

Shkai'ra made a sound, mostly groan but with the hint of a whimper in it. "It's meant to keep things *out* and let offal *through*—there's a spring holding it closed; it hinges out. *Pull.*"

Megan cursed herself silently; there was a limit, and her mind was loosing resilience under the cudgeling she had been taking. Anger made her wrench sharply on the grille; there was a rending pop as the laminated wooden spring gave way.

"Just a few feet, and then into a lighted room," she whispered back to Shkai'ra. *Goddess, to be clean . . .*

19

The Adderchief slammed a palm down on the polished surface of the table. The sound fell into a silence that filled the cellar room; among stolen finery and bare dew-weeping walls.

Around the table the aristocracy of the Adderfangs sat, their eyes lost in the shadows of their hoodmasks. They were the elite of their kind; aristocrats among thieves, assassins, alley bravos; overlords of protection rings, banks, the houses that satisfied tastes so curious that even Fehinnan law looked askance. Their organization was ancient by Illizbuah reckoning, which stretched back to reach times when the shape of the continents themselves had changed. There were rules, laws, a tradition of decorum. This display of emotion was unseemly. Behind the masks, certain calculations of power began to shift.

"Two of our best dead," the Adderchief continued. "On a standard mission, with only two clients—she used the antiseptic terminology of the trade—"and those sleeping. And an Adderfang killed in plain view—with his own fungus grenade!"

They winced at the humiliation. And face was important; their reputation was their livelihood. The Northside Serpentchief spoke, greatly daring:

"The red-haired barbarian . . ." He let the phrase trail off; no need to remind the Adderchief of the fiasco at Raisak Staaiun last year; no doubt the reference would not be lost on those considering new leadership either.

The Adderchief's voice was much calmer when she answered, and for the first time that evening the man was frightened.

"That," she said in carefully measured tones, "is not spoken of in my presence. Not more than once."

The gathering tension was broken by a voice; not from any of the six darklords. They rose to their feet and spread out with smooth economy, and an observer with eyes to see would have noticed that they had lost little of the alley skills in their years of mastery.

The sound came from the garbage chute, in the wall against which their council table had been pushed.

". . . hinges out," they heard. "*Pull.*"

There was the click of a miniature crossbow being cocked, and the first bolt slid from the magazine into the groove, its point dull and tarry.

It was a shock to be free of the confining tunnel. Megan lay for a moment, panting, under the table before turning to help Shkai'ra. It was then that she heard the small sound. She froze. That had been a weapon, a weapon like . . . She looked up and stared along the crossbow shaft into the eyes of a crouching figure in a black hood. From beneath the table she could see the legs of six more.

Shkai'ra followed her, staggering as she crawled with the aftershock of adrenaline exhaustion. Slowly, she looked up, and sighed.

"Oh, sheep*shit.*"

The Adder kicked the last of their clothes into a corner and turned to finish tying Shkai'ra. Megan's breath hissed between her teeth as she pulled on the bindings. Her arms were strained behind her back, hands tied to the feet and thumbs to toes. Lying on her back, her full weight lay on her wrists, sending sharp, random pain shooting up her arms.

"We go to pick grapes and the rivers run wine." The Adderchief laughed softly. "Five thousand gold we will get from the General Staff. Three thousand from the tight-arse priests." Her voice caressed. "Revenge best of all." She leaned forward and began heating a knifeblade in the glass chimney of the alcohol lamp on the table before her. "A shame to spoil the temper of a good blade, but guests are always dropping in before the facilities are ready. Thoughtless of you, Red-hair . . . and for the love of the Sun's

shadow, throw some water over them; meeting over a
sewer is bad enough, without it crawl in with us."

The one had finished with Shkai'ra and rolled her on
her back, her knees spreading in an uncontrollable reflex
to ease the pain of unnaturally strained limbs. He gripped
her above the hips and looked up at the leader.

"Not yet," that one laughed, muffled behind the black
hood. "Later, when she needs cheering up."

Megan felt hate and rage flare up in her. She strained
again, gasped as the icy water splashed over her, shook
her head, and spat at the figure before her. "*Kouritz
H'Rokatsk!* Your mother died of leprosy before you were
conceived!"

The Adder backhanded Megan quite casually as she
turned to watch their chief. A green light flared in Megan's
eyes, and she fell silent, seeking something, anything, to
fix her power on. Nothing.

The Adderchief knelt by Shkai'ra, considering. The others gathered closer. Shkai'ra's face was expressionless as
the metal touched and sizzled briefly on the upper curve of
one breast. The Adder gave a deep sound of satisfaction.
"Don't talk too soon," she said happily.

Megan pulled harder on the twine securing her thumbs,
as the sizzle filled her ears and the scent of scorched meat
drifted out into the humid closeness of the room. She
could feel the stiff, harsh fiber cutting into the skin, but if
only she could pull . . .

She sagged a second; then what? A roomful of armed
assassins against her. She strained again, and her nails
grated on the stone beneath her. At the harsh sound
everything went still. *Pull?* she thought. The directionless
fury cooled suddenly to an icy knot within her, and her
mind stopped its fruitless thrashing. By straining her hand,
she could just use her nails . . . so. She ignored the
cramping in her hand and felt the threads stretch and snap
as she snicked through the first few. Not allowing her
hands to fall free, she turned her gaze around the room
and assessed her chances. We are going to die, she thought,
but which one goes with us? The one tormenting Shkai'ra
was just too far away, with others between. She turned
her head to look at the one who had struck her and slowly
began to shift her weight.

One of the black-clad figures glanced up uneasily. "Ah, Darkness," he said. The Adderchief looked up. "I think I can hear the little crawlers in the waste chute."

There was a barely perceptible stirring motion, quickly checked. The Adders spent much of their working lives below the surface, in the huge network of tunnels, sewers, and blind basements that spiderwebbed beneath the streets, pumped free by the giant windmills along the walls. The labor of generations had pushed through new connections; there were chambers down in the below that had no direct connection with the light, and many a householder lived unknowing above. There were boundaries and territories in the sunless roads, and wars fought in darkness. The crawlers were the fear that never left those who passed their time below; no menace when you could shut a barrier on them, or run, but to be trapped with no way to block an entranceway . . .

Irritated, the Adderchief lifted the knifeblade and studied it for a moment before reheating. "The grate is closed, and the spring is new," she said.

Shkai'ra's eyes snapped back from the infinitely remote place within her where they had been focused. Consciousness returned, and there was a hard, delighted malice in the carrying tone she used.

"Not since we broke it climbing in," she said.

The Adderchief hesitated as the others wheeled to stare at the opening in the wall. The first of the crawlers dropped with a click to the flagstones of the floor and scuttled about. Her hand wound in Shkai'ra's hair, and she tensed to draw the other woman forward onto the glowing iron. That moment frozen between fear and hate was her undoing. The Kommanza's head snapped sideways and her teeth sank into flesh; she could feel tendon and artery beginning to yield as she gripped and worried, heedless of the pain in her bound hands. The assassin lord shrieked, as much in surprise as in pain; it took her long moments to free herself, and blood trickled thickly from the ugly wound on her knifehand.

At the assassin's cry, Megan leaped, her hands arching out in a swift slash that tore through her target's face from brow to chin. She felt fluid spray across her fingers and her claws catching, slowed by the muscles but sinking to the bone as fatty tissue shredded away.

The woman staggered back screaming, hands clasping the ruins of her face. "My eyes! My eyes!" The black hood showed ragged, sodden edges through her fingers, and bright blood splattered her hands—blood and other fluids.

More crawlers had dropped from the hole, lashing in the feeding frenzy brought by the scent of blood. The assassins were moving with the uncanny swiftness that was their safety. Megan's cramped limbs failed her as she tried to finish the one, and she fell. She never saw the blow that felled her; she only felt the stunning pain that blossomed in her back, a spining kick that knocked her into the wall. The world blacked out for a second.

The Adderchief alone paused at the door. "Remember me, Jahlini Buhhfud's-Kin," she taunted. "As long as the crawlers give you time. They won't eat your hair; the priests will pay us for that, at least. Hearty appetite!"

The door slammed on the sound of her laughter, leaving them in the darkness and the sound of scales on stone. Below, the grate hung loosely against its mornings; each scrambling push of crawlers forced it open long enough for a few to pass, before the weight of the others dropped it back again. Soon the press passing through would float it wide open on a sea of backs; for a moment only a hand of the tiny reptiles could pass at a time.

Shkai'ra twisted to crush one of the crawlers that had found her in the dark. "Megan! Megan!" she called, then, "Yie! Cowget bastards! Megan!"

"No . . . no need to shout," Megan gasped, desperately trying to regain the wind that had been knocked out of her as she levered herself up, first on her forearms, then knees, finally staggering to her feet.

Shkai'ra heard the table go over with a crash and a sliding scrunching noise as it was pushed against the wall. "Say something, so I can find you," Megan said.

"*Get me loose!*" It was an instant's work to free Shkai'ra, and a bit longer to relight a lamp. They spent a hurried moment bracing the table; the tunnel was narrow, and there would not be enough of the reptiles pushing on the surface of the wood blocking the entrance to shift it. The crawlers already in the room were easy enough to deal with; a hard quick stamp and a sound halfway between a crunch and the bursting of a ripe tomato followed. Even this close to the sewers the smell was heavy; the ruptured digestive tracts were foul with the food the crawlers scavenged from the city's wastes.

At last they paused, silent except for deep panting breaths. Shkai'ra leaned back against the wall, wincing but accepting the pain for the support. Her eyes strayed to the door, and a meditative look came into them. And slowly, a smile flashed among the bruises and drying blood.

The guards outside the Council door were bored. It was a high honor to guard such a meeting; common shivpushers could not dream of it. And there had been excitement enough, when all the Darkones had come boiling out. The Southside Serpentchief had been badly wounded by someone or something. But the cryptic command to guard the prisoners while the crawlers finish them had been baffling. What prisoners?

Still, they knew better than to question an order from Adderchief Jahlini herself, especially with one of her supporters removed from power so suddenly. It would have been nice to have a few screams, though. . . .

It was weak, exhausted. The guards nodded at each other and crouched down expectantly.

Surprisingly, words followed. "Oh, please . . . the grate—it must have closed—there aren't any more coming, but—ah, no! I'm tied—"

One of the guards rose to his feet and laid a hand on the handle of the thick plank door. His companion stopped him.

"Yo' out yo' taany ratfuck maahnd?" she drawled in thick New City patois.

"Wha shoul' the darkones gi' all tha fun?" he said petulantly. " 'saads, order was to let crawlers gnaw 'em. No mo' crawlers, we goin' do it."

She nodded reluctantly. He approached the door with caution, pressing his ear to the wood and hearing nothing but a low moaning and a sudden cry of pain. Satisfied, he opened the door a tiny crack, standing well back; the other Adderfang poised to kick it shut and slide back the

bar. He saw only Megan, lying bound on her back, stirring and sobbing slightly. Behind the hood, his grin spread.

"Nääce," he said. "Ev'n all bash' up. No need to kill
fast. . . ." Together, they strode into the room.

They never saw the Kommanza at all.

When they woke moments later they had been roughly
bound with the fragments of the prisoners' ruined clothes.

"Nääce," was Megan's comment. Shkai'ra grinned down
at them. "Sorry we can't stay and entertain you," she said,
"but like thoughtful hosts you've already provided that."
She kicked the table away from the hole, and they bolted
the door behind them.

The screams did begin soon.

"Now what? We've our weapons, assorted wounds and
blood, and not much else. Once we find a way out, you
think we can walk the streets like this?" Megan asked.

Shkai'ra shrugged. "Well, with those manacle scars and
the battering, you could always claim to be an escaped
slave."

"Well, what can you see? Darkness take it! I want out of
this warren. Is that the way out?"

Shkai'ra turned from the peephole, light falling in a thin
shaft into the darkness of the cramped corridor. She turned
to her companion, a half-grin showing white in the gloom
of the corridor. "There's a room out there, all right . . .
from the decorations, I'd say a joyhouse on the Street of
Dubious Delights."

"Better than the sewers."

Shkai'ra felt carefully around the edges of the panel;
there was a sharp click and it swung inward. Before them
was a sea of garishly colored pillows, broken here and
there by waist-high padded platforms of varying shape. It
was L-shaped, and a chorus of moaning and slapping sounds
came from around the bend.

"Door's probably that way," Shkai'ra said.

"Shall we interrupt?"

The customer was a woman in her middle years and
immensely fat, on her knees amid a pile of pillows. Several of those were needed to support the lithe young boy
crouched behind her, his hands clenched in rolls of tissue
as he thrust with steady metronome regularity. There was

little chance of the woman seeing the two naked and bloody figures, as her eyes were closed and her face buried between the legs of the girl who lay before her. That one did see them, and raised startled brows at the sight of the edged metal in their hands.

Shkai'ra raised a finger to her lips and pointed toward the door with the tip of her saber. The girl nodded, leaned back into her nest of pillows, and resumed a series of artful moans, interrupted by bites at a peach she selected from a nearby bowl. Shkai'ra speared another with her sword as they padded by. Megan quirked up one corner of her mouth as they slipped by. *So what did you expect in a joyhouse?* she asked herself. *Incense and piety?* She slipped out the door behind Shkai'ra and closed the door softly. The mosaic was cool on the feet as they passed a number of closed doors. She nudged Shkai'ra. "Do they keep a tally of who enters? If not, then two more customers who had been, ah, a trifle enthusiastic, in the baths wouldn't be noticed, would they?"

The taller woman pursed her mouth. "Hmmm," she mused. Her eye lit on a cool blue hanging of light cotton. She ripped it down with a jerk of her wrist and began wrapping their weapons in it.

"Remember," she said, throwing an arm around Megan's shoulders and practicing a slight stagger, "we're drunk. Sing in the shower, but let's not stay too long. And if we complain about our clothing being destroyed, we can probably get a couple of tunics. I know the management in places like these; I did a stint as a bouncer in one when I was down on my luck, once."

"Sing? I have a voice like a raven!"

"So be an *inconsiderate* drunk."

20

The Street of Dubious Delights roared around them as they staggered from the joyhouse doorway. Lamplight and windowglow ran across the busy pavements; after the close incense-scented silence of the inner rooms, the smells of sweat and dung and garlic struck like a fist at taut nerves. They both knew that a crowd was the best hiding place, but something old and blind within urged them to run, to seek out silence and darkness.

The two women leaned against each other, feet weaving and voices raised in discordant snatches of song. Two more foreign sailors would attract little notice, except from the pickpockets and slavers; scars and weapons would persuade them that these were best left alone, even with a small keg split between them. They passed the darkened mouth of an alley between two garish shopfronts, and reeled in among the fruit rinds and the smell of stale urine.

Megan tugged fretfully at the cheap cotton of the whore-house tunic, brightly printed with what a Fehinnan would consider erotic patterns. "I'd like to get out of this wiperag," she began, then swayed to one side and began quietly vomiting against a wall. There was a limit; across half this huge and alien city, to kill and kill and kill, and cower in sewers like a hunted rabbit . . .

The sudden image of a murderous bunny turning at bay with a dagger in its teeth brought a half-hysterical chuckle that turned to a curse as she spat the taste of bile from her mouth.

"Fortunate that we didn't eat before this began," she

said. Wordlessly, Shkai'ra laid her hand for a moment on the back of the Zak's neck.

"Now," Megan continued, "I want to hole up somewhere. And shake for a sennight." She looked up at the brightening stars with mild amazement. "Only a little after sunset!" she said.

Shkai'ra nodded. "Warrior's time," she mused. A shake of the shoulders. "Best we go."

"Shka'ira?" Megan said quietly.

"Hmmm?"

"Don't you think it might be a good idea *not* to go back to the Wayfarer? Even if they haven't picked up on the fact that we've gotten out and had us followed, they will be watching the inn and each other." They were still a few blocks away from the Weary Wayfarer, near the docks, having swung around to approach the inn from another direction than that of the New City. The streets down here were narrower and the poured-stone light posts fewer. Once or twice Megan saw a shattered lantern, glass scavenged from the broken stump. The taste of bile was still raw in the back of her throat as if she had scoured the membranes with sand, and she could smell it when she inhaled.

The blond woman was silent for a moment, eyes following the road and rooftops in automatic animal wariness. "Best we do," she said. "If possible. It's a big city, but hard to hide in if the right people are looking for you. Anywhere else, I'd not know the ways in, more chance of being caught off guard."

Ahead, three figures had halted under a lantern. It was dim; there was only an impression of tawdry-bright tunics under dark cloaks, eyes and teeth in brown faces. Hands moved, and voices were raised in hissing argument. And a sudden darting flicker, a wet grating and a brittle *snap*; the sound of a tempered-glass stiletto striking and breaking on bone. One of the figures staggered, and the others moved in practiced unison. A swift kick behind a knee turned the wounded stagger into a fall; another gripped a wrist and pulled while he stamped on the victim's throat. Both figures looked up as the women approached.

Shkai'ra raised an eyebrow and inclined her head as they passed, her hand on the hilt of her saber; Megan kept her eyes to the front, a knife tapping idly on her knuckles. The thieves looked at each other. One opened a toothless mouth in puzzlement, before moving to help his companion drag their victim by the heels into a lightless alley. The lolling head rolled on the cracked concrete, a fly settling industriously on one open eye.

"And they won't just try to kill us again," Shkai'ra continued, musing. "*Eh*, they'll assume we've stashed the message and it'll come out if we die or vanish. *Ka*, too open an attack would reveal things to the Sun-on-Earth, and this *must* be a faction fight below that level, or we'd already be on the flaying tables. So they have to snatch us, for torture, without creating too much of a fuss. Not easy. Better if we got in unseen, yes, but what really worries me is the priests setting spooks on us."

"How good are the wizard-priests?"

Shkai'ra snorted. "At what, mounted archery? I couldn't tell a spook pusher from a spavined pimp—you'll have to handle that."

"Damn tricks is all I have," Megan said, casting a look back over her shoulder where the thieves had disappeared, leaving only the drag marks in the damp of the street, and thrust the dagger back into its sheath with a snick. "Foolery with winecups, twistings of light and shadow . . ." Her voice trailed into silence. "Could you get in unseen, alone?" They stopped in a puddle of dark in an alcove where one building jutted out. Megan sneezed at the odor of cat piss and almost missed Shkai'ra's snort.

"Can the Sun rise? What do you have in that small mind of yours?"

"Keep an eye out for trouble while I think." At this Shkai'ra shrugged and turned to peer down the street.

"Don't think too long."

"Cohrse nahht, Gaaimun." At the rumbling bass at her back, Shkai'ra shied violently and whirled, sword already arcing out. The tall, burly, scarred Fehinnan porter made no move to dodge as the edge swept horizontally through his neck nearly two meters above the pavement, and said, in Megan's voice, from considerably closer to the ground, "Will this pass, in the dark?"

"Well, I'll be a sheepraping offspring of a nomad leper," Shkai'ra swore, peering more closely. The edges of the figure seemed a little blurred; she squinted, and saw her companion's figure beneath, as through muddy water.

The illusion vanished. Megan stood before her, wiping sweat from her forehead. "Tiring. Especially in warm weather. But there will be less effort when the image is what people expect to see."

"Ahi-a," Shkai'ra said, tapping her chin. A cold smile bent the wide, thin-lipped mouth. "Do you know what an oxgoad is?"

The pile of wicker cages reached the full five-meter height of the main kitchens. Below stretched the orderly chaos of tiled floor, stretches of wooden counter, and the great multiple brick hearths; the hen pheasants clucked and circled wearily, as if resigned to their fate. A violent squawking brought the attention of an undercook.

He saw the black-furred figure crouched in the second tier. "It's *him!*" he cried, through the hiss of fires and thudding of cleavers. "The demon!" And he threw the first object that came to hand. As this chanced to be a stuffed and roasted salmon fresh from the bakeoven, a shrill scream followed the fish as it whirled through the oil-smoke haze.

The salmon smacked flatly into the brick wall behind Ten-Knife-Foot. This alone might not have distracted him; a paw outstretched through the lattice of a cage was only a hairbreadth from the cowering and hysterical form of a quail in the far corner. The shower of scalding oily droplets was sufficient to attract his attention.

Following instinct, the cat streaked for the top of the pile. An equally unthinking reflex drove an undercook with a surface burn on his palm to attempt to climb the pile after the four-footed nemesis of the Wayfarer's kitchen staff. Even braced against a wall, the thin withes were inadequate to his weight, and the pile exploded outward.

And most of the cages were secured only by straw. The oddly muffled sound of four and sixty woven cages thudding down over table and hearth and vat was lost under the noise of near twice as many birds freed and driven frantic in the same moment. A large turkey, with the wit of its race, made a perfect ballistic trajectory into one of the great ceramic vats that lined the opposite wall. A few brief flailing strokes of its wings distributed enough smoking-hot peanut oil on the near-naked skins of the kitchen slaves to send half a dozen screaming and leaping into the center of the floor. Chickens landed and scurried, clucking. The quail and pheasants circled above, liberally bedewing the trampled food and leaping servants below. And one, with more presence of mind than the rest, fluttered in to perch on the highest object available.

Unfortunately, this was the centerpiece of the kitchens, an elaborate confection of spun sugar, crystallized caramel, ginger, and flake pastry, all adorning a centerpiece of froth-whipped cream and brandied sliced gooseberries. The bird landed, clutched, was entrapped, and sank layer by layer to lie thrashing amid the berries and cream, until its claws scrabbled through the pastry shell and spilled the fruit on the bare feet of Glaaghi, the head cook. There it formed a complement to much of the superstructure clinging to her face and shoulders.

She scraped the sticky goo out of her eyes just in time to see a fleeting black shadow, hampered by the hysterical pheasant in his mouth, dart between the legs of one of the burned kitchen slaves. He staggered as the cat hit him and tried to lift his other leg into the air as well, as a flailing wing hammered him across the shin. He fell into another servant, and both tumbled back to hit the edge of the trestle table holding that evening's late dinners, out of the way until they could be delivered to the common room. The table arced like a released catapult, plastering the entire results of an evening of careful work against the opposite wall.

With a bellow that almost silenced the pandemonium, Glaaghi snatched a cleaver from the block just behind her and, skidding in fruit, feathers, pheasant dung, and sugar, went after Ten-Knife-Foot.

"Killing's too good for you, you scraping of a whore's scabs! I'll make cat soup without doing you the good of cutting that verminous, mange-ridden throat! I'll . . ." The tirade became a wordless roar.

The head cook was heavy, but capable of a good turn of speed once started. And unlike the cat, she saw no necessity to weave among feet and tables. Through the shrieking ruins of what had, not sixty seconds before, been a busy but well-ordered kitchen, she plowed with the ponderous inevitability of a knight's destrier. Ten-Knife-Foot had been making for the main stairs to the upper levels. Glaaghi's course made that impossible, and the cat turned and ran for the ladder-stair that descended to the storage level bellow. Most traffic to the bins was by the counter-weighted lift in the far corner of the great room, or by the steep ramp from the rear laneway, of course.

Ten-Knife had the pheasant gripped closely, at the base of the throat; there had been no time to attend to killing it, and the frenzied battering of its wings forced the cat to keep his head high as he weaved his way through the milling feet and down the rough wooden treads. It also slowed him enough to keep Glaaghi only a little beyond a cleaver-swing behind. Several were attempted.

Good practice, Megan thought. She was trembling with the effort of keeping up the image, reaching to prod the slow oxen walking to her left. *But I should have hidden with Shkai'ra.* As the cart of new linen rumbled around the corner and down the incline to the door of the under-cellar she could just make out the flicker of movement that marked the drawing back of one of the watchers who waited for the small dark woman. Or the tall red-blond; together or apart. A Fehinnan porter and his laundry interested him not at all. "All right?" she muttered as the cart creaked to a stop, below.

". . . hot!" Shkai'ra's answer was muffled by the bales of linen bedding, but Megan caught the last word. With a grunt, she swung open the door that would block them from outside view and dropped the image, shaking hands and shoulders to loosen muscles tense and fatigued by concentration. There was a surf-roar of noise, somewhere in the bowels of the inn; she wondered vaguely what it might be as she turned to help Shkai'ra move the bales and get out.

The undercellar was dim. Little could be seen of Ten-Knife-Foot save for the flutter of pheasant wings as he raced across the littered floor and bounded to the top of the oxcart. There he paused, sniffed deeply, cast a glance over one shoulder at the looming figure of Glaaghi, and began throwing sheeting aside with flying paws, *mroewling* around a mawful of feathers.

Tense and made sensitive by the stain of maintaining an image for much longer than she'd ever done before, Megan caught a blast of cat-thought . . . *big-one, safe, help big smelly big big watch-out, help feather spit, eat-good, help big bright-sharp, hide, run, hide, here safe, hide-with, help run, angry, SNEEZE feathers, HELP* . . . Shkai'ra's hand snaked out between the bales, snapped the pheasant's neck, and pitched the cat to the other side of the cart over Megan's head. "Stupid beast, go away!" she said.

Glaaghi thundered past Megan, leaning casually on the cart, and beyond, no longer able to track the cat by the sound of the shrieking bird. A last wild swing at the disappearing tail sank into taut linen perilously close to a red-blond lock of hair.

"Thank you, but I don't need any help," Shkai'ra said, rising and throwing off a bale of sheets with her shoulders.

Glaaghi raised the cleaver and opened her mouth to shout. Gray eyes met hers, and she remembered what the upperservants had related of this one's room. Remembered that there was another world beyond the kitchens; beside a dead Adderfang, a head cook was not of great account. She bowed and withdrew.

In a comfortable corner of the roof, far above, Ten-Knife-Foot settled down to rid his pheasant of the irritating feathers.

21

As the door closed behind them, Megan headed reflexively for the bed, tired and aching in every limb, but forcing herself to stop and check the warding on the room. She regarded the ward sign, the thread-thin band of silver outlined in red, both now close-held in a thicker band of

blue. Someone much more powerful than she was rein-
forcing her spell, subtly and with care. Someone she had
felt before. Megan looked over at Shkai'ra and said nothing. None but the most powerful would even think of
checking for these wards; perhaps only their God-King
could see them, should he be interested—at least from
what everyone's reaction was when the Avatar was mentioned.

Every pillow, from both beds, was piled against the
framework between two of the posts, forming a nest just
below where Shkai'ra's sword hung. In the middle of this
Megan sat curled, with the sheet pulled up close. She
frowned at her nails and resumed rasping at one of them,
not satisfied with the edge. Shkai'ra looked up from a
cushion where she had been painting her scratches and
abrasions with the brown liquid from the bottle in her
hand, almost flinching as it stung in each wound. "You'll
wear them away if you keep that up."

"Hmm." Megan's reply was only an affirmative mumble
that showed she wasn't really listening. "I'm quite sick of
this. This is *not* my idea of a restful stop in my journey
home."

"Hah," Shkai'ra snorted. "You'll rest when you're a
withered ancient of forty or fifty snows. If we live that
long, I'll join you by the fire!" Megan nodded absently,
tossing the pouch they had retrieved from Harriso, when
the army's offer had seemed to be the best.

"There is only one person that we could possibly give
this message to without getting our arms and legs pulled
off before having our throats cut."

"But she'd turn us into frogs . . . or those slimy worms
that live under rocks. I don't want to live the rest of my
life catching flies!" Shkai'ra said, only half in jest.

"Look," Megan said shortly, dangling the pouch by one
string. "This I *cannot*—understand?—*cannot* break. And
both the priests and the army faction have had a good shot
at killing us. Every time they lose face they'll try harder
next time. They have to, from what you tell me."

A baffled voice drifted in from the corridor rather plaintively. "Why am I carrying this tray?"

Megan nodded to remind Shkai'ra, who got up and

jerked the door open. Her frustration showed plainly the way she snapped at the servant. "Room four!" She grabbed the tray and slammed the door shut.

The servant stood looking at the door and then at her hands, counting slowly on the fingers; she looked up and down the corridor, counted again, turned the hand over to count a third time, and finally shrugged and went downstairs.

Shkai'ra stood a second by the door, then put the tray down and wrenched the cork out of the bottle. "Well, then. The priests won't stay bought, nor the General-Commander, and we can't buy the Adderfangs in the first place; we just have to be better than they are for a while."

She chuckled again and poured the cups full. "Life won't be so bad with webbed feet." A laugh, as she drank the red wine. "And I'll pick out my lilypad. Hard on Ten-Knife; pheasant are scarce in the swamps."

The cat looked up from the bed, then closed his eyes again. He was lying on his back, paws splayed, stomach comfortably rounded. A pink and reminiscent tongue lapped once at his jowls.

Shkai'ra tore the leg off a duck. "Not enough here to slow us down; only one bottle," she said mildly. Finishing with a comfortable belch, she crossed to her room and returned dragging a chest. Licking grease off her fingers, she kicked the latch free. "But this time I'm taking some precautions."

She lifted the lid with a toe. Inside, neatly wrapped in waterproof bindings, was a set of Kommanz cavalry armor, the gear worn by horsearcher-lancers on the prairies of the Red River Valley. Flared helmet with a long nasal; back-and-breast of four-ply lacquered bisonhide on fiberglass; laminated thigh and armguards of the same; greaves; round shield.

"With all that? The clatter will wake next century's dead. And if we have to climb . . . best cross your war-horse with a cat. Or a fly."

Ten-Knife came to nose hopefully at the box, sniffing at the familiar scents of leather and oil and varnish. "Mrrrrrr-eooow?" he said.

"No, lazy one, you don't get to see the countryside from horseback," she said. To Megan: "I'm quite nimble in this, but you're right. *This* is what I wanted."

She pulled a rosewood case from its clip along one side of the box. Inside was a curving shape of wood and horn and fiberglass, a little over a meter long. The central grip of the bow was hardwood, carved and shaped, with a cutout to allow shafts to pass through the centerline of the weapon. The thick laminated arms ended in offset bronze wheels; the string passed over them, adding pulley and camming action to the power of the draw. Four long arrows snapped into a quickdraw quiver along the grip, and thirty more were in the round leather tube she slung from the small of her back.

The weapon turned in her hands, dark and shining and lovely, coming alive as she strung it with a complex tool of bronze and horn. From the box she strapped on the armguards of her armor, and slipped a bone ring over her right thumb. Then she drew to the ear, thumb lapped over the cord and hand locked around it.

"Kill at a thousand paces with this," she said. "Penetrate armor at half that; the drawstrength is two-thirds my bodyweight. Up close, the shaft will go right through a horse and kill you on the other side."

Megan padded over and tested the string with a few fingers. "Nice to be able to knock them out farther away. If we see them first." She turned to the window, easing it open. The warding should keep anyone from looking; it would take a light shining out in darkness to break that. Across the way . . .

"Shkai'ra, the ones with the blowguns are still waiting across the way, I think," she said.

The tall woman snapped her shotpistol closed and tucked it back into her sash. "Six gets you one they're still dogging the back, too."

"Then how will we get to Yeva?"

"And you the acrobatic one," Shkai'ra said, raising a finger until it pointed at the ceiling. "Until we get a few blocks away, then catch a pedicab."

Megan snorted lightly. "If you can overcome your fear of heights, long one," she said.

Megan moved silently over the hard slick tile of the roof, faint moonlight melding her dark clothing into the colorless wash of night. Above, the huge soft stars glowed in a sky of scattered cloud. This was Low Town, the tenements of the poor, smelling of bad drainage and fever and slum. And the occasional mansions of wealthy kinfasts whose trades battened on the swarming humanity crowded here; those were well guarded.

Shkai'ra followed, almost as agile, but with an occasional clatter of boot on baked clay. *More heights, and never a big enough lead to get down*, she thought. Her face was set; in the Zekz Kommanz the highest thing was a warrior's lancepoint, and she did not like the roof road.

"Is this . . . really needful?" she whispered. "I haven't heard them for a while, and the streets would be much faster."

Megan motioned her to silence and poised, her eyes closed. It had rained recently, and the tile was dusty-damp, smelling of earth. She strained hearing: a squeak. Her mind collated the sound, ran through chambers of data; memory was important to one who had survived in a world of giants by wit and stealth. *Cork, squeaking on a wet surface*.

An image flashed into her consciousness, the Adderfang dropping down onto the windowledge beside her. The cork-soled sandals and the sound of him shifting his weight as he struggled for balance, in the instant before she swept him to his death.

"No, it isn't *really* necessary, loud one," she whispered. "If you don't mind having *them* above you."

The red-maned head flashed around. Lips skinned back; she sank down beside her comrade. They lay and peered back across the roof, only their eyes showing over the ridge. Coolly, their gaze swept over acre upon acre of jumbled roof, like a relief map of the mountains, broken here and there by the dimly lighted trench of a road.

Moonlight and knife-edge shadow flattened the city-scape into a pattern treacherous to the eye. They both waited with the hunter's endless patience, taking slow deep breaths, their attention traveling steadily from the farthest to the nearest point in smooth controlled arcs.

Megan saw the figures a bare fraction of a second earlier, black-clad, stealing noiseless from one puddle of deep shadow to darker ones. There flashed before her eyes the basement room and the sizzle of her Akribhan's flesh, and the intense desire to watch them all die shook her. Her hand clenched reflexively, driving nails into the tiles, loosening to fall to the knifehilt. The shadowy figures vanished, reappeared, flitting.

The Kommanza laid her hand on Megan's where it was drawing forth the knife. "Don't want to let them get that close," she mouthed, as Megan's attention snapped to her; she tapped the bowcase slung across her back. "Let's fight *and* run," she said defusing the rage shining in the Zak's eyes. Her words even drew a grim smile as Megan nodded.

It would be well to cut the odds a little, and the pursuers were on their trail anyway. Vindictiveness would make them more careless. *I never liked running*, Megan thought.

Shkai'ra squirmed farther down the roof and touched the wheelbow in its leather case, running knowing fingers over the familiar weapon. The pulley wheels at either end responded smoothly to her gentle tug, spinning silently on well-oiled bearings. Shooting from a solid roof would be easy, after a galloping horse.

She drew the meter one and a half of bowstave from its case with a convulsive move that sent her sliding two armlengths down the low-pitched rooftop. Swearing softly, she wormed her way back to the rooftree. Megan was on her back, staring along the long edge of the roof and the broader street that had blocked their way, no longer striving for control but thinking. "Don't take too long," she said.

"Then tell 'em not to move around," the archer answered sardonically, taking a quick look over the ridge. The pursuers were closer now, about two hundred yards. The first had paused on a rooftop, risking exposure for a better chance at spotting the quarry. It was a bad choice.

Shkai'ra edged back, far enough that she would be hidden kneeling, and nocked a shaft. She rose, taking a deep breath and emptying her mind of everything but the task, feeling muscle and nerve balancing arcs and trajectories in a process far below the surface of thought. Practiced from birth, the art cut channels in the synapses; all you had to do was get out of the way and let them function. She *knew* the smooth arc of the arrow, the target, the sudden jolt as the two met. The nock of the arrow drew to her ear. The point came up, elevated for the arching shot. There was a rattle and clack as she loosed and the long string of the wheelbow hummed through the pulleys.

The sound must have carried to the target; he came up from his crouch, head darting this way and that as he sought the source of the unfamiliar sound. He was still seeking a second later when the shaft sliced down vertically out of the night. Sound carried well, here above the muffling walls and streets; they could clearly hear the crunch as the three-bladed hunting head slammed into his neck just inside the collarbone, and the single muffled grunt. That was all, before the body collapsed loosely and slid out of sight along the reverse slope of the distant roof.

The Adders were determined, with Jahlini's anger to face if they failed. Over that ridge boiled a dozen of them, running openly now that their quarry had revealed itself.

Shkai'ra's hands moved with blurring speed; the second shaft pinned an Adder as she leaped from one roof to the next. The massive power of the heavy bow stopped her in midair, and the body dropped straight down three stories to the pavement. The third arrow drilled through the back of a knee as the nightstalkers took cover; the fourth knocked chips of tile into the eyes of an incautious one who turned to peer from behind a roof ridge.

"Not bad, at that distance and in darkness, without good footing," Shkai'ra mused happily. She had never been judged more than a passable archer among her own people: the saber was her favorite weapon.

"Stop singing your own praises and come on," Megan hissed, her voice harsh with frustration. The knife was a good weapon, but it lacked reach. "I've spotted a route that will give us some time."

She slid down the roof, caught at an ornament, and landed cat-footed on the high courtyard wall below. The Zak teetered a moment, standing in the slant of the V of obsidian knives laced along the wall's top, and glanced at Shkai'ra.

"Come on," she continued impatiently. The razor flakes of stone were angled to prevent searching hands from climbing over the boundary, not to stop a walker from traveling along it. Carefully, steadily, she paced along it, then halted. Her eyes flicked left. The courtyard gaped, a high building beyond it, joining at right angles to the low corner-block they would climb to from this wall. An agile pursuer might well . . . *would* use that building, and leap to the one she and the Kommanza sought. She looked back at her companion and flashed a single smile before running nimbly along the remainder of the route. She would need a place to rest and concentrate.

Shkai'ra blinked at the expression on the Zak's face, shrugged, and dropped to the wall. Her larger feet were more awkward in the narrow slot of footing; one glass blade broke and clattered to the courtyard. She looked down to see a dozen tiny hairy dogs dance out beneath. Their eyes were bright black buttons as they yapped and squealed at the figures above.

Like noisy mops with legs, Shkai'ra thought. *So, the Slinkers should be . . .*

Just then there was a crunch, and one of the dogs fell silent. Its final *yipe* was astonishing, from an animal so small. *Slinkers,* Shkai'ra thought, concentrating grimly on maintaining her balance. She had never liked the two-stage alarm system favored by Illizbuah's richer merchants and vicelords. The nails-on-slate squealing of the dogs was bad enough, but the giant two-meter weasels gave her a spider-on-skin distaste that had little to do with their deadliness. A tiger was more dangerous, but somehow cleaner; and she would not care to be the slave assigned to the kennels, soundless enchanted whistle or no. *And it's wasteful of dogs,* she thought. *Even if they do order the little fuzzballs in job lots.*

Reaching the roof, she hauled herself up beside Megan, ducking her head to wipe her face on the short sleeve of her tunic.

"I thought you were in a hurry," she said in a whisper. "Why delay now?" Her hand went out, then was snatched back as if from live coals. It was like trying to grasp ball lightning. Megan traced a figure into the tile with the point of her dagger and slashed the palm of her hand. With an emphatic gesture her bloody hand descended into the rune as a low hum began, a note that shuddered on the edge of hearing, impossibly deep for one so small.

The Adders were coming across the diagonal with frightening speed, moving with smooth precision, like human spiders, each hand and foot placed with finicky delicacy. Their final leap down from the higher building was a marvel of fluent authority. So much so that for a moment Shkai'ra too seemed to see a carven ledge where their grasping fingers reached.

Unfortunately for the assassins, there *was* no ledge. They were close enough for the women to see a paired expression of unbelieving despair on their faces, mouths straining slackly under the black masks. The confident skill of their movements turned to a frenzied scrabbling for nonexistent fingerholds as they scraped down the stucco toward the eager chitterings below.

The screams were brief.

The third scrambled on the tiles, flailing to shed momentum before it carried her over the edge of the courtyard. Alert brown muzzles and bright red eyes followed with disappointment as she teetered on the eave, then catwalked back over the roof ridge.

Shkai'ra looked down, to see a long shadow disengage from the pack and run with humping swiftness back toward the kennel. The moonlight was treacherous, but the Kommanza was fairly certain there was a leg in the creature's mouth. *Mad, like all the mink tribe*, she mused.

"Hunger's the best sauce," she murmured, and turned to the Zak. "Useful trick. Now, I think, they *will* be annoyed."

The remark passed unheard. Megan's breath slowed, and her eyes lost a look of focus on something unseeable. The hum spiraled up into silence; she jerked at her hand, and it came free of the tile with a slight hesitation, as if stuck to the clay. Yet there was no sign of a wound on her hand or mark on the roof. . . .

"Hmmm?" she said, and gestured vaguely behind her in the direction of the New City market square. "That's the way, from here."

The Zak looked down into the courtyard. Chitterings and ripping sounds told of a quarrel over the Adderfangs, and all the dogs were silent. Even the last, as it moved in a straight line across the flagstones, desperate speed in its leg-blurring scamper. The form that undulated smoothly behind it gave every appearance of leisurely disinterest as it gained. Megan smiled.

22

Miles of roofs later, Megan dropped from the limb of a chestnut tree onto the creaking shingles of a tall building. She wiped bark from her hands; they crouched, looking back along their track from the vantage of the fourth-story height.

Shkai'ra rubbed gingerly at one buttock. "Hope the Glitch-damned thing thing wasn't poisoned," she said.

"Don't worry," Megan replied. "That was streets ago; you would have stiffened and fallen if it was." She paused and touched one raw-scraped cheek, wincing. "Dogsucking offspring of darkness, but I feel as if I've been beaten all over with a club!" She paused again, an expression of disgust creeping over her features. "What on earth is that stink?"

"Zaik knows. Burning sugar, maybe?" Her eyes scanned backward. "Those last three are persistent, considering how we've whittled them down this night; if we could only be sure of enough lead, we could take to the streets and outrun them—"

She froze. Slowly, her head turned to face Megan's. They sank down on the rough, splintery surface of the shingles. Even over the cloying thick sweetness in the air, they could smell the dusty, sharp odor of dry rot.

"Three?" Shkai'ra said.

"Then why are we *running*?" Megan replied.

Shkai'ra raised herself on one elbow, until her eyes were just level with the rooftree. "It's taking them a long time," she whispered.

Behind them a power windmill turned idly, disengaged,

its eggbeater blades a figure-eight curve against the bright
southern stars. Shkai'ra's eyes narrowed in thought.

And a knife burst up through the thin sun-warped shingles, exactly in the spot her throat had been a moment
before. At full extension the point of the blade kissed the
skin under her chin, enough to start a tiny trickle of blood.
The black-clad arm withdrew, too swiftly for her to seize
and break.

She sprang erect; her saber snapped out and down
through the papery squares of cedar below her. No result;
they must have had a quick escape planned. Arrows would
be useless. She whipped the shotpistol from the small of
her back, thrust the long barrels through the rent, and
slapped her other wrist on the grip for support before
pulling both triggers.

There was a rending *kang*, and twin tongues of flame
lanced down into the darkness; the heavy weapon bucked
convulsively in her hands, a solid impact that jarred back
into her shoulders. From below there were yells of surprise, fright, and pain. She grinned savagely at that.

"Pellets are too light to kill at a distance," she said. "My
last shot, too—but *they* don't know it. Come on, down and
in," she called, turning and half running, half sliding
toward the eaves of the low-pitched roof. "There'll be an
opening under the roof. We can't let them get out into the
darkness."

The Zak followed, feather-light and soundless where
Shkai'ra's boots brought muffled crunching. The overhang
of the roof was slight, and beneath it louvered vents gave
out into the night. There was light from within; belike the
owners of this place kept that and a night-watcher on
hand. Neither would have accomplished much against an
Adderfang.

They gripped the eaves, backflipped onto the sloping
surface of the ventboards that opened in a half-V to the
outer air, and paused, surveying what lay within. The
place might have been a tenement or mansion, four centuries ago when the New City had been first enclosed. Now
it had been converted to a manufactory, for the making of
the cheap hard candy Illizbuah's lower classes loved. A
huge circular vat filled one end of the floor, four stories
below; others of smaller size were grouped down the

walls, two sets of three separated by a raised plankwalk. The interior had been gutted, save for structural timbers bracing the concrete-block walls, and a few for cranes and hoists.

At their feet lay a sparse network of such rafters. A ladder led down to the second floor, where there was merely a skeletal tracing around the central opening, and a decked timber floor along one wall where a hoist door stood open beside a swingout crane. The three Adderfangs turned incredulously from the platform.

"I'll take the ladder," Shkai'ra said. Her quiver was empty, and that was her only distance weapon. Megan nodded, and headed purposefully toward a dangling pulley-and-hook arrangement that swung out over the center of the building's interior.

The ladder was simply an upright timber that had had crosspieces pegged on, leading down to a foot-wide horizontal beam. Shkai'ra took the inside, putting the wood between her and the Adderfangs, and made speed by dropping straight down with an occasional grab to slow herself. It was only twice man-height, and she wanted to have sound footing on that beam before the blackcoat was within striking distance. After that, she did not await much trouble; the assassin would be more at home fighting here where one step to the side would end fifteen meters down on flagstones, but long knife against a Kommanz cavalry saber was no contest.

The assassin had the same thought. As he ran cat-certain along the narrow beams toward the ladder he unlimbered a weapon quite unlike a knife. It was a chain, two meters in length; the last half of the links had outer edges honed to a razor edge, and the tip ended in a ball of spikes. A fighting-iron, and deadly if well used.

The end curled around the ladder and came within a hairbreadth of taking the Kommanza's face with it when it withdrew. Shkai'ra saved herself with an astonishing sideways leap onto the horizontal beam; she landed off-balance, and beat a shuffling retreat to keep the whistling length of metal out of reach. The figure in black handled the strange killing-tool like a master, keeping it whirling in a great fan of figure-eights that put moving metal between every inch of his body and Shkai'ra's long curved sword.

She backed, feet groping for balance, right foot forward, poised to lunge. This was like the standard footfighting-without-shield stance, using the menace of the point to substitute for a defensive weapon. But the need to remember the gap on both sides of her was a continual nagging distraction, interfering with the smooth automatic flow of trained response. And the chain was the natural enemy of the sword; it could be thrown hard against the edge, and used to drag the bladewielder off balance. And once balance was gone half the fight was lost; and *this* thing could curve right around a parry and cripple you. On flat ground, or in armor, or with a shield, she would have felt confident enough. As it was . . .

No shadow of doubt showed in face or stance or poise. Her mouth was slightly open, breath even, eyes slitted and wary. The blade poised, then flashed out at the vulnerable spot where the hands whirled the chain. He jerked back, but used the same motion to pivot the swing of the fighting-iron down toward her feet. It would slice them open above the boots, or wrap around her ankles and throw her off. She leaped straight up and cut, but there was no force behind it when a good landing was so crucial, nor time to draw the slash. A line of red opened on his upper arm; the eyes behind the hood widened slightly at her speed. She gave ground, feet still moving in a fast light shuffle. He followed, and raised the chain at an angle; the death-circle of his swing now centered at eye level, angling out toward her.

Megan had run along the beam to the spot opposite the loading doors. Her position was too exposed and vulnerable for wisdom, but she hoped that the sheer outrageousness of that would throw them off. Apparently it did. She dodged a shuriken as if it were a thrown knife in a cniffta game and reached the center of the beam. The sheave pulley was locked at the top by a friction block, rope coiled on the wood and dangling down. She seized the coil and looked to see one assassin heading for another ladder. The other watched them all coolly, and directed. Megan's hands had gathered the right amount of rope . . . she hoped. She leaped straight back, allowing the beam itself to pull her into the correct arc to knock the one straight out the doors, or crush her against the crane. Neither worked.

As she swung, the younger assassin spun around and brought up a blowgun, while the other leaped out of her way. She was just too close to change direction and arched past. As she missed she felt the jar as a dart sprouted in the rope by her arm; her other hand swept around with the trailing end of the rope. The hook on the end of it almost missed as well, but took the young Adderfang under the chin. Her weight dragged him across the floor to fall toward the vats below, but the snapping of his neck prevented the jawbone from tearing out entirely. The body hung somewhere between the second and third floors, twitching spasmodically as nerves died in the already dead body.

Megan landed in a roll on the loading-bay platform and came to her feet, knife in hand, to front the leader of this group. She stared into eyes gone black with hate and thought, *Of course, I've killed her guildkin . . . as I will kill her.* Her boots grated on the dust and grit that had collected up here; it smelled of ragweed and dust, drowning in burned sugar. It was still furnace-hot up under the roof, and she could feet the sweat prickling on her lip and running down her face as she watched the assassin before her. *Let her think it is fear-sweat.* Above the mask, dark eyes glinted, and Megan could almost feel the baring of teeth that she could not see. To the side she heard the struggle between Shkai'ra and her opponent, harsh gusts of breath and scuff of leather on wood, but she couldn't shift from the death that threatened. Here, with feet of space echoing below, the speed and quickness that could compensate for the other's reach would be nearly useless.

An outsider would have seen nothing fearful in the figures of the two women facing one another save, perhaps, the knives gleaming in their hands. The only moves they made, at first, were slight shiftings of the feet and hands. Eyes locked on her opponent's, Megan raised her dagger a fraction of an inch, playing through the possible sequence that would end with the knife buried in the Adder's guts, and found it instantly countered. Play and counterplay . . . every move, even to the constriction of

eyes, vital to the death of the other. Not flashy or showy at
all, but the one who failed first would die.

Testing, Megan twitched the hand farther from the
other, another knife suddenly appearing in it to spin
toward her. The Adder leaned aside and countered, her
blade tearing the cloth over Megan's thigh as she retreated with the same blinding speed that the assassin
showed. All of ten seconds had passed, feint and counter;
both were breathing hard. The hollow sound of the thin
floor warned Megan that she couldn't retreat much more;
the edge was too near, just a few feet behind her.

The Adderfang allowed herself to be distracted for a
fraction of a second by the clang of steel on steel on the
beams across the building. That was enough. As her eyes
flickered back to Megan, the Zak feinted again. The Adder
lunged to counter and committed herself. A flurry of movement and the assassin sprang back out of range. A tearing
sound had marked contact, and the cloth of the assassin's
hood gaped open at throat height, though Megan's blade
still showed clean.

Dogsucker! Megan thought. *That one should have done
it. This one is as fast as I am. A trick is what I need . . .
and a good one.* Again the game had begun, the Fehinnan
determined not to be taken in once more.

The edge was just about a bodylength behind Megan,
and she could hear the bubbling vat below. She realized
that this would have to end quickly. Her idea was dangerous. She began to drop her guard as though tiring. She
allowed her eyes to shift and made her breathing harsh.
She licked her lips and began to edge back, showing
classic signs of fear and tiredness. Her counters to the
other's moves slowed, and she let fear show on her features. Behind the mask of her face she watched the assassin accept the messages she was sending. When the Adder
was sure enough to begin forcing her toward the edge, she
backed and flung the dagger at the assassin as if her nerve
had broken.

As her hand shifted to the throwing position, the other
lunged and came in for the kill. Megan fell back, trying to
avoid the knife, but taking it in the shoulder rather than
the throat; she locked crossed hands around the assassin's arm, then rolled. The Adderfang was moving forward

already, couldn't stop, she flew over Megan's head, assisted by a boot in the belly. Shock just had time to dawn in her eyes, changing to panic, as she realized that she was not going to land on this level.

Megan followed through, feeling the edge of the floor hit her at chest height. She threw herself forward and hung, held by the leverage of her outstretched arms and her claws dug into the wood, the grating shock of the knife in the bones of her shoulder graying the room out. The assassin fell, spiraling down, reaching to catch something, anything. She landed in the main vat with a sticky splash, the force of her fall driving her under. She flailed to the surface, screaming horribly as the boiling sugar pulled her down again. She thrashed as if to climb the air, flesh already loosening from the heat. A last clenching of a gray hand and she was gone. Megan swung one leg up onto the edge and lay there a moment on her belly, panting. She watched a drop of her blood follow the Adderfang, then her head snapped up to Shkai'ra's fight. Dark One take the knife! She pulled herself up and dragged the thing in her shoulder loose, stuffing cloth into the wound to stanch it. The knife was bent where it had turned on the bone; useless. She pushed the pain to the back of her mind and ran through the maze of beams to help her comrade.

Shkai'ra had been backing steadily before the whirring menace of the chain. They had edged around the corner and were on one of the slanting diagonals that angled back toward the long walls of the factory; soon the concrete blocks would be at her back.

Zaik eat him, she thought. *That thing has too much reach, and he's too good. Stalemate, but only as long as I can retreat.*

She hawked a thick glob of phlegm from her dust-dry mouth—and cut backhand for his throat. He struck: the chain wrapped itself around the blade in a shrinking circle of blur. With a wrench, he hauled forward to throw her off the beam.

Shkai'ra had been waiting for that; she spat into his face, used the pull to leap forward into the corps-à-corps, and used the sudden slack on her sword to strike savagely inward with the eaglehead pommel.

Blinded, off-balance, the Adderfang then showed he

was a combat master, not merely skilled. There was only one possible move that would restore the tension-grip of his weapon on her sword; he took it, and leaped backward and down for the next level and the longitudinal beam that ran nearly beneath them. The chain sprang taut as his weight plummeted downward, and he used the inertia of Shkai'ra's body to swing himself to a secure landing.

The Kommanza did not even have the option of dropping her blade; it was secured to her wrist by a hide loop. She fell from the beam, twisting in midair as her fall once more brought slack into the chain. The long steel slid free with a slithering rasp, but there was no time to bring her feet back beneath her. With a monstrous, flesh-straining effort she caught the first-story beam as she fell, the sword dangling loose from its strap, her body hanging beneath the timber baulk. Her opponent's face was hidden behind the mask, but she could detect his taut grin from the set of the narrow strip across his eyes. Her mind still functioned, smoothly turning over alternatives; would keep doing so until the heart ceased. From below came waves of sticky, unbearably sweet fumes, stifling hot. Ahead of her, behind the Adderfang pacing forward under cover of whirling iron, a black shape hurtled downward to the great vat at the head of the factory; there was a single hideous scream.

She ignored it: it was not relevant to the battle computer her mind had become. *Maybe I can bring my legs up and kick at his ankle*, she thought. It would mean enduring at least one bone-shattering strike from the knife-edged chain, but if she could override the pain . . .

Splinters drove into face and arms as she hugged the wood, jackknifed, poised a boot. There was little chance she could hold on with a broken arm, still less with her skull laid open, but the alternative was to let go. And below, the smaller overflow vat bubbled.

Megan took in the scene even as she began to sprint for the ladder. And realized that there would be no time. The assassin's chain clinked as he shook it to assure free play; Shkai'ra tensed for the ultimate move.

There seemed to be a great deal of thought as Megan's body moved. A memory of the Adder leader's scream as she struck the boiling sugar. A knife laid hilt-first in her hand. Her own voice: *my Akribhan*.

There was only one possible move; half a dozen steps along the central beam gave her momentum, and she leaped out and down. An extra story's height gave her arc the distance needed; the assassin took the full force of her body in the moment before his upflung metal whip could slash down on Shkai'ra's hands. Her bootsoles shocked into bone, halting her in midair as the energy of her falling body was transferred to the man's heavier frame. The assassin fell sideways; the flailing chain wrapped itself around his neck as he plunged. A crack of breaking bone sounded as he landed on his back across the edge of the vat.

Megan fell, straight down, as if a floor had disappeared from beneath her. Time slowed to a crawl as her hands reached out for the beam under which Shkai'ra hung; her nails scraped wood in passing as her eyes locked with the Kommanza's. The Zak's closed.

Oh, shit, Shkai'ra thought. The small body fell past, shoulder blotched with red. She twisted her head to see Megan land in the soft, syrupy goo of the smaller holding vat, and lie twitching for a second before sinking.

The frozen instant seemed to last forever. Then she noted that the Zak had not sunk at once—the sugar could not be fully liquid. Bubbles broke the surface, and even as a hand groped through into air Shkai'ra was heaving herself to the beam and knotting a dangling rope around her waist. With an almost physical effort she thrust away the thought of scalding, treacly liquid candy forcing its sluggish way past nose and mouth. *Not time to sing her deathsong yet*, she thought desperately. *But if she can't remember to keep her mouth closed I'm going to kick her next incarnation's arse*.

She pushed herself off the beam, swooping down to halt with a jerk that left her heart in her mouth; or it might not have been solely that. Heat lay on her skin like liquid; she gritted teeth and thrust her arms into the vat.

"Ai!" she gasped, groping. Not hot enough to scald the skin off, but . . .

She used the disciplines of the Warrior's Way to thrust the sensation way, and the thought of what it might do to her hands. In the Zekz Kommanz, those who could not conquer physical pain did not live long enough to grow warrior braids.

The hot candy burned, flowing thickly into Megan's eyes and nose and ears, weighing every limb with pain, heat that clung and seeped. Megan pushed the blackness aside and wondered why she was not dead; reflex blew air past her teeth and then clamped lips shut. She struggled and thrashed to reach the surface as the candy forced its way into the corners of her mouth. *Burning, always burning.* Instinct turned her face down into the cooler lower strata. Air exploded from stressed lungs, and for a moment her mouth and nose were clear. She remembered hearing that drowning was a gentle death—*who told them so?* Her hand broke surface for a moment, then it was lost, and the knifewound weakened her. Nausea overwhelmed her; the hands in her hair seemed like first dream of death.

Shkai'ra filled her lungs, gripped; her whole body arched in a steady, controlled convulsion as she pulled her comrade from the syrup's embrace. Eyes stared blindly, rims white. The air came out in a long *hugggggggn* of effort, as the smooth sheaths and straps of muscle stood out on arms and shoulders and back, hard as tile under the skin. The Zak's shoulders broke the surface, and Shkai'ra transferred her grip to the belt, hands scrabbling for purchase in the soft slickness of hardening candy. The legs came free; the larger woman twisted against the rope around her waist, turned the other over her arm, and jerked her under the diaphragm to force any blockage clear of the breathing passages. The pulse under her hand beat quick but strong.

Shkai'ra looked up once she was sure that the limp weight in her arms was not dying. Suddenly, she realized that she was hanging straight as a plumbline over the center of the vat, all sides equally out of reach.

This, she mused, *is going to take some thought.*

Megan's eyes lost their glaze as full consciousness returned. Shkai'ra knelt beside her, sponging the gummy contents of the vat away from her face with a dampened cloth; the expression on the hawk features was amused and almost tender.

"You're undersized," she said with a slow smile, laying a hand beside the other's face. "Maybe I should throw you back?" Then, more seriously, "If you do something like that to me again, I might get *really* angry."

Megan grasped the hand, and felt some of the small hairs behind her ears pull out by the roots as they stuck. Irritation, relief, and a crazed amusement at living roused her more than the blessed feeling of cool air on her skin.

"Do *to* you? As if it wasn't bad enough to nearly get me drowned in *water* . . ."

Slowly she sat up in the circle of Shkai'ra's arm, and realized that they were leaning against the overseer's walkway. She turned to her companion and made mock-threatening hitting motions. "And if you ever make me risk my skin like that again, I'll refuse to cry your name to the wind." The sweet stench had a strange undertone now, and the body of the young Adderfang overhead jerked slightly lower as another ligament tore. Megan began to pry hard caramel from her fingers. "*Versht za?* Do you understand?" She caught her lip between her teeth as the burns under the candy became painfully obvious. "I'd better not try to pull this off . . . my skin would come with it." The ridiculousness of the situation hit her, and she began to laugh, leaning into the circle of Shkai'ra's arm. "In . . . in . . . candy! What a gruesome joke."

Shkai'ra wolf-grinned in response. "You can't be too bad, then." She looked around at the scattered bodies. "Gods and demons, the candy is going to taste odd this month . . . and we both look like we've been through the tiger once already. Let's get going; but from now on we *walk* to see your tame spook pusher. On *solid ground*, and leave the rooftops to the pigeons."

Megan tried to stand, staggered in a wave of dizziness. Shkai'ra threw a supporting arm around her shoulders and clamped a hand under the opposite armpit.

The Zak tried to shrug off the arm, staggered again, and gripped at the back of her comrade's tunic. "Thank you," she said.

Shkai'ra grunted noncommittally, wincing at the pain of a pulled leg muscle as she took the first step toward the door. She set the pace carefully; they could both ignore pain if they must, but the body did not give its warning lightly, and there was little danger of pursuit in the immediate future.

The street outside was dark; the lanterns did not survive long in this part of the New City, and the merchant princes of the municipium were stingy about their replacement. They cut an odd figure, both bloody and torn, powdered with dust and woodchips and new scabs that cracked across as they moved. Megan was spitting to clear her mouth and dragging at bits of hard candy on her eyelids; Shkai'ra walked with the saber naked in her hand, and the sleeve of her tunic was sodden and flopping to the elbow, more than enough to deter any predators attracted by their wounds and weariness.

As she hung on to Shkai'ra's arm, Megan felt very strange. She dismissed it as the aftereffects of the fight and the close brush with death. She set herself to keeping up to the slow pace that Shkai'ra set, thinking that the hot, pulsed feeling in the wound would fade now that the bandage was on.

Outside, the cooler air was a relief, as the moon finally rose to light their way. The burning sensation and shortness of breath didn't fade but spread in slow waves centering on the wound. The night swam in front of her eyes and grew darker, shot with patches of colors that couldn't be there. Megan set her teeth and ignored it. If it was what she thought, then resting wouldn't help; only the sorceress could. It was growing harder and harder to force herself to breathe.

They were almost to the Old City gates before Megan staggered again; her knees buckled, and Shkai'ra swayed as her friend's weight came fully on her arm.

"Ahi-a, what is it?" she inquired.

"My—shoulder," the smaller woman gasped.

Shkai'ra leaned her back in a puddle of light to examine it. The injury was a typical puncture wound, deep and narrow; the wadded cloth and the hardening syrup had prevented much bleeding. It had begun to close by the time she had put a temporary pressure bandage on it, back at the factory. Painful, and bone-deep, but it should not be giving her this much trouble, not without having hit a major artery. And there had been no nerve damage;

Megan moved the arm too well for that. The Kommanza had been dealing with wound trauma most of her life; she was puzzled, until she saw the faint bluish discoloration around the edges of the wound, and convinced herself that it was not a trick of the pale uncertain flame of the lantern. She rocked back on her heels, gone white about the mouth, and let out a shuddering breath. The smell of the sudden fresh sweat that broke out on face and flanks and armpits was rank in her nostrils.

"Poison," she said quietly. "I thought . . . it usually acts so fast, but the cloth, and then the sugar . . . probably got most of it." She paused and added with startling intensity: *"We've got to get to the spook pusher!* Can you walk, kh'eeredo?" To herself she added: *And when we get there, she's going to help or learn the look of her own liver*.

"Walk? Of course not," Megan murmured. The thin ghost of a smile strayed across her mouth. "But I can crawl, if I have to."

Shkai'ra bent to pick her up; not that she could carry the Zak far in her present condition, but . . .

The sound of rubber-shod wheels on the brick pavement brought her head up with a snap. The three-shaaid gang-pedicab, the pedalers pumping with predawn weariness.

"Ahi-a, halt!" she cried, then cursed vilely as she realized she had spoken the tongue of the northwestern steppes. Fatigue pressed on her, burning in her joints; her mind seemed to be moving like sheets of glass separated by wet sand. She repeated the call in Fahinnan, waving the meter-long length of steel for emphasis.

The pedicab was typical of its type, a four-seater carriage of light wood and leather on spindly wheels, pulled by a pyramid of toilers standing over pedals geared with ceramic and hardwood that powered back to the rear axle. It was a cumbersome vehicle, and the human engine was tired; still, they moved with remarkable speed. The whole clumsy apparatus seemed to circle in its own length and begin to accelerate back the way it had come. But for a moment inertia held it, straining.

Shkai'ra moved. Faster than was natural; almost faster than could be believed: she had called on the last reserve against extremity, nearly gone ahrappan, berserk, body

powered by a hysterical strength that might have pulled
muscle loose from bone. With an effort that cost almost
the last shreds of sanity she forced herself not to plunge
the saber between the rear pedaler's shoulderblades. Instead she laid the crusted edge against his throat.

He looked around, and screamed. Millimeters from his
eyes was . . . not a face, a mask. Lips thinned to vanishing
peeled back from teeth bared almost to the angle of the
jaw. Foam spattered, hot and rank; eyes showed the whites
around the entire edge. And even in his terror, he knew
astonishment that a human voice could speak from that
frightfulness, in syllables of grating ash.

"New City—House of Terhan's-Kin—*now or die, get of
a nomad pig. Pick her up and go!*" The voice almost
spiraled up into a falsetto shriek. Almost, but not quite
into the blood trill of the Kommanza zh'uldaz; and Shkai'ra's
neck quivered with the effort of denying the killing squeal.

The doorguard of the house of the Terhan's-Kin lay
beside the bronze-strapped portals. He whimpered, sobbing as his hands tried futilely to stem the bubbling from
the deep diagonal cut on his inner thigh. There had only
been the one, for the Old City was well policed; he had
not stopped Shkai'ra for long.

Now she stood before Yeva, representative of the Guild
of the Wise, and stared into the blind white eyes. She was
without fear, not even truly conscious. The disciplines of
the Warrior's Way had stood her in good stead, and the
training of the Warmasters that many did not survive; it
allowed her to call on reserves down to the cellular level,
and keep drawing until the last were exhausted. And she
was using them recklessly, had become animate Purpose;
in this state she could continue until the blood vessels in
heart and brain burst loose from their moorings.

Megan lay very quietly. The bluish discoloration had
spread, and she was having trouble breathing. For the last
two kilometers Shkai'ra had been holding her, forcing air
into and out of her lungs with pressure under the
diaphragm.

She said nothing to the magician. No words were necessary, and she was beyond words. Silence. Yeva leaned

forward from her nest of cushions and laid a hand on Megan's forehead.

In the darkness somewhere a newly familiar voice called and faded. The blackness was shot with blue and flashes of stars. Out of the pit of her mind, Megan rose on the fog in a whirlpool of ghosts and dead things. She floundered, lost in the night, and called for her father. He came, but only as he had died, a sacrifice in the arena. He raised a flayed hand to her and was swept past her to disappear into the black. She followed, falling endlessly screaming into the depths of her mind, surrounded by the hated and the loved things in her life; and still she fell. And fell. And fell.

A hand touched her in the darkness. She turned, or seemed to, and saw the shadowy figure of the sorceress Yeva beckoning. Sure that this was another of the misty shadows that offered false assistance, she almost did not heed. Then the voice called her name again and spoke. "Young-kin. Your time of growth is not yet on you. There is one who calls. One who still needs. You should not pass this way, for I bar it to you. *There* lies your way." She pointed into the mist, then her image swelled and pulsed, blurring as it blocked the way out of the bottom of Megan's mind, whirling into an intense bloom of light. Megan threw her hands before her face and thought, *One who calls?* A bright sword danced before her eyes, light gleaming off its curve, pointing the way that Yeva's image had indicated. Faint as a curlew's cry on the wind came the sound of her name, shredded and tattered but still hers. She gathered the shards of herself together and called back. "*I* come." She stood now in darkness and realized that she stood only in her mind. Vaguely she could feel something beneath her; for a dizzying moment she was both standing and lying, then with a wrench she pulled another name from the dark, hurled it before her and followed it like a slung spearshaft out of the night. "*SSSHHHHKAAAAAIIIIRAAAAAA!*"

For a long moment little had seemed to happen and the sorceress just held her pose. Then the Zak's chest heaved, paused, settled into a more normal rhythm. The bluish

tinge began to leave lips and fingers; not quickly, but the
normal pink began to creep back. And the angry red of
burns somehow looked more superficial, as if only the
upper layer of the skin had been parboiled, and not the
layers of subcutaneous fat and muscle beneath.

Yeva withdrew her hand, "So," she whispered. "The
body knows the secrets of its own healing. We merely show
it the way." She could feel the minute particles in the
blood seeking out and neutralizing the toxin that had been
spreading, clogging the tiny flashes of nerve transmission;
felt the fluids moving and isolating heat-damaged tissues.
She urged the process forward; it was natural, as natural as
the underlying entropy urging toward dissolution and death.

Shkai'ra's gaze stayed fixed and inhuman, until the signs
were unmistakable. Then the automatic process of release
began, the implanted commands loosening their hold on
heart and glands and organs. Overload signals screamed
inward to their receptors. As she began to crumple toward
the floor she could feel the Warmaster's voice, echoing
down the decades: *For everything there is a price*.

What a headache coming, she thought with a last flicker
of rationality before her skull struck marble. And heard
Megan murmur her name, softly.

23

When Megan woke she lay a moment just savoring the
languid feel of simply lying on a soft surface, still feeling a
bone-deep tiredness in every limb. Her thought drifted as
lazily as the drowsy buzz of a cicada that she heard in the
distance. Until last night's events replayed themselves for
her. She sat up abruptly and clutched the edge of the
divan as dizziness swept over her. Her knife harness lay

under her hands, tangled in the light sheet that had covered her. A light robe that had apparently lain on the bed by her feet now lay on a patterned stone floor. This was definitely not the Weary Wayfarer.

Shkai'ra lay to her right, snoring slightly, her hands grasping the strap of her scabbard, on another divan similar to the one Megan now sat on. Plants filled the room with whispery rustlings as they brushed against each other and the skylight, moving gently in the breeze that blew from the open windows to the double doors at one end of the room. They also stood partly open, revealing a glimpse of a garden outside. Sunlight slanted into the room, and as the plants moved, they cast cool green shadows across the low table that stood before her, bearing a red glass decanter and three goblets.

She felt as if her tongue were wrapped in dusty wool, and her breath rasped her throat dry. The decanter, condensation sliding down the glass, drew her like a lodestone. Her legs were shaky, and she stumbled once before she sank down by the table and seized the pitcher. Water flowed down her throat in a cool rush, and it took an effort of will to stop before she made herself sick with drinking.

Ach, she thought, *that is the closest I've ever been to Death and still cheated her*. She looked over at Shkai'ra, who slept on, oblivious. Her skin was burned still, but only as if she had fallen asleep in the sun in late afternoon, while the dagger wound gave off faint twinges of a weeks-old injury. Her head ached, but the water soaking into dehydrated tissues would ease that soon. She refilled the goblet and sipped again, slowly.

Now. Someone must have seen to putting us to bed, and cleaning us up, she thought wryly. *The last one I remember is Shkai'ra, but she was in no shape to help herself, much less me. That leaves the sorceress. Then this must be the merchant's "guest" house. Not really a good place to stay long. After all, the Merchants' Guild had a hand in setting the assassins on us, unwittingly or not. They all play their own games. So. Yeva is the one with answers, if she will give them to us.*

Megan got up, swayed, and sat down just as rapidly. *Later.*

"A good thought, young-kin. A healing depletes all the

reserves." At the now familiar chuckle so close by her, Megan flinched reflexively, then sheepishly put the knife back in its place.

"Your pardon, Teik—Lady. I'm sure you understand my unease."

"The sorceress nodded. "My name is Yeva—please use it. Formality ill becomes kin-in-power." She sat on one of the cushions, the second goblet already by her hand, but empty. She smiled at Megan and continued, "And if we are of alike power then you would drink with me."

"Gladly—but alike power? As an eating knife compares to a longsword!" Megan's caution was already falling before her curiosity. "If I might ask, how *do* you do the appearing-out-of-nowhere trick?"

"Trick it indeed is. It's much like your warding. A 'turning away of the mind,' and very simple, really. Has no one taught you these things?"

"Simple." Megan looked down at her hands, turning them over as if she had never seen them before. "Often, simple things are the hardest to do." She gripped the edge of the table and was up on one knee, raising her hands to shield her eyes. "Knowing that there is no Blood or Steel between us, the thing that yet binds is Power. So do I, called Whitlock, answer the debt I owe you and freely give . . ."

"*No.*" Yeva's voice rang sharp, all warmth gone. "I do not accept this debt, for it does not exist in my eyes. I own no one, by no intent. The binding of friendship is all that I take from you. But I will not bid you in any way."

Megan had rocked back on her heels at Yeva's abrupt interruption. "In honor I can't do anything else! I owe you my life. You *refuse* what I freely give?"

"Yes." Yeva held her hands to the smaller woman, palm up. "Come. Freely. And 'see' with me. Leave the anger and try to understand."

Bluish-white light played gently around the hands she held out to Megan. For a moment there was silence as the Zak looked down into the light flowing in the long-fingered hands. Slowly she reached out to cover Yeva's hands with her own. As they came into contact, the scarlet light flared in Megan's hands, brightening minute by minute to an orange glow. They sat, surrounded by a soap-bubble swirl of light, blue and red, as they warily shared what they knew, colors deepening as trust grew. Megan could not or would not remember what passed between them. Her mind, still reeling from the close brush with death, felt, for an instant, the inquiring murmur of the others in the guild as they became aware of the rapport, but the alienness of the way they thought and felt and believed rang through her mind. With a cry she wrenched her hands free, snatching them close to her chest. She was trembling slightly, white showing around her eyes, as Yeva sat back slowly. "You see?"

Megan nodded mutely. All chance of speaking easily to Yeva, of learning, had been shattered by the overwhelming tide of information that she could not assimilate. *Facts* she had, but no meaning or context to understand them. All seemingly useless.

A moment passed, enough for a ray of sunlight to shift and warm them both. Megan shook herself. "I've always depended on steel, anyway."

Yeva smiled, at once cool and compassionate. "I have found a weapon with an edge sharper than any steel. Yourselves."

Megan shrugged. "Only death has the sharpest edge, they say."

The sorceress's voice took on a briskness. "You will need to turn it, then. After defending that scrap of paper you found by . . . chance . . . the others will not believe you could surrender it. Each seeks the credit of using it to ruin their mutual enemies." Her fingers tapped the base of her goblet. "Best awaken your lover, before we speak further of this. A night and a day and a night again of sleep should be sufficient."

Megan's legs trembled less as she bent over Shkai'ra and reached a hand toward her shoulder. Then she reflected on the tight grip the sleeper kept on her swordhilt, stepped back a pace, and called.

The Zak looked down at the bladetip poised beneath her chin, then at Shkai'ra. "A little jumpy, aren't we?" she asked.

The Kommanza brushed sleep out of her eyes and laughed softly. She looked around for the delight of *seeing*. "I know we're not dead or I wouldn't feel so terrible." The

sword slid back into the sheath with a slithery rasp, and
Shkai'ra gingerly felt her head.

"Yes, it's still there. Do you think a goblet of water
would help?" Megan asked innocently.

"Now why would I want to wash? Wine is what one
drinks." She swung her legs to the floor and shuddered,
holding her temples. "On second thought, water would be
better." At Megan's chuckle she pretended a glare that
dissolved into a grin.

"If I may interrupt . . ." Yeva's voice broke in, dryly.
"There is still a slight problem to be discussed." One hand
gestured gracefully to the cushions. "Sit. I have called for
more water. As your 'healer' I suggest you eat something
light. Fruit, perhaps." Her voice brooked no thought of
objection, and the two moved slowly to the table.

Shkai'ra opened her mouth but was forestalled. "Since
you owe me her life and yours, I suggest that you watch
what you say to me." Laugh lines crinkled around Yeva's
eyes. "Your feelings toward the, ah, spookers, as you put
it, are known to us."

A servant padded in bearing a tray with another pitcher
and a bowl of fruit. She set it down on the table, looked
around, and clicked her tongue in disgust at the rumpled
sheet on the floor. Yeva reached out to forestall Megan's
comment and spoke. "I thank you, but you may leave the
bedding until later." The woman started and stared around,
obviously not seeing them. "Leave me," Yeva continued.

The servant bunched her tunic under nervous hands.
"Lady, my master asks if all is to your liking and . . ." She
was backing toward the door, her eyes scanning the interior.

Yeva's voice was impatient. "Yes. I need nothing else.
Now go!" With that the woman bowed and was gone,
followed by laughter.

"He never learns. Never. He still tries to force his
bondlings into spying on me. Still, she only heard your
laughter, mixed with mine. That should only be another
strange tale to tell about me, and they are not aware of
your presence. Only Bors knows, and him I would trust; I
do trust." She cocked her head and laid one finger to her
cheek, "looking" at Shkai'ra. "You were about to say?"

"Just that I never quarrel with someone I owe a debt to,
at least not for the first day." Shkai'ra reached to fill the

goblets with the new pitcher, felt of it, and snorted. "Phagh. Not only is it water but warm as well." When she poured the cups clouded as if ice had formed on them. Shkai'ra looked up to catch the glance that passed between Megan and Yeva. "More tricks. For something that angers so many people, you two are pretty free with it." She rinsed her mouth and swallowed. "So. A problem?" She leaned back and waited while Megan sipped and watched the other two.

Yeva looked down at the goblet before her, so casually filled, and at the women who would drink with one called Abomination by the Sun-priests. She smiled to herself. Bright souls these two had, outlanders though they were. That much she had seen in the scrying-ice a sennight ago.

"We had decided that a message was necessary, for your safety."

Shkai'ra threw her head back and poured the goblet down her throat, trickles running from the corners of her mouth. "Good as the Red River in spring," she murmured. Then:

"True enough. Nobody believes that something they want that badly doesn't exist anymore. Ever hear of a mercenary believing a farmer who swore there *wasn't* silver buried under the hearth?" She glanced across at Megan. "You still have it?"

For answer the Zak produced the parchment slip. "What *does* it say?"

Yeva passed her hand over the shifting script as it lay on the stained rosewood of the table. There was a curious sensation, as of a *click* a finger's breadth behind the eyes. Megan picked up the much-folded slip and read. Her face lost all expression; after a moment, her shoulders began to shake. Shkai'ra took it from her fingers and read the common Fehinnan lettering.

"'*Yes*'?" she said. "'*Yes*'! For *this* we've been chased, knifed, nearly eaten alive, tortured, soaked in shit . . ." Her voice trailed off, hesitating between fury and laughter.

Yeva spread her hands and smiled with an impish glee. "Well, the Merchants' Guild asked us if we would take a hand in matters; we decided to, so . . . *yes*."

The Kommanza dropped her head into her hands and began to laugh; then she fell over on the pillows and beat

hands and feet against the fabric, gasping as helpless tears
ran down her face.

"Ai, ai!" she wheezed. "I haven't seen anything so good
since the drunken nomad drowned in a mead vat at Solstice Fair, the year I left Stonefort. Heroes we were,
leaping from roof to roof like eagles, slaying all in our
path—for a treasure of great price. 'Yes'! 'Yes'!"

Megan sank back on the cushion, almost lying down,
laughing so hard that she almost couldn't breathe. "Would
it . . . have been any better . . . if it had . . . had been
'No'?" And she wiped tears away from the corners of
her eyes.

Through gasps Shkai'ra managed to say, "Or even
'Maybe'?" And she fell over again at the idea, wheezing.

Megan smoothed wisps of hair away from her face and
straightened the cushions she sat on. "Ach, a story to tell
children . . . but not one that priests or army would
believe." She picked a slice of melon from the bowl and
bit into it, catching a fragment at the corner of her mouth.
"Now what are we to do to pull them off our trail?"

Shkai'ra rose, pulled out Swift-Kiss, and began polishing
the already bright steel carefully. "We've already thought
of leaving the city, but . . ." She put the sword down
across her knees and began ticking off points on her fingers. "*Eh*, the ports are watched and we would have to
travel by horse or foot, both slower than river or sea. *Ka*,
if the army succeeds in starting this war of theirs then the
countryside will be mobilized and not very healthy for
outlanders, even mercenaries. I, for one, do not care to be
a conscript in their Glitch-taken holy war. *Sh'ra*, they've
already tried to kill us; even if they catch us elsewhere,
that wouldn't stop them from doing it then." She looked
up. "Enough points?"

"Too many," Megan said. She looked up from where
her nails tapped on the tabletop. "We can't stay in hiding
forever. And I *cannot* stay here. It's too bad that we
couldn't just give them all the message. After all, what
good would it do them?"

"But none of them would believe that the message was
just one word," Yeva broke in. "It wouldn't be convincing
enough . . . That might be our answer!" She looked over
their heads, smiling. "If they all got what they *expect*,

then they would be convinced, wouldn't they?" Her gaze lowered to the other two. "Do you think you could see that all three factions got a glimpse of the message?"

Megan suddenly felt as if her mind had started working properly again. The pieces of this plot fell into place, and she began a slow smile at the thought. "Give them a lie they will believe, rather than the truth they cannot." She slapped the table. "I'm sick of being the quarry; let us turn the tables."

"Put a weasel in the henhouse, with the right message," Shkai'ra said enthusiastically. "Hmmm, but each will need a different emphasis—what if they compare notes?"

Yeva tapped a long finger on her chin. "Shoes from a leatherworker, steel from a blacksmith—and for the impossible, a magician."

Simple enough, she thought. *The material is already sensitized. Now, what is it that the powerful of this city fear most of all? Ah, of course. . . .*

She arched her hands over the parchment and raised the patterns in her mind. They hung before her consciousness in a slow-circling three-directional maze, an intricate knot of light strands. Now, this corresponded to the basic human mind set—all the recipients would be human, of sorts. Here, the common character elements; a line of suspicion, a loop of treachery. She had known a gulltaker once, in her youth as a hedge-wizard; he had told her that it was nearly impossible to run a successful scam on the honest, although such were fortunately rare. This would apply the same principle; she inserted the last of the subliminal clues, tapped energy from her environment, and sent her mind plunging through the matrix of the spell. Possibility warped, and *might* became *is.*

The two adventurers felt a momentary clenching, and a sudden chill. Megan felt the surge of energy spiraling into the focus and almost, almost saw what was happening. A glimmer of something not quite there, caught out of the corner of an eye. She wanted power so badly that she could taste it; then cast the idea away. *So she cannot teach me,* she thought. *I am a Red-witch and will remain one. Living on the edge of a knife is good enough.*

"There," Yeva said. "Take it and read, remembering the lie."

Shkai'ra scanned the now-lengthy message, pursing her lips and raising a brow. Megan took it in turn.

"Fascinating," she said. "You, apparently, have been corresponding with Habiku to sell me to slavers *again*. The man has no imagination."

"And you are taking the priests gold, for me," Shkai'ra added, turning to the sorceress. "This is a *fangaz'i whul pukkut*," she said. "A sheep-bitten wolf."

"For you," Yeva replied. "Not for those whose nourishment is treachery. We call them 'mind-that-sees-lurkers' —*paahnit*. They will believe."

Shkai'ra's teeth drew back from her teeth in an expression that bore no relation to a smile. "The Fehinnans like a circus," she said. "Now they'll have one the size of a city."

Yeva turned her eyes to Megan's smile, if it could be called that, and nodded. "Perhaps you could use some assistance? I believe that your rooms at the inn are still being watched, by everyone, and I cannot shield you here much longer. It takes as much power to keep up your invisibility over a long period as it does reaching out over a distance . . . or into the temple. Take counsel between you—I will not really be here for a moment." With that it was as if she withdrew herself and was . . . gone. Her body still sat with them, one of its hands lightly clasped around the base of the cup.

Megan turned a thoughtful eye on Shkai'ra. "I find myself with a strange appetite for more discussions of philosophy. . . ." She trailed off and raised a questioning eyebrow at the Kommanza.

"Probably the safest place in this stone warren," she mused. "When?"

Megan poked a finger into her hair; it crackled. She mumbled under her breath, picking at patches of congealed sugar sticking tightly to her abraded skin.

"Not until I've had a bath. Many baths."

"Just a little candy; the sooner the . . ." She sat up, stood, gripped her head in shaking hands, and sat down again. "On the other hand, perhaps we should rest a little," she continued, gritting her teeth against the heaving of a rebellious stomach. The reserve against extremity was not tapped without a price. The Kommanza sank back resentfully, closing her eyes.

"Although I'd like it better if the resting were a different place," she said softly after a moment's pause. The magician seemed . . . otherwhere, at present, but she remained cautious. "Not that this one hasn't dealt well with us, but I don't—"

"—*like* spook pushers," Megan finished with weary humor. "And I don't particularly like to swim, but we'll both do what we hate if we have to." She rose, wincing, and stood beside the blond woman's side. "Me to the hot water, if I can wake our hostess; you to sleep, Akribhan."

Shkai'ra rolled onto her side and sighed, curling into the crisp cool surface of the linen sheets. Sleep relaxed the hard, wary lines of her face; for a moment it was possible to see her as she might be at peace, unthreatened. Megan stood a moment in silence, just looking, then put out a hand to hover just over Shkai'ra's shoulder. She felt the heat radiating from her, and as a sound came from behind them, snatched the hand back.

"You care much for this one." Yeva's comment was quietly spoken, and not a question. "A good person to have at your back."

"So I thought."

"Well then. As a guest, as my master reminded me, I also can have guests." She paused, color tingeing her pale cheeks. "I should have realized it before. No matter. The servant can show you the way." She clapped. "I don't think I have to tell you to move slowly."

"Ach, moving at all is the problem." Megan bowed slightly. "I still would like to speak with you, once I cease feeling like a smashed clockwork toy." And Yeva's cool amusement followed her out of the sunny room, like the scent of lavender.

Like a great sperm whale broaching from the depths, the Weary Wayfarer's head cook lumbered up the stairs. Servants shrank against the walls as she passed, gawking at the afternoon tea tray in her hands. It had been many years since Glaaghi had carried anything heavier than a ladle, or a whip.

She slowed as the bare concrete and stone of the work-

ing quarters gave way to paneling and tile; that aspect of
the old manor had needed little change when the Weary
Wayfarer had become a business as well as a home to its
owners. One of the upperservants stopped her.

"The owners wouldn't appreciate this," he said appre-
hensively. Old highlander tattoos showed on his cheeks,
but years in captivity had worn the soft dialect of coastal
Fehinna into his tongue.

Glaaghi grunted. She was a free employee, and highly
valued; the masters might own her kitchen, but it was
hers. She waved the tray.

"Trouble in two-west-five," she said. "Not taking trays,
and the lazy fishbrains can't tell me why." She plodded
stolidly on, uneasy in her feast-day tunic, and conscious
that it diminished her. In leather apron and clout she was
a figure of terror; with blue cotton on her shoulders she
was a fat, middle-aged servant woman.

"Well, *I* will find out what's going on. Even if they
prefer that only the younger, comelier servants wait directly on guests, and are offended by *me*." Still, she was
careful not to tread too heavily and not to knock against
anything.

The stairs creaked under her weight, and she remembered why she had stopped coming up to this level. If
someone had been standing down the hall, he would have
seen Glaaghi's head and massive shoulders emerge from
the stairwell, Titanlike. Even out of her realm the head
cook was impressive. Not for nothing did the underserv-
ants call her the Sea-Cow behind her back, being very
careful to be out of earshot.

She stopped in front of second-west-four and looked
down at the tray in her hands. "Two-west-four has their
tray. Only four rooms on this floor. And why am *I* carrying
this tray?" She shifted the tray to one meaty hand and
scratched her head, counting. "One, yes. Two, yes. Three,
no breakfast tray today. Four has theirs." She looked
down at herself and her puzzled frown deepened. "Now
why would I dig out my festival tunic and do something
strange like come upstairs?" She lumbered back down the
stairs still muttering. "Festival? Maybe that's it. A festival
trick. But why am I carrying this tray?"

The upperservant was still where she had left him.

"Here. You take this. This isn't my job." He looked puzzled as well.

"What?" he said, trailing in her wake as she headed back downstairs. "Didn't they take it?"

"Didn't who take it?" Glaaghi asked.

"Why, second-five-west," he said.

The head cook stopped on the stairs, one hand on the balustrade. "I, I don't remember," she said. "I must have spoken to someone. Yes. I must have." She sounded more confident. "That is an extra tray. Take it downstairs. I have work to do, and good tunics don't mate well with grease."

24

Megan gnawed on the end of her pen, then carefully drew in another line. *"There,"* she said. "Hmmm, it still isn't very complete."

Shkai'ra scowled. "You'll need more information than that, if you're to get our little scrap of paper into the temple," she said. "Not just floor plans; the organization, and what approaches would work."

"At least you've agreed I'm the one to deal with the priests," she answered.

"Little people are better at hiding. And neither of us could pass for a local, but you're closer. Agreed: you for the temple, me for the Iron House. But how are we going to do an in-and-out with the Adderfangs? With the contract, both of us are kill-on-sight bladefodder." She prodded a finger at the paper. "And we don't even know enough for *this*."

There was a dry cough from the hearth. Harriso looked up from his teapot. "Although elderly, I am not *quite* on my pyre," he said. "For the temple, recall what I was: guidance I can give. And the Beggar King has often sent me to deal with the Adderfangs."

He crossed the little room and gently lifted a stone from the irregular wall. The niche within was dank, but the documents were safely enclosed in a bag of greased leather, tightly sealed. "Now, with your help, red-hand—"

"Now wait a minute, Harriso," Megan cut in sharply. "Granted that all you say is true . . . I, for one, don't wish to expose anyone else to the risk. Besides, even if we succeed in pulling the hairs from these skunks' tails without damage, we can always leave. This is not our home, though perhaps it is becoming yours," she said in an aside to Shkai'ra. "But afterward the survivors are likely to have long memories and come looking for you." She paused. "I won't do that by involving you more."

Harriso's ruined eyes swung toward her. "Child," he said in a voice soft with power, "I have lived . . . eighty turnings of the Sun. Many more than most. All that I loved died long ago; memories and words, memories and words."

He paused. They might almost have thought him asleep, but for the schooled stillness of his cross-legged stance. "Because I have bent with my fate, do not presume to believe that I welcome it. Two things remain to my hand. Those chance-met friends I have made, here in this second world, my second life." His voice dropped, caressingly. "And my enemies. While they are, I am. We are bound, closer than lovers, closer than kinmates or parents. This"—he touched the pouch that bore the message—"puts me within reach of them again. Let me bring us to our ending. And give a fitting farewell gift to those who saw more than a blind beggar."

Megan's lips parted slightly, then closed in silence. Shkai'ra dropped a hand lightly on her shoulder. *Deathpride,* she thought.

Harriso poured the tea and set the cups out with the quiet gestures of ritual. The three sat, guttering firelight casting highlights from below on the harsh cheekbones of the Kommanz steppe, glistening on curtains of raven's-wing hair. They drank.

"So. Now that you infants have listened to the voice of

wisdom"—the wrinkled face lost its inhuman serenity in a smile of friendly mockery—"consider the coming Purification in the Temple. All of Illzibuah will be there, or that part that can cover its nakedness and contribute to the Servants' treasury. A small, *agile* person might do well."

"I suppose that a warhorse plunging around in the crowd would be rather obvious," Megan said. "A Purification? If the crowd is that big, it might be my best chance. When?"

"Three days from now. Enough time for me to pay . . . a visit to the ones the current Reflection of the Effulgent Light finds useful tools. Yes, by all means, the Silent Knives first. That will clear the way for you, red-hand; drop the pomegranate of discord among the warriors, to scatter its seeds. Then, before any but vague rumors of turmoil spread, we send the message of disharmony to the Reflection. And watch the results among them all; revenge is a dish best eaten cold. It will be some time before the survivors have the leisure to seek out the authors of their troubles."

Shkai'ra blinked and choked on the last sip of her tea. "Harriso, you were wasted on these dwellers-in-stone-warrens," she said. "You should have been a Granfor Warmaster; you have just the devious, nasty mind. When I asked for your aid, I wasn't expecting you to set our strategy."

The fire had died, and even several pots of the tea were not enough to keep hoarseness from their throats. Harriso stood, moving unerringly in the semidarkness, and began to sling a blanket curtain across the middle of the hut. Megan paused in fluffing a pallet.

"Elder," she said in a thoughtful tone, "it seizes me that one thing is lacking in your plan."

The blind man inclined his head toward her. "And can it be found, on such short notice?"

"If I know anything at all of the underside of cities, yes," Megan said, her eyes focused unseeingly on the dim shape of Shkai'ra pulling off her tunic. "A small, swift, daring, inventive, and very, very greedy child."

"Excuse me again, young one, but is the Shadowed One *still* busy?" The Adderfang apprentice looked up sourly from the records spread on the low table at the stooped

figure of the old beggar leaning on his staff before him.
The small boy who had led him here had not ceased
moving once since they had arrived, and had contributed
greatly to his decision that the Beggars' Guild could wait,
for a change. *Sunstruck, blind old fool*, he thought. *Three
times I've lost my place. Adventure in the Assassins' Guild,
hah! Might as well be a priest.* He probed again at the
aching molar with his tongue and broke his silence.

"Yes! My Shadowed, Luko, is *very* busy today and is
likely to be so for another finger-width of the candle, so
could you *kindly* sit down? And keep the boy quiet." As if
on cue the urchin spoke up again.

"Grandfather, I hafta go to the jakes, the latrine I mean.
I hafta, *now!*" He tugged at the beggar's cloak and set up a
whine that carried around the room.

"Why Dahv, you know your kin-mother told you . . ."
The old one's maundering died away as the two were
escorted down the hall by another apprentice, who looked
just as thrilled as Luko's.

*By the Sun's shadow, the two are enough to drive you
mad*, he thought. And what could be so important that he
wouldn't even mention the insult of being kept waiting?
Harriso, yes, that was the blind one's name. Not a frequent contact, but logical. After all, who better to deal
with dwellers in shadow than one blind? It showed the
Beggar King's understanding of his place. He turned back
to his papers and wondered if Luko would be in a better
mood now that the madam had been in to pay the protection. When they got back maybe he ought to risk disturbing him. How many throwing stars could he *have* in his
office, anyway?"

Officious child, Harriso thought, as they were led back
to the waiting area. Luko was normally much easier to see
during the evening hours than this.

He felt Dahvo's hand on his arm and thought that the
boy played his part well. If they believed a clan or kinfast
stood behind them, perhaps it would make them hesitate
a little before killing them. *Ai*, he sighed mentally, the
Adders were too fond of killing these days. Subtlety was
what they lacked. It had been otherwise in his youth.

Harriso felt the sour expression on the apprentice's face;
not at all unlike an acolyte serving in the outer chambers

of the temple, even to the petty pleasure he took in keeping a supplicant waiting. At last he sighed, laid down his pen, and scratched at the door of the sanctum before entering. The blind man strained hearing honed in darkness; there was a muffled bellow and a sharp *thunk* of steel on wood.

". . . *and if you won't stand still for it, bring it back!*" the voice said, and bellowed again: laughter this time. The heavy door swung open and the apprentice waved them through; his hand shook slightly as he did, and a fresh scar showed white against the pitted inner surface of the door, at neck height.

Harriso walked slowly in, more slowly than needful, with a hand on the shoulder of the boy. Rooms were largely a matter of smell to him; this one was stale sweat, cane spirit . . . yes, and perfume overlying sex-musk. The Adderfang's voice sounded, round and thick and heavy; there was an impression of meaty forearms thick with hair, and wet jowls. The tone was still shark-jovial from the lethal baiting of a moment past.

"Well, old no-eyes, does the Beggar King complain of our tax again? Or have freelances been at the bowls once more?"

Dahvo shifted under his hand; Harriso could tell that he was glancing around, impressed. The garishness must be truly hideous. The old man spoke softly.

"Perhaps my business should remain confidential, One in Darkness," he said. The Adderfang snorted heavily and leaned on the wicker backrest behind his cushions. It creaked heavily.

"Then why bring the boy? Unless as a present for me."

"He is my eyes and ears," Harriso said absently. Then: "There was a commission for . . . those-who-remove, recently. Concerning the recovery of a missing object?"

The backrest creaked again, and stopped. Harriso could hear the man's breathing catch and pant; the sharper scent of fear was in his sweat. Silently, the blind man produced a folded paper from his robe; at a warning squeeze Dahvo took it gingerly between thumb and finger to deposit it on the Adderfang's desk. The boy returned to his position. The rustle of stiff paper unfolding was plain to sensitive ears, but Harriso squeezed again.

"He's unfolded it now, Grandfather. Now he's started to read."

"Porpoiseshit!" the Adder gasped, and slammed the paper face down on the desk; a fact which was noted in the same clear treble. He had always been one of Jahlini's supporters; that had gotten him this sinecure in Guild Liaison, when he grew too heavy for active commissions. But if she heard he had read this . . . whatever it was . . .

From the Servants of the Effulgent Light . . . Thank That Which Coiled in Darkness he had stopped.

"How did—" He stopped, took several quick breaths, and a long pull at a bottle of cane brandy hidden beneath a cushion. A moment later he regretted that; it was happening too often these days. Decision crystallized.

He yanked at a cord. The door opened, and the apprentice side-flipped through, landing in guard stance and looking astonished as nothing edged flew in his direction.

"Get the Adderchief," Luko began, his voice an octave higher than usual. "Tell her that Luko will pay with his liver and lights if it isn't more important than *anything* she's doing now. No, you fool, leave the door open!" It would be hard enough to convince her that he hadn't heard, done, or read anything as it was.

They sat for long minutes of echoing silence, Luko sweating still more, jamming thick hands against each other to still the urge to reach for the black glass bottle; Dahvo fidgeting; Harriso serenely motionless. Very faintly, he smiled; the taste of intrigue and danger and great events was not one he had thought to enjoy again, and he found that the appetite had not vanished so thoroughly as he had imagined. *Like most cravings,* he thought. *Or even pain. One becomes so accustomed to the need that it vanishes from consciousness, until the possibility of satisfaction appears.*

The apprentice did not reappear. Instead, Adderchief Jahlini herself slid through the door. Harriso knew the smell, dry and old and somehow reminding him of wet metal and ratfur. She spoke no word as she crossed to the desk and flipped the paper over.

Luko burbled, a safe three paces away, with his face carefully averted. "Not a word, Darkest!" he stuttered. "As soon as I knew, believe me . . ."

"Oh, I believe that, Luko," she said softly, returning the paper to the desk and smoothing it down with one hand. The other curled fingers toward the slit under the right armpit of her tunic. "Not even you would be fool enough to bring me to this, when your name is at the top of the list."

The knife she drew was not large—a handspan and a half, slightly curved, with a hilt of dimpled bone. Luko's black jacket parted soundlessly; the point slid in just under the floating rib and drew down and across, finishing with a twist.

He fell, and she stove in his larynx with a sandaled heel. "No dying words from *you*," she said coldly.

Her eyes moved to Harriso and the child, and even in his darkness he felt them. His reply was cool and dry. "Consider, Commander of Silent Knives, that *I* at least cannot read the product of any pen; nor can this child of the streets. And further, will sources of information be forthcoming if your reward is a journey to the sewers to dine with the crawlers?"

She stood silent. Suddenly, Dahvo ran forward, kicking at her shins and pounding at her waist with small fists.

"You leave Granther alone!" he cried. "I don't like you! You smell!"

There was a hard smack as she backhanded the child into a sobbing huddle on the floor. *Not worth my time,* she thought as the gray face of Luko's apprentice peered through the door. "Get me the . . . no, the *Assistant* Master of Terminations. And my guards!" *Who would have thought so many?* she muttered, ignoring the old man as he helped Dahvo to his feet, leaning on the desk. He sidled out the door as black-masked figures began to pour through it.

Harriso went to hush Dahvo and found him already quiet. The boy sniggered slightly. "She didn't even hit me as hard as Ma does. Did that bit good, din't I?"

"Yes, Dahvo. Now come—this place is too close for my liking."

"How? They blindfolded me on the way in and led us both. I'm lost."

"This way." Harriso turned around a corner, hearing the *fttt* of blowguns behind them, coming closer. He pulled Dahvo into a doorway and listened to the sounds of Jahlini's housecleaning. It sounded as if many were going to die in this; each one deserved it.

Blindfolds worked well with those dependent on sight. Everyone forgot that the blind remember. Out of darkness then, the blind man led the boy.

The heavy smell of frying food told him that they were near the exit . . . or entrance, as the case might be. The latch clicked and the small door swung open.

"Now, Dahvo, be my eyes for a short time again. Has anyone moved the box from below or disturbed anything?"

"No, but I think the fight's following us." He sounded a little nervous.

Harriso smiled and stepped to the box below, to the small barrel, and then to the floor. "We have time. Close the door." He could hear the muted rustle of conversation and the clatter in the kitchens on the other side of the door.

A thump and Dahvo was down as well. "Come along. You shall have your reward for playing my grandson. You shouldn't get hit for not making your quota today. Maybe even tomorrow, if you're careful."

They moved through the kitchen and the restaurant, weaving between seated patrons, cushions, and low tables. As they got to the door, Harriso squeezed the boy's shoulder and pressed the bit into his hand that Megan had given him to pay the boy. There was an unkitchenly clatter from the kitchen and a figure fell through the fishbone curtain, blackclad, rigid and stiff, with a small dart pinning the hood to the throat. The restaurant cleared with lightning speed as panicky diners realized that the Adders were fighting among themselves. Some nearly stumbled over an old beggar who sat by the corner of the building, shaking his bowl, crying, "Alms! Give and the Light shine on You! Alms . . ."

25

Sammibo could hear the gate lieutenant's nasal voice echoing down the entrance corridor of the Iron House long before the portals came in sight. There was little traffic here after sunset, and discipline enforced silence. *For most*, the staff officer thought. *That youngker is making enough racket for himself and twenty other fools.*

"It's obvious, little Rahlini; the great red cow doesn't understand the high speech. She didn't even look up after that last insult—graciously delivered as it was."

The Fehinnan softened his step as he paced past the faded stains around the side entrance, smiling. He caught Shkai'ra's eye over the shoulder of the lieutenant and the hapless private who was a forced witness to his baiting of the outlander. Shkai'ra leaned at her ease against one of the doorposts, ignoring the light drizzle that soaked her tunic; her back rested against time-blackened oak, brass-strapped, towering four bodylengths above her. The gate underofficer turned to her again.

"And how long will you wait for the officer?" he said, in labored city patois. Under his breath he added: "Offspring of a sow and a shark," in the formal tongue. But very softly; the foreigner's passivity had made him bold, but there was something about the scarred hands thrust into her belt that contradicted it.

Shkai'ra jerked her head slightly to indicate Sammibo, and cleared her throat. "I see," she said, in officer-class Fehinnan with a slight burr, "that you're still using lapdogs and imbeciles for guard duty."

The lieutenant abruptly became a model soldier. "Ah, sir," he began.

"And still stuffing pikeshafts up their ass to make 'em stand straight," the Kommanza continued.

"So, do you take him out on the practice field, or shall I?" Sammibo said, with a gesture halfway between a salute and a wave.

"Nia, pillow-soldier, he's not worth the trouble. Vultures might puke on his shadow; I can't be bothered." She cast a wink at the private, who clutched her pike and stared solemnly ahead as bright spots appeared on her cheeks. The barracks would be amused tonight.

Shkai'ra flipped a ball of hard rubber from her belt and began squeezing it, tossing it to the other hand every tenth contraction. Pushing past the rigid lieutenant, she leered and whispered; his braced attention quivered.

Her grin faded as they entered the hall. Lanterns and reflectors barely touched the dimness; around them the great pile of stone and brick and glassbound concrete hunched in on itself, hugging its darkness. The Iron House was not the oldest building in Illizbuah; the foundations of the Sun Temple went back before the Godwar, before the world was changed and broken. But it was the only structure of its era that had not been rebuilt out of all recognition. Long years had passed since its builders piked cannibal bands back from the four-story walls; the crumbled concrete of another cycle had been dragged from ruins to make its mortar. It had always been a fortress; the smells of sweat, oil, polish, and musty cold stone made a composite aura, the smell of power. Not a place of laughter.

"You're laughing in the shark's mouth," Sammibo said. "Insisting on giving it to the High Commander personally. She bears no overwhelming love for you." All that while they had been passing through the thickness of the outer wall. At the first cross-corridor of the warren a guard detail fell in about them, full-armored.

Shkai'ra shrugged. All that stood between her and a spearpoint between the shoulderblades was her appraisal of her opponent's cast of mind. That, and luck. She made the gesture with her swordhand out of habit, but uneasily. There had been too much luck about of late, both good and bad; the gods must be taking a close interest in this fight. Gods, or . . .

"You mean, she has the malice of a viper," the Kommanza replied, snapping her attention back to the matter at hand.

Sammibo winced and glanced around, the reflex of years on the fringes of the High Command. One of the guards had twitched; that might be a trick of the eye, and body language was difficult to pick out under a leather-and-fiberglass suit stretching from pate to foot. Sammibo decided that Smyna trusted him exactly as he did her.

"She also . . . ." Shkai'ra let the comment trail away. Baiting the Fehinnan was amusing, but she had no desire to ruin him. "She gives me the money, she gets"—she tapped her belt—"this."

Sammibo stroked a satin-gloved finger down his mustache and adjusted the fine green linen of his dress tunic. "Well, at least let me *hand* the message to her," he said unhappily. "No need to remind her of your presence more than is necessary."

They paused at a colonnade to watch a group of mercenaries; from the equipment, Shkai'ra judged them to be the headquarters company of a Kaalyn light cavalry regiment. Sun slanted down the fifty meters of airwell above them, catching on the blue-honed heads of the javelins slung in hide buckets across their backs. A company of regular Fehinnan infantry watched, drawn up in what the manuals called an honor guard formation; the troops knew it as "suspicion guard."

"Hiring, I see," she said. Silently, she extended a hand with the parchment.

Sammibo took it with a sigh of relief, tucking it behind the sky-blue of his sash, under the tache of his broad-bladed infantry shortsword.

"Don't try to read it, Sammibo," she said.

"It's eyes only." He shrugged.

"Sammibo, when they carry you to the pyre you'll pick the pallbearer's pockets, just to see what's there. *But this was written by spookers.*"

There was a slight check in the staff officer's stride before he said smoothly: "Duty forbids, in any case."

"But you would have tried."

"Well . . . perhaps. Good intelligence is the heart of military science."

Toward the centrum of the fortress some effort had

been made to modernize the interior; murals and colored-marble floors clashed jarringly with doorframes graven in demon faces. Incense fought with mold; guards stood at four-meter intervals, unmoving; the air had a greasy, cold-soup chill. It was familiar, from her days as a commander of irregulars. *We Kommanz have a name for treachery,* she thought. *But we don't have to look to our backs in battle.* She made to spit on the flagstones, then reconsidered.

They halted for a moment at the ancient, brass-strapped doors. There was a line of discoloration at about chest height, very faint; this was where the guard had made its last stand two centuries ago, when the Maleficent's troops had become the only hostile army ever to set foot in the Iron House. On either side sentries stood, statue-immobile; Shkai'ra watched with interest as a fly crawled across one's face and over a motionless eyeball. The discipline was impressive, although a little showy to a Kommanza; her people lived by bow and lance and had no energy to spare for fripperies.

Sammibo darted a glance at her as the door swung open, its twice man-height moving soundlessly on oilwood bearings. She was too calm, he thought; but it was hard to be sure.

The chamber within was vaulted, a wedge-shaped segment of a circle two tiers in from one of the outer towers. Soft indirect light came from panels in the roof; Shkai'ra noted the narrow decorative slits that rimmed the ceiling. More than decorative; she would have wagered an eye that there were winch-wound siege crossbows up there, covering every movement in the room.

Smyna sat at on a low padded bench, overlooking the massive map table that was the centerpiece of the huge headquarters chamber. Around stood a clutch of staff officers and senior unit commanders, moving counters with long-handled rakes. Since her own people used a similar system, the Kommanza took in the dispositions with a single glance.

Odd, she thought. *Most of the foot concentrated around the city. Easier to supply on navigable water, of course, but why not farther up the Iamzs Valley, if they're planning a campaign in the south?*

The commander of Fehinna's capital garrison looked up

with a slight, cool smile. Shkai'ra could feel Sammibo tensing at her side; she did not delude herself that he would lift a finger if the general ordered her cut down on the spot, but it might cause a little regret.

Not that Smyna would. The Kommanza had never been a real threat to the General Commander; nobody in her position *could* be. Chance had given her the opportunity to cause her some trouble and embarrassment . . . *Smyna's eyes staring from the mask of mud and blood as bright arterial blood pulsed from the leg wound, her fist stained red on the pressure point*.

No, Smyna would never grant her the dignity of ordering the sort of hasty execution others would; that would imply real fear and hence respect. It would be far more to her taste to see the outlander groveling for a minor scrap, ignore her with lordly disdain. And not even notice her sword. Gray eyes met black for a moment, and then the westerner looked away, casually. It would not do to let Smyna see her lack of regret, and no Fehinnan aristocrat gained or held this much power by being a fool.

The General Commander turned to Sammibo, ignoring the barbarian commoner, raising a slim brow. Shkai'ra noted sardonically that for all her calm, she was the only one present wearing even partial harness, chain gorget and steel breast-and-back, part of the priceless suit that was one badge of her office.

The staff officer wordlessly extended the parchment. Smyna waved it toward her chief aide, a stocky, bouncy figure hovering at her right.

"Such trouble," she said. "For a trifle." She reached for a cup of chilled pomegranate juice on a tray held by the nearest soldier-servant. Her attention strayed from the map table to a file folder in her lap.

Shkai'ra was acutely conscious of the staff officer standing with the message in hand; time slowed and she could feel the sweat trickling down from her armpits over her flanks, chilling in the cool air that fans brought up from the basement, the rankness carrying faintly through harsh incense. The dim, rich colors of the room seemed intolerably bright. Her breathing remained calm and even, and the gray eyes traveled with deceptive casualness across the room, noting the position of each human and object

with drilled, unconscious speed. Soldiers; she was a warrior, and the next few minutes would show the significance of that.

The aide unfolded the parchment and read, casually at
first. Then he stopped with a deep hoarse grunt, the
sound a mailed cestus driving into the pit of his stomach
might have brought forth.

"*Why!*" he shouted, raw disbelief in his voice. "I was
the only one you could trust—!"

He stumbled backward. Rage replaced fear on the heavy
features, and his hand went to the hilt of his blade.

Smyna had scooped the parchment from the floor. The
cool, regular detachment of her features became very ugly
as she scanned the short lines. The animal reflex that
drove her into a fighting crouch saved her life as her aide's
sword skittered over her shoulderpiece and plowed across
her upper arm in a blow that would have ended in her
neckbones if she had not moved.

"*So Fehinna needs a General Commander more 'pious
and reverent to the Servants of the Light'* " she said in a
deadly whisper, as the long cavalry sword slid free in her
good hand. The voice rose to an insane shriek. "*Kill him!*"

The room tensed, but the expected bolt did not flash.
The aide laughed and drove forward in a lunging thrust
that she stopped only with a desperate twisting leap.

"Did you forget who sets your guard?" he inquired
nastily. There was a deep bass throb from the hidden
gallery that ran around the council chamber, and a heavy
bolt plowed chips from the floor inches from his foot. A
moment later there was a wet crunching sound, and an
arm thrust limply through the slit. It hung, and dripped
red slowly on the priceless carpets. Confused shouts and
the clash of metal followed through the arrowslits.

The staff officers had frozen at the clash of steel, immobilized by the shock of total incredulity. The field commanders were less hesitant, and more used to sudden
emergencies. Forming a knot, they backed toward the
portals, raising a shout.

"Treason!" they cried. "Guard, *guard!*"

They had reckoned without the atmosphere of headquarters. Sudden disciplined action, here, suggested fore-
knowledge of the plot. The crossbows hummed.

Prudently, Shkai'ra had dropped behind a massive wooden map chest, dragging Sammibo with her for additional cover. She grinned into features gone liquid with dazzlement; beyond him she saw one gray-haired staff officer doggedly crushing the throat of another with her map pointer, oblivious of the dress dagger buried in her midriff.

"Such madness!" she laughed, the sudden shrill wild giggle of her folk. He shrank from the blaze of orgiastic pleasure in her face as she looked out over the scene. "Such chaos!"

She suddenly grew calm. One of the dying field officers had swung the doors open, leaving a glistening trail as he slid down the mottled ebony. "I'm for the outside, Sammibo," she said, in a somehow merry snarl. "Glitch godlet of fuckups be with you—this is his realm—and for the sake of some good times, hide under the table!"

A darting rush brought her to where Smyna and her second-in-command dueled among the ruins of their hopes. She stooped, swept up the parchment, twirled, and ran for the door, the impetus of the backkick she snapped at Smyna's knee speeding her on her way. Deliberately, she did not draw steel; that would force potential obstacles to keep their blades for their opponents, when the sight of a bright edge out of the corner of their eye might have drawn a blow. She whirled through the fight in an almost-dance, cleared the last half-dozen paces with a striding run, and dove headfirst through the open portals, confusing both the crossbowmen behind and the halberdiers before. Landing on crossed forearms, she bounced to her feet and ran; no time now to pick directions, but it would be best to be on the expanding outside edge of the sphere of chaos she had exploded.

26

There was no problem blending with the crowd. Megan's problem was moving against it; the Avenue of Triumphal Arrogance was blocked for two kilometers back from the square, and the mass of humans and vehicles moved in slow inchworm jerks. The subtropical sun beat down vertically, with a pitiless white light that threw the scanty shade black and knife-sharp at the edges. Megan could feel it soaking into her skin, as palpable as the sweat that stuck the tunic to her back and turned her loincloth to a sodden raw-chafing rag; body heat joined it; marble-faced concrete radiated its share back into the throng. The heavy smell of massed sweat was thick in the humid air, and hot white dust stirred by thousands of feet.

She could feel hotter air puff up from her collar with every halting step. The press was worse than a theater or arena crowd in F'talezon; and these were aliens. Any close contact brought a slight overfall of emotion and thought, unshielded; there was the constant soft pressure of bodies and minds forcing their way into her own sphere of selfness. With an effort she forced her attention on details—a small boy being berated for coming to the ceremony unwashed; someone nearby who had been eating onions, strong ones.

With a skill learned in the childpacks she wriggled forward and nudged against the back of a knee. The man staggered. "Apologies," she muttered, slipping past. "I stumbled." A narrow space between two goldsmiths let her through; there were advantages to small size, whatever the big redhair thought. She imagined Shkai'ra in this oilpress and her lips quirked slightly as she ran a wet hand over a slick forehead.

She stopped again in a knot where two litters jostled for position. The wayservants jostled and strove to outshout each other, vainly; for all their curses and thumpings, the litters were jammed. Some of the crowd ahead were beginning to look and mutter, clutching resentfully at bruises. Even with meek clerks and law-fearing storekeepers, there were limits to what could be done with a hot, irritated Illizbuah mob. The litters were placed down with a thump, and one noble leaned out from the shade of her awning to talk to her neighbor. She looked maddeningly cool in a tunic of multicolored silk ribbons tacked together every handspan; even the lapdog that panted beside her heightened the contrast. Beside the litter the bearers crouched, necks bent to keep their wooden fetters from pulling on galled throats. They panted in jerks, strings of gummy dry saliva hanging from their lips.

Megan glanced down. There were many things missed by simple failure to pay attention to what was underfoot; being closer to the ground than most, she was less prone to that error. The litters were nearly a meter off the pavement on their legs, most of that showing as inviting black gap between stone and the underside of the padded couch. And the wayservants were all ahead. . . .

The shade was welcome. Megan relaxed into the comparative coolness and watched the ankle's-eye view of the crowd. There seemed to be too many here of equal rank for the shouts of "Way, way for the Brightness Iaasac's-Kin" to have much effect, however many upperservants flourished the ivory batons of their status. Most of the respectable part of Illizbuah was here; all those with guild or kin. And some of the less respectable as well. Shouts of "Stop, thief! She has my pouch!" rose above the dull surf-roar of the crowd. The sharp clear sound was a shock, through that pounding of white noise; she thought warily that this would be the perfect place for an assassination, where no small betraying sound would be heard before the blade struck. The better thieves must be having a fine day of it. She suppressed the sudden crawling feeling along her spine. *I'm going into the temple to slap the cobra on the nose*, she thought irritably. *What are a few assassins to that? Besides, they've had chances enough to slay me*. Although that last was part bravado, she admitted to herself. She had been very lucky. Or . . . had it been luck? A shrug: she would never know what Power had been at her side.

Snatches of conversation drifted through the slats overhead. "The market for hides is booming, and we *cannot* get supplies . . ."

". . . but Kinmother! . . ."

". . . a new sheersilk tunic from Ch'in for the next festival . . ."

The Gaaimun in the next litter leaned over, tugging pettishly at the fringe of his striped awning. Megan wrinkled her nose at a wave of too-sweet scent, and felt the boards creak above her head as the woman there shifted backward. *Something we agree upon, at the least,* the Zak thought.

"Don't you think it's just a *trifle* too hot to really enjoy a Purification? One feels as if one's burning oneself. Although this is supposed to be a *particularly* disgusting heretic."

"Oh?" the woman above drawled with studied disinterest.

"Oh yes! She tried to teach that the Divine Effulgence was nothing more than a ball of glowing rock—and that *it* went around the earth, rather than the Ineffable Truth's teaching, that we circle about the God."

"Oh," came the reply. The Zak could feel both the Gaaimun shift as they drew the suncircle on their breasts.

Ignorant foreigners, Megan thought impatiently. *Of course the Guardian of Lives makes the sun shine. If it were glowing rock, the Dark One would have put it out. Silly thing to get burned for.*

She craned her head out from under the litter and looked ahead. The road broadened before her, fanning out in a delta shape as it joined the square.

"Ah, Jaahno, run over to that vendor and get me a cup of . . . What's this under your litter, Maahgli? A new pet?"

Glancing out, Megan met the gaze of her shade's occupant, their faces inches apart but reversed; she noted how the Fehinnan's silver-wound hair trailed in the dust as she knelt on the cushions and peered with bafflement under her conveyance.

"What," she said in outraged tones, "are *you* doing

under there, taking . . ." She groped for a word "Taking *my* shade without permission?"

She really looks very much like a sheep, Megan thought. *If sheep wore silk ribbons and jewelry. Nice piece of silver-and-turquoise . . .*

"Enjoying *my* road," the Zak replied. "If you *must* come and put your litter on it."

The Fehinna's puzzlement was giving way to real anger. Megan reached out and tweaked her nose sharply, then scuttled out crouched, weaving through the crowd at knee height. Given nimbleness, small size, and a ruthless willingness to hurt, it was possible to move with some speed, much faster than a search party of tall-standing officials, even with the weight of authority behind them. It was what she was counting on.

Behind her outraged shrieks told of disorganization spreading. That had been childish, but then a childhood spent stealing buckles in the River Quarter was far from the worst training you could have for a time like this. *And it will give that dull person something to entertain her tedious friends and relations with.*

The interior of the temple was almost as bright as the square, where the gilded dome had left phantom afterimages dancing across her eyes. The contrast with the darkness of the entrance tunnel was dazzling, and calculated. All four of the great lenses in the dome were uncovered, sending beams stabbing down through four hundred meters of air blue with incense to break blindingly off the circular gold-and-crystal sunburst Holy of Holies atop the central altar. A handbell silenced the congregation as they crowded to the barrier that kept the central dome free. There was no sound but the soughing of their breath and the deep, rapid chanting of the choir grouped around the balcony that girdled the dome one hundred meters above their heads.

The great jeweled sun-shape began to turn, smoothly, soundlessly, on jeweled bearings. The fierce light was thrown back in huge swirling patterns, through the hazy air, dappling the stern faces of the onlookers and the glossy interior of the vast building. A long-drawn *AAAAHHHHHHHHHH* broke from twenty thousand throats.

From the eastern door, the entrance of the rising Sun, came the procession of the priests. The Reflection of the Beneficent Light himself was there, about him the gold-colored robes of the Inner Circle, each with a globe of purest crystal in one hand. They moved into the clear space about the altar, their sandals whispering in a swaying rhythm on the yellow marble, their left hands flashing up to stretch toward the sun.

The sound of their chanting rose, clear and deep: "Continuance of Life! Continuance of Life! On High, on High, the Sun grants Continuance of Life!"

Behind followed younger priests, whirling about the procession. There were a thousand of them; half gripped handbells of brass in their right palms; half rang bells of crystal and silver, an eerie tinkling resonance under the deeper tone of the metal. Their left hands swept tall unlit candles of deepest red through the air as they danced; the young faces were blank, ecstatic, beyond humanity as they traced an intricate pattern across the floor around their seniors.

Behind came red-robed priests, burly men and women who walked with a long measured stride alive with the consciousness of power. The Hands of the Effulgent Light carried the heretic among them, roped under the arms and suspended on long poles to twist above the heads of the crowd. She wore a white robe with a stylized pattern of flames rising toward her face. The victim was unmarked; Megan could even see that all the finger and toenails were intact. But she was . . . not unconscious, for her eyes were open, and she moved. It was the pattern of movements that was strange, odd jerks and twitchings as if the human's limbs were trying to flex in directions not allowed for in their design. The priests set her down before the altar with a jar, and she gave a single scream.

Megan was never to understand the impulse that made her reach out to "touch" the woman's mind. She recoiled, even before the knowledge of what she felt seeped through. There was familiarity to the touch. Like the Sniffer. *Once, as child, she had seen the ants at a nestful of hatchlings. . . .*

The sacrifice writhed against her bonds as the redrobes bore her back and fastened her to the central spine of the altar's disk. That rose, now, from the spinning gold, and showed itself to be plain hard steel, black and smooth. The robe ripped away, and the crowd fell to their knees, heads bowing like a ricefield in the evening breeze. Megan did not glance down; she had full opportunity to see the changes that had begun in the other's body. The victim's head rolled back, and she howled. Not a scream, but a thin screeching keen, and the skin bulged out in the beginning of a sack beneath her jaw as she rose.

A ripple went through the crowd. The Zak raised her eyes with theirs to the apex of the dome, smelling the fear-sharpness of her own sweat over the sickly musk of the incense. Half an hour ago, she might have convinced herself that she played a dangerous game. That was then; here, there was no escaping truth.

It took a moment for the significance of the shapes she saw to snap into a picture behind her eyes. Slowly, slowly, a massive lens was lowering from its niche at the very summit of the dome. Gilded chains thicker than a man's arm supported it, as it dropped with fluid precision to the center of the great space and swiveled, hunting. Then it intersected the four beams from the fixed lenses, and a fireburst of light sprang into being below it. Brighter than the sun; Megan's eyes averted themselves by reflex, to the corona of trembling air that surrounded the point of focus. The chanting of the priests slowed; the young acolytes stood quietly in their ranks, swaying, their bells chiming with infinite softness, like crystalline leaves in a forest of glass. They rose and fell in harmony with the unhuman cries of the heretic as she raised gradually into the region of fire.

Megan wrenched herself free of the growing swell of fascination and dread that washed at the edges of her mind. *This was not what I came to do*, she reminded herself grimly. But there could be no better time.

She sidled over to one of the junior priests stationed at the barricade between populace and hierophants. She tugged at his sleeve, gently, then more forcefully, as his rapt face remained locked on the scene above their heads. "Elder Brother . . ."

"*Pay heed and do not disturb the Light!*"

"But, Elder Brother, I feel the need to bare my sinful thoughts . . ."

"Not *now*," he said, his voice still vague with the blank-
ness of the drugged. His hands made small fluttering
gestures, but he did not take his eyes from the rising
pillar. It was far from the spot of incandescence, but there
was a new note in the screams, and the bells of the
acolytes rose to complement it. What the priests had
strapped to the altar might be no longer human, but it
could feel pain.

Megan seized a hand, dug her thumb into a nerve
cluster, and pressed the scrap of paper into his palm. The
man started violently. The Zak was amazed; with that grip
he ought to be twisting paralyzed on the floor.

"Outlander, if this is not important . . ." he began,
glancing down at the writing. His eyes snapped open;
Megan could see the pupils swell and shrink to dots as a
galvanic jerk ran through his body. Screwing up his eyes,
he averted them from the script as if to deny they had
ever lain there.

"Stay here!" he gasped, panting, and blundered off across
the floor of the altar space. At any other moment swift
murmurings would have followed swifter action from his
superior. Now there was no reaction, even when he nearly
blundered into a bellringer in the panic haste of his flight.

Megan showed shark's teeth as she watched the young
priest repeat, more diplomatically, her efforts to arouse
attention. The upperpriest responded well, once his junior
waved the message before his eyes. He staggered, and
would have fallen but for a strong young arm to hold him
upright. The Zak was tempted to stay and watch the
progress up the table of ranks; there should be increasing
terror with every step upward, as those who might be
genuinely feared if they knew too much were reached.

She turned and began her rapid squirm through the
crowd. Resolutely, she kept her face turned from the
point above. The screams of agony were shriller now, and
on each the upper choir came in faultlessly, one octave
below, the deeper tone prolonging and carrying the sound
of pain across the echoing chamber. Woman and trembling
light met; there was a moment of silence, then a steam-
driven *fuff* as the moisture exploded out of the body. The
pure carbon that remained burst into flame, and the pillar
sank back toward the altar. The acolytes chimed their bells

in a relaxing dissonance and danced forward to light their candles, before sweeping out in a flower pattern to hand them to the waiting congregation.

Megan could feel the huge tension release the crowd, letting them sink back into selfhood. Still, she reached the doors before the crowd itself could begin to move. Even slowed by shock, the temple security forces should be moving soon.

But by then I'll be in the alleys, she thought. *And the Reflection will have troubles of his own.*

The Second Priest, Kayhri, mounted the steps to the High Priest's level with the strangest mixture of haste and reluctance. The Chancellor had finished the major ceremony and had left for his apartments before the Sun-forsaken message had reached her. The great doors of the temple had already been ordered open to allow the minor ceremonies of the Seven Nights of Exultation Unhindered by All Tedious Ordinance to continue.

Great Light, she thought, I *would* be the one to have to bring it to him. The faster I do so the safer . . . and also more dangerous. *Divine Sun guide* me. . . . Her thought trailed off as she tapped on the first door of the Inner Sanctum, nodding to the young orange-robe who opened the door. *That idiot Ehlvaio didn't even think to have the bearer of this detained.* Perhaps he could see the justice in being kitchen staff again. . . . She stood on the mat before the door, genuflected to the image of the Sun at eye level, and entered quietly.

This was not the audience chamber, but one that had a balcony looking out into the dome itself. Below the main platform ran another walkway that the guard-priests alone had access to. Cubilano sat at the exact center of the opening in the wall and surveyed the crowd that was drifting to the doors not yet open.

She bowed at his back and waited, then cleared her throat nervously.

Cubilano did not turn from his contemplation of the scene below the balcony, but his voice was chilling. "You disturb my Communion with the Sun after such an occasion?"

"Reflection of the Divine Light, forgive this one that is less than the shadow that creeps . . ."

"Enough! Forgiveness is given to those who come to the point!" Very slowly he turned his gaze on the hapless replacement of his chosen successor.

Fascinated, the Second Priest stretched forth the hand with the scrap of paper in it, her eyes locked on her superior's. "Brightness . . . the message of the Guild of the Da—"

Struck speechless by the sudden motion, she froze as the paper was snatched from her. He scanned it and his face, which had been still before, hardened to stone. "So, treachery. . . . Where is the purveyor of this?"

Kayhri swallowed and thought of the condition of her soul. "She was not . . . not detained, Brightness." The rest of the words came in a rush that died away awkwardly. "I will see personally to the lower one's discipline, Brightness; he really should have . . ." Her words lay in the thick silence on the floor. Dimly she could hear the counterweights creak as the great doors began to swing open in the temple below, and the renewed crowd mutter as it shifted forward toward the outside. She braced herself for what was coming. She had never seen the High Priest move so fast, without the deliberation that was normally his, as when he had snatched the message from her.

There was the small sound of paper crumpling. She opened her eyes and saw that his were no longer fixed on her. He leaned forward over the edge of the enclosure and signaled to one of the redrobes.

"Younger Brother, there is another heretic in the temple. I trust that you will do much better than the last time." His voice rose just a fraction, and the icy edge was enough to make the guard-priest blanch. "Less than two days ago . . . No, Kayhri, stay." He turned back to the redrobe. "Send another of the Hands to me. Go! And stop the doors, now." The crushed message was cast down without a second look. He knew what it said, and that was enough. Kayhri was not going to like her penance. . . .

Megan looked out from behind one of the pillars by the doors. They were just starting to swing open, and she had

to restrain herself from being among the first to leave. That
would have silhouetted her between two groups of Fehinnans, the worshipers leaving and the next batch awaiting
their turn.

Fishguts, she thought with disgust as the uproar began
behind her. Not altogether surprising, but she had hoped
for a longer period of disorganization. *Someone* in this pile
must be competent.

Priests were trying to herd the congregation into order
as they streamed toward the opening portals; they stopped
midway through their arc, and murmurs of irritation broke
out, almost loud enough to drown the amplified call from
the corridor roof above their heads.

"Hearkening and Obedience!" The traditional shout of a
temple herald brought slow silence. "Hearkening and Obedience! The Divine Light has revealed to Her Reflection
that among our faithful ones lies a Shadow, an outcast of
the Dark. This one takes the form of an outland woman,
smaller than most, black of hair but fair of skin. All faithful, look about you! Examine your neighbor! If it is the
one in need of Purification, draw apart from her. Touch
her not! Point to the Darkness, that we may restrain it!"

Fresh tumult broke out. Megan drew deeper into the
shadow of her pillar and watched the crowd that spilled
through the corridor and down the temple steps break up
into circles. Any short woman with fair skin seemed a fair
target; she saw one blond ringed, and several men. Megan
was not surprised, being familiar with the ways of crowds.
Her eyes darted about.

A thin trickle of worshipers was still threading out the
door, the heedless and impatient. There were not enough
to provoke more than a quick scanning glance from the
Hands who had begun to fan out through the mass of
humanity. One was a prosperous merchant, spare and
thin; his wayservant held a priest in argument as the
master halted briefly before sweeping out. A young girl
held the trailing end of his feather cloak from the floor,
just in front of the pillar. Merciful, Megan was careful to
keep the razor-tipped ends of her nails clear as she clamped
the carotids.

The servant woke a few minutes later, sitting propped
against a temple pillar, with a splitting headache, wonder-

ing what the commotion was. Megan busied herself arranging the fall of cloth quite carefully as they passed the ring of priests into the heat of the square. The merchant had not noticed his change of servant except for an irritable growl when she had jerked at the cloth as the servant fell. They proceeded down the steps to his litter. Megan's neck prickled and she expected to hear the shout of discovery any second. She kept her pace slow, matched to the dignity of the merchant, who turned to step into his conveyance.

"What? . . . You're not . . ." he sputtered.

"Did you know that several threads are loose here?" Megan said. She leaped forward from the steps above, going right over his head as he ducked reflexively, the cloak flung completely over his head. "See for yourself," she said, and burst through the litter, scattering cushions into the crowd. She heard laughter begin as the man struggled to right his clothing to see his assailant, waving his arms in the air, hindering the attempts of his entourage to help him.

She reached the center of the crowd, and rather than continue running and drawing attention to herself, stopped and after edging around began craning her neck and asking taller folk what was happening, all the while unobtrusively moving them forward while she moved back. Now . . . the alley should be around here somewhere. . . .

The Hands of the Effulgent Light surged out of the temple. The slow, steady surge of purposeful movement in the crowd was giving way to eddies of disquiet; the security priests clubbed and pushed their way toward the center of disturbance, hindered by the clumsy help of the pious crowd. The square locked tight into a straining mass of flesh, grilling in the heat, misted by white dust. Noise rose, to a shrill bewildered roar. Over it rose the slithering multiple crash of shod hooves on slick stone pavement as a squadron of lancers cantered into the square from the southeast entrance.

The horses were nervous, with a contagion caught from their riders. An expert might have seen a slight raggedness in their ranks, but the priests were not experts and

busy besides. One broke free of the press and ran to grasp
the bridle of the commander.

"Fellow Servant of the Light," he began. "We have to
seal off—"

The lancepoint from the second rank took him high in
the chest with a hard snapping sound as the four-sided
pyramid-shaped head punched through a rib. The priest
looked down incredulously, then staggered back off the
point with a wet bubble of suction. He was still staring at
the spreading stream when the squadron commander
spurred close and cut twice. The second drawing cut was
across the back of his neck; the sword caught between two
vertebrae, and the body hung for a moment until the
weight pulled it free.

"Sun and General Commander Smyna! Sun and General
Commander Smyna!" she called, and the troopers took it
up raggedly. *"Treason! Treason in the temple!"* The squadron spurred forward, one or two horses stumbling and
sliding over the body of the priest.

Another section of troops double-timed into the square
from the eastern exit; infantry this time, with crossbows
and the close-quarter stabbing spears of the marine
detachments. The cavalry commander wheeled her mount
to watch as the crowd poured away on either side like
water cleaving before a ship's prow; the square would be
empty soon, which suited her well. Cavalry needed room
to maneuver, and a sitting horse was an easy target. Around
her, brief combat flared; the Hands were not trained or
equipped for open combat, and the citizens who had joined
them were worse than useless. Screams drowned the
battleshouts.

She spurred forward to greet the marines and take
command. There was just time for her to realize her mis-
take before the crossbow bolt slammed under the noseguard
of her helmet; it punched through bone and brain to bury
itself in the sponge-and-cork backing on the other side.

"Treason! *Rebellion in the Iron House!*" the leader of
the infantry called. His troopers swept forward, firing
from the hip and then closing on the riders, whose mounts
spun in caracole among the crowding bodies. Most of the
Hands were down, and only a fraction of the crowd turned
to join the temple loyalists. But a fraction of that crowd

was thousands, and their hands moved for the lancers. Behind them the last of the priests retreated up the broad stairs of the temple, stave and chain striking on lanceshafts and swords; they stood, and fought, and died so that the great bronze doors might swing shut on the battle. And the cavalry retreated before the mob and the marines, their backs to the closed portals.

Even the horses went down under the weight of the mob, screaming in fear over the crowd roar. People fled the renewed bloodshed, clutching children and weaker kin, their festival finery spattered red. Elaborate masks crunched underfoot, blood oozing through empty eyesockets.

In the alley Megan almost couldn't distinguish festival sound from the fight noise rising behind her. *Ach, these fish weave their own net,* she thought. She stepped aside to allow a troop of dancers with torches and ribbons past her. They were laughing, and a few were singing and staggering slightly already in their dance, clutching at each other. Megan thought that they should encounter the new riot just around the corner of the square.

She cut through a small park, almost stumbling over the couples in the grass. The crowd here was closer, and she stopped by a fountain to look for a rapid way through. She stepped to the rim and leaped for one of the dryer ornaments higher up. The stone under her hands was slick, as she went from fountain to low balcony, then up the side of the building, she noted that the color of the water was changing from blue to green. *Festival,* she thought. *We'll give them festival.*

27

Megan lay at her ease on the tiles, chin resting on cupped palms. Shkai'ra leaned back against the shallow slope of the roof, sipping from the ironglass flask. The red baked clay of the roofing was gritty beneath them; the warm-earth smell of it mingled with the rank smell from columns of smoke that rose like pillars into the late-afternoon sky. From the fourth-story roof they could see a dozen major fires, and the clamor of the firefighting squads mingled with the sounds of combat and riot—and even of celebration; this was a large city, and most of the citizenry were reluctant to sacrifice their festival.

The chaos in the streets was abating, as squads of the Elite Guard sallied from the palace quarter. Yet the faction fights still ran through the city, along street and alley, in chambers and close places beneath the earth. It would be days before the Sun-on-Earth's troops flushed the last holdouts into the light; much that was done this sennight would never be known.

The two women lolled above; they had an excellent view of the roads about, and their high perch made it unlikely that those who fought or fled would pass by.

Cat-content, Shkai'ra stretched. "Like nobles at the cage fights," she said, handing her companion the flask.

"There wouldn't be much loot down there anyway," Megan replied, sipping and replacing the cork. "Coppers, and too many people striking at random. If someone kills me, I want it to be *meant*."

Shkai'ra bent a casual eye on the scrimmage below. There was a small public garden; they could see figures dodging among the planters and shrubs, treetrunks and curbstones. Brief glimpses of black cloth, street tunics, the mottled green of camouflage paint on army leather armor. Harsh breathing of humans in desperate effort and fear of death; rutching of hobnails on brick.

"I think," Megan said reflectively, "that message is still dangerous—dangerous as a plague carrier—and it is still floating around, somewhere in the temple." Her eyes dipped to the pavement. "Ahhh, good stroke! Now duck! Tsk, tsk, too late. That must *smart.* . . . Where was I? Oh, if any of them should start putting the facts together, and realize who planted it . . ." She peered into the gathering dusk between the buildings. "Amazing how long someone can live with the intestines hanging out, isn't it?"

Shkai'ra chuckled and called out softly, "Stop trying to stuff them back *in*, man." She shook her head. "Still, they always try, don't they?"

"Perhaps Yeva has that answer as well. After all, some magics can be released from a distance."

"You and that spooker with the funny eyes." Shkai'ra looked down at Megan. "I have a spooker as a lover, and she wants to talk to the other shaman. Ahi."

Below, a priest stole furtively behind the knot of soldiers who stood panting and bleeding over the dead assassins. Her hand scattered a fine mist of powder; seconds later one soldier shook her head and another staggered, his features contorting into a rictus of hate. With shrieks of insane fury they fell on each other, striking blindly. A shortsword sheered off most of the priest's face as she turned to run, quite by accident.

"Not a bad sort, as shamans go," Shkai'ra concluded grudgingly. She swiveled herself over the rooftree and slid down the opposite side on her stomach, dropping lightly over the edge and landing, with springy resilience, on a small balcony.

"Coming?" she called softly.

Almost at that moment Megan landed lithely on the balcony railing, which put her eyes nearly on a level with her comrade's.

"You bellowed?" she said. And was slanting down the side of the building before the Kommanza could answer. Shkai'ra looked after her, cursed, and paused to thrust her sandals through her belt.

They were level as Megan leaped across to the lower roof of the next building. Shkai'ra grinned as she began to skirt the central courtyard, stepping quick and light along the eaves just above the terra-cotta rain gutters. The smaller woman sped ahead again, down into the courtyard and along the top of a board fence.

"If you will take the *wide* road . . ." she called from a story higher on the roof of the next house.

Their speed grew, and with it a wild and reckless exultation. Shkai'ra leaped, and the rest of the journey was scattered fragments. A cat staring at her disdainfully from a ledge she traveled along hand over hand. A shred of vine tearing loose from under her hand, and a pot crashing down from its windowsill to shatter on the roadway.

They outdistanced the Elite Guard squads, and the quiet they brought. That moved out in a wave from the palace of the Sun-on-Earth, making little distinction between revelers and rioters, except that the latter were more prone to stand and fight, and therefore die; the celebrants of the festival scattered with a drug-bright uncaring, to resume their play elsewhere. The streets were slick with blood, and wine; bodies knotted together in love or death. And at the last there was only the quiet of the richer sections of the New City, where celebrations were private and guards kept the peace.

Milampo's estate fronted on the Street of Sweet-Scented Shade Nourished by the Gold of the Sun. Chestnut trees lined the courtyard walls along it, meeting to mesh their leaves together over the pavement. The long green tunnel rustled softly in the light evening breeze, full of shadows and the smell of leaves. They slid down a wall, fingers and toes gripping, and dropped to the concrete.

"We've been—" Shkai'ra began, then pulled Megan back into the shelter of a doorhouse. A group of assassins flitted down the street, moving from tree to tree; they were in place for an assault on the merchant's house just as a squad of soldiers rounded the corner.

"Nasty weather lately," the Kommanza whispered, as a shortsword flashed by their refuge. The flying point swung a trail of red drops that hung in a perfect arc before spattering on the whitewash above their heads; in the darkening light the blood was black against the glimmering paleness. Shkai'ra slid the latticed door closed; a risk, but it was unlikely that the preoccupied fighters would notice the slight movement. "It's raining sharp objects. Best we let these good folk finish their business before we knock."

Megan leaned into her companion's shoulder and sighed happily. *So nice to see a fight and not be involved,* she thought. Then: *Goddess, I must be more tired than I thought!*

The combat settled; in the last purple dusk of twilight they could barely see flies settling on wounds and eyes. Shkai'ra opened the door, and they stepped over a lax arm that lay before it, a throwing star slipping languidly from relaxing fingers into a pool of blood that no longer grew.

"Where was I?" Shkai'ra mused. "Ahi-a, we've been lucky. Or the hand of a god has been on us, or a spirit, or . . ." She nodded toward the merchant's house, still reluctant to name the occupant. Names gave power. "You like that one, don't you?"

Megan's hand idly traced the grafitti scratched into the courtyard wall—"Hail profit"—and a crude picture of the Reflection involved with a mule.

"Indeed . . . if matters had been different. I might have been her student . . . disciple, perhaps."

But we think too differently, a stubborn inward honesty said. *Illizbuah and F'talezon are six months' sailing apart, but the Guild of the Wise and the Lake Quarter are farther still.*

"Give me steel anytime," Shkai'ra grumbled, hammering on the portal with the hilt of her dagger. "Killing people by . . . thinking . . . is, ah, *sloppy,* somehow."

The door-slit at eye level opened, and a frightened child's face peered through.

"Boy! Send to your master's guest, the Wisdom Yeva, and tell her that the *message-bearers* have returned. Quick now! She might be angered if you keep her waiting."

There was the sound of a stool overturning, and the patter of bare feet on flagstones. Shkai'ra nodded. "Easy enough to seize which name brings the fear-sweat in that household, and it isn't the master's." She snickered.

"You are quick enough to use the *name* of power, when

it suits you," Megan said slyly, bringing a rueful shrug
from the Kommanza.

They waited. A bee wandered sleepily in the flowers of
a vine that overgrew the walls; garden-scent blew to them,
overriding the street odors of dung and death. Megan
pushed herself upright and listened, head to one side.
"Hola, he returns. And with one even smaller than himself. The merchant must have found grown folk too expensive to keep replacing."

The child led them through the half-familiar strangeness
of the garden, and into the main wing of the house.
Guards and servants were absent, perhaps hiding in their
quarters, or gone to find richer pickings than a trader's
pay in the chaos of the streets. But the interior was almost
painfully bright, with lanterns and a spendthrift's hoard of
wax tapers.

Megan shuddered at some of the colors and decided
that she much preferred the Weary Wayfarer's more subdued taste. Suddenly she was sick of the inlay on inlay and
overornamentation. Simple, clean-cut stone, that was beautiful for its own sake, would have been better. *Like home*,
she thought.

Milampo Terhan's-Kin was hopping from one foot to
another—an interesting sight, in one of his bulk. His
round brown face was flushed and shiny with sweat as he
waved small, beringed fists in the air. The color of his face
almost matched the thick varicose veins that writhed across
his spindly legs; they in turn set off the bright orange silk
ribbons that wound upward to his knees to secure his
sandals. A purple tunic from Ch'in hung stiff with argent
embroidery, cinched by an acid-green velvet sash. The
costume was considerably crumpled, by both figure and
unaccustomed exercise.

"Peace!" he shouted to the mage beside him. "Peace!
Trade will be ruined for a year; my kin will be levied twice
over for damage repair and municipal service—the recon-
struction taxes will be *worse* than a war, with our competi-
tors left to steal markets! And you—"

Yeva moved her fingers slightly, and Bors stepped forward. With no trace of effort he lifted her out of the
wheeled chair; in her white gown of linen she seemed a

child, cradled against his breast. The disquieting white
eyes turned on the merchant with the amused tolerance of
an adult for a relative's spoiled and noisy offspring.

"Peace," she said. She raised a hand to indicate the two
warriors. "Here are those who carried our *message* with
such skill and daring. Do they not deserve praise and
reward?"

The merchant turned and regarded the two women. His
first reaction was a drawing back and a glance about for his
guards; he had the fear and aversion of the rich for those
who live by violence and practice their banditry openly.
What he saw was not reassuring; tall scarred blond outlander, with the worn hilt of her saber under one palm;
small swift darkling, less obviously foreign, but with a cold
amusement on her face. They smelled of sweat and smoke,
of things the Terhan's-Kin had labored long generations to
force out of their lives. He set his shoulders, and was
somehow more than an overdressed fat man squealing at
fate.

"Magician you may be," he continued quietly. "But you
have no right to make a jest of my life, and the lives of my
kin and guildsibs. Are we playthings to you?"

Yeva paused, surprised. Her eyes closed for a moment
of thought, then strayed to the two who waited with an
alert, wolfish patience. The merchant was a man without
justice, but his accusation bit a little.

"Yet you asked our aid," she said gently. "You cannot
cavil at the manner of it; we warned that it might not be to
your liking. These two—"

"—probably tried to sell my life to the highest bidder
on a scrap of paper!" Milampo said.

"Certainly," Shkai'ra said. "But they wouldn't stay
bought." Megan kept a considering silence, her eyes roving the surface of the room.

Yeva sighed imperceptibly. "There are things here which
you cannot know," she said. "I may not tell; nor could you
understand if you heard." She turned to the two. "And for
the . . . paper you left on the temple floor, do not concern
yourself. That has been attended to."

Shkai'ra nodded stiffly. She did not relish the feeling of
an unseen hand behind her strivings, but there was little to
be done.

"Out of my house!" Milampo stormed. It was an act of considerable courage, and his hand shook as it pointed to the door. "And take your greasy thugs with you!"

Yeva signed to Bors. "I go," she said. "And warriors of such . . . perception and resource will doubtless find their own recompense."

As Bors strode from the room, Milampo suddenly realized that his means of leverage was leaving. He started after the servant and the magician, calling something about compensation. Shkai'ra looked after the merchant and the mage with interest; Milampo was sweating and trotting to keep pace with Bors's long strides, his yapping complaints reminding her forcefully of a terrier she had once seen harassing a warhound.

He seemed to have forgotten their presence completely; natural, or perhaps Yeva's last gift. Her eyes followed the three out into the corridor; this led naturally to a cool, appraising examination of the interior of the room. It was interesting. The floor of this entry hall was glowing, pearly Baihma marble, except for a twelve-meter oval in the center, which was clear heavy glass over a pool of fantastically colored fish. The walls were hung with Pensa tapestries and hex signs, where they were not crowded with shelves full of knickknacks. Milampo's taste seemed to run to solid-gold yoni with emerald centerpieces, along with carved-jade jaguars, figures of swans and leaping dolphins done in a blue glaze, crystal goblets tastefully inlaid with his name in tiny rubies, and other items less restrained. A granite plinth bore a silver statue of the merchant himself in one-quarter scale; quite accurate, except that the artist had left out twenty years and about a hundred pounds. A scent of costly incense drifted on the air, overpowering the smoke and stench from the festival and riot-torn city. Cool air gusted up through ducts, from the chamber below where slaves pedaled endlessly to power the fans.

Shkai'ra tapped a fingernail against her teeth. Megan hefted an alabaster vase that held a white powder and several silver straws. A moment, and she turned to find her motion echoed by the other woman. Their eyes met, and Shkai'ra's mouth stretched in a slow grin.

"We'll need a sack," the smaller woman said.

*   *   *

"No, no, that's too heavy. Just pry out the gems."

"What, and ruin this thing of deathless beauty?" was the snide reply.

"You—yes, you, the greasy one with the double chins. Pick that up and . . ."

"A pity we don't own a horse."

"Oh, we will."

The guard had been doubled at the gate of the Weary Wayfarer's Hope of Comfort and Delight; no more was necessary. Here along the harborfront, sensible rioters, arsonists, looters, and celebrants knew better, even in a drug-fogged state. Even if one got past the guards, there were the guests. . . .

Megan halted and stared fixedly at the pikeshaft that swung down to bar her way: it was at about chest height for most, which put it on level with her eyes. She could see clearly the nicks of brighter wood in the haft where a blade had stuck. She turned her eyes to the doorguard, the gaze flowing slow and gelid up the length of the weapon to rest on those of the pikeman. *Which one of his eyes goes?* she thought, and a spark of red flickered in the black of her pupils.

The woman was tiny, he thought, but . . . His face flushed hot, then cold. The shaft swung up. Wordless, Megan stalked on through into the busy courtyard.

Shkai'ra followed, leading the burdened horse with a slow, ratcheting clatter of hooves on brick. Smiling, she rested a hand on the trembling guard's shoulder.

"Smart man," she said. And laughed with genial cruelty as he sank back against the wall.

28

"God Among Us, the prisoners have arrived."

Aygah the Forty-first, Avatar of Her, rose from the chair. That was one of several low shell-shaped things slung in frames of tubular steel. There were no Fehinnan sitting cushions here in the private audience chamber; the furniture was solid, waist-height, of plain blond ashwood polished to a silky finish; the only touch of luxury was a throw rug over a couch, northwestern snowtiger, pale and silky and beautiful. The room itself was cool smooth stone on three sides, the fourth open to a view of terraced gardens and the Iamz, flowing molten beneath the dawn sun. The morning breeze blew through the open wall and its low balustrade, smelling of flowers and the brackish water of the tidal estuary.

Aygah sighed and slowly finished the cup of tea as Smyna and Cubilano were thrown down on the hardwood boards at his feet. They lay prone, unbound; the guards stepped back to the walls and stood at an easy parade rest. Neither would dream of moving; the God's presence pinned them more thoroughly than any spearpoint.

The petulant adolescent face of the Sun-on-Earth turned to the wall. A print hung there, strange to Fehinnan eyes. A grassy slope, and a two-story house of wood; on the lawn a dark-haired woman, face turned away from the viewer.

"*Damn*," he muttered, in a language no human being had spoken in a hundred generations. "*Almost got it right this time.*" He transferred his attention to the figures at his feet, and suddenly . . . changed. Stance, the tension of hands and body, expression, all underwent a subtle transformation. In a corner, the crouching scribe wrote steadily: no word of the God was insignificant. All must be recorded, for the temple to plumb their oracular meaning.

He walked over to the two lying on the floor, his face somehow contriving to look much older; his voice changed, straining for a baritone that the body could not reproduce. "Riots," he said. "During the holy festival. *My* holy festival." He began pacing around the room, apparently arguing with himself over the two failed conspirators, the voice and stance changing as he spoke, often with dizzying speed.

"As the Sun-on-Earth . . . no, you fool, *I'm* the Sun-on-Earth, and I say . . . no, both of you are wrong. *We* are the God—STOP IT! all of you! This is confusing the issue! Riots, disruption. Remember that. All of us, remember and stick to the point! Well, If we insist . . . I suppose.

"Oh, you have been a very naughty girl."

A senile voice won out and the God stood looking down at Smyna. "You . . . lost the war? No, that was that awful woman a few centuries ago. . . . Ah, the riots!" Mumbling, the God paced across the two of them, paying them no more heed than rolled-up rugs on the floor. With a sudden fluid move the God turned. "You wanted to start a holy war. Without my (our! . . . Go away and leave me alone. This is important) express permission. As well as causing discord in the Iron House (wasn't that her grandfather? No. No. This is today; now. Not four hundred years ago. Pay attention, can't you?), also killing many of the hands that I need to carry out my plans for Fehinna." The decisive voice faded again into the argument of many, and Aygah continued pacing.

"Got to find a better way to edit," he muttered. "Maybe use amnesiacs? No, no, too risky, might get stuck in a brain-damaged hulk." His voice was abstracted, turned inward. The body jerked, turned, strode briskly to the clerk in the corner and took paper and pen.

"No, no: why don't you write something *useful*," a new voice said. A woman's voice, with an archaic lilt to the spacing of the syllables. She dashed off a line and handed it back to him; the slow, unhumanly graceful pacing resumed.

The priest-scribe looked down. She was a scholar of

sorts, and recognized the cursive script in use before the Maleficent's time, before Fehinnan received an overlay of Pensa loan-words. *Thi Sunne-Suyr-Grawnd baihi Traiwly madde.* She paled, looked up to be certain those eyes were no longer on her, and scratched the offending line out. Had not the God once said: "I am large: I contain multitudes"?

The God-King came to rest near Smyna, standing on one of her outstretched hands, without noticing. There was a crackle, and beads of cold sweat broke out above Smyna's upper lip. She made no sound.

"*Look at me, woman,*" the Voice said. She knew that Voice; it was that aspect of the God called Must-Obey. She looked up into the eyes, and felt herself falling, whirling away into a blast of contending voices; an image formed in her mind of huge dusty storehouses heaped with treasures and trash, glittering in decay. There was no resistance in her; three thousand years of submission lay behind her, generation on generation.

"Oh, I see. Yes, overenthusiastic. What *was* it that you did? Oh, yes—killed the shaatheayds. No, they say shaaids now, don't they? And all those fires, and the soldiers fighting each other. Bad girl."

Aygah's face turned to the door. "General," he said crisply. A figure in green stepped in and saluted, bowing low and going to one knee with his face to the floor.

"Are those . . . hillbillies . . . tribesfolk, whatever, still being troublesome up in the Blue Ridge country?"

"Yes, God Among Us," he replied evenly.

"I really must do something about that," Aygah muttered, abstracted once more. "Poison gas? No, I already did that, and it didn't work. Plenty of time." The tone became crisp once more. "This one," he said, resuming his pacing and kicking Smyna absently in the ribs as he passed. "Send her out there, have her kill them. All of them, and don't let her back until it's done. Now go away, you foolish woman." Smyna crawled backward from the room, leaving faint bloodmarks where her injured hand pressed the boards. A silent servant appeared, buffed the spots with a cloth, and slid away.

"A shepherd," Aygah said. "That's what I intended the High Priest to be . . . Chancellor, my right hand . . .

when I created the office." He looked down at the man. "Fifty thousand dead, then a Purification disrupted by one woman, priests; MY HANDS killing soldiers and being killed. Raising taxes on staples to finance this little dream of yours? This is shepherding my flock? Perhaps I should give you to our enemies. You'd help them right into surrender."

A harsh bark of laughter, and he circled Cubilano slowly. "Why did we start that? The shaven heads? Oh, you don't remember either. Well, it was a long time ago . . . you were the God only two hundred years before I was. Back to business." The boy sighed and tapped Cubilano's head with one foot. "Look at us, fool. We decide when the world is ready for Our benevolent rule. The Fehinnans as my chosen will be enough, for now." The voice darkened. "And you have the presumption to tell me what to do, with your little schemes? There is very little I can do to you that you haven't done or seen done. . . . Ah." The God lifted his head as if listening to an internal dialogue. "Yes. Good that you reminded us. It was religious fervor that drove you to this. Commendable, in small quantities. The cannibals of the islands and south coast need to hear the word of the Sun. I think *you* are just the person to do the job. I never want to see your face again. If I do, *Right Hand*"—sarcasm rang heavy in his tone—"I'll have it removed."

He turned to the general who knelt by the door. "Advice. This one was supposed to give us good advice. We'll need a new adviser, new Reflection of the Effulgent Light, new Right Hand, new Chancellor, new everything. Wasn't—" He looked down at Cubilano. "I said I didn't want to *see* you again, tiresome fellow!" The man who had been High Priest crawled from the room; Aygah reflected that the man had seldom felt more genuine fear. "Didn't I tell you to fetch the old one—the one before that one— what was his hame, Arrri, no Harriz, something like that? I'll see him in a few hours, or whatever."

Absently, the God turned back to the table and turned a paintbrush in his slim fingers, his eyes straying back to the painting on the wall. "Next time I'll get it right," he said. "I may not have Andy's talent, but I've got lots of time."

*   *   *

In the corridor outside, Cubilano stumbled to his feet. Perfect humiliation had burned his face to a certain purity; the dark eyes looked inward, blind. Blinder than the ruined eyes of the figure who leaned on his staff among the line of those waiting for audience; Cubilano might have passed him by if the staff had not reached out to tap him on the chest.

The blind man's aquiline nose flared slightly. "Didn't recognize your old fellow student, then, Cubi?" he said, very softly. Cubilano jerked; nobody had used that nickname since the training classes in the temple, forty years gone. Forty years of struggle and effort.

"But I recognized *you*," the blind man said. "By smell. *Scrape the chickenshit off your clumsy feet, serfkin!*"

The taunt lanced home, through all the years of mastery: a child's cruelty, to the small boy lost and friendless among the children of the great ones. Cubilano had spoken scarcely a word, in all the time since the guard came. Now he cried out and raised a hand to strike. The spearhead dipped down and touched delicately at the base of his throat; he looked up along it into bored, cool young eyes under the helmet brim. His shoulders slumped, and he shuffled off down the corridor, and for the first time his walk was an old man's.

The soldiers of the Elite Guard were not too rough with Smyna: fanatics they might be, but soldiers were soldiers. The officer of the detail was almost friendly, in a distant way. The guard did not need to fear that her treason would prove contagious; he sent for the palace garrison surgeon, to splint the hand, and waited patiently while it was done.

"So, it's the border for you," he said.

And once the hand's healed, a fast horse and over the mountains, she thought. Not much of a chance; the Painted People of the mountains had little love for her breed, but a better path than a lifetime of raid and patrol work. And once overmountain in Kaina . . . well, there was always a market for swords. *General-Commander of the Righteous Sword, then a mercenary at two bits the month*, she thought. Bitterness was acid at the back of her throat.

"Do me a last favor?" she said, putting down the winecup

and watching unmoved as the fingers were forced back into their rightful positions.

"Depends," he said warily.

She flashed a bright smile that gave him a brief flicker of disquiet. *Lucky this one's going*, he thought. *Truly, the God is wise*.

"Just pass on to my kinfast: 'It was the red-hair's doing.' We've a previous debt with her. This makes it worth following up."

He shrugged incomprehension. "It seems little enough," he said, and hitched at his belt. "Time we were going; it's a long ride to Chaarsvaahl."

Jahlini wrenched the long knife free from between her opponent's ribs and came erect, shaking tense shoulders. The dim flickering light cast shadows across the interior of the disused warehouse; the ranks sitting quietly on their heels beyond the fighting circle were motionless, patches of deeper black.

Usually there was a certain formality to meetings of the Adderfang Dark Council. Today that had been dispensed with. There were too many empty seats, and too many wounded; the Southside Serpent-Chief sat propped between henchfolk, one eye gleaming fever-bright from the white bandages that covered her face. Patches showed redly wet, rimmed with dirty yellow discharge; her breath came in a rhythmic bubbling. The two supporting her shifted uneasily as that brought a faint hint of corruption, sweet and cloying. Who would have expected a human to have *claws*? They were uneasily conscious that their overlord was now in a minority; Jahlini had few supporters among the sector lords, now.

The chief of the Adderfangs rose from the body, gasping. *Too old*, she thought, conscious of the burning cut along one arm. *Too old, if only one passage leaves me winded*.

"That settles it," she said hoarsely, scanning the black-masked shadows-within-shadows. This was even more poorly lit than tradition demanded, and it smelled of the docks, coffee and molasses and timber-baulks. The usual meeting place had proved to be known to the Intelligence Section; ten globes of lungrot had gone down the ventilators, fol-

lowed by commando squads in gasmasks. *But they wouldn't
follow us into the tunnels*, she thought with a flicker of
triumph. *We can rebuild*.

"We can rebuild. We go to the cellars, fight off the
other brotherhoods, then we rebuild—"

The Southserpent made a wet noise of assent. Jahlini
looked in her direction and cringed slightly at the hate in
the single eye, glad it was not directed at her. There was
little left of her face; Jahlini would have sworn it was
impossible to live a day with those wounds, much less a
week. And the claws that had gouged just come out of the
sewers; the rot, Dark Shining One, the *rot. . . . But the
red-hair is mine*, she thought. *When we have the time.
The gates are watched, they can't get out*.

"Rebuild?" a man's voice snarled. "When the others
have taken our protection circuits?"

"The smuggling?" another continued.

"Two of our joyhouses have been torched—and we don't
have enough blades to protect them!"

Another figure stepped up to the edge of the circle,
knelt to touch her knife to the line, and sprang in, fresh,
tossing the blade from hand to hand. Behind her, there
was a rustling as others moved to stand in line.

"Rebuild, with a new Adderchief," the challenger said.
"Must be, oh, a dozen here with kniferight."

Jahlini sank into a crouch. *But how many would try it,
after I kill this one?* she thought. Her lungs burned, and
the blood from her arm turned the sleeve sodden on her
arm.

29

The jeweled message egg spun across the floor, trailing
a length of silver chain and a large black tomcat providing
momentum. Megan felt it bounce sharply off one ankle,
then whirl under the bed; from beneath the mattress came
rattling bangs and the cat's satisfied whuffling as he picked
the toy up and moved it to a new spot by the door.
Ten-Knife-Foot settled himself carefully, adjusting all four
paws, then batted the sphere of diamond-studded silver
against the oak panel. There was a hollow boom, and the
ornament rebounded; the cat gave a small jump of delight
and retrieved it to begin the process again.

The Zak turned a ruby idly in one hand, flipping it
gently over each knuckle, holding it up to admire the
tawny crimson reflections in its depths. *Pity I couldn't
take the setting,* she thought. *I wonder where Milampo
got the idol.* It was an even greater pity it had been
one-eyed. A jingle drew her attention to the center of the
bed. Shkai'ra had just upended another counting-house
bag over her head, and a spray of tradewire and foreign
coins tumbled down, slivers of red-gold lost in the long
mane that fell past her shoulders.

"I've always wanted to do that," Shkai'ra said, a little
sheepishly, glancing sidelong at Megan sitting cross-legged
on the window ledge. Bouncing off the bed, she crossed to
where a mass of rainbow-colored silks lay tossed about.
The tunic she was wearing was a bright green with orange
fringes; she pulled it over her head, rummaged in the
pile, and held up another critically. Stretching, she rose to
her toes and let the heavy dense-woven silk fall into place,
sighing at the feel of the smooth fabric on bare skin. This

one was a blue just short of black, the sleeves flaring to
end above her wrists, the knee-length hem sewn with
small bullion medallions that kept the drape smooth along
the long taut curves of her body.

Well, how do you like *this* one?" she asked, buckling on
a broad leather belt, tooled with vine leaves picked out in
gold.

Megan looked up and smiled. "I like that. Much better
than the red one before that. It clashed with you. That
one shows you off."

She cast a critical eye on the pattern of gems on the
white stone ledge before her and carefully placed the ruby
into the design. "You want to see something funny? Come
on."

She went into the warded room, picking through the
minted bits for the silver, opening one of the windows.
"Watch." She carefully aimed and tossed a bit into the
midst of a group of revelers who were hitting each other
over the head with bladders, elaborate festival costumes
suffering under the wobbling blows. A second's pause as
they realized what had hit the pavement; then a frantic
scramble to grab the silver. Megan chuckled and tossed
another bit into a group about twenty feet from the first.
"Even without warding, if you're careful, no one *ever*
thinks of looking up!"

The Kommanza laughed. "Godlike beneficence," she
said. "More so, all the gods I've met are stingy as starving
coyotes." She picked up a heavy round Pensa coin, chis-
eled into fretwork, sighted, and flicked it off the head of a
staggering reveler two stories below. The man in the
fishmask staggered still more, looked down at his feet, and
fell to his knees. He picked up the coin and gripped it
between his thighs, puzzling, until they saw him raise
both hands in the Fehinnan attitude of prayer.

Shkai'ra leaned back against the opposite end of the
window opening and tucked her feet beneath her. "That
dark-brown looks good . . . a little drab for festival clothes,
but good."

Megan looked down at her tunic and adjusted the sleeve,
tugging at the small red embroidery. "Festival? It's comfortable, and dark. What do I want with anything more?"
She was honestly puzzled.

"Well—" Shkai'ra bent and seized a handful. "You might try this—or this—or *this*—" Laughing, she pitched one tunic after another over the small form, the folds of thick smooth cloth settling over her like huge orchids in a jungle of flowers.

"Hey! Ach. Stop!" Megan sat down suddenly, overburdened with cloth, and pulled away the one lodged over her head. "I suppose they are nice. Like this one." The silks and satins were sliding to the floor, pulled by their own weight, except for the honey-colored one across Megan's lap. She ran her hand over it as if it were a cat and said thoughtfully, to the air, "This one reminds me of Shyll . . . in winter before the summer sun washes the hair color away. . . ." Her voice trailed off as she stared down at the cloth, her hand mechanically continuing the slow stroking motion.

Shkai'ra's grin faded. "Megan . . ." she began, almost shyly. "There's . . . I've been an exile for a long time. I'm twenty-and-six snows; five years since I left the Zekz Kommanz, a long time to wander without a roof. There's . . . an estate. Not far from here; good pasture, and the pomegranates are sold by name. Back a ways, I put a, hmmm, down payment on it. The owner lives elsewhere, and owes me a favor. The manor is nice; not large, but, well—room enough for two, and to spare. More later, but . . ."

"The harvest festival will be beginning soon," Megan said. "And the river will be slowly starting to grow its skin of ice. The north wind will blow from the steppe, carrying winter in its teeth. . . . I have a revenge. And kin." She looked up at Shkai'ra. "Come with me. Only for a short time. I want to show you my home." She half reached out a hand to Shkai'ra, who had gone very still.

The Kommanza started to speak, then leaned her head against the windowsill for a moment. "Mine are a homefast folk," she said softly. "I have friends here . . . even though none so close as you, who I've known only this tennight. And . . . I know this place; the wounds of my homeroots are only now scarring. Must I cut them again?" She looked up, and astonishingly the cold eyes glimmered in the afternoon light. She held out a hand, palm upward. "Stay?" she asked, a plea without hope.

*   *   *

It was late. Megan raised her head from her knees and stared blindly into the darkness. Across the alley, on a ledge, two gleaming coals glinted; the eyes of a cat. She scrubbed angrily at the corners of her eyes. Water lapped quietly at ships and docks and pilings, below the niche she had found on this rooftop. It smelled like home. The quiet call of the ship watch drifted up to her ears.

I cannot stay. And I cannot demand that she come with me. This is her place, and I am as strange here as she would be there. I cannot stay. Goddess, weaver of lives . . . curse you. It hurts.

She was perched where she could just see the massive four-master that had arrived yesterday. She looked sound enough, and the general air on board was quiet and calm . . . a timber run up the north coast, then across through the islands of the Great Sea. She would be on it when it left.

I want to scream and smash things . . . kill someone, hurt someone as much as I hurt. She stood up and started back to the Weary Wayfarer, using difficult and dangerous ways across the roofs so she wouldn't have time to think. The new guard on the roof just nodded as she slipped past him. His silence had been bought with one of Milampo's gemstones.

She walked along the quiet corridors, her boots noiseless on the rugs, feeling sleep soaking the building. Every other lamp was lit, reflecting warmly on the wood-mosaic walls.

She settled into the curve of Shkai'ra's back a short time later, careful not to wake her. As she drifted to sleep, her thought was sorrow for leaving along with joy at going home, strange and bittersweet. A tear slid down one temple and was lost in her hair.

30

The wineshop was half-sunk into rubble. Not ground; there was little in the harbor district of the Old City; this was the ruins of past cycles. It was dark inside, cool, musty and heady with the smell from the vats lining the back wall. Shkai'ra ducked her head beneath the low beams, staggered slightly, swayed back erect.

"Wine," she said to the proprietor. "Wine, strong an' cold." Her voice was slurred, and the staccato gutturals of her birth-speech were heavy in it.

The owner peered at the big foreigner. Most customers here ordered wholesale, and knew their vintages. This one . . .

"One-twenty-fifth silver for a liter crock," he said. That was outrageous, but the disturbances had raised prices generally.

Bloodshot gray eyes flickered over him; he could sense that they used him only as a resting point, focused on some inward thing. A hand tossed a minted bit on the table. A *gold* bit. A *whole* gold bit. Enough for a tun of Aahngnaak that would need four horses to pull it. The shopkeeper felt a sudden chill; nobody treated money they had earned that casually, and this was no aristocrat. He whispered sharply to a kinchild.

"A stonejug: the Maanticell, quickly." That was a frontier vintage, respectable but not distinguished, the sort of wine a magnate would serve at a banquet.

Minutes stretched, and he watched the impassive hawk face. She had plainly already seen the bottom of the goblet more than once, but there was little of the slackness of wine; merely a cold grimness that settled like a mantle around her shoulders. The sleeves of her fine blue-black silk tunic fell back, and he looked at the thin white scars on forearms that rippled as her fingers moved on the worn bone hilt of a curved sword.

There was a clatter from the street door, and a ragged urchin slipped through the screen of wooden beads at the foot of the stairs; the doorward panted behind him.

"Pardon, Kinelder, he—" She swiped with her staff. "Come *here*, little limb of darkness!"

The child dropped flat under the swing with a skill born of long experience, rolled across the flagstones, under a barrel raised on timber slats, and tugged at the red-haired foreigner's tunic hem, grubby fingers closing on the round gold-thread mandrels that hemmed it. The shopkeeper closed his eyes and winced; he was a kindly man, and would not wish serious harm even to a shaaid cub doubtless come to see what he could pilfer. A clip across the ear would have been enough.

Astonishingly, there was no blow or cry of pain. He peered, and saw the bright head bent as the woman in the blue tunic went down on one knee. The boy grinned and shifted from foot to foot, reveling in his importance.

". . . more trouble than an ape, Dahvo," she said.

"No," the boy whispered, in a clear carrying tone. "Said you'd want to know: 't old blind gimp bowl-shaker, tha know? Big one now. He—"

The woman grabbed him sharply by the forelock; the words dropped to a murmur. When she straightened again, her face had changed. She smiled, and the shopkeeper recoiled as she vaulted the vat with a smooth raking stride, landing easily. The wine arrived; she swept it up, weighed the stoneware jug thoughtfully, then tucked it under her left arm. "No use wasting good liquor," she muttered thoughtfully. "Or letting it get in the way." Her eyes rested appraisingly on the stairs as her mind ran through the layout of the street above.

The boy scurried up and tugged at her again, at the tooled leather of her weapons-belt this time. She started from her tactician's reverie and grabbed him by the scruff of his neck.

"What, pest?" she asked, with what was almost a chuckle in her voice.

"Ol' bowl-shaker, he say tha'd give me a bit," he said
hopefully, wide-eyed, with a look of total trust. The woman's eyes flicked back to the granite risers of the staircase,
each worn almost to a U by sandaled feet.

"And you came without being paid in advance?" she
asked. "No, here's your bit." She fished blindly in her
pouch and pressed the result into his small, hot palm. He
stared, and for once had no words.

She took the scabbard of her saber in her left hand,
holding it horizontal to the ground for the fast draw-and-
strike. "Stay here," she said. "Not much chance they're in
place, but it could start raining hurt." And was gone,
taking the slope in a bounding run that left only a faint
tap-tap of sandal leather on stone beside it. There was a
blare of light and noise from the street as the door swung
open, and a smell of dust; then the cool, fruity darkness of
the cellar-store returned.

"Sun in Her Glory!" the owner of the store muttered.
His gaze fell to the boy, who started, tucked the gleaming
sliver of metal in a loincloth that looked to have started its
career as a dishrag, and began to edge toward the exit.

"You can keep your reward, child of the streets," the
shopkeeper said. The slum boy looked unconvinced, but
there was nobody between him and escape. "It must have
been mighty good fortune you brought."

Dahvo scratched his head, examined the result, and
cracked it between thumbnail and forefinger. "Dunno,"
he said, puzzled. "The message—'Fear the revenge of the
defeated, and take ship for your life.' Na much good about
that, izzit?"

"Twenty?" The head supply clerk arched his brows.
"*Twenty* breakfast and afternoon trays returned unused
from second-five-west?" He pursed thin lips and rolled the
cork-covered surface of his pen between ink-stained fingers.

Glaaghi scowled. The tiny attic office crowded around
her, smelling of paper and dust, lit by a single skylight
bright with morning through its coating of grime. The
occupant fitted easily into the room; barely thirty, she
knew, but looking older. He was pale, a legacy of his
Newfaai father; thin brown hair receded from his forehead
over pinched features.

"Do you realize," he continued, "just what the cost of—" He paused to examine a list. "The cost of ten times ten double eggs, corncakes, syrup, tea, coffee, lemonade . . ."

"Which you use for blood—I can see it boiling in your veins," she sneered heavily. "I tell you—" She hesitated. "I tell you there's something *strange* about second-five-west. I sent Ehaago there; he came back with the tray. A day in the sweatbox, and he 'forgot' again!"

The clerk sniffed and steepled his fingers. "The fact remains, with the disturbances, prices have risen. The Weary Wayfarer's Hope of Comfort and Delight is not a charitable organization, and we must *all* pull together to control costs. Prices have risen *steeply* with the disturbances. Now, a deduction from your *very* generous stipend—awk!"

Glaaghi closed a hand on his shoulder and another on his elbow, big work-roughened hands sinking into the flesh of a small man who had spent many years squatting behind his table. That overturned, and she led him to the door on tiptoe.

"So, I'll *show* you," she said.

"But, but—put me down, woman!" His attempt to free himself was futile.

He looked about the corridor. "But why deliver five trays to a four-room floor?"

"You can say that to . . ." They both started. The clerk passed a hand over the back of his neck in unconscious reflex at a feeling of cold wind touching his skin. The world blurred and shifted, as a pressure they had not felt lifted from their perceptions.

The cook looked down at the clerk. "Didn't you just say, four rooms?"

He nodded again. "Of course—" He stopped, with a mental sensation of running into a concrete wall. "But . . . there are five rooms here! There are five on *all* the floors. I . . . forgot. *And I remember forgetting.*"

They both drew the circle of the Sun on their breasts. For a long minute they stood and stared at each other, implications running through their minds like rabbits before the hounds.

"There's always a certain amount of wastage," the clerk said thoughtfully.

Glaaghi nodded. "Not waste! The hogs get it, and the servants what they won't eat!" She nodded again, with enthusiasm.

He tapped at his chin. "In any case, the room fee covered it."

Glaaghi waited through a musing silence.

"Well, we need to order the new rugs. And arrange protection from the new Darkchiefs."

"And no mystery here, eh?"

"Mystery?" the clerk said, arching his brows once more. "Of course not. And now, Mother, I think we both have business to attend to." He minced decisively down the corridor.

31

Megan tilted her head back against the mast and looked up, up to the dizzying height where the sails were being released from the port bindings; quick-release knots were tied at the reef points of the smaller sails, and the larger ones loose-hauled. The rigging was swarming with crewfolk, almost as tiny as the gulls wheeling raucous above. The breeze was offshore, running with the beginning of an ebb tide, but still the air bore a hint of open sea.

She looked down at her hands, lying on her crossed legs, warm in the sunlight. *Why so cold and empty?* she thought. Her goods were stowed, with a minor ward to make sure that no straying hands discovered reason for them to disappear. The ship was making ready to cast off on the shipmaster's word, and the pilot stood by the wheel. She was going home.

So why the tight feeling under the breastbone? It was absurd; even Shkai'ra would laugh. Shkai'ra. *You did say* goodbye, she reminded herself. *You did leave the kin-giftknife with her, so there's still a link. It isn't as if she died; life will continue. . . . So why do you feel so alone?* she asked herself sardonically.

There was the usual last-minute confusion at the boarding plank; a kinfast of furtraders was late, and their folks were dashing up with bundles in their arms. The sailors avoided them with practiced nimbleness, until a brace hauling on a line chanty-walked backward into a servant scooping spilled beads off the deck; there was a curse from the petty officer, and the sound of a rope's end encouraging the landsman to mind his step. The shipmaster shouted over the side as the rowtug bobbed alongside, looking woodchip-small beside the great windjammer.

Tide at full flood soon, Megan thought. *We'll be underway in twenty minutes, with the favoring wind.* And more easily than the mankiller lanteen rigs her people used.

The Zak surged to her feet and strode to the rail, as if to leave hollowness behind. Leaning on the teak, she looked out over the docks. *Alien.* All strange, even the smells, too warm and spicy beside the cold riverports of her memory. She wanted to *be* home; not *going* home, but being there. She drove one nail into the hard wood and watched the teak splinter up around it, oblivious to the clatter of low-geared winches behind her raising a spar.

I told her I'd miss her. It's not even a couple of hours yet. Damn. Going nowhere in circles if I don't stop.

She forced herself to concentrate on the ship; there should be useful hints, here. *Let's see.* Square rig above, fore-and-aft below, staysails . . . A young crewwoman skipped nimbly along a spar, far above.

Wouldn't Shkai'ra have just cringed at being that high, she thought with the beginning of a smile. *And done it anyway—damn!* Wistfully: *But I wish I could have shown her a RI.*

The horse shied. *Bastard kinless cowturd*, Shkai'ra thought savagely. There had been no time to saddle, barely enough to throw the frame for the heavy saddlebags over the restive animal.

Just the sort of handless cow that a merchant would buy, ran through her mind as she edged it snorting and rolling its eyes, through the gate and into the street. *All looks and nerves, no stamina or sense*. This was the sort of beast that shied at a blowing leaf or a shadow; Zailo Unseen alone knew what—

The horse did a standing jump, all four of its slim legs shooting out in an equine starfish. It landed, bucked hugely, and bolted. Shkai'ra's legs clamped home effortlessly; she had ridden from the age of three, and nothing short of a warhammer could throw her, even bareback. The saddlebags pounded against the horse's shoulders: from one came an enraged *ERR-EHRO-HWAW-ERRRR* as Ten-Knife had the air squeezed out of his lungs in midhowl. Chickens, children, and pedestrians bolted from her path; she retained enough control to swerve around a cart laden with early-season watermelons and baskets of peaches. That prompted a thought; the curved sword slipped into her hand, rose and fell with a solid *tchik* of steel into pine as she slashed the ropes holding the rear gate in place. Behind her there was a roar of falling fruit, the wet sounds of melons striking stone, a wail of peasant anguish; twelve span of oxen tossed their heads and lowed plaintively as she dashed by. Then she was around the corner and onto Delight Street; it would not be wise to gallop here, with the Watch so thick. She reined in and risked a glance behind.

There was no obvious pursuit; the remnants of fallen factions would not dare to operate in the open, not yet, not while there was a chance of catching her in the streets. She used the point of her saber to twitch a blowgun dart out of her mount's haunch, then reined it in sharply with one hand. Behind her, down the Laneway of Impeccable Respectability, came the joyous screaming of the street children as they swarmed over smashed melon. The Kommanza looked up through heat-haze to the morning sun; she had a little time, and there would be few faster than a rider to follow. The main gates would be watched, of course, but there were too many ships and too much harbor, if she did not linger to haggle for passage.

Swing south to the harbor, she thought. *Then west. Sure as there's pus under a scab, they'll be after me soon.* She heeled the merchant's show-beast into a slow canter, threading her way among wagons and carriages and pedicabs. The dart had probably been poisoned, but horses had more body mass than humans, it should last. And then whoever ate it was welcome to the bellyache.

The docks and warehouses of the Northern Adventurers were crowded; half a dozen sizable craft were leaving on this tide, and twice that number of coasters were making ready to beat north from port to port. The air was pungent with the smells of sugar and wine, dried fruit and heavy cheap rum; bales of cotton cloth and crates of tools and weapons stood by. Muscle-powered cranes ratcheted; carts rumbled by on ironwood rails, coasting down inclines from the upper stories of the warehouses. Porters trotted up gangplanks, bent double under their burdens, naked skins shining; an overseer stood by with her whip's jagged ceramic beads dangling against one leg. There were carts and wagons aplenty; few looked up at another rider, even one forcing her way through the throng with unmannerly haste.

Wish I could use my saber, Shkai'ra thought. But that would be madness; not only was there the Watch to think of, but sailors were not as meek as most city Fehinnans. It would have been more useful to unlimber her bow, in a running fight like this. These easterners did not understand horsearchery. . . .

The weight of the animal forced a way for her among the crowd. It was winded now, favoring the right forehoof, muzzle low and trailing streaks of foam. There was more on the front of her tunic, spattering it where it was not dark with horse sweat. That brought an absurd pang; she had *liked* that dark silk. . . .

The beast lurched and staggered sideways. *Poison,* she thought. Horsewoman's reflex brought her legs up. The animal splayed its hooves, attempting to recover; one knee buckled, and it went over on its side, kicking wildly. The bystanders scattered from the hooves. Shkai'ra darted in, swearing, thankful that it had collapsed on the gold and armor rather than her cat. She seized the leather strap connecting the bags, waited for a heave, and pulled it free.

"You," she snarled, catching a bystander by the collar. "Where's the *Gullwinged Gainsnatcher?*"

"*There*" the woman choked, pointing. "Just casting off—*leggo.*"

Shkai'ra threw the saddlebags over one shoulder and looked behind her. There were half a dozen figures pushing their way through the crowd; hard-faced, looking uneasy in their civilian tunics of unbleached cotton. Two carried bundles wrapped in rags, and the shape suggested crossbows. She craned, using her height recklessly; yes, others with hats on heads that might be shaved. She did not bother to check for Adderfangs; if they wanted to be unseen, they would be. One of the first party spotted copper-blond hair over the dark crowd. She could see yellow teeth barred in a pockmarked brown face.

She turned, kicked a man with a seabag on his shoulder behind the knee, forced her way into the space he left, and shoved. It should be easier for one than a group, she thought. There was a weary *errowr?* of protest from one saddlebag.

The gunwale under Megan's hands was starting to take on the appearance of worm-eaten barnboard, splinters stiking up in random directions. One of the crew had ventured to protest, pausing in her way along the deck, and was greeted with an icy stare and the slow, reflexive crooking of one hand. The crewwoman decided that the gunwale could always be sanded smooth later, and took her eyes elsewhere while she still had them. Megan looked out over the crowd and vaguely wondered what could be blocking the way down the road, just in sight around the edge of the oil jars and livestock cages being loaded on the next ship. Something was disturbing the flow of the crowd, and heads were starting to turn.

The third and fourth ropes were just rattling on deck when an outraged shout rose from the spot where the traffic was blocked. *More interesting things*, Megan thought. *That's one thing I won't be sorry to leave behind.* A snide voice in the back of her mind commented that she would probably go mad very shortly of boredom. She sighed and looked down at the scratchings on the rail.

The crowd thinned out toward the water's edge, where the piers projected out from the dock like the teeth of a comb; there were too many carts for toes to be jammed so closely together. The *Gullwinged Gainsnatcher* was two piers west; the Kommanza could see her masts and stays, swaying as the tug pulled her head out into the basin. But she had not cast completely free, not yet. A pile of cotton cloth stood before her, twice head height; cheap garish stuff printed in the bright patterns the northern forest and sea-land tribes of Newfaai and Naiskat loved. She went straight at it, not even slowing her run, up and over the steep-sided pyramid of cloth. As she reached the summit there was a deep musical throb, and something half-visible went *thrup* by her shoulder.

She slipped down, braking with her heels; another bolt slammed through the space her spine and breastbone had occupied a moment earlier; the skin between her shoulders roughened into lumps. Then she was flashing along the clear space beside the departing ship, toward the great cable that still stretched from a concrete bollard to the stern of the ship. It was the last, holding the three thousand tons steady while the tub brought the ship's stem into the current. The longshore crew stood ready to hit the release catches; tension pulled the meter-thick sisal taut, squeezing water in a steady spurting flow out of the fibers.

Shkai'ra felt the breath panting deep and swift into her lungs. There was no time, not with a repeating crossbow behind her. And eight meters of water between her and the deck . . .

Her teeth grated painfully as she leaped from dock to bollard and out along the cable; the thick hawser seemed suddenly thread-thin as it stretched ahead to weave through timber baulks below the rail. Below, the ebbing morning tide sucked hungrily at the oaken piles of the dock.

At the scream and thrum of weapons, Megan's head snapped up, just in time to see bright copper hair flash, then Shkai'ra pelted through a clear spot. *Running as if she could outrun crossbows,* the Zak thought. A bolt skittered by, shattering on a stone column, and the Kommanza was up on the rope connecting the ship and the dock. The scene froze with the longshoremen standing, mouths agape, staring at this madwoman.

"Move!" Megan cried. "If you freeze you'll fall!" Her voice was seemingly lost. "Move!" she screamed. And other running figures were now visible. One stopped to kneel and take careful aim.

Shkai'ra's feet gripped at the rough surface of the sisal through the thin leather of her sandals. Natural balance and warrior training took her out above the hungry water, foot curving swiftly before foot in a walk that was half a skip. *Got to keep going fast,* she thought. *Like tumbling or a swordhand throw. Faster you move, easier to balance.*

She was halfway between dock and ships, and even the weight of the hull could not deny the hawser a slight curve. And there was a massive sudden impact below her right shoulder, the blow of a sledge swung overarm. She felt a sharp prickling as the point of the bolt touched her skin, a tip of metal through the saddlebag and the steel helmet it contained. With a monstrous wrenching effort she seemed to leap and twist in midair, coming down straddle-stanced along the rope, crouching. Her balance was saved, but the position immobilized her for a crucial brace of seconds. She looked back, to see the crossbowman kneel and sight; looked at her own death.

Something snapped in Megan's mind. The lost, cold feelings surged up, becoming raging flames, forge-heat. Living elsewhere with Shkai'ra alive was bearable. Her Akribhan dead? Her hands leaped forward almost of their own volition, one pointing to the crossbowman, the other raised to sky where the Sun shone. The man threw back his head and howled, flinging the weapon from him, tearing his clothes and hair, screaming that he was on fire, his skin blistering and turning black, cracking open, though no flames were visible. He threw himself into the harbor, still screaming.

Steam rose.

Shkai'ra darted the last ten steps to the railing; her muscles had still been moving, even with the certainty of death on her. Behind, there were screams and frantic prayers and a sickeningly appetizing smell of roast pork; the crowds exploded away from the place of magic like quicksilver on glass. But not many had seen, and it would take time to spead word. The Kommanza cleared the rail with a vault, tossed her burden to the planks, and dove, pulling the slight figure of the Zak down with her. Another bolt buzzed by overhead and sank a handspan deep in the rearmast; others followed, and a blowgun dart. Then the whole great fabric of the ship lurched as the longshore crew slammed their mallets into the releases of the bollard. There was a sudden alteration in the movement as the *Gullwinged Gainsnatcher* slid out into the harbor basin and swung toward the open river; above, canvas crackled as the crew unrove the topgallants to put steerage way on her; she heeled, and the keel bit water.

Megan lay limp beneath Shkai'ra as the Kommanza raised herself on one elbow; they were out of projectile range now. Her eyelids fluttered, and a small sound escaped her.

Shkai'ra slowed her breathing with an effort. "I changed my mind," she said. The thin mouth moved in a quirk. "Sea voyages are so healthy."

One of the bosuns strode near, a belaying pin tapping at the hilt of his knife. The blond woman jingled her pouch, and let the other hand drop to her swordhilt. Beyond, a small black head poked free of a saddlebag, glanced about, then retreated to lie glaring from the sheltering darkness, eyes darting from side to side.

Megan's eyes snapped open, and she tried to raise herself on one elbow, not succeeding very well. "Flames," she said, and smiled.

About the Authors

S. M. STIRLING was born in 1954 in Metz, Alsace—which is French or German territory, depending on one's point of view. Since then, places of domicile have included Europe, North America, and various parts of Africa. Languages are English, French, a smattering of Swahili and Afrikaans, and several tongues which will not be spoken for several millennia yet. Diversions range from travel, cooking, obscure wines, cats, karate (green belt, Shotokan and Tao Zen Chuan), horses, and sailboats through baroque music, sex, and literature—not necessarily in that order. Currently under construction are two further fantasy novels dealing with Shkai'ra's early career. Social interests center on the Bunch of Seven, a Toronto-based writers' group.

SHIRLEY MEIER was born in Woodstock, Ontario, in 1960. As a child, she read every science fiction and fantasy book in the library, used interlibrary loan to get others, and pestered the librarians to distraction to buy more. (She gave them lists.) Ms. Meier is willing to try anything at least once and is actively involved in reading, karate, chess, learning Go, baking bread, riding (rent-a-horse), and costuming. She is a founding member of the Bunch of Seven, a Toronto based writers' group. She claims to paint badly, play the violin worse, and exhibit severe withdrawal symptoms when prevented from putting words on paper.